DEAD SOULS

DEAD SOULS

NIKOLAI GOGOL

Translated from the Russian by

Bernard Guilbert Guerney

Introduction by René Wellek

HOLT, RINEHART AND WINSTON, INC.

New York Chicago San Francisco Atlanta
Dallas Montreal Toronto

Seventh Printing, June, 1966

Translation copyright 1942 by The Readers Club
and 1948 by The George Macy Companies, Inc.
Introduction copyright, 1948, by René Wellek
Typography Design by Stefan Salter
Manufactured in the United States of America

ISBN: 0-03-009900-5

34567890 065 19181716151413121110

INTRODUCTION

TO

DEAD SOULS

WHOEVER comes to the reading of Gogol's *Dead Souls* with preconceptions of the nature of the Russian novel based upon a reading of Dostoevsky and Tolstoy will be surprised and delighted to discover something very different. Here is a comic epic, a gallery of portraits, a loosely assembled travel story with little psychology, no tragic conflict, no debates concerning God and immortality.

The plot of *Dead Souls,* published in 1842, is based on conditions of Russian serfdom as they existed early in the nineteenth century. Its hero, Chichikov, "neither stout nor thin, neither old nor young," travels around the country and interviews landowners in pursuance of a fraudulent scheme. He offers to buy up "dead souls," i.e., the male serfs who had died since the last census, but for whom the landowners were still compelled to pay the head tax. Acquiring these "souls" cheaply or free of charge, he hoped to raise a large loan by mortgaging the paper transfers. We meet first the landowners he visits: the sugary Manilov, the stupid, suspicious woman Korobochka, the dashing wild braggart Nozdrev, the bearish and boorish Sobakevich, the grotesquely horrible miser Plushkin. We get glimpses of the venal officials in the small provincial town, of the gossipy, featherbrained ladies, the smelly valet Petrushka and the drunken coachman Selifan. The figures are drawn with such vividness that they have become as familiar to Gogol's countrymen as Pickwick and Babbitt are to us.

Taking the novel as a realistic "panorama" of the Russia of the day, Gogol's contemporaries either protested against it or welcomed it as exposing the backwardness of the landowners and the corruption of the officials. Though Chichikov's scheme looks improbable, it appears that there were actual cases of landowners who bought "dead souls" in order to accumulate enough serfs necessary to qualify for the establishment of a distillery on their estates. Gogol always proclaimed that he never had drawn anything from pure imagination, that he succeeded best when he drew from real life. But he worried over the criticism directed against the accuracy of the book. In a preface to the second edition (1846) he appealed for corrections and materials for a continuation. He studied statistics and travel books in preparation for a new trip through Russia. Belinsky, the foremost liberal critic of the time, praised *Dead Souls* as a "purely Russian, national work, drawn from the depths of the nation's life, ruthlessly revealing its reality"; and Herzen, the famous revolutionary, entered in his diary that he had met Gogol's people wherever he went and had seen them hundreds of times. Thus Gogol became the model of the "Natural School" of Russian writers.

Since the late nineteenth century, however, this conception of Gogol and *Dead Souls* has been attacked by critics associated with the Symbolist movement: by Rozanov, Merezhkovsky, Bryusov, and Bely. Gogol, they argued, has nothing to do with realism or naturalism. He is a writer of the imagination, a dreamer. His world is that of a puppet show; his figures are a gallery of grotesque caricatures, comic and tragic masks, "hollow men," the projections of Gogol's own tortured, divided soul. To this interpretation Gogol himself lent some support with the statement that he "transferred the majority of his vices and weaknesses to his heroes, laughing at them in his tales and thus got rid of them for ever." And he has told the story of reading the first chapters of *Dead Souls* to Pushkin, who had originally suggested as a suitable subject the anecdote about the buying of dead souls. Pushkin laughed but then saddened and exclaimed: "How gloomy is our Russia!" But Gogol protested that Pushkin had not realized that it was all "nothing but caricature and mere fancy." These later critics thus reject any interest in Gogol's social and religious ideas. Russian literature after Gogol, they argue, must be interpreted rather as a reaction against his work than as a continuation of it.

But are these two views—here stated in extreme form—really irreconcilable? To consider a novel a mere sociological document is assuredly to take a crude view of the relation between literature and society. Gogol's art is fantastic, even mythic. Each figure in his gallery is drawn in the sharp outlines of a caricature: here a nose sticks out, there some whiskers, here a paunch and there a chin. Frequently the figure has traits of an animal: thus Sobakevich is a bear, Plushkin a spider. The people are seen as growing out of their surroundings or are assimilated to the objects around them. In Sobakevich's house the very furniture says: "I, too, am Sobakevich." Even the blackbird in the cage bears great resemblance to Sobakevich. The dogs and the hurdy-gurdy are as much part of Nozdrev as his whiskers, his red cheeks, and his boasting. Plushkin's wild neglected garden matches his soul, which has gone to seed. The book is written in an exuberant style quickly shifting from the sublime to the comic and back again. Similes are sometimes longer and more elaborate than what they are supposed to illustrate. We cannot forget the church choir evoked on the occasion of barking dogs, or the squadrons of flies settling on a loaf of sugar in the sun which serve as a simile for the tail-coated gentlemen at a ball. As if on the margin of the book there is a curious life of little figures which flit by never to reappear: the lieutenant of Ryazan who was trying on his fifth pair of boots in the middle of the night or the sturdy peasants in Sobakevich's list of "dead souls."

Yet however we stress the imaginative exuberance of the book, we cannot deny that it is related to the reality of the times and the reality of human nature. Gogol's profound insight cannot be refuted by such computations as a Russian professor, Vengerov, made, of the very short time Gogol actually spent in the provinces of Old Russia. The social significance of *Dead Souls* lies in its imaginative criticism of the decaying Russian landowning class, the venal officials, the petty small-town life. Chichikov himself is the symbol of self-satisfied mediocrity and cunning greed. Like all great art, Gogol's is both local and universal. It depicts the Russia of the early nineteenth century, but also the human greed and meanness, stupidity and brutality, affectation and corruption to be found everywhere. It is both a social satire and a work of high imagination.

As it stands, the book is self-contained and coherent. It concludes with Chichikov's flight from the town and the famous address to Russia: "Whither art thou soaring away?" We should not need to know anything about the author or the continuation he planned, if there were not asides and allusions to himself and hints, toward the end of the book, of new things to happen. But even these asides are mostly little essays: reflections on Russian snobbery, feminine education, the Russian love of French and of overeating. Older novelists claimed this privilege as they wanted to gain their readers' confidence and make them feel that they are manipulating the story. There is only one strictly autobiographical passage, the address to Russia from "my alien, beautiful, far-off place." But of Gogol's life we need to know only that he had left Russia after the performance of his play, *The Inspector General,* in 1836 and was wandering about Europe. *Dead Souls,* though begun about 1835, was written mostly at Vevey, in Paris, and then in Rome. Rome undoubtedly is in his mind when he contrasts the South, its palaces, ruins, and gleaming mountains with the desolate Russian steppe.

Very late in the book there are hints of a continuation: the somewhat incongruous story of Chichikov's youth is apparently an afterthought which suggests a different characterization of the hero. At one point, the author hints even that in Chichikov's "chill existence is contained that which will cast man down into the dust and on his knees before the wisdom of the Heavens." Obviously, Chichikov was to be reformed and, according to one report, converted by the Czar himself. Gogol took very seriously the criticism of patriotic friends and foes that the book contained only "negative" characters. He wanted to make up for this deficiency by depicting "positive" social types in the sequel. He began even to think of *Dead Souls* as a kind of *Inferno,* merely introductory to the *Purgatory* and *Paradise* of his new Undivine Comedy. Once Chichikov is jokingly compared to Dante, when a petty clerk, his

Virgil, shows him to the desk of the Court House where the purchase deeds are to be concluded.

Gogol did write a second part of *Dead Souls*, but burned the manuscript a few days before his death. What has been preserved, and is commonly reprinted as the second part, represents a rejected version of the continuation, written in the early forties. Every admirer of Gogol will admit that these fragments are deeply disappointing. There are serious gaps in the narrative, and Gogol seems to have lost his power of characterization. Chichikov is hardly the shadow of his former self, and the new figures of landowners are mere mouthpieces for pious platitudes. Even the ideas preached are shoddy or put into the mouths of the wrong persons: the perfect landowner Kostanzhoglo advocates only the ideals of efficiency in terms hardly different from those of the Western capitalistic world Gogol condemned so strongly. A merchant and millionaire lectures on Christianity and retirement from the world, and a prince concludes the whole with a long harangue against bribery. Only one episode, that of Petukh, a stout, hearty, overeating gentleman whom Chichikov meets floating in a pond, is worthy of the first part. This so-called second part has not been included in this edition.

We can account for Gogol's failure, at least in part. His inhibitions were psychological and psychopathic, but they were also genuinely spiritual. Gogol underwent a development which brought him to the point where he thought of himself as a great moralist and preacher, the propounder of a philosophy which, in many ways, anticipates Dostoevsky's faith in the Orthodox Church and in Holy Russia. He published a volume of *Selected Passages from a Correspondence with Friends* (1847) which raised a storm among liberals and earned him Belinsky's denunciation as a "preacher of the knout, apostle of ignorance, defender of obscurantism and darkest oppression." But there was no conversion, no "apostasy," for we can see the germs of these ideas in Gogol's early works. Nor need we share Belinsky's indignation. Gogol's religious philosophy was no mere obscurantism, but rather has affinities with the French Catholic social philosophies of the time. The fragment of a drama, *Alfred*, even shows some sympathy with a constitutional monarchy. But the artist in Gogol could not survive this overpowering religious and moral passion sharpened by doubts and self-lacerations.

The present-day reader may go on from *Dead Souls* as first published in 1842 to read stories such as the *Great Coat* (1842) and the play, *The Inspector General* (1836). He may even enjoy Gogol's early collections, *Evenings on a Farm near Dikanka* (1831–1832), and *Mirgorod* (1835), strange mixtures of Ukrainian folklore and gruesome romanticism. But *Dead Souls* is Gogol's greatest work, unique and original. It has some literary antecedents, of course: the rogues' novel, the travelogue, the humors of Sterne, the characters of Goldoni and Molière. Gogol called his novel a "poem" because it aspires to be a comic epic like Fielding's *Tom Jones*. Yet centrally Gogol is an astonishingly individual and original author. The artistic value of *Dead Souls* surely is not in the plot, the psychology, or even the ideas, but in the rich texture, the vivid detail, and its ultimate vision of the world: gloomy but also grotesquely comic.

New Haven, Connecticut   RENÉ WELLEK
June, 1948

BIOGRAPHICAL AND

BIBLIOGRAPHICAL NOTE

Nikolai Vasilievich Gogol was born in 1809 in Sorochintsy in the Government of Poltava, not far from Kiev, in the Ukraine, as the son of a small landowner. He was educated in a near-by provincial town, Nezhin, and came to Petersburg in 1828. For a time he was in the civil service and lectured on history at the university. He left Russia in 1836 and lived mostly in Rome, very retired and almost alone. He made, however, several trips to Russia and in 1848 went to Palestine on a pilgrimage. His last years were spent in Odessa and in Moscow, where he died in 1852.

There are three books on Gogol in English: Janko Lavrin's *Gogol* (New York, Dutton, 1926), primarily a deft psychological study of the man; Vladimir Nabokov's *Nikolai Gogol* (Norfolk, Conn., New Directions, 1944), a whimsical essay, with good translations, which expounds the view that Gogol was a writer of grotesques; and David Magarshack's *Gogol* (New York, Grove Press, 1957), a full and well-written biography. There are shorter useful chapters in D. S. Mirsky's *History of Russian Literature* (New York, Knopf, 1927), in Helen Muchnic's *An Introduction to Russian Literature* (Garden City, N. Y., Doubleday, 1947), in Marc Slonim's *The Epic of Russian Literature* (New York, Oxford University Press, 1950), and in V. Zenkovsky's *A History of Russian Philosophy*, trs. George L. Kline (London, Routledge and Kegan Paul; New York, Columbia University Press, 1953), vol. 1. There are two excellent articles by Dmitri Chizhevsky, "Gogol: Artist and Thinker" in *The Annals of the Ukrainian Academy of Arts and Sciences in the United States*, vol. II, No. 2(4), 1952, pp. 261-78, and "The Unknown Gogol" in *The Slavonic Review*, vol. XXX, 1952, pp. 476-93.

TRANSLATOR'S NOTE

It is gratifying to see a Russian classic in a new version, believed to be the most complete translation in any language. This edition is the fourth, and the first revision of Part I (the only one given here); all available texts have been consulted in its preparation and a considerable amount of material hitherto untranslated into English has been included. Thus the famous *Tale of Captain Kopeikin*, hitherto either prefaced with some such apology as "To reproduce this story with a raciness worthy of the original is practically impossible," or generally thrown overboard altogether, has, in those cases where it was Englished at all, been given invariably in the perverted version which Gogol was forced to substitute to save his whole book from being forbidden publication, and in which the Captain is made the villain and butt and the officials the philanthropic heroes; here, for the first time in English, the real tale is presented as based upon the author's first, suppressed version, with all due consideration given to the version usually Englished. Also, in addition to many passages, some of them quite long, hitherto scamped in translation or not translated at all, the reader will find an entire chapter (the tenth, in this translation) which has never, to the best of the translator's knowledge, appeared in English before.

No more than a dozen (or a Devil's dozen) of Russian words have been used throughout. These are so well known that it would have been feeble to use approximations in their stead. Measurements and weights have been ruthlessly computed into equivalents familiar to the reader; but, since it is as downright silly for muzhiks to be making change in dollars and cents as in shillings and farthings (or francs and sous, or even marks and pfennigs), they have been allowed to retain their own currency: a ruble under the Czars was worth practically half a dollar or two shillings; a kopeck is still one hundredth of a ruble.

Before releasing the reader to the delights that follow, the translator must make his usual request for criticisms, comments, corrections and opinions concerning his work: they will all be deeply appreciated.

BERNARD GUILBERT GUERNEY

New York, N. Y.
June, 1948

CHAPTER ONE

A RATHER HANDSOME, light traveling carriage on springs rolled into the gates of an inn in a certain provincial capital, the kind of carriage that is favored by bachelors: retired lieutenant-colonels, second captains, landowners possessing a hundred souls or so of serfs —in a word, all those who are called the fair-to-middlin' sort. The gentleman seated in this carriage was no Adonis, but he wasn't bad to look at, either; he was neither too stout nor too thin; you couldn't say he was old, but still he wasn't what you might call any too young, either. His arrival created no stir whatever in the town of N—— and was not coupled with any remarkable event; all the comments it called forth came from two native muzhiks standing in the doorway of a pot-house across the way from the inn, comments which, however, had more to do with the carriage itself than with the man sitting in it.

"Look at that, will you?" said one muzhik to the other. "What a wheel! What do you think, would that wheel make it to Moscow, if need be, or wouldn't it?"

"It would," answered the other.

"But it wouldn't make it to Kazan, I'm thinking—or would it?"

"Not to Kazan, it wouldn't," the other answered.

And with that the discussion ended.

Also, as the carriage drove up to the inn it encountered a young man in white dimity trousers, quite narrow and short, and a swallow-tail coat that made a brave attempt at being in the mode, revealing a dickey fastened with a brummagem stick-pin of bronze, in the shape of a pistol. The young man turned back, looked the vehicle over while clutching at his cap, which had been almost carried away by the wind, and then went on his way again.

As the carriage drove into the yard, its occupant was met by one of the tavern help (or *servers,* as they are called), so very lively and spry that it was downright impossible to make out what sort of face he had. He dashed out nimbly, napkin in hand, a long figure himself and wearing a long frock-coat of linsey-woolsey, its back so high that it reached almost to the very nape of his neck, tossed back his hair, and nimbly led the gentleman up and along the entire wooden outside gallery to show him the chamber that God had provided for him. The chamber was of a familiar kind, inasmuch as the inn was also of a familiar kind—that is, precisely such as all inns in provincial capitals, where for two rubles a day the transients receive a restful bedroom with cockroaches peeking out of every corner like so many black plums and with a door, always barricaded with a bureau, leading to an adjoining apartment, which apartment is always taken by a fellow-guest who is taciturn and placid yet exceedingly inquisitive, interested in knowing all the details about the latest transient. The outward façade of the inn corresponded to its interior; it was a very long building, of two stories; the lower one had not been stuccoed and exposed its small dark-red bricks, which, while they had grown still darker from the cruel changes of weather, were nevertheless rather grimy in their own right; the upper was painted yellow, of a never-varying tint; below were shops stocked with horse-collars, ropes, and hard, brittle cookies. The corner of one of these shops—or, to put it better, its window—was occupied by a vendor of hot mead, with a samovar of ruddy copper and a face as ruddy as his samovar, so that from afar one might think that there were two samovars standing in the window, if only one of them were not sporting a beard as black as pitch.

While the transient gentleman was inspecting his room his belongings were carried in; first and foremost, a small trunk of white leather, somewhat scuffed, indicating that this was not the first time it had been out on the road. The small trunk was brought in by Seliphan, the coachman, a squat little fellow in a short sheepskin coat, and by Petrushka, a flunky, a lad of thirty in a loose, much worn frock-coat, evidently a hand-me-down from his master's shoulders, a lad somewhat austere at first glance, whose lips and nose were on a very large scale. After the trunk, they carried in a small casket of mahogany with marquetry of Karelian birch, a pair of shoetrees, and a roasted chicken wrapped up in blue paper. When all these had been carried in, Seliphan the coachman set out for the stable to see to the horses, while Petrushka the flunky began settling himself in the tiny anteroom, a very dark cubby-hole, whither he had already brought his overcoat and, together with it, a certain odor all his own, which had been also imparted to the bag he brought in next, containing sundry flunkyish effects. In this cubby-hole he set up against the wall a small and narrow cot with only three legs, putting on top of it a skimpy simulacrum of a pallet, as lumpy and flat as a pancake (and, perhaps, just as greasy), which he had succeeded in wangling out of the owner of the inn.

While the servants were arranging things and fussing about, the gentleman went down into the common room. What these common rooms are like every transient knows well: there are always the same calcimined walls, darkened at the top from chimney smoke and glossy below from the backs of sundry transients, but still more from those of the indigenous traders, inasmuch as the merchants came here on market days in their sixes and their sevens to imbibe their well-known glass or two of tea; the same sooty ceiling; the some luster, dingy from smoke, with a multitude of pendent bits of glass that leapt and bounded and tinkled every time a waiter dashed across the worn-out oilcloth mattings, deftly swinging a tray on which was perched as great a host of tea cups as you might find of birds on a shore; the same pictures, covering an entire wall and done in oils—in a word, everything the same as you would find everywhere; the sole difference was that one picture depicted a nymph with such enormous breasts as the reader, in all probability, has never beheld. Such a sport of nature, however, occurs in various historical pictures, although no one knows at what period, or whence, or by whom they were imported among us in Russia—now and then, perhaps, by our grandees, those lovers of the arts, who must have bought them up in Italy upon the advice of the couriers who had driven them about.

The gentleman threw off his cap and unwound from around his neck a woolen, tricornered neckerchief of all the hues of the rainbow, of the sort that is folded for married men by their wives, with their own fair hands, to the accompaniment of prudent counsels on how they ought to muffle themselves; as for who performs that office for bachelors I cannot say with any certainty—God knows what shifts they are put to!—I never having worn such neckerchiefs. Having unwound it, the gentleman ordered his dinner. While the various dishes usual to taverns were being served up to him, such as cabbage soup with small dumplings of puff-paste (the latter purposely preserved for weeks at a stretch for the particular benefit of transients), brains with peas, sausages and sauerkraut, a roast pullet, dill pickles, and the eternal sweet pastry of layered dough, which is always at your service—while all this was being served to him, either warmed over or simply cold, he made the tavern waiter retail to him all sorts of small talk concerning such things as who had kept this tavern before and who was keeping it now, and whether it yielded much income, and whether the host were a great scoundrel, to which the waiter made the usual answer: "Oh, he's a great hand at a swindle, sir!"

Even as in enlightened Europe, so in enlightened Russia as well there are at present rather many worthy persons who can never dine in a tavern without having a chat with the waiter and at times even having a bit of fun at his expense. However, not all the questions this transient gentleman put were idle ones; he inquired, with the utmost particularity, about the officials in the town: who was the Governor of the province, who was the Chairman of the Administrative Offices, who was the Public Prosecutor—in short, he did not pass over a single bureaucrat of any importance; but with still greater particularity, if not downright concern, did he make inquiries about all the prominent landowners: how many serf-souls each one owned, how far out of town he lived, even what his character was like and how often he drove into town; he inquired closely about the state of the region—whether certain diseases weren't prevalent in that province, such as epidemic fevers, deadly agues of one sort or another, smallpox and things of that sort, and all this he asked in such a way and with such particularity as to indicate that his interest was something more than mere curiosity.

There was something substantial about the ways of this gentleman, and whenever he blew his nose he did so exceedingly loudly. No one knows just how he did it, but just the same his nose resounded like a trumpet. This point of merit, apparently a perfectly innocent one, won, nevertheless, a great deal of respect for him on the part of the tavern server, so that every time he heard this sound he would toss back his hair, straighten up with greater deference and, inclining his head from the heights, ask was the gentleman wishin' somethin'.

After dinner the gentleman partook of a cup of coffee and seated himself on a divan, resting his back on one of the cushions (which in Russian taverns are stuffed with broken bricks and cobblestones instead of resilient wool). At this point he took to yawning and asked to be shown up to his room where, lying down for just forty winks, he fell asleep for a couple of hours. Having had his siesta, he wrote on a slip of paper, at the request of the tavern waiter, his rank as well as his first name and his last, for reference to the proper quarters: the police department. As the server went down the stairs, he spelled out the following on a slip of paper: "Collegiate Councilor Pavel Ivanovich Chichikov, landowner, traveling on private affairs."

While the server was still spelling out the note, Pavel Ivanovich Chichikov himself set out to look the town over and, it would seem, was quite satisfied with it, since he found that it in no way yielded to the other provincial towns—the paint on the stone houses was the usual yellow and just as hard on the eyes, while the paint on the wooden houses showed as a modestly dark gray, quite unexceptional. The houses were of one story, of two stories, and of a story and a half, with the everlasting mezzanine which, in the opinion of the provincial architects, is ever so handsome. In some places these houses seemed lost in the midst of a street as wide as a field and among never-ending wooden fences; in others they got into a huddle, and in such places one could note a greater movement of people and greater animation. One came across signs that were all but washed off by the rains, showing pretzels and boots; occasionally these signs depicted blue breeches and the signature of some tailor or other who hailed from 'Arsaw; here was a store with caps and forage caps, and the inscription: "Vassilii Fedorov—from Abroad"; over there, a depiction of a billiard-table with two players, togged out in the sort of frock-coats worn in our theaters by those guests who come on-stage in the last act. The billiard players were portrayed taking aim with their cues, their arms twisted backward somewhat, and with bow-legs, for all the world as though they had just finished cutting a caper in the air. Under this was inscribed: "This Way to the Academy."

Here and there, right out in the street, stood stalls with nuts, soap, and cookies that looked like soap; occasionally one came on a cookshop, with a depiction of a rotund fish with a fork stuck therein. But most frequently of all one noted the time-darkened two-headed imperial eagles, which by now have been replaced by the laconic inscription: "Liquors at Retail." And the pavement was rather poor everywhere.

Chichikov also looked in at the town park, consisting of the puniest of trees, which had taken but poorly to the soil, propped at the bottom with boards placed in triangles and very handsomely painted in a glossy green. However, although these trees were no higher than reeds, the newspapers, in describing certain gala illuminations, had said of them that "Our city has been graced, thanks to the solicitude of the Municipal Director, by a park of shady trees whose spreading boughs provide coolness on a sultry day," and that, during the ceremonies, "it was most touching to observe how the hearts of the citizens throbbed in an excess of gratitude, while torrents of tears streamed forth as a mark of appreciation for His Honor the Mayor."

Having minutely questioned a policeman on post in a sentry-box as to what was the nearest way of going, if need be, to the cathedral, to the government offices, to the Governor's, Chichikov set out for a look at the river which flowed through the middle of the town; on his way thither he tore off a poster tacked up on a post, so that, upon his arrival at home, he might give it a thorough reading; eyed closely a lady who was not at all hard to look at as she passed over the wooden sidewalk, followed by a boy in the uniform of a military school with a small bundle in his hand; and after once more casting an eye over everything, as though to memorize well the lay of the land, he set out straight for home and his room, being deferentially helped up the stairs by the tavern waiter.

Having regaled himself with tea, he sat down at a table, called for a candle to be brought to him, took out of his pocket the poster and, holding it close to the candle, fell to reading, puckering his right eye just a trifle. However, there wasn't a great deal of anything remarkable in the broadside: a drama by Kotzebue* was being presented, Rollo to be played by one Poplevin, Cora by Mlle Zyablova, while the other personæ were even less outstanding; however, he read the names of the whole cast through, getting down even to the tariff on parterre seats, and also learned that the poster had been printed at the printing press of the Administration of that province; next he turned the sheet over, to find out if there might not be something on the other side as well, but, finding nothing, he rubbed his eyes, folded the sheet neatly, and put it away in his traveling casket, wherein it was his wont to store everything that came to his hand. The day was (unless I am mistaken) brought to a close by a portion of cold veal, a bottle of beet-cider, and sound slumber, with the air-pump going full blast, to use an expression current in certain localities of our widespread Russian realm.

The whole of the following day was dedicated to paying calls. The new arrival set out to call on all the high officials in town. He paid his respects at the office of the Governor who, it turned out, was just like Chichikov, in that he was neither stout in body nor thin, who wore the decoration of Anna about his neck, and concerning whom it was even being hinted that he would be proposed for a Star; he was, however, a good-hearted fellow and even occasionally embroidered fancywork on tulle with his own hands. Next Chichikov set out for the Vice-Governor's; then he called on the Public

---

* Kotzebue, August Friedrich Ferdinand von (1761–1819). In Russia from 1781 to 1795; from 1798 to 1800 Court Dramatist in Vienna; on return to Russia in 1800 sent to Siberia for one of his works but soon recalled and appointed Director of the German Troupe in Peterburgh. In 1819 he was sent to Germany, where he was slain on suspicion of espionage. Wrote more than 200 plays, sentimental, rhetorical—and enormously successful in their day. *Trans.*

Prosecutor, on the Chairman of the Administrative Offices, on the Chief of Police, on the tax-farmer, on the superintendent of the government manufactories. . . . It's a pity that it's somewhat difficult to mention all the mighty ones of this earth, but it will suffice to state that the newcomer evinced an unusual activity in the matter of calls: he put in an appearance to attest his respects even to the Inspector of the Board of Health and the Town Architect. And after that he still sat for a long time in his light carriage trying to call to mind to whom else he ought to pay a call, but it turned out that there were no more bureaucrats in that town. In his conversations with these potentates he was able to flatter each one most artfully. To the Governor he hinted, as though by the bye, that when one entered his province it was as if one were entering into a paradise: the roads might have been lined with velvet, they were that smooth, and that those governments which appointed wise dignitaries were deserving of great praise. To the Chief of Police he said something most flattering in regard to the policemen on post; while in his chats with the Vice-Governor and the Chairman of the Administrative Offices, who were still only State Councilors, he addressed each one a couple of times, in error, as Your Excellency, which proved very much to their liking. The consequence of all this was that the Governor extended him an invitation to attend an evening-at-home he was having that very night; the other bureaucrats, for their part, extended their invitations—this one to dinner, that one to a round of boston, a third to a cup of tea.

The newcomer, as it seemed, avoided saying much about himself; if he did say anything, it was in general terms, with a perceptible diffidence, and his speech on such occasions would take a somewhat bookish turn as he explained that he was the most insignificant worm in this world and unworthy of arousing much concern; that he had gone through a great deal in his day; that he had endured much for the sake of righteousness while in the service of his country; that he had many enemies, who had even made attempts at his life; that now, desirous of finding peace and quiet, he was seeking a choice spot where he might settle down at last, and that, upon his arrival in this town, he deemed it his bounden duty to attest his respect before its foremost dignitaries. And there you have everything that the town found out about this new personage, who very shortly thereafter did not fail to show himself at the Governor's evening-at-home.

His preparations for this evening-at-home took up two hours and a bit over, and in this matter likewise the newcomer envinced such an attentiveness in grooming as is hardly to be met with in general. After a brief after-dinner snooze he ordered water and a wash-basin to be brought and for an exceedingly long time scrubbed both his cheeks with soap, making them bulge out with his tongue; next, after taking a towel from the shoulder of the tavern waiter, he wiped his full face thoroughly, beginning with the back of his ears, but only after first snorting a couple of times in the tavern waiter's very face; next, he put on a dickey in front of the mirror, plucked out with tweezers a hair or two that stuck out of his nose, and immediately thereafter was clad in a frock of a scintillating bilberry-red hue. Having thus clothed himself, he drove off in his own carriage, rolling along through streets infinitely broad yet lit only by the scanty light from windows glimmering here and there.

The Governor's residence, however, was illuminated as if for nothing less than a ball; there were carriages with lamps, a brace of gendarmes before the driveway, post-boys calling in the distance —in a word, everything was just right.

Upon entering the main hall Chichikov was compelled to narrow his eyes for a minute or so, since the brilliance of the candles and lamps and the ladies' gowns was terrific. Everything was flooded with light. Everywhere one looked black frock-coats flitted and darted by, singly and in clusters, as flies dart over a white, gleaming loaf of refined sugar in the summer season, on a sultry July day, as an aged housekeeper standing at an open window cleaves and divides the loaf into glittering, irregular lumps: all the children, having flocked together, are looking on, curiously watching the movements of her roughened hands as they lift up the maul, while the aerial squadrons of flies, held up by the buoyant air, dart in boldly, as if they owned the whole place and, taking advantage of the crone's purblindness and of the sun that bothers her eyes, bestrew the dainty morsels, in some places singly, in others in thick clusters. Sated with the riches of summer, which spreads delectable repasts at every step even without such windfalls as this, they have flown in not at all in order to eat but merely to show themselves, to promenade to and fro over the mound of sugar, to rub either their hind- or their forelegs against each other, or scratch with them under their gossamer wings or, having stretched out their forelegs, to rub them over their heads, and then once more to turn around and fly away, and once more come flying back with new harassing squadrons.

Chichikov had hardly had time to look about him when his hand was already seized by the Governor, who presented him on the spot to his good lady. Here, as well, the newly come guest did not fail to keep up his end: he delivered himself of some compliment, quite suitable for a man of middle age whose rank was neither too great nor too small. When the dancers who had paired off for the evening crowded everybody to the walls he, with his hands clasped behind him, contemplated them very attentively for a few minutes. Many of the ladies were gowned well and in the latest mode; others had put on whatever the good God may have allotted to a provincial capital. The men here, even as everywhere, were of two kinds: one consisted of those who were as slim as slim could be, who were fore-ever fluttering about the ladies; some of these gallants were the sort that one could only with difficulty tell apart from the dandies of Peterburgh, having much the same side-whiskers, combed with quite a deal of thought, although the faces of some, while comely and oval, were quite smooth-shaven; they all seated themselves next to the ladies just as airily as the Peterburghers, spoke French just as the others did, and, just as the others, made the ladies laugh: everything was done just the way it is in Peterburgh.

The other sort consisted of stout men, or of such men as Chichikov—that is, not what you might call any too stout, but by no means slim, either. These, in contrast to the others, eyed the ladies askance and backed away from them and were constantly looking this way and that, to see if one of the Governor's servants were not setting out the green-baize tables for whist. Their faces were full and round, some of them even with moles, while here and there one

came across a fellow who was pock-marked as well; they did not
dress their hair either in top-knots or in curly locks, or in the *may-
the-Devil-take-me* mode, as the French put it; their hair was either
cropped short or slicked down, while their facial features were for
the most part rounded out and strong. These were the officials, the
bureaucrats, highly regarded in the town. Alas! The stout ones
are able to manage their affairs in this world better than the slim
ones can manage theirs. The slim ones work for the most part on
special missions or are merely carried on the rolls and gad about
hither and yon; their existence is somehow all too easy, ethereal,
and altogether insecure. But the stout ones never take up posts
that are off to one side, but always those that are right in line,
and once they come to roost anywhere, they will roost securely and
fast, so that though the perch may crack and bend under them yet
they will never fall. They are not fond of outward glitter and
show; the frock-coats upon them are not so deftly cut as are those
of the slim ones; but then they do have God's own plenty in their
little tin boxes. A slim fellow won't have, in the space of three
years, a single serf-soul that isn't mortgaged; the stout man plods
along, slow but sure, and, lo and behold you, somewhere at the end
of the town a house has appeared, bought in his wife's name; then,
at the other end of the town, another house; then, a little way out
of town, there's a hamlet, and after that even a country seat, with
all the adjuncts of landed property. Finally the stout man, having
served God and sovereign, having earned the respect of all, leaves
his service, moves to a new place, and becomes a landed proprietor, a
fine Russian squire, noted for his hospitality, and not merely lives,
but lives gloriously. And after him his slim heirs again try to see
how fast they can let all the paternal goods go down the drain.

It would be impossible to conceal that reflections of almost this
nature were occupying Chichikov while he was looking over the
social gathering, and the consequence was that he at last joined
the stout ones, among whom the personages he encountered were
nearly all familiar ones: the Public Prosecutor, whose eyebrows
were quite black and bushy and whose left eye had something like a
habitual wink, just as though he were saying: "Let's you and me,
brother, go into the next room—there's something I want to tell

you," but a fellow who was, nevertheless, serious and taciturn; the Postmaster, a short little man to look at, yet a wit and a philosopher, and the Chairman of the Administrative Offices, quite a judicious and amiable man. All of them welcomed Chichikov as an old acquaintance, to which welcome he responded with bows, done somewhat to one side but on the whole not without an agreeable air. It was among them that he made the acquaintance of a quite obliging and affable landowner by the name of Manilov and of a certain Sobakevich, who seemed somewhat clumsy at first glance and who began the acquaintanceship by stepping on Chichikov's foot and then begging his pardon. Here, too, a place-card for a whist table was thrust into his hand, which card he accepted with his unvaryingly polite bow.

They seated themselves at the green-baize table and never got up until supper. All talk ceased abruptly and utterly, as is always the case when people dedicate themselves to some really worth-while occupation. Although the Postmaster was quite loquacious, even he, once he had picked up his cards, immediately made his face assume a cogitative expression, sucking his lower lip under the upper and keeping it there all the time the game was on. When playing a court card he would strike the table hard with his hand, adding, if the card was a queen: "Get along with you, you old shrew!" and, if it were a king: "Go on, you Tambov muzhik!" As for the Chairman of the Administrative Offices, he would add: "Why, I'll knock his mustache off! I'll knock his mustache right off!" At times, as the players slammed their cards down on the table, certain expressions would escape them: "Ah, come what may—might as well play diamonds if there's nothing else"— "Spades, dig in!"—or simply exclamations denoting the various diminutives and pet names with which they had, within their own circle, rechristened the four suits.

At the conclusion of the game they disputed, as is the wont, quite loudly. Our newly arrived guest disputed as well, but with an extreme finesse, so that all perceived that while he was disputing he was at the same time doing so most agreeably. Never did he say: "You led," but: "You were pleased to lead; I had the honor of covering your deuce," and the like of that. In order to win his opponents over still more concerning some point or other he would, at every opportunity, offer them a pinch from his silver-and-enamel snuff-box, at the bottom of which they noticed two violets, placed therein to impart their fragrance to the snuff.

The attention of the newcomer was especially taken up by Manilov and Sobakevich, who have been mentioned above. He immediately made inquiries about them, calling the Chairman of the Administrative Offices and the Postmaster a little to one side. The few questions he put demonstrated that this visitor possessed not merely curiosity but judiciousness as well, for first of all he made inquiries as to how many serf-souls each one of them had and what condition their estates were in, and only after that did he ascertain their names and patronymics. In a short while he succeeded in absolutely enchanting them. The landowner Manilov, not at all an elderly man yet, with eyes that were as sweet as sugar, and who puckered them up every time he laughed, lost his head over Chichikov. He shook his hand for a very long time and begged him most convincingly to honor him by coming to his village, which, he said, was only some ten miles from the city limits, to which Chichikov replied, with quite a polite inclination of his head and a sincere handclasp, that he was not only ready and very willing, but would even consider it his most sacred obligation to do so. Sobakevich also said, somewhat laconically: "I beg of you to come to my place also," with a scrape of his foot, shod in a boot of such gigantic proportions that its equal was hardly to be found anywhere, especially in these times, when doughty wights are beginning to die out even in Russia.

The following day Chichikov set out for a dinner and an evening at the home of the Chief of Police, where, three hours after dinner, everybody sat down to whist and played until two in the morning. There, among other things, he made the acquaintance of Nozdrev, another landowner, a man of about thirty and a sprightly fellow who after an exchange of three or four words began *thou*'ing him. He was likewise on *thou*'ing terms with the Chief of Police and the Public Prosecutor, and treated them as close friends, but just the same when they sat down to play for big stakes the Chief of Police and the Public Prosecutor scrutinized the tricks he took with the utmost attentiveness and kept an eye on almost every card he played.

The evening of the day after that Chichikov passed at the home of the Chairman of the Administrative Offices, who received his friends in a dressing-gown that was somewhat greasy, even though there were two ladies (let us call them that) among the guests. Subsequently Chichikov was at an evening given by the Vice-Governor, at a grand dinner at the tax-farmer's, at a modest dinner at the Public Prosecutor's (which, however, had cost as much as the grand one); at the Mayor's after-mass cold buffet luncheon, which was likewise worth any dinner. In short, he did not have to remain at home for a single hour, and he would come back to his room only to sleep. This newcomer had a never-failing presence of mind, somehow, and showed himself to be an experienced man of the world. No matter what the conversation might be about he always knew how to keep it going; if the talk was about a stud-farm he would speak of a stud-farm; if they happened to speak of thoroughbred dogs, he would impart very sound observations on that subject; if the conversation had to do with an investigation being carried on by the Treasury Department, he demonstrated that juridical quiddities were also not unknown to him; if the discussion was about the game of billiards, he did not let his auditors down in that game, either; if they happened to speak of virtue, he would discourse about virtue too, and discourse exceedingly well, so that tears actually welled up in his eyes; if the talk was about distilling hard spirits, he knew what was what in hard spirits also; if it dealt with customs inspectors and clerks, why, he passed judgment about them likewise, as though he himself had been both a clerk and an inspector. But it was remarkable that he was able to clothe all this with some sort of sedateness, that he was able to conduct himself well. He spoke neither too loudly nor too low but in a manner that was just what it should be.

In a word, no matter which way you looked at him, he was a very decent fellow. All the officials were pleased by the arrival of this new personage. The Governor expressed himself clearly on the subject, that he was a well-intentioned man; the Public Prosecutor said that he was a man of affairs; the Colonel of Gendarmes, that he was a learned man; the Chairman of the Administrative Offices, that he was an experienced and meritorious man; the Chief of Police, that he was a meritorious and an amiable man; the wife of the Chief of Police, that he was the most amiable and the most courteous of men. Even Sobakevich himself, who rarely spoke well of anybody, after arriving rather late from town and having already completely undressed and got into bed by the side of his gaunt wife, said to her: "I had supper at the Chief of Police's evening-at-home and made the acquaintance of a Collegiate Councilor by the name of Pavel Ivanovich Chichikov—a most pleasant fellow!" To which his spouse answered "Hmm!" and gave him a kick.

Such was the general opinion, quite flattering to him, which was formed concerning the newcomer in that town, and it was maintained until such time as a certain strange characteristic of his, as well as an enterprise (or, as they put it in the provinces, an *escapade*) that he embarked on, both of which the reader will soon learn about, threw almost the whole town into utter bewilderment.

CHAPTER TWO

THE newly arrived gentleman had been living in the town for more than a week by now, driving about to attend modest evenings-at-home and dinners, and in that manner passing his time, as the expression goes, very pleasantly. Finally he decided to extend his visits beyond the town and to call on Manilov and Sobakevich, the landowners to whom he had given his word to do so. Perhaps he was urged thereto by another, more essential reason; a matter more serious, nearer his heart. . . . But concerning all this the reader will find out by degrees and in its own due time, if he will only have the patience to read the narrative offered him—a very long one, which has yet to expand more sweepingly and broadly as it draws to that end which crowns the matter.

An order was issued to Seliphan the coachman to harness the horses in the familiar carriage early in the morning; Petrushka the flunky was ordered to stay at home, to keep an eye on the room and the small trunk. It would not be superfluous for the reader to make the acquaintance of these two bondmen of our hero's. Even though, of course, they are not such very prominent personæ and belong to what is called the secondary or even the tertiary category, and even though the chief actions and mainsprings of this epic are not based upon them, and may concern and implicate them but lightly here and there, yet the author is exceedingly fond of being circumstantial in all things, and even though he himself is a native of Russia, he wishes, in this respect, to be as thorough-going as any German. This, however, will not take up very much time and space, since it will not be necessary to add a great deal to that which the reader already knows—to wit, that Petrushka walked around in a loose brown frock-coat that was a hand-me-down from his master, and that he had, as is usually the way among people of his calling, a nose and lips done on a large scale. He was by temperament taciturn rather than talkative; he even had a noble impulse toward enlightenment—i.e., the reading of books, the contents of which presented no difficulty to him whatsoever; it was all one to him if the book dealt with the adventures of an enamored hero or whether it was simply a dictionary or a prayer book—he read everything with the same attentiveness; if a hand-book on chemistry were to be thrust under his nose he wouldn't have spurned it either. It wasn't what he read that pleased him, but rather the reading itself or, to put it better, the very process of reading—look and behold you, some word or other inevitably cropped up from out the welter of letters, even though, at times, the Devil alone knew what that word might mean. This reading was generally performed in a recumbent position, in the entry, on his cot and pallet; the latter, owing to this circumstance, had become as flat and thin as a wafer. Besides his passion for reading he had two more habits that comprised his two other characteristic traits: that of sleeping without undressing, just as he was, in that very self-same frock-coat, and

16 ·

of always having about him a certain atmosphere that was peculiarly his own, somewhat redolent of quarters that had been long lived in, so that it sufficed for him merely to set up his cot somewhere, even in a room that had not up to then been lived in, and to drag therein his overcoat and worldly goods, and it would immediately seem that people had been living in that room for ten years or so. Chichikov, being quite a sensitive man, and even in certain cases downright squeamish, upon drawing in a whiff of the air in the morning, through a nose refreshed by slumber, could only make a wry face and say, after a shake of his head: "The Devil alone knows what you're up to, brother; you're sweating, or something. You ought to go to a public bath, at least." To which Petrushka would make no reply and try to busy himself with some immediate task: he would either pick up a clothes brush and go to where his master's frock-coat was hung up, or simply begin tidying up something or other. What were his thoughts the while he went silently about his tasks? He may have been saying to himself: "You're a fine fellow, too; you never get bored with saying the same old thing over and over and over. . . ." God knows, it is hard to know what a slave servant thinks about while the man who owns him gives him a lecture. And there, for a start, you have what can be told about Petrushka.

Seliphan the coachman was an altogether different sort of man. . . . However, the author is quite conscience-stricken about taking up the time of his readers for so long with people of a low class, knowing, by experience, how unwilling they are to be introduced to the low strata of society. For that's how the native Russian is: he has an overwhelming passion for scraping up an acquaintance with him who may be but a single step above him in rank, while a nodding acquaintance with a count or a prince is for him a better thing than to be on the most intimate terms with a real friend. The author actually feels dubious about his hero, who is only a mere Collegiate Councilor, after all. There is a likelihood that Court Councilors, say, may condescend to know him; but as for those who have already clambered up the grades of General This and General That, these, God knows, may even bestow upon him one of those contemptuous looks which man proudly bestows upon anything that may be crawling like vermin at his feet, or, which would be still worse, will pass him by with an unconcern that would be lethal for the author.

However, no matter how exceedingly grievous either the one procedure or the other would be, we still must come back to our hero. And so, having issued the necessary orders the evening before, after awakening very early in the morning, after a wash-up and a sponge bath from head to foot (something that was ordinarily gone through only on Sundays, and this day happening to be a Sunday), after shaving himself so closely that his cheeks became truly satin-like, as far as smoothness and glossiness were concerned, and donning his frock-coat of scintillating bilberry hue, and then a great-coat lined with selected bearskins, he at last descended the stairs, supported now on this side, now on that, by the tavern servant, and seated himself in his light carriage. The said carriage thundered out of the gates of the inn and into the street. A priest who was passing by doffed his hat; several street urchins in thoroughly soiled shirts held out their hands, to a chorus of "Kind sir, give something to a poor orphan!" The coachman, having noticed that one of them had a great fondness for hitching on behind, lashed him with his whip, and the carriage was off, bouncing over the cobbles.

Not without joy did Chichikov behold the striped toll-gate in the distance, informing him that the paved way, even as every other torture, would soon be at an end; and, after having bumped his head quite hard a few more times against the body of the vehicle, he was at last rolling along on soft earth. Hardly had the town retreated when (quite the usual thing among us) there unrolled on both sides of the road vistas of a wild preposterousness: hummocks, fir groves, small, squat, sparse undergrowths of young pines, charred stumps of old ones, wild heather, and such-like nonsensical rubbish. One came upon villages all strung out in a single line, with huts that looked like weather-beaten woodpiles, covered over with gray roofs, the wooden fretwork decorations underneath them resembling hanging towels with embroidered designs. A few muzhiks in short sheepskin jackets were, as usual, yawning as they squatted on benches placed before the gates; countrywives, with stout faces and their breasts caught up by shawls, were looking out of the upper windows; out of a lower window a calf would peer, or a sow might be poking out its unseeing snout. In brief, the sights were of a thoroughly familiar nature. Having passed the tenth mile, Chichikov recalled that, according to Manilov, his village must be thereabouts, but the eleventh mile flew by as well and yet the village was still not to be seen, and had it not been for two muzhiks that they chanced to come upon Chichikov and his coachman would hardly have hit upon the right direction.

In response to the query whether the village of Zamanilovka was far off, the muzhiks doffed their hats, while one of them, who was brighter than the other and adorned with a beard shaped like a wedge, answered: "Is it Manilovka, mebbe, and not Zamanilovka?"

"Well, yes, Manilovka."

"Oh, Manilovka! Why, soon as you drive on for a mile more you'll come smack on it—that is, sort of straight to the right."

"To the right?" the coachman echoed him.

"To the right," said the muzhik. "That will be your road to Manilovka; as for Zamanilovka, there ain't no such place whatsoever. That's what it's called—it goes by the name of Manilovka, that is; but there ain't no Zamanilovka hereabouts at all, at all. When you get there, you'll see a house up on a hill, of stone, two-storied—the manor, that is, where the squire himself lives. And that there is your Manilovka; but as for Zamanilovka, there ain't no such place whatsoever hereabouts, nor ever has been."

They set off in search of Manilovka. Having driven for well over a mile they came to a turn in a country road; but they covered another mile, then two and three, it seemed, yet there was still no two-story house of stone to be seen. At this point Chichikov remembered that when a friend invites you to call on him in his village, only ten miles out of town, it means that it must certainly be twenty miles distant.

The village of Manilovka could hardly lure many people by its location. The manor house stood all by itself out in the open—that is, it was on an elevation exposed to all the winds of heaven that might chance to blow; the slope of the hill upon which it stood was covered with closely clipped turf. Two or three clumps of lilac bushes and yellow acacias were scattered over it, in the English manner; birches, in small groups of five or six, reared their small-leaved, rather scanty tops here and there. Under two of these one could see an arbor with a low green cupola, blue wooden columns, and an inscription reading: *A Temple for Solitary Meditation;* somewhat lower was a pond, covered with green scum, which, how-ever, is no great matter of wonder in the English gardens of Russian landowners. At the foot of this hill, and partly up the slope itself, criss-crossing and showing darkly, stood gray little log-huts, which our hero, for some reason unknown, fell to counting that very moment, and of which he counted more than two hundred. No-where among them was there a bit of a tree growing, or any sort of greenery; everywhere there were only logs to be seen. The view was animated by two countrywives, who, with their gowns hitched up and tucked in all around, were wading up to their knees in the pond, dragging by two wooden grapples a torn dragnet, wherein one could glimpse a couple of entangled crayfish and the gleam of the captured dace; the women, apparently, were at odds and were having high words over something. Showing darkly to one side, somewhat at a distance, was a pine forest of some depressingly bluish tint. Even the very weather had quite fittingly put itself out: the day was neither clear nor cloudy, but of some dove-gray tinge, such as you can find only upon the worn uniforms of soldiers in garrison, those troops that are, on the whole, peaceful, but never entirely sober of Sundays. To round out the picture there was not lacking a rooster, that harbinger of changeable weather, who, dis-regarding the fact that his head had been pecked through to the very brain by the beaks of other roosters over certain affairs of gallantry, was clamoring at the top of his voice and even beating his wings, as bedraggled as old straw matting.

As he was driving up to the courtyard, Chichikov observed the master himself, standing on the porch, in a coat of green châlons cloth, with his hand at his forehead, cupped over his eyes as a sunshade the better to see the approaching vehicle. As the light carriage neared the porch, his eyes grew merrier and merrier and his smile expanded more and more.

"Pavel Ivanovich!" he cried out at last, as Chichikov was alighting from his carriage. "So you have at last managed to remember us!"

Both friends kissed most heartily and Manilov led his guest inside. Although the time during which they will be passing through the entry, the anteroom, and the dining room is somewhat brief, nevertheless let us try if we can't somehow utilize it to say a thing or two about the master of the house. But at this point the author must confess that such an undertaking is a very difficult one. It is considerably easier to depict characters that are on a grand scale: there you just dash the pigments onto the canvas with a full sweep—black, blazing orbs, beetling eyebrows, a forehead furrowed by a deep crease, a black cape (or one as scarlet as fire) tossed over the shoulders—and your portrait is done; but you take all these gentlemen, now, of whom there are so many in this world, who are so very much like one another in appearance, and yet at the same time, when you take a close look, will be seen to have many exceedingly elusive peculiarities—why, these gentlemen are dreadfully difficult to do in portraits. Here you will have to strain your observation hard, until you compel all the fine, almost imperceptible traits to emerge before you and, in general, you will have to force your eye, already well exercised in the science of prying, to penetrate as deeply as possible.

God alone, perhaps, could tell what sort of character Manilov's was. There is a species of men labeled as *so-so, neither here nor there*, or, in the words of the proverb, *neither fish nor flesh nor good red herring*. Perhaps Manilov as well ought to be included in their number. He was a striking man, to look at him; the features of his face were not devoid of amiability, but there was apparently far too great an overdose of sugariness about it; in his ways and turns of speech there was something that wheedled for your good graces and friendship. He smiled ingratiatingly and was blond in an ashy sort of way, with blue eyes. During the first minute or so of a conversation with him you could not but say: "What a pleasant and kindhearted man!" The minute after that you would not say anything at all, while the third minute you would say: "The Devil knows what's going on here!" and walk away as far as ever you could; if you didn't, you'd feel a deathly spell of the blues coming on. You could not, no matter how long you bided your time, ever get an eager word out of him, or even a challenging one, for that matter, such as you may hear from almost anybody should you broach a matter that touches him to the quick. Every man has some ambition of his own: the ambition of one may turn on wolfhounds; to another it seems that he is a great lover of music and amazingly sensitive to all the profound passages therein; a third may be a great hand at putting away a huge dinner; a fourth feels that he can play a better part in this world, even though that part be but a fraction above the one assigned to him; a fifth fellow, whose aspiration is more circumscribed, sleeps and dreams of how he might promenade on a gala occasion with some aide-de-camp, showing off before his friends, his acquaintances, and even those who aren't acquainted with him; a sixth may be gifted with a hand that feels a preternatural urge to bet big on an ace or deuce of diamonds, say, while the hand of a seventh simply itches to set things to rights wherever he may happen to be, to get under the skin of a station master or stage-coach drivers. In short, everyone has something all his own, but Manilov didn't have a thing. At home he spoke very little and for the most part gave himself up to meditation and thought, but what he thought was, likewise, known only to God—maybe. It could not be said that he busied himself about the estate—he never so much as drove out into the fields; the estate got along of its own accord, somehow. When his steward would tell him: "It might be a good thing, master, to do so and so,"—"Yes, that's not a bad idea," he would usually answer as he puffed away at his pipe, pipe-smoking being a habit he had formed at the time he had served in the army, where he had been considered the most modest, the most considerate, and the best-educated of officers. "Yes, just so, that's not a bad idea," he would repeat. When some muzhik would come to him and, scratching the nape of his neck, would say: "Master, give me leave from my work, so's I can earn enough for the taxes," —"Go ahead," he would say, puffing away at his pipe, and it never even entered his head that the muzhik was going off on a bender.

At times, as he looked down from the front porch on the courtyard and the pond, he would get to talking of what a good thing it would be if one were to up and tunnel an underground passage leading out of the house, or build a stone bridge across the pond, on both sides of which there would be shops, and have merchants sitting therein and selling all sorts of small wares that the peasants needed. As he spoke thus his eyes would become exceedingly sweet, while his face assumed the most contented expression. However, these projects ended, after all, with mere talk. In his study there was always some book lying about, with a bookmark laid in on page 14, which he had been steadily reading for two years by now. There was perpetually something lacking about his house: the furniture in the dining room was splendid, upholstered with the smartest of silk materials, which had certainly cost quite a bit; but there had not been enough of it for two of the easy chairs, and those two chairs stood there upholstered in ordinary matting; however, the master, for several years at a stretch, kept warning every guest with the words: "Don't sit down on those chairs; they aren't ready yet." In some of the rooms there was no furniture whatsoever, even though there had been some talk of it during the first days after his marriage: "We'll have to see to it tomorrow, my pet, and have some furniture placed in this room, if only temporarily." Toward evening an exceedingly exquisite candlestick of patinated bronze, with the three Graces of antiquity and an exquisite escutcheon of mother-of-pearl, would be brought in and placed on the table, and right alongside of it would be put some invalid of common copper, lame, twisted all to one side, and covered all over with winding-sheets of tallow; the incongruity of this, however, struck neither the master of the house, nor its mistress, nor the servants.

His wife . . . however, they were perfectly content with each other. Despite the fact that more than eight years had elapsed since their marriage, each one of them still kept bringing to the other either a slice of apple, or a bon-bon, or a nut, and would say in a touchingly tender voice: "Open your little mouth wide, dearest, and let me put this tid-bit in it." It goes without saying that the little mouth was on such an occasion opened very gracefully. When a birthday was due, surprises would be prepared—some sort of tiny beaded pocket-case to hold a toothpick. And quite often as they sat on the divan, suddenly, for no known reason on earth, he abandoning his pipe and she whatever she may have been working on (if it happened to be in her hands at the time, of course), they would impress so languishing and prolonged a kiss upon each other's lips that one could, while it lasted, smoke a small straw-stemmed cheroot to the end. In a word, they were what is called happy. Of course, it may be remarked that there are many other things to be done about the house besides preparing surprises and indulging in prolonged kisses, and one could put a great many questions. Why, for instance, was the kitchen run so stupidly and shiftlessly? Why was the larder rather empty? Why was the housekeeper such a thief? Why were the servants slovenly in person and such drunkards? Why did all the house help sleep so outrageously long, and carry on dissolutely all the rest of the time? But all these are low matters, whereas Mme Manilova had been well educated. And a good education, as everybody knows, is acquired at boarding schools; and at boarding schools, as everybody knows, there are three major subjects which constitute the basis of all human virtues: the French language, indispensable for domestic happiness; the pianoforte, to afford pleasant moments to one's spouse; and, finally, that which really pertains to domestic science: the knitting of purses and other such surprises. However, there do occur sundry refinements and variations in methods, especially at the present time; it all depends for the most part upon the good sense and the capabilities of the boarding school head-mistresses themselves. In other boarding schools the major subjects may be given in such order that the pianoforte comes first of all, the French language next, and domestic science only after that. And at times it may even so happen that the first in order is domestic science—i.e., the knitting of birthday surprises —then the French language, and the pianoforte only after that. The methods vary. It might not be out of the way to make one more remark . . . but, I confess, I am very much afraid to talk about the ladies, and besides that it's high time I returned to my heroes, who have been standing for several minutes now before the doors of the drawing room, each urging the other to enter first.

"Don't disturb yourself for my sake, if you please," Chichikov was saying. "I shall follow you in."

"No, Pavel Ivanovich, no—you are my guest," Manilov was saying, indicating the door with a wave of his hand.

"Don't put yourself out, please—don't put yourself out; do go in, please."

"No, really, you must excuse me; I would never allow such a pleasant, cultured guest to go in after me!"

"You have too high an opinion of my culture. . . . Please go in!"

"Well, now, do be kind enough to go in first."

"But why?"

"Well, now, just so!" said Manilov with a pleasant smile.

Finally both friends went through the door sideways, crowding each other somewhat.

"Allow me to present you to my wife," said Manilov. "My pet, this is Pavel Ivanovich!"

It was only now that Chichikov observed a lady whom he had utterly failed to notice while he had been so busily scraping and bowing to Manilov in the doorway. She wasn't bad to look at, and becomingly dressed. A negligee of some finely woven silken material, pale in hue, sat well upon her; a slender, small hand hurriedly tossed something on the table and clutched a cambric handkerchief with embroidered corners. She rose up from the divan on which she had been sitting. It was not without pleasure that Chichikov approached to kiss her tiny hand. Mme Manilova assured him, even lisping somewhat, that he had made them very happy by coming, and that not a day passed without her husband's calling him to mind.

"Yes," Manilov proclaimed, "she even used to ask me all the time: 'How is it your friend does not come?' 'Wait, my pet,' I would tell her, 'he'll come.' And so at last you've actually honored us with your visit. Really, now, you've afforded me such delight . . . like a day in May . . . a birthday of the heart. . . ."

Chichikov, hearing that matters had already reached the stage of a birthday of the heart, actually became somewhat embarrassed and modestly protested that he had neither a renowned name nor even a distinguished rank.

"You have everything," Manilov interrupted him with the same pleasant smile, "you have everything—and even a bit over."

"How did our town strike you?" asked Mme Manilova. "Have you spent your time pleasantly there?"

"A very fine town, a splendid town," Chichikov responded, "and I have spent my time very pleasantly; the society there is most cordial."

"And how does our Governor strike you?" Mme Manilova persisted.

"A most estimable and amiable man, isn't he?" added Manilov.

"Perfectly true," said Chichikov, "a most estimable man. And how he has put his very heart into his work—what a grasp he has of it! One can only wish that there were more people like him."

"How skillful he is, don't you know, in receiving anybody, in observing delicacy in all his actions." Manilov contributed his bit with a smile and, in his delight, all but closed his eyes, like a tom-cat when you tickle him lightly behind his ears.

"A most obliging and pleasant person," Chichikov went on, "and what a clever, artistic chap! I could never even suppose such a thing, but how well he embroiders all sorts of designs for the house! He was showing me a purse, his own handiwork—there's hardly a lady who could have embroidered it as cleverly as he did."

"And the Vice-Governor, now, what an endearing chap he is, isn't he?" asked Manilov, again puckering up his eyes somewhat.

"A most worthy person, most worthy!" Chichikov responded.

"And, if I may ask, what did you think of the Chief of Police? A most pleasant person, isn't he?"

"Extremely pleasant, and what an intelligent, what a well-read man! We played whist at his place together with the public Prosecutor and the Chairman of the Administrative Offices until the last roosters left off crowing. A most worthy person, most worthy!"

"Well, now, and what is your opinion of the Chief of Police's wife?" added Mme Manilova. "A most pleasing woman, isn't she?"

"Oh, she is one of the worthiest women I know of!" Chichikov rose to the occasion.

Following this, they did not omit the Chairman of the Administrative Offices, nor the Postmaster, and in such fashion went over nearly all the officials in the town, who all turned out to be the most worthy persons.

"Do you spend all your time in the village?" Chichikov at last put a question in his turn.

"Yes, for the most part," answered Manilov. "Occasionally, however, we drive into town for the sole purpose of seeing some cultured people. You'd become rusticated, you know, if you were to lead a cloistered life all the time."

"True, true," said Chichikov.

"Of course," Manilov went on, "if only one had some good neighbors; if, for instance, one had some such person as one might chat with about the amenities of life, about good usage, or if one had some scientific pursuit or other that would kind of stir the soul, lend one wings to kind of soar with, as it were. . . ." At this point he wanted to express something additional but, perceiving that he had become all tangled up in verbiage, merely fluttered his hand in the air and went on: "In that case, of course, village life and solitude would have very many pleasant points. But there is absolutely no one. . . . All one can do is dip now and then into the *Son of the Fatherland.*"

Chichikov evinced utter agreement to this, adding that there could be nothing more gratifying than living in solitude, taking delight in beholding Nature's pageantry, and occasionally reading some book or other.

"But do you know," Manilov added, "that everything, if one has no friend to share it with—"

"Oh, that's true, that's perfectly true!" Chichikov interrupted him. "What do all the treasures in the world signify in that case! *Do not treasure money; treasure the company of good men,* as a certain sage has said."

"And do you know, Pavel Ivanovich," said Manilov, making his face assume an expression that was not only sweet but actually cloying, like the sort of mixture which an adroit worldly doctor has laced unmercifully with saccharine, imagining that he will gladden his patient thereby, "that in such a case one feels a certain spiritual enjoyment, in a kind of way. . . . As, for instance, right now, when chance has afforded me the happiness—a rare, exemplary happiness, I might say—of chatting with you and of enjoying your pleasant conversation—"

"Come, what sort of pleasant conversation am I capable of? I am but an insignificant person, nothing more," Chichikov protested.

"Oh, Pavel Ivanovich! Allow me to be frank—I would joyfully give up half my property to have but a part of those good qualities which are yours!"

"On the contrary, for my part I would consider it the greatest—"
No one knows to what lengths this mutual outpouring of sentiments on the part of these friends would have gone, if a servant had not entered and announced that dinner was waiting.

"Pray go in," said Manilov. "You must excuse us if our dinner isn't of the sort that's served in parqueted banquet halls, in capital cities; we do things in a simple fashion, after the Russian way—nothing but cabbage soup, yet offered with an open heart. Go in, please."

Here they disputed for another spell as to who was to go in first, and at last Chichikov edged into the dining room.

Two little boys were already standing in the room—Manilov's sons, who had reached the age when children are already allowed to sit at the family table, but still in high chairs. Their tutor, who was hovering over them, made a polite bow and smiled. The hostess took her seat behind the soup tureen; the guest was seated between the master of the house and its mistress; a servant tied napkins about the necks of the children.

"What darling little children!" said Chichikov, after one look at them. "And how old may they be?"

"The elder is eight, while the younger passed his sixth birthday only yesterday," Mme Manilova informed him.

"Themistoclius!" said Manilov, turning to the elder, who was striving to free his chin, which had been tied up in the napkin by the waiter. Chichikov raised his eyebrows somewhat upon hearing such a name—only partially Greek, inasmuch as Manilov, for some unknown reason, had given it the *ius* ending—but made an immediate effort to resume his usual expression. "Themistoclius, tell me, which is the finest city in France?"

At this point the tutor turned his full attention on Themistoclius and it seemed as if he wanted to penetrate into the boy's very head through his eyes, but finally became perfectly reassured and nodded when Themistoclius answered: "Paris."

"And what is our finest city?" Manilov asked again.

The teacher again became all attention.

"Peterburgh."

"And what's another great city?"

"Moscow," answered Themistoclius.

"What a clever darling!" Chichikov commented on this. "I must say . . ." he went on, at once turning with a certain air of amazement to the Manilovs. "Of such tender years, and yet already possessed of such knowledge! I must tell you that this child will have great abilities!"

"Oh, you don't know him yet!" Manilov responded. "He has an extremely keen wit. You take the younger, Alcides, he isn't so apt; whereas this little chap, the minute he comes across anything—some tiny insect, some little bug—why, his eyes simply light up all of a sudden and start darting to and fro; he'll run after it and draw your attention to it at once. I intend to have him go into the diplomatic corps. Themistoclius," he went on, turning to the boy anew, "do you want to be an ambassador?"

"Yes, I want to," answered Themistoclius, munching bread and letting his head loll right and left.

At this juncture the waiter who had been standing behind him wiped the ambassador's nose, and it was very well he did so, otherwise a most considerable drop of foreign matter would have plumped into the ambassador's soup. The table-talk began: about the pleasures of a tranquil life, interspersed by comments from the lady of the house concerning the theater in town and the actors there. The tutor looked at the speakers most attentively, and as soon as he noticed that they were about to smile he would open his mouth at the precise moment and laugh assiduously. Probably he was an accommodating fellow and wanted in this manner to repay the master of the house for good treatment. Once, however, his face assumed a stern look and he rapped sternly on the table, fixing his eyes on the children seated across the table from him. This was really called for, inasmuch as Themistoclius had bitten Alcides' ear, and Alcides, having shut his eyes and opened his mouth, was all set to begin bawling in a most piteous manner: but, sensing that this might easily lead to being deprived of a course, restored his mouth to its previous state and, with tears in his eyes, fell to gnawing at a mutton bone, which made both his cheeks glossy with grease.

The hostess very often turned to Chichikov with the words: "You aren't eating a thing; you have helped yourself to very little—" to which Chichikov would answer every time: "Thank you very much—I'm full. Pleasant talk is better than any course."

By and by they got up from the table. Manilov was in exceedingly benign mood and, with one arm protectingly about his guest's shoulders, was about to steer him thus into the drawing room when the latter suddenly declared, with quite a significant air, that there was a certain urgent matter he had intended to discuss with him.

"In that case allow me to invite you into my study," said Manilov, and led him off to a small room, one of its windows looking out on the blue-tinged forest.

"This is my den," said Manilov.

"A pleasant, cozy room," said Chichikov, having cast his eye over it. And the room really wasn't devoid of a pleasant atmosphere; the walls were done in some charming bluish tint, on the grayish side; there were four chairs, one easy chair, a table on which a book was lying, with a bookmark inserted therein, which book we've already had occasion to mention, and several papers covered with writing; but there was more of tobacco there than of anything else. It was there in all shapes and forms: in paper-boxes, in a tobacco jar, and, finally, simply strewn in a heap on the table. Also, lying upon both windowsills, were little mounds of ashes knocked out of pipes and so disposed, not without pains, as to achieve very handsome little rows. It was obvious that, on occasion, this must have constituted a pastime for the master of the house.

"I would ask you, if you will allow me, to make yourself comfortable in this easy chair," said Manilov.

"I'll take a plain chair, if you'll allow me."

"Allow me not to allow you that," said Manilov with a smile. "I keep this easy chair especially for any guest of mine; you must take it, whether you like it or not."

Chichikov took it.

"Allow me to treat you to a small pipeful—"

"No, I don't smoke," Chichikov answered affably and with an apparent air of regret.

"But why?" asked Manilov, likewise affably and with an air of real regret.

"I haven't formed the habit, I'm afraid; they say that pipe-smoking gives one asthma."

"Allow me to inform you that that is a prejudice. I even believe that to smoke a pipe is far healthier than to snuff tobacco. We had a lieutenant in our regiment who never let a pipe out of his mouth, not only at table but even, if I may be allowed to say it, in all other places. And now he's forty and over but, God be thanked, he's in such good health that it couldn't be better."

Chichikov observed that things like that did happen, most certainly, and that there were many things to be found in nature which were inexplicable for even the broadest mind.

"But first allow me to make one request—" he uttered in a voice about which there was a suggestion of a certain strange (or almost strange) intonation, and immediately thereafter, for some unknown reason, glanced over his shoulder. "How long ago was it your pleasure to submit a tally of your serfs to the Bureau of Audits census?"

"Why, a long time ago, by now; or it might be better to say that I can't recall when."

"How many of your people have died since the last time you submitted a tally?"

"Why, I can't tell; it would be necessary to ask the steward about this, I suppose. Hey, there, fellow! Summon the steward here; he ought to be around today."

The steward appeared. He was a man of under forty, clean-shaven and used to wearing a frock-coat and, apparently, one who led a tranquil existence, inasmuch as his face had a sort of puffly full look, while the yellowish tinge of his skin and his little eyes indicated that he knew only too well what downy comforters and featherbeds were like. One could see right off that he had gone through his career much the same as all seigniorial stewards do: he had been formerly simply a lad about the house who knew how to read and write; then had married some Agashka, a housekeeper who was her mistress' favorite; had become a manager in his own turn, and after that actually the steward. And having become steward he acted, of course, as all stewards do: he hobnobbed with and cultivated the friendship of those folk in the village who were better off, and added to the burdens of those of the poorer sort; he awoke when the morning was going on nine, and then took it easy till the samovar came and he had his tea.

"I say, my good fellow, how many of our people have died since the time we submitted the figures for that last census?"

"Why, how do you mean, how many? There's been many dying off since then," said the steward, and hiccuped at the same time, shielding his mouth by slightly cupping his hand over it.

"Yes, I admit I was thinking the same thing myself," Manilov chimed in with him. "Very many have been dying since then—precisely!" Here he turned around to Chichikov and added once more: "Exactly so—very many."

"But what, for instance, would their number be?" Chichikov inquired.

"Yes, how many do they number?" Manilov chimed in.

"Why, how is one to say what their number is? For no one knows how many of them died off; nobody kept any count of them."

"Yes, precisely," said Manilov, turning to Chichikov. "I also supposed that the mortality had been great; there's absolutely no knowing how many have died off."

"You will count them over, please," said Chichikov to the steward, "and make a detailed list of them, with their names."

"Yes, all of them, with their names," echoed Manilov.

"Right, sir!" said the steward and went out.

"And for what reasons do you need this?" asked Manilov when the steward had taken his leave.

This question, it seemed, was a difficult one for his guest; some sort of strained expression appeared on his face, actually making it turn red—a straining to express something that it was not entirely easy to put into words. And truly, Manilov at last heard such strange and extraordinary things as human ears had never heard before.

"For what reasons, you ask? Here are the reasons: I would like to buy some people—" said Chichikov, then stammered and did not finish what he was saying.

"But allow me to ask you," said Manilov, "how would you wish to buy these people: with land, or simply to take them with you—without land, that is?"

"No, it isn't the actual peasants I am after," said Chichikov. "What I wish to have is the dead ones—"

"What, sir? Pardon me . . . I am somewhat hard of hearing; I thought I heard a most peculiar word—"

"I propose to acquire the dead people, who, however, would be designated as alive in the Bureau of Audits," said Chichikov.

Right then and there Manilov let his chibouk crash to the floor, long stem, red clay bowl and all, and for several moments remained with his mouth still gaping. Both friends, who had so recently discussed the pleasures of a life of friendship, remained motionless, staring into each other's eyes, like those portraits which in the old times used to be hung facing each other, one on each side of a mirror. At last Manilov picked up his chibouk and, as he was bending down, looked up into Chichikov's face, trying to catch a possible smile or something of the sort on his lips, to see if he weren't jesting; but there was nothing of the kind to be seen—on the contrary, Chichikov's face seemed to be even more dignified than ever. Then it occurred to Manilov that perhaps his guest might have gone out of his mind by some chance, and he looked at him intently with fear. But his guest's eyes were perfectly clear; there was no wild, restless fire in them, such as darts through the eyes of a mad person; everything was seemly and proper. No matter how hard Manilov tried to consider how he was to act and what he had to do, he still could not think of anything better than letting the smoke dribble out of his mouth in a very tenuous stream.

"And so I would like to know if you could let me have such people, who are not actually living, yet alive insofar as legal form is concerned, by transferring them to me, or ceding them, or in whichever manner may be best to your way of thinking."

But Manilov became so confused and muddle-headed that he merely kept staring at him.

"It seems to me that you find the matter a difficult one?"

"I? . . No, that's not it," said Manilov. "But I can't grasp . . . pardon me . . . I, of course, was unable to receive such a brilliant education as is, so to say, to be perceived in your every movement; I do not possess the high art of self-expression. Perhaps in this case . . . in the explanation which you have just now put forth . . . there is concealed some other . . . perhaps you were pleased to express yourself thus for the sake of a good style?"

"No," Chichikov caught him up, "no, I mean the matter to be taken just as it is—that is, I am referring to those souls who are now definitely dead."

Manilov was utterly at a loss. He felt that there was something that he had to do, some question that he had to put, but what that question was the Devil alone knew. He wound up, at last, by again letting the smoke out, this time, however, not through his mouth but through his nostrils.

"And so, if there is nothing in the way, we can with God's grace get down to making out the purchase-deed," said Chichikov.

"What—a purchase-deed to dead souls?"

"Oh, no!" said Chichikov. "We will write down that they are alive, just as they are actually entered in the census of the Bureau of Audits. I have made a habit of not deviating in any way from the civil legal code; even though I have had to suffer on that account during my service, yet you must excuse me: an obligation is to me a sacred thing; as for the law, I stand in reverent awe before it."

The last words proved to Manilov's liking, but he still could not, no matter how he tried, penetrate the gist of the matter itself and, instead of replying, took to sucking away at his chibouk so hard that, at last, it began to gurgle like a bassoon. It seemed as if he were trying to draw out of it an opinion concerning such an unheard-of situation; but the chibouk merely gurgled and emitted its death-rattle and nothing more.

"Perhaps you are entertaining certain doubts?" asked Chichikov.

"Oh, I wouldn't want you to think so—not in the least! What I am saying has nothing to do with my having any prejudgment concerning you—any critical attitude, that is. But allow me to put this to you: won't this enterprise—or, to use a more comprehensive expression, as it were—won't this negotiation, then, be out of keeping with the civil regulations and the ultimate welfare of Russia?"

At this point Manilov, lifting his head somewhat, looked very significantly into Chichikov's face, exhibiting on every feature of his own and especially on his tightly compressed lips an expression so profound that, in all probability, its like was not to be seen on any human countenance, with the possible exception of some far too clever prime minister and, even so, only at a moment when he is engaged in some particularly brain-racking affair.

But Chichikov merely remarked that such an enterprise, or negotiation, would in no way be out of keeping with civil regulations and the ultimate welfare of Russia, and a moment thereafter added that the Treasury would actually derive benefit therefrom, since it would receive the legal stamp-duties.

"Do you really think so?"

"I think that it will be a good thing."

"Ah, if it's going to be a good thing then it's an entirely different matter; I have nothing against it," said Manilov, and became utterly reassured.

"All that remains now is to agree on the price—"

"What—did you say anything about a price?" Manilov was off again, and then paused. "Can you possibly suppose that I am going to accept money for souls that, in a sort of a way, have done with their existence? Since you have already gotten such a, so to say, fantastic whim, then for my part I assign them to you without any financial interest in the matter and will take the costs of the purchase-deed upon myself."

It would be a great reproach to the historian of the events recorded herein if he omitted to state that after hearing Manilov utter such words his guest was overcome with pleasure. No matter how dignified and judicious he may have been, nevertheless at this point it was all he could do to keep himself from actually cutting a caper in the air, something like a goat's, which, as everybody knows, is something that is done only under the strongest impulses of joy. He turned so hard in the armchair that the woolen material of its cushion burst apart; as for Manilov, he was regarding him with a certain perplexity. Chichikov, prompted by gratitude, instantly poured out such a flood of thanks that the host became embarrassed, turned all red, went through a deprecatory gesture with his head, and, only at long last, declared that all this was really nothing, that he would actually like to prove in some real way the inclination of his heart, the magnetism of the soul; but as for giving away the dead serf-souls, they were, in a sort of way, so much trash.

"They are far from being trash," said Chichikov, squeezing Manilov's hand.

At this point a very deep sigh escaped him. He was, it seemed, in a mood for heart-felt effusions; it was not without feeling and expressiveness that he uttered, at last, the following words: "If you but knew what a service you have rendered by giving this apparent trash to a man of no lineage or breeding! And really, what haven't I endured? Like some bark or other, tossed amid the ferocious waves. . . . What oppressions, what persecutions have I not experienced, what woe have I not tasted of! And for what? For that I kept to the ways of righteousness, for that my conscience was clear, for that I extended the helping hand both to the homeless widow and to the poor, wretched orphan!"

At this point he himself had to dab away with his handkerchief at a tear that coursed down his cheek.

Manilov was touched, but utterly. The friends kept squeezing each other's hand for a long spell, and for a long spell gazed in silence into each other's eyes, in which the welling tears could be perceived. Manilov simply did not want to let go of his friend's hand and went on squeezing it so ardently that the latter by now did not know how to rescue it. Finally, having imperceptibly jerked it away, he said that it might not be a bad thing to put through the purchase-deed as soon as possible, and that it might be a good thing if he himself were to see what was going on in town; then he picked up his hat and fell to bowing and scraping in farewell.

"What? You wish to go already?" asked Manilov, suddenly coming to himself and becoming almost frightened.

At this juncture Mme Manilova entered the study.

"Lizanka"—Manilov turned to her with a somewhat plaintive air—"Pavel Ivanovich is leaving us!"

"It must be because we have wearied Pavel Ivanovich," Manilova answered him.

"Madam! Herein," said Chichikov, "herein, right here"—at this point he placed his hand on his heart—"yes, herein shall always dwell the pleasant time I have passed with you! And, believe me, there would be no greater bliss for me than to live with you, if not in the same house with you then, at least, in the closest vicinity to you."

"But do you know, Pavel Ivanovich," said Manilov, to whom such an idea appealed very much, "that it would really be a fine thing if we were to live thus together, under the same roof; or if, in the shade of some elm or other, we were to philosophize about some subject or other, were to go in for something deep!"

"Oh, that would be living in paradise!" said Chichikov, with a sigh. "Good-by, madam!" he went on, approaching Manilova to kiss her tiny hand. "Good-by, my most esteemed friend! Do not forget my request!"

"Oh, you may rest assured," Manilov told him. "I part with you for not more than two days."

They all went into the dining room.

"Good-by, my darling little ones!" said Chichikov, catching sight of Alcides and Themistoclius, who were preoccupied with some little wooden hussar, who by now lacked both an arm and his nose. "Good-by, my dear tots! You must excuse me for not having brought you a present, for I must confess I did not know that you were on this earth; but now, when I come, I'll bring you something, without fail. For you, Themistocles, I'll bring a sword. Do you want a sword?"

"I do," answered Themistocles-Themistoclius.

"And for you a drum. A drum for you, eh?" Chichikov went on, bending toward Alcides.

"Yeth, a trum," Alcides lisped in a whisper and with his head bent down.

"Very well, I'll bring you a drum, and what a glorious drum! It will always be beating *boom-boom! Boom-boom-bang!* Good-by, my little pet! Good-by!" Whereupon he kissed the boy's head and turned to Manilov and his spouse with restrained laughter, such as is always turned on for the benefit of parents, thus letting them in on how innocent the desires of their children are.

"You ought to stay, Pavel Ivanovich, really," Manilov remarked when they had already come out on the front steps. "Just look at those clouds!"

"They're only small clouds," was Chichikov's reply.

"But do you know the way to Sobakevich's?"

"That's the very thing I want to ask you."

"If you'll allow me, I'm going to tell your coachman right now." Whereupon, with his unvarying courteousness, Manilov told the coachman how he was to go, and even used *you* once, instead of *thou*, in talking to him.

The coachman, upon learning that he would have to pass two turns on the road, and turn in only at the third, said: "We'll find the way, Your Honor," and Chichikov was off, to the prolonged accompaniment of bows and much waving of handkerchiefs on the part of his hosts, who finally had to raise themselves on tip-toes to watch their departing guest.

Manilov remained standing on the front staircase for a long time, his eyes following the receding carriage; even when it was altogether out of sight he still stood there, puffing away at his pipe. Finally he went indoors, sat down on a chair, and gave himself up to meditation, his soul rejoicing because he had afforded a slight gratification to his guest. After that his thoughts passed on imperceptibly to other matters and wound up God knows where. He was thinking of the felicity of a life of friendship, of how fine it would be to dwell with one's friend on the bank of some river or other, after which his imagination began building a bridge across this river, then a most enormous house, with so lofty a belvedere that one might see even Moscow from it, and he also thought how fine it would be to quaff tea there of evenings, out in the open air, and to discourse on pleasant subjects of one kind or another; after that he imagined that he and Chichikov had arrived in fine carriages at some social affair, where they were enchanting all and sundry with the affability of their behavior; next, the Sovereign, apparently having learned of so great a friendship as theirs, had elevated them to the rank of generals and, after that, in the very end, his daydreams were of God knows what—things that he himself could make neither head nor tail of, no matter how hard he tried. Chichikov's strange request put a sudden end to all his reveries. The thought of it refused, in some peculiar way, to jell in his head; no matter how he turned it over and over, he could not make it clear to himself, as he sat there all this time and puffed away at his pipe, which occupation lasted until it was high time for supper.

CHAPTER THREE

CHICHIKOV, meanwhile, in a spirit of contentment, lolled in his carriage, which had long since been tooling along a highroad. From the preceding chapter it is apparent by now what constituted the main trend of his likes and inclinations, and therefore it is little to be wondered at if in a short while he surrendered thereto, body and soul. The projects, calculations, and schemes, indications of which strayed over his face, must have been most pleasant, evidently, inasmuch as at every moment they left their traces in a contented smile. Absorbed in them, he paid no attention whatsoever to the fact that his coachman, who was likewise gratified with the reception he had received from Manilov's domestics, was making quite sound observations to the dappled off-horse on the right. This dappled horse was powerful sly and was merely putting on a show of pulling his load, whereas the shaft-horse, a sorrel, and the other off-horse, a light chestnut in color, who was called Assessor because he had been acquired from some tax-assessor or other, put all their hearts into their work, so that one could actually note in their eyes the pleasure they derived therefrom.

"Keep on with your smart tricks, keep right on! But watch out I don't outsmart you!" Seliphan was saying, rising a little and giving the sluggard a taste of his whip. "Just keep your mind on your work, you German breeches-maker! You take the sorrel horse, there's a horse to look up to; he does his duty; I'll give him an extra measure of oats right willingly, because he's a horse you can look up to; and Assessor, now, he's a good horse, too. . . . There you go, there you go—what are you twitching your ears for? You just listen, you fool, when someone's talking to you! I ain't a-goin' to teach you nothin' bad, you ignoramus! Look at where he's goin'!" Here he again gave him a taste of his whip, adding: "Ugh, you barbarian, you! You damned Boneyparte, you!" Then he shouted at all three: "Hey, there, my darlings!" and flicked all three, but no longer as a form of chastisement, but just so's to show them that he was satisfied with them. Having given them that pleasure, he again turned his lecture upon the dappled horse: "You've got a notion you can hide from me the way you're carrying on. Oh, no, you've got to live accordin' to the ways of righteousness if you mean to be looked up to. There, over at the squire's where we were just now, the people are a fine lot. I take pleasure in conversing, if there's some fine person to converse with; I'm always good friends with a fine person—right friendly; whether it comes to drinking a dish of tea or having a snack, I'm right willing, if it be with a fine person. Everybody looks up to a fine person. There, our master is looked up to everywheres because—do you hear me?— he done his duty in serving the government, he's a Collidjit Councilor, he is—"

Discoursing thus, Seliphan at last went off into the most remote abstractions. If Chichikov had lent an attentive ear he would have learned many particulars referring to him personally; but his thoughts were so taken up with their main theme that it was only a deafening thunderclap which forced him to come to himself and look about him: the whole sky was overcast with clouds, and the dusty post-road had become spattered with drops of rain. Finally there came the peal of a second thunderclap, louder and nearer by now, and the rain burst suddenly, as if out of a bucket. At first, taking an oblique direction, it lashed one side of the carriage, then the other; next, changing its method of attack and becoming per-fectly vertical, it drummed right on the carriage top; the drops, finally, began pelting the occupant's face. This made him screen himself by pulling down two leather curtains with two round little windows, intended for the contemplation of the views along the road, and give orders to Seliphan to drive faster. Seliphan, who had also been interrupted in the very midst of his harangue, realizing that this certainly was no time to dally, immediately dragged out from under his box some sort of wretched garment of drab cloth, threw it over himself, grabbed the reins, and shouted to his troika, who were barely putting one foot in front of another, for they felt a pleasant enervation after the instructive discourses they had heard. But Seliphan, no matter how hard he strove to do so, could not recall whether he had passed two turns in the road or three. Having considered, and recalling the road to some extent, he surmised that the turns had been many, all of which he had let slip by. Since a Russian will always promptly find a course of action at decisive moments, even though it be without going in for any remote considerations, Seliphan turned to the right at the first crossroad he came to, shouted to his horses: "Hey, there, my honored friends!" and started off at a gallop, giving but little thought where the road he had taken might bring him to.

The rain, however, seemed to have set in for a long spell. The dust lying on the road was rapidly churning into mud and it became harder and harder with every minute for the horses to draw the carriage. By this time Chichikov was beginning to worry seriously, since such a long time had passed without his seeing Sobakevich's village. According to his calculation it was high time for him to have gotten there. He kept looking out on this side and on that, but the darkness was such that one might as well have been blind.

"Seliphan!" he said at last, thrusting his head out of the carriage.

"Yes, master?" Seliphan answered.

"Look around now—maybe the village is in sight."

"No, master, it's nowheres in sight!"

After which Seliphan, swinging his whip from time to time, launched into a song—well, you couldn't call it a song, exactly, but it was something so long drawn out that there was never an end to it. Anything and everything had gone into it: all the encouraging and urging cries which horses are regaled with all over Russia, from one end of it to the other; all sorts of adjectives without the least discrimination, but just as they came to the tip of his tongue. Thus things reached such a pass that he began to call his horses, at last, his "secretaries."

Meanwhile Chichikov began to notice that the carriage was swaying every which way and dealing him the most violent of jolts, which enabled him to sense that they had turned off the road and were, in all probability, straggling over a freshly furrowed field. Seliphan, apparently, had surmised as much himself, but was saying never a word.

"Why, you scalawag, what road are you taking?" asked Chichikov.

"Why, master, what is one to do at a time like this? It's so dark there's no seeing the whip even!" Having said this he made the carriage careen so that Chichikov was forced to hold on with both hands. It was only then that he noticed that Seliphan was rather fuddled.

"Hold her, hold her—you'll turn the carriage over!"

"No, master, how could I ever turn it over?" Seliphan protested. "That's not the right thing to do, to go turning a carriage over, I know that right well of my own self; why, I'd never even think of turning it over, nohow." Thereupon he began to turn the carriage a little, and kept on turning and turning it, until at last he had turned it over entirely on its side. Chichikov went smack into the mud on his hands and knees. However, Seliphan managed to halt the horses, although they would have halted even of themselves, because they were much spent. Such an unforeseen occurrence utterly amazed Seliphan. Having clambered down from his box he took his stand in front of the carriage, placed his arms akimbo, and while his master was wallowing in the mud and striving to scramble out of it, he pronounced, after due deliberation: "Look, now, if it didn't go and turn over after all!"

"You're as drunk as a cobbler!" Chichikov told him.

"No, how could it ever happen that I should be drunk! I know it isn't the right thing to be drunk. I did have a chat with a friend of mine, because one can chat with a fine person, there's nothing bad about that; and we had a bite together. A bite isn't a thing that does anybody any harm; one can have a bite with a fine person—"

"And what did I tell you the last time you got drunk, eh? Or have you forgotten?" Chichikov asked him.

"No, Your Honor, how could I ever forget? I know my duty by now. I know that it isn't the right thing to be drunk. I just had a chat with a fine person, because, you see—"

"Why, I'll take and flog you so's you'll know what it means to chat with a fine person!"

"Just as Your Grace wishes," answered Seliphan, who was ready to agree to everything. "If I've got to be flogged, then let me be flogged; I'm not at all against it. Why not be flogged, if one deserves it? That is as the master wills. Flogging, now, is a needful thing, for otherwise the muzhik would get spoiled; order must be maintained. If one deserves it, then go ahead with the flogging—why not?"

To such reasoning the master was utterly at a loss for an answer. But at this juncture it seemed as if fate itself had decided to have compassion upon him. Barking was heard in the distance. Chichikov, heartened thereby, ordered the coachman to give the horses the whip. The Russian driver has good intuition which he uses instead of eyes; it is because of this that there are occasions when, shutting his eyes tight, he will merely jolt along with might and main yet will always fetch up somewhere in the end. Seliphan, without seeing a thing, set his horses in such a straight line for the village that he stopped only when the shafts of the carriage ran right up against a fence and there was absolutely nowhere else to drive. The only thing Chichikov observed through the thick pall of the driving rain was something that resembled a roof. He sent Seliphan off to seek out the gate, which search beyond a doubt would have lasted for a long time if, in Russia, in place of doormen, savage dogs were not employed, who announced him so resonantly that he had to stick his fingers into his ears. A light gleamed in a small window and reached in a misty beam to the fence, indicating the gate to our wayfarers. Seliphan took to hammering upon it and in a short while some sort of figure, swathed in a drab peasant overcoat, opened a wicket and thrust itself out therefrom, and the master and his serving man heard a countrywife's hoarse voice: "Who's that knocking there? What are you carrying on like that for?"

"We've just come, mother; let us stay the night," Chichikov informed her.

"Look, what a nimble-footed fellow," said the old woman, "and what a time to come! This ain't no wayside inn for you; there's a landed proprietress livin' here."

"What are we to do, then, mother? We've lost the way, you see. Surely one can't sleep out in the open fields on a night like this."

"Yes, it's a dark night, and a bad one," Seliphan put in.

"Keep still, you fool," Chichikov told him.

"But who might you be?" asked the old woman.

"I am of the gentry, mother."

The phrase "of the gentry" apparently made the old woman pause and think a while.

"Wait a bit, I'll tell the mistress," she announced, and a minute or two later was already back with a lantern in her hand. The gates were unlocked. A small light gleamed in still another window. The carriage, having been driven into the courtyard, came to a stop before a small house which, owing to the darkness, it was difficult to have a good look at. Only one-half of it was lit up by the light issuing from the windows; one could also see a puddle before it, directly in the light from the same windows. The rain beat loudly upon the wooden roof and ran down in gurgling streams into a barrel placed below. In the meantime the hounds were chorusing in all sorts of voices; one of them, with his head thrown back, brought his notes out in such a drawn-out way and with such zeal that it seemed as though he were receiving God knows how high a salary therefor; another was chopping his notes hastily, like a village sexton; among them tinkled, like a jingle-bell on a mail coach, an indefatigable treble, probably that of a young puppy; and all this, finally, was topped by a bass, probably an old fellow, endowed with a stalwart canine nature, inasmuch as he rumbled in his throat, the way a canorous basso profundo rumbles when a choir recital is at its very height: the tenors rise up on their tippity-toes from their strong desire to bring forth a high note, giving out with their all, and letting that all escape and soar to the rafters as they throw their heads back, while he alone, thrusting his unshaven chin deep into his cravat, squatting and sinking almost to the ground, lets his note come forth from there, which note makes the windowpane rattle and emit a jarring tinkle. Judging by the canine chorus alone, made up of such superb musicians, one could have supposed that this small village was quite a considerable one; but our drenched and chilled hero had no thought for anything but a bed. The carriage had barely come to a full stop when he had already jumped out on the small porch, swayed, and almost fallen. Again some woman or other came out on the porch, somewhat younger than the one before but resembling her very much. She led him indoors.

Chichikov took a cursory glance or two about the room: it was done in rather old and poor striped wall-paper; there were pictures, showing some nondescript birds; between the windows were small, antiquated mirrors, with dark frames in the form of curled-up leaves; each mirror had either a letter, or a pack of cards, or a stocking tucked away behind it; there was a wall clock, with flowers painted on its face . . . it was beyond his strength to notice anything more. He felt that his eyes were becoming stuck together as if somebody had smeared them with honey. A minute later the mistress of the house entered: an elderly woman, in some sort of night-cap, hastily put on, with a piece of flannel about her neck; one of those motherly creatures, petty landed proprietresses who are forever complaining tearfully about poor crops and their losses as they keep their heads somewhat to one side, yet who at the same time accumulate, bit by bit, their tidy little hoards of money, in little money-bags of bright ticking, tucked away in various bureaus. In one little bag they'll put by themselves all the silver rubles; in another the dear little half-ruble coins, and in a third the quarter-rubles, even though it may seem, when one looks there, that there's nothing in the bureau save linen and sleeping-jackets, and balls of thread, and a cloak with the seams ripped apart, destined for a subsequent transformation into a dress, if the old dress should burn through somehow during the baking of cookies and the frying of all sorts of fritters for the holidays or should become utterly threadbare of its own self. But that dress will never burn through and it will not become utterly threadbare of itself; thrifty is the little crone, and the cloak is fated to lie long thus in its ripped state, and then come down, through a last will and testament, to

· 45

the niece of a female second cousin, together with all sorts of other rubbish.

Chichikov made excuses for having disturbed them by his unexpected arrival.

"Not at all, not at all!" said the hostess. "What a night for God to bring you to us! Such a nasty storm out. . . . You ought to have a bite of something after your travels, but it's so late at night I can't cook anything for you."

The hostess's words were interrupted by a strange hissing, so that the guest was frightened at first: the noise sounded as if the whole room had filled up with serpents; but after a glance upward he became reassured, inasmuch as he surmised that the wall clock had gotten a notion to strike. The hissing was immediately followed by a death-rattle, and at last, summoning all its forces and making a supreme effort, it struck two, which sounded as if someone were walloping a cracked pot with a stick, after which the pendulum started off again clicking away calmly as it swung to the right and to the left.

Chichikov thanked the hostess, saying that he did not need anything, that she should not put herself out in any way, that outside of a bed he did not ask for anything, and wanted to know only what locality he had strayed to, and whether it was far from here to the village of Sobakevich, the landowner, to which the old woman replied that she'd never even heard such a name, and that there wasn't any such landowner.

"Do you know Manilov, at least?" asked Chichikov.

"And who might Manilov be?"

"A landowner, mother."

"No, I never happened to hear of him; there isn't any such land-owner."

"What landowners are there around hereabouts, then?"

"Bobrov, Sviniïn, Kanapatiev, Kharpakin, Trepakin, Pleshakov."

"Are they well-to-do or not?"

"No, father o' mine, there's none that are any too well off hereabouts. This one might have twenty souls, that one thirty, but as for those who might have a hundred or so, you'll find none of that sort hereabouts."

Chichikov perceived that he had come to the backwoods for fair.
"Is it far to town, at least?"

"Why, that will be forty miles or thereabouts. I feel so sorry that
I haven't anything for you to eat! Would you care for some tea,
sir?"

"Thank you, mother. I need nothing except a bed."

"True enough; after a trip like that one needs to rest—very much
so. So you just dispose yourself right here on this divan, sir. Hey,
Phetinia, fetch a featherbed, some pillows, and a sheet! What a
night God has sent us, what thunder! I've had a taper burning before a holy image all night long. Eh, father o' mine—why, your
whole back and one side is caked with mud like a boar's; wherever
did you manage to get yourself so filthy?"

"Glory be to God that getting filthy was all I did; I ought to
render thanks to Him because I didn't break all my ribs."

"The blessed saints, what you must have gone through! But
maybe you ought to have your back rubbed with something?"

"Thanks, thanks! Don't put yourself out; the only thing is, you
might order your wench to dry out and clean my clothes."

"Do you hear that, Phetinia?" said the mistress of the house,
turning to the woman who had first come out to the travelers and
who by this time had already managed to drag in a featherbed and,
having plumped it up with her hands on both sides, had loosed a
whole deluge of feathers all over the room. "You take this gentleman's great-coat together with all his other garments and after
first letting all of them dry out in front of a fire, as we used to do
for the late master, you can then brush and beat them out well."

"Right, ma'am!" Phetinia kept saying, as she spread a sheet over
the featherbed and placed the pillows.

"There, now, there's your bed, all ready," said the hostess. "Good-
by, dear sir; I wish you good night. But maybe there's something
else you might be needing? Maybe, father o' mine, you're used to
having somebody scratch your heels at bedtime? My dear departed
husband could never fall asleep without that."

But the guest passed up even having his heels scratched. The
hostess went out and he at once hurried to undress, giving Phetinia
all his doffed panoply, great-coat as well as all the other garments,

· 47

and Phetinia, having wished him good night in her turn, dragged off all this sodden gear. It was not without pleasure, when he was left alone, that he eyed his bed, which reached well-nigh up to the ceiling. Phetinia, it was evident, was a past mistress of the art of fluffing up featherbeds. When, by standing up on a chair, he clambered into the featherbed, it sank under him almost to the floor, and the feathers, crowded out of their confining covering, flurried to every corner of the room. Putting out the candle, he covered himself with the calico comforter and, curling up into a pretzel under it, fell asleep in a split second.

When he awoke the morning was already rather far gone. The sun was shining through the window right into his eyes, and the flies that had been peacefully asleep on the walls and ceiling the night before now all turned their full attention upon him: one perched on his upper lip, another on his ear, a third was maneuvering to settle on his very eye; as for one that had been incautious enough to squat near a nostril he, being half asleep, drew it up his nose, which made him sneeze hard, a circumstance that was the cause of his awakening. Casting an eye over the room, he now noticed that the pictures were not all of birds; among them hung a portrait of Kutuzov, that most popular commander, while another, done in oils, was that of some old man or other, the red cuffs on his military uniform being of the sort that were sewn on at the time of Czar Paul I.

The wall clock again emitted its hissing sound and struck ten; a feminine face looked in at the door and disappeared at the same moment since Chichikov, having wished to sleep comfortably, had thrown off absolutely everything. The face that had looked in seemed to him somewhat familiar. He began cudgeling his brain as to who she might be, and at last recalled that this was his hostess. He put on his undershirt; his clothes, dried out and cleaned by now, were lying near by. Having dressed, he walked up to the mirror and sneezed once more, so loudly that a turkey-cock who had strolled up to the window—for that window was very close to the ground —began gobbling something at him suddenly and very rapidly in his odd speech; probably it was "God bless you!"—which Chichikov acknowledged by calling him a fool. Having approached the window, Chichikov fell to contemplating the sights it offered; the window looked out practically on the poultry-yard—at least the narrow little yard before the window was densely populated by poultry and all sorts of domestic animals. Of chickens and turkey-hens there was no end; among them a rooster promenaded with measured strides, tossing his comb and turning his head from side to side, as though he were trying to lend an attentive ear to some-thing; a sow and her family also bobbed up right on the spot, and right on the spot, while rooting through a midden-hill, she gobbled up a chick in passing and, without perceiving this, went on putting away watermelon-rinds in a systematic sort of way.

This small barnyard, or poultry-run, was bounded by a board fence, beyond which stretched away extensive truck-patches planted to cabbages, onions, potatoes, sugar-beets, and other such domestic produce. Apple trees and other fruit trees were scattered here and there over the truck-patches; these trees were covered over with nets as a protection against the magpies and sparrows, the latter flitting obliquely from place to place in perfect clouds. For the same reason of protection several spread-armed scarecrows had been put up on long poles; one of them was sporting a night-cap that had belonged to none other than the mistress of the house her-self.

Beyond the truck-gardens came the huts of the serfs, which huts, although they had been built helter-skelter and were not restricted to regular streets, nevertheless indicated, as Chichikov had noted, the well-being of their dwellers, inasmuch as they were properly looked after: the deal on the roofs, where it had become too weather-beaten and time-worn, had in all cases been replaced with new; nowhere were the gates or wickets hanging askew; while in each of those covered sheds that faced him he noted a cart standing, almost new and kept in reserve; in some sheds there were actually two of these carts.

"Yes, this hamlet of hers isn't at all such a small one," he said to himself, and proposed right then and there to have a good talk with the owner of all this and to make her closer acquaintance. He looked through the crack of the door through which she had thrust in her head and, seeing her seated at a tea table, entered her room with a cheerful and amiable air.

"Greeting, my dear sir. How did you sleep?" inquired the hostess, rising a little from her seat. She was dressed somewhat better than yesterday, in a dark dress, and was now minus her sleeping-cap; but there was still some sort of rag bound about her neck.

"Fine, fine!" said Chichikov, taking an easy chair. "And what about you, mother?"

"I slept but poorly, father o' mine."

"How is that?"

"Sleeplessness. The small of my back keeps on aching without a let-up, whilst one of my legs, from the ankle up, has a nagging pain all the time."

"That will pass, that will pass, mother. You mustn't mind it."

"May God grant that it pass. I rubbed on lard, now, and put on a compress with turpentine, too. And what would you like to have with your tea? There's some fruit brandy in that flask."

"Not a bad idea, mother; guess we'll try a little of the fruit brandy, too."

The reader must have noticed by now, I think, that Chichikov, despite his amiable air, was nevertheless quite more free and easy of speech with her than he had been with Manilov and did not at all stand on ceremony. It must be said that if we Russians haven't yet caught up in a thing or two with the natives of other lands, we have on the other hand gotten way ahead of them in social behavior. There's no enumerating all the shades and refinements of our be-havior. The Frenchman or the German could never in a lifetime either surmise or comprehend all its peculiarities and nuances; he will use almost the same tone and the same language in speaking both with the money-bags worth millions and the man who keeps a tiny tobacco-shop, even though at soul he will, of course, crawl and cringe and fawn enough before the former. But that's not the way we do things: we have men so wise and adroit that they will speak to a landowner possessing but two hundred serf-souls in a way altogether different from that in which they will to one who possesses three hundred of them; while to him who possesses three hundred of them they will again speak not in the same way as they would with him that has five hundred souls; while with him that has five hundred souls the manner of their speech will again differ from that used to him that has eight hundred; in brief, even if you were to go up to a million, you would find different shadings for each category. Let's suppose, for instance, that there is a certain chancellery in existence—oh, not here, but in some Never-Never Land; and in this chancellery, let's suppose, there exists a Director of the Chancellery. I ask you to have a look at him as he sits there among his subordinates—why, out of awe you simply wouldn't be able to let a peep out of you. Hauteur and noblesse . . . and what else doesn't his face express? Just pick up a brush and paint away: Prometheus, Prometheus to the life! His gaze is that of an eagle; he ambulates with a smooth, measured stride. But that self-same eagle, the moment he has stepped out of his office and nears the study of his superior, a sheaf of papers tucked under his arm, flutters along like any partridge, with all his might and main. In society or at some evening-at-home, provided that all those present are not so very high in rank, Prometheus will even remain Prometheus to the very end; but let there be present someone ever so little above him, such a transformation will overtake our Prometheus as even Ovid himself could never think of: he's a midge, even smaller than any midge; he has been transmogrified into a grain of sand; "Why, this just can't be our Ivan Petrovich!" you say to yourself as you look at him. "Ivan Petrovich is ever so tall, while this is not only such a squat little fellow but such a thin one, too; the other one speaks loudly, booming away in his bass and with never a laugh out of him, while the Devil alone knows what this one is up to: he cheeps like a bird and keeps on laughing with never a stop." You walk up nearer and take a closer look—and sure enough, if it isn't Ivan Petrovich! "Oho, ho, ho!" you think to yourself. . . .

However, let's get back to the actors in our drama. Chichikov, as we have already seen, had decided not to stand on any ceremony whatsoever, and therefore, picking up his cup and lacing his tea with the fruit brandy, led off with: "That's a fine hamlet you've got, mother. How many souls are there in it?"

"There's a little short of eighty souls in it, father o' mine," his hostess informed him. "But the trouble is that times are hard: there, last year, too, the crops were so poor that may God preserve us from their like again."

"However, your muzhiks are a sturdy lot, to look at 'em; their huts are strongly built. But allow me to ask your name. I was so absent-minded . . . arriving so late at night—"

"Korobochka—relict of a Collegiate Secretary."

"Thank you very much. And your first name and your patronymic?"

"Nastasia Petrovna."

"Nastasia Petrovna? A fine name, that, Nastasia Petrovna. I have an aunt, my mother's sister, who goes by that name."

"And what's your name?" asked the landed proprietress. "Why, you must be a tax-assessor, I guess?"

"No, mother!" Chichikov answered with a smile. "I guess I'm no assessor, but just traveling on my own little business affairs."

"Ah, so you're a commission buyer! What a pity it is, really, that I sold the honey so cheaply to the merchants, for now, father o' mine, you'd surely have bought it off me."

"There, now, honey is just what I wouldn't have bought."

"What else, then? Hemp, maybe? But then I've but little of it now, either dressed or raw—only twenty pounds or so in all."

"No, mother, it's a different sort of goods I'm after. Tell me, have any of your peasants been dying off?"

"Oh, father o' mine, eighteen of them!" said the old woman, with a sigh. "And those that died were all such good folk, all fine workers. There's been an increase since then through births, true enough, but what's the good in 'em? They're all such small fry. And then the tax-assessor came along. 'The tax, now,' says he, 'pay so much for each soul.' They've died off, yet you've got to pay the tax on 'em the same as if they were alive. Only last week my blacksmith was burned to death—what a skilled blacksmith he was, and a master keysmith, to boot."

"Why, did you have a fire, mother?"

"God saved me from that calamity; a fire would have been still worse. No, he burned up of his own self, father o' mine. Something caught fire within him, somehow—he'd been drinking overmuch

--there was just a small blue flame coming out of him; he kept on smoldering and smoldering all over, and then turned all black, like charcoal—and yet what an awfully skilled blacksmith he was! And now I've nothing to ride out with—there's no one to shoe the horses."

"God's will is in all things, mother!" said Chichikov with a sigh. "One mustn't say anything against the wisdom of God. Let me have 'em, now, Nastasia Petrovna!"

"Whom, father o' mine?"

"Why, all these souls that have died off, now."

"But how could I let you have them?"

"Why, just so. Or, if you like, sell them to me. I'll give you hard cash for them."

"But how can one do such a thing? Really, I can't make head or tail of this. Or is it that you'd be after digging them up out of the ground?"

Chichikov saw that the old woman had strayed far afield and that it was absolutely necessary to make clear to her just what was what. In a few words he explained to her that the transfer or purchase would be merely a paper transaction and that the souls would be listed as living.

"But whatever would you be wanting them for?" asked the old woman, staring at him with her eyes popping out.

"That, now, is my own affair."

"Yes, but they're dead now."

"Yes, but who's saying that they're alive? That's the very reason why they're a loss to you, because they're dead; you keep on paying taxes on them, whereas I now rid you of all bother and of having to pay those taxes. Do you understand? And not only do I rid you of that but I'll give you fifteen roubles to boot. There, is it clear to you now?"

"Really, I don't know," the hostess uttered hesitatingly. "After all, I've never sold any dead souls."

"Naturally! It would have been rather something like a miracle if you had sold them to anybody. Or do you think that there's really some good to be got out of them?"

"No, I don't think that! Of what good can they be? No good of any sort. But that's the very thing that troubles me, that they're dead now."

'My, but she seems to be a hard-headed hag and set in her notions!' Chichikov thought to himself. Then: "Look, mother! Do but consider this well—why, you're ruining yourself, paying a tax on a dead serf as if he were alive—"

"Oh, father o' mine, don't even talk of it!" the landed proprietress caught him up. "Only three weeks ago I paid in more than a hundred and fifty rubles, and gave the assessor some palm oil as well."

"There, you see, mother! And now take into consideration merely the fact that it will no longer be necessary for you to give palm oil to the assessor, for now it will be I who'll pay taxes on these dead souls—I, and not you; I take all the liabilities for taxes upon myself; I shall even execute the purchase-deed at my expense, do you understand that?"

The old woman went into deep thought. She perceived that the deal certainly seemed an advantageous one; only it was far too novel and unusual, and for that reason she began to entertain strong fears lest this purchaser might take her in, in some way; for he had come God knows whence, and in the dead of night, at that.

"Well, what is it, mother—shall we shake hands on the bargain, eh?" Chichikov was saying.

"Really, father o' mine, I've never yet had occasion to be selling dead folk. I did let some live souls go to Protopopov, something like three years back, it was—two wenches, at a hundred roubles each —and he was right grateful; they turned out to be such splendid workers that they can weave napkins by their own selves."

"Yes, but it isn't live souls we're talking about, God be with them! It's dead ones I'm after."

"Really, I'm afraid, since it's the first time I'm doing such a thing, lest I take a loss, somehow. Maybe you're fooling me, and they are . . . now . . . they're worth more, like."

"See here, mother . . . eh, how can you be like that! What can they be worth? Look at it this way: why, they're nothing but dust. Do you understand, now? They're simply so much dust. You take any worthless thing, any least thing at all, now, a common rag, for instance, and even that rag has a value: it will, at the very least, be bought by a paper-mill; but this dust, now, is of no use on earth. There, tell me yourself, of what use is it?"

"Well, now, that's true enough. Yes, it's of no use whatsoever; but there's only one thing that stands in my way—that they're dead, after all."

"May the Devil take her! What a blockhead—her head must be made of oak," said Chichikov to himself, by now beginning to lose his patience. "Try and come to terms with her! She's making me sweat, the damned old hag!" Here, taking out his handkerchief, he began mopping the sweat that was now actually beading his forehead. However, it was in vain that Chichikov was getting worked up about her: at times you'll come across a man who is highly respected, and is even in the government's employ, yet when it comes down to doing business with him will turn out to be a perfect Korobochka. Once such a man gets a notion into his head, there's no earthly means of your overcoming him; no matter how many arguments that are as clear as day you may present to him, they'll bounce off him the way a rubber ball bounces off a wall. Having mopped his sweat Chichikov decided to try if there weren't some other way of setting her on the right path.

"Mother," he said, "you either don't want to understand what I'm telling you, or you're purposely talking the way you are just to hear yourself talk. . . . I'm giving you fifteen roubles cash, in government notes, do you understand that? Why, that's money. You won't pick that up in the gutter. There, now, own up, what price did you sell your honey at?"

"At twelve rubles for each thirty-six pounds."

"You're taking a small sin on your soul, mother. You never sold it at that price."

"I call God to witness I did!"

"There, you see? But it fetched that price because it was honey. You'd been storing it up for nigh unto a year, maybe, having to work hard and being put to all kinds of trouble and a lot of bother; you had to drive about, rob the bees of the fruit of their labor, and then feed and keep them the whole winter through in your cellar, whereas dead souls are not of this world. Here you applied no effort on your part; it was God's will that they leave this world, causing a loss to your estate. So you received for your toil, for your effort, a matter of twelve roubles, but here you get something free and for nothing, and not merely twelve roubles, mind you, but fifteen, and not in silver, but all in lovely blue government notes."

After such potent persuasions Chichikov hardly doubted that now the old woman would, at last, give in.

"Really, now," answered the landed proprietress, "mine is but a poor widow woman's lot! It would be better if I mark time a bit; maybe the merchants will come riding this way, and I'll see what the prices for dead souls are like nowadays."

"This is a disgrace, a disgrace, mother! This is simply a disgrace! There, now, whatever are you saying? Just stop and think it over for yourself! Whoever is going to buy them from you? There, what use could such a purchaser put them to?"

"Well, maybe they can come in handy around the place somehow or another, by some chance—" contradicted the old woman, but never finished her speech, letting her jaw drop and staring at him almost with fear as she waited anxiously for what he might say to that.

"Dead folk around the place! So that's where you've fetched up! Going to scare the sparrows off with them of nights in your truck-garden, perhaps, or what?"

"The power of the Cross be with us! What dreadful things you're saying!" the old woman let drop, crossing herself.

"What other work would you want to put them to, then? But that doesn't matter, really, for the bones and the graves all remain with you: the transfer is only on paper. Well, what's it going to be? What do you say? Let's have your answer, at least."

The old woman again went off into deep thought.

"Well, what are you thinking of, Nastasia Petrovna?"

"Really, I still can't decide what I am to do; I think I'd better sell you the hemp."

"But what has hemp to do with it? Good heavens, I'm asking you about something else entirely, yet you shove hemp at me! Hemp is all right in its own way; if I come another time I'll take the hemp off your hands as well. Well, what is it going to be, Nastasia Petrovna?"

"Honest to God, this is such a strange commodity, so unusual!"

At this juncture Chichikov lost every last shred of patience, picked up his chair, banged it down in exasperation, and hoped the Devil would take her.

The landed proprietress became inordinately frightened of the Devil. "Oh, never mention him, God be with him!" she cried out, turning all pale. "It was only three days ago that I dreamt of him all night long, the accursed one! I got a notion before bedtime of telling fortunes by cards, after saying prayers, and so, evidently, God must have sent him as a punishment. How vile he appeared! Why, his horns were longer nor a steer's."

"What I wonder at is that devils don't come to you in your dreams by the half-score! I wanted to do this solely out of mere Christian love of humanity. Here I saw a poor widow woman working herself to death, enduring poverty. . . . Why, may you drop dead and fall through the ground, you and your whole confounded village! . . ."

"Oh, what dreadful curses to be wishing anybody!" said the old woman, looking at him with fear.

"Why, one can't find words vile enough for you! Really, and without meaning the word in a bad sense, you're like a dog in a manger; it can't eat the hay itself and it won't let others eat it. I was about to buy up your farm produce, of whatever sort, inasmuch as I also supply the government on contracts—" Here he lied a bit, and even though he did so in passing and without any ulterior consideration, he nevertheless met with unexpected success. Those government contracts had a strong effect on Nastasia Petrovna; at any rate, when she spoke it was already in a conciliatory tone.

"Why, whatever did you get so all-fired angry for? If I'd known beforehand that you're so apt to get angry I never would have argued with you at all."

"As if there were something to get angry about! The whole thing isn't worth a tinker's curse, and you think I'm going to get angry over it!"

"Well, if you like, I'm ready to give them up for fifteen roubles in government notes! Only look you, father o' mine, about those contracts, now: should you have occasion to get flour, either rye or buckwheat, or any groats, or any slaughtered cattle, don't you take advantage of me, please, in that case."

"I won't, mother," he told her, but in the meantime was brushing off with his hand the sweat that was coursing in whole streams down his face. He inquired of her if she didn't have some trusted agent or acquaintance in town whom she might empower to put through the purchase-deed to the dead souls and do whatever else might be necessary.

"Why, of course! The son of Father Cyril, the Dean, works in the Administrative Offices," said Korobochka. Chichikov asked her to write him a letter of authorization, and, in order not to put her to any extra trouble, even undertook to compose it.

"It would be a good thing," Korobochka was thinking to herself meanwhile, "if he were to take my flour and cattle for his government contracts. I ought to get on the right side of him; there's still some dough left over from yesterday, I might as well go and tell Phetinia to make some pancakes. It might also be a good thing to bake an unleavened turn-over with eggs; they bake turn-overs well in my kitchen, and it doesn't take much time, either."

The hostess left the room to put into execution her idea about the turn-over and, probably, also to round it out with other creations of home baking and cookery, while Chichikov walked into the parlor where he had spent the night, in order to take the necessary papers out of his casket. Everything had long since been tidied up in the parlor; the luxurious feather-bed had been carried out, and a table, with a cloth on it, placed in front of the divan. Putting his casket thereon, he rested a while, inasmuch as he felt that he was all in a sweat, as if he were swimming in a river of it; every stitch he had on, from his undershirt to his stockings, was wringing-wet.

"Eh, but that damned old woman has well-nigh killed me!" said he, having rested a little, and opened the casket. The author feels that there are readers so inquisitive that they wish to know even the plan and the interior arrangement of this casket. By all means, why not gratify them? Here it is, the interior arrangement: in the very

middle was a soap dish; behind the soap dish six or seven very narrow divisions to hold razors; then square receptacles in the corners
for a sand-shaker and an ink-pot, with a boat-like, hollowed-out
little shelf to hold quills, sticks of sealing wax, and whatever articles might be quite long; then all sorts of little partitioned receptacles, with lids and without, for objects that were rather short;
these were filled with cards—visiting cards, funeral announce-
ments, old theater tickets, and the like, which had been put away
as souvenirs. The entire upper tray, with all its partitioned com-
partments, could be lifted out, and underneath it one came upon a
space taken up with piles of paper, in folio; then came a small secret
money-drawer which, while it had no perceptible opening, could
nevertheless be pulled out from one side of the casket. It was always
so hastily pulled out and pushed back all within the same minute
by the owner that one could never tell with certainty how much
money there was in it.

Chichikov immediately bestirred himself and, having trimmed
a quill, fell to writing. It was at this point that his hostess entered.

"That's a fine chest you've got there, father o' mine," said she,
sitting down near him. "Bought it in Moscow, I guess?"

"Yes, in Moscow," answered Chichikov, writing away.

"I just knew it; everything there is made well. Three years ago
my sister brought me back some warm little boots for the children,
such well-made stuff that they're wearing them to this day. My
goodness, what a heap of stamped paper you've got there!" she went
on, after a peep into his casket. And really, there was not a little
stamped paper in it. "You might make me a present of just one
teeny sheet! For that's the very thing I lack; I might have to
petition one of our courts, and yet not have anything to write
it on."

Chichikov explained to her that this paper was not of that sort; it
was intended for the execution of purchase-deeds and not for peti-
tions. However, in order to pacify her, he gave her some sheet or
other with a ruble stamp on it. Having written the letter, he gave
it to her to sign and asked for a short list of the dead serfs. It turned
out that this landed proprietress kept neither records nor lists of
any kind whatsoever, but she did know the names of almost all her

serfs by heart. He made her dictate these to him right then and there. Certain of the peasants amazed him by their family names, but still more by their nicknames, so that every time he heard them called out he had to pause before writing them down. He was especially struck by a certain Petr Saveliev Neuvazhai Koryto (No-Respect-for-the-Pig-Trough), so that he could not help saying: "What a long name!" Another had appended to his name Korovii Kirpich (Cow-Dung Brick); there was one who turned out to be simply Kolesso Ivan (John the Wheel).

As he was finishing his writing, he sniffed the air slightly and caught the enticing aroma of something hot, made with butter.

"I beg of you to have a bite," said his hostess. Chichikov looked around him and beheld, already standing on the table, small mushrooms, patties, hasty pudding, scones, tarts, pancakes, and wafers with all sorts of baked additions—baked chopped onion, baked poppyseed, baked curds, baked clotted cream—and Heaven alone knows how many other things were there.

"This is an unleavened turn-over with eggs!" the hostess informed him.

Chichikov drew up to the unleavened turn-over with eggs and, after speedily eating half of it and a bit over, duly sang its praises. And, really and truly, although the turn-over was tasty of itself, yet after all the fuss and fret he had had to go through with the mistress of the house it seemed still more tasty.

"And won't you have some pancakes?"

In answer to this Chichikov rolled up three of the pancakes together and, having dipped them in melted butter, dispatched them into his mouth, after which he had to wipe his lips and hands with a napkin. Having gone through this performance three times, he asked his hostess to order his carriage harnessed. Nastasia Petrovna immediately sent off Phetinia, giving her orders at the same time to fetch some more hot pancakes.

"Your pancakes are most tasty, mother," said Chichikov, buckling down to the hot ones as soon as they were brought in.

"Yes, they make them well in my kitchen," said the hostess, "but here's the trouble: the crop was poor; the flour isn't what it might have been. . . . Why, father o' mine, why are you in such a hurry?" she asked, seeing that Chichikov had already picked up his hat. "Why, your carriage isn't harnessed yet."

"They'll harness it, mother, they'll harness it. They harness it fast when I'm around."

"Well, then, if you'll be so kind, don't forget me when it comes to filling those contracts."

"I won't, I won't," Chichikov kept saying, stepping out into the entry.

"And aren't you buying any lard?" asked the mistress of the house, following him out.

"And why not? I do buy it, only that will have to come later."

"I'll have lard too, around the Christmas holidays."

"We'll buy, we'll buy, we'll buy everything, and we'll buy lard as well."

"Maybe you'll be after needing feathers. I'll be having feathers, too, about St. Philip's Fast."

"Fine, fine!" Chichikov kept saying.

"There, you see, father o' mine, your carriage isn't ready yet, just as I said," his hostess remarked as they came out on the front steps.

"It will be ready, it will be ready. Do but tell me one thing— how does one get out on the main road?"

"Now, how am I ever to do that?" the hostess wondered. "It's such a complicated thing to explain, there's such a lot of twists and turns, unless I was to send a little wench with you, to show you the way. For I guess you've got room up on the box where she might sit—"

"How else!"

"Yes, that's what I'll do, I'll let you take a girl along—that little wench of mine knows the way. Only, look you, don't you go and carry her off; some merchants have already carried one off from me."

Chichikov assured her that he would not carry off the little wench, and Korobochka, set at rest, now began overseeing everything in her yard: she stared hard at the housekeeper, who was carrying a wooden dipper of honey out of a store-room; at a muzhik who had bobbed up at the gates, and little by little she withdrew entirely into the life of her household. But why busy ourselves so long with Korobochka? Whether it be a Korobochka, or a Manilova, whether the mode of life be domestic or not, let's pass these things by. For isn't everything in the world arranged with wondrous whimsicality? The gay can in an instant turn into the sad, if one stand and contemplate it overlong, and then God knows what odd notions may not stray into your head. Perhaps you may even take to thinking: "Come now, does Korobochka really stand so low on the infinite ladder that leads humanity to perfection? Is the chasm so great that divides her from her sister, who is so inaccessibly fenced in by the walls of an aristocratic house, with perfumes floating over its cast-iron staircases, a house gleaming with brass, and glossy with oriental rugs; her sister who yawns over an unfinished book until such time as she starts out for a visit to some witty social gathering, which will furnish her with an arena where she may brilliantly show off her intelligence and express thoroughly re-hearsed ideas, ideas which, according to the laws of fashion, will amuse the whole town for a week; ideas having nothing to do with what is going on in her house and on her country estates, both household and estates being in utter confusion and going to wrack and ruin, thanks to her ignorance of domestic science, but ideas having to do with whatever political upheaval is brewing in France, with whatever direction modish Catholicism may have taken?" But let these things pass, let them pass! Why talk of all this? But why, then, amid thoughtless, gay, carefree moments, does another, won-drous strain of thought flash of itself within us? The laughter has not yet had time to fade completely off your face, and yet you have already become a different person in the midst of the very same people, and your face has already become illumined with a different light. . . .

"And here's the carriage, here's the carriage!" Chichikov cried out, catching sight, at last, of his carriage driving up. "What were you fussing about so long, you blockhead? Your head hasn't cleared of yesterday's drink yet, it seems."

Seliphan had no answer to this.

"Good-by, mother! Well, what about it, where's that little wench of yours?"

"Hey, there, Pelagea!" the landed proprietress called out to a little girl of eleven who was standing near the front steps, in a dress of some homespun material, dyed and glossy, with bare feet which from a distance might have been thought shod, so plastered with fresh mud were they. "Show the gentleman the way."

Seliphan helped the little wench to clamber up on his box, which she did after first making the step intended solely for the owner's foot all muddy with her own and only then scrambling up to the high perch and settling down there near the driver. After her Chichikov himself put his foot on the step and, making the carriage tip to the right, inasmuch as he was rather on the heavy side, finally settled down himself, saying: "Well, now everything's set! Good-by, mother!"

The horses started off.

Seliphan was morose all the way and, at the same time, very attentive to his work, which was always the case with him whenever he had done something wrong or had been drinking. The horses were wonderful to behold, they were that well curried and groomed. The collar upon one of them, which up to now had almost always been put on with such a rent that the oakum peeped out of the leather, was now skillfully mended. During the whole way Seliphan was taciturn, merely lashing out with his whip from time to time, and not addressing any diatribes to the horses, although the piebald horse would have liked, of course, to lend an attentive ear to something instructive, inasmuch as at such times as these the reins always dangled somehow listlessly in the hands of the usually loquacious driver and his whip strayed only pro forma over their backs. But all that could be heard issuing from the grim lips on this occasion was monotonously unpleasant outcries, such as "There, now, you crow-bait, there! Keep on gaping, keep it up!" and nothing more. Even the sorrel himself and Assessor were dissatisfied, not having heard themselves called, even once, either *darlings* or *Your Honors*. The piebald felt most unpleasant lashes on his fuller and broader parts. "Look you, how worked up he is," thought the piebald to himself, cocking up his ears somewhat. "He sure knows where to whip you! He won't lash you straight across the back, but picks out just the very spot that's most sensitive, flicking your ears or lashing you under the belly."

"Do we go to the right now?" Seliphan turned to the little girl seated beside him, putting the question in the driest of tones and pointing out to her with his whip the road, darkened from the rain, between the vividly green rain-freshened fields.

"No, no, I'll show you when we come to it," answered the little wench.

"Which way do we go now?" Seliphan asked after driving on for some time more.

"Why, that way," answered the little wench, pointing with her hand.

"Oh, you!" said Seliphan. "Why, that *is* to the right; you don't know your right hand from your left!"

Although the day was a very fine one, the ground had become miry to such a degree that the carriage wheels, churning it up, soon became wholly covered with it, as if with felt, which slowed the carriage down considerably; in addition to that the soil was clayey and unusually clinging. Both the one and the other were the reasons for their having been unable to get out of the maze of cross-roads before noon. Without the little wench it would have been difficult to accomplish even this, inasmuch as the roads crept off in every direction, like a catch of crayfish when you dump them out of a sack, and it would have been Seliphan's lot to drive about at random, this time through no fault of his own. In a short while the little girl pointed with her hand to a structure showing darkly in the distance and said: "And there's your highroad!"

"And what's that there building?"

"That's an inn," said the little wench.

"Well, now we'll make the rest of the way by ourselves," said Seliphan. "You get along home."

He stopped the carriage and helped her get down, muttering through his teeth: "Hey, you black-footed little thing!"

Chichikov gave her a copper coin, and she ambled off on her way, contented with merely having sat up on the driver's box.

CHAPTER FOUR

As he was driving up to the tavern, Chichikov ordered Seliphan to stop for two reasons: on the one hand, to give the horses a chance to rest, and, on the other, to have a bite of something and fortify himself as well. The author must confess that he is quite envious of the appetite and stomachs of this sort of people. All the top-notch people living in Peterburgh and Moscow mean absolutely nothing to him—people who spend their time in thoughtful planning of what they may eat tomorrow, and what sort of dinner to contrive for the day after, and who sit down to this dinner not otherwise than after having popped some pills into their mouths, people who gulp down oysters, sea-spiders, and other such wondrous cates, and eventually wind up with having to go to the baths at Carlsbad or to take the medicinal waters in the Caucasus. No, these gentry have never aroused any envy in me. But you take some of these fair-to-middlin' gentlemen, who will call for ham at one stage-post, a suckling pig at a second, and at a third for a slice of sturgeon, or some sort of sausage baked with onions, and then, as if they hadn't eaten a thing all day, will sit down at a full table, at any hour you like, and tackle sterlet chowder, with eel-pouts and soft roe, so hot it hisses and burbles as they take it into their mouths, followed, as a sort of chaser, by a fish pie with millet porridge, or cabbage dumplings, or a pie baked of young catfish, so that even an onlooker must needs work up an appetite—now, these gentlemen really are enjoying an enviable gift from Heaven! More than one top-notch gentleman would sacrifice in a moment half the number of serfs he possesses and half his estates (mortgaged and unmortgaged, with all the improvements both foreign and domestic), just to have such a stomach as the fair-to-middlin' gentleman possesses. But that's where the trouble lies, that one cannot acquire, either for any sum of money or for any estate (either with improvements or without),

such a stomach as you will find a fair-to-middlin' gentleman possessed of.

The wooden, time-stained inn received Chichikov under its shed,
narrow and small but hospitable, supported by short turned
columns of wood that looked like antiquated church candlesticks.
The inn was something in the nature of a Russian hut, only on a
larger scale. Cornices of fresh wood, with fretwork designs, under
the roof and around the windows, stood out in sharp, lively, and
motley contrast against its dark walls; pitchers with flowers were
daubed on the shutters. Having clambered up the narrow wooden
steps Chichikov made his way into a spacious entry, where he was
met by a door opening with a creak and a stout old woman in bright
calico who said: "This way, if you please!" Within the main room
he came upon all the old friends everybody meets in modest wooden
inns, of which there are not a few erected along our waysides, to
wit: a samovar covered with a hoar-frost-like patina; walls of
smoothly adzed pine; a three-cornered cupboard with tea pots and
tea cups in one of the corners; small porcelain eggs, gilt, hung up on
blue and red bits of ribbon before the holy images; a cat that had
recently had kittens, a mirror that reflected instead of two eyes
twice that number and, instead of the face, some sort of wafer or
other and, finally, fragrant herbs and cloves, stuck around the
images in bunches so dried up that he who wanted to sniff them
found no other reward than having to sneeze.

"Have you got a suckling pig?" was the first question Chichikov
addressed to the country-wife standing before him.

"We have that same."

"With horse-radish and sour cream?"

"With horse-radish and sour cream."

"Bring it on!"

The old woman began bustling about and fetched a plate, a napkin that was starched so much that it buckled like dried tree-bark,
then a knife, the bone handle of which had turned yellow and the
blade of which was as thin as that of a pen-knife, a two-tined fork,
and a salt cellar which it was impossible to set upright on the table.

Our hero, as was his wont, immediately entered into conversation
with her and questioned her thoroughly: whether she herself ran

the inn or if it had another owner, and how much income the inn brought in, and whether her sons lived at the inn, and was her eldest son a single or a married man, and what sort of wife had he taken unto himself, had her dowry been large or no, and had the bride's father been satisfied, and hadn't he been angry because there had been but few presents at the wedding—in fact, there wasn't a thing that he passed over. It goes without saying that he was curious enough to learn what landowners there were to be found thereabouts, and learned there were all sorts of landowners: Blokhin, Pochitaev, Mylnoi, Cheprakov (a colonel, he was), and Sobakevich.

"Ah! You know Sobakevich?" he asked, and heard, right then and there, that the old woman knew not only Sobakevich but Manilov as well, and that Manilov was a bit more refined, like, than Sobakevich was: he'd order a chicken to be cooked at once, and would ask for a bit of veal also, and if they happened to have any sheep's liver he'd ask for sheep's liver as well, yet would take only a taste of everything; this Sobakevich, on the other hand, would order only one dish, but then he'd eat up all of it and even ask for an extra helping for the same price.

As he was thus conversing over his suckling pig, of which only the least morsel remained by now, he heard the rattling wheels of some vehicle that had driven up. Looking out of the window he saw, halted before the inn, an exceedingly light carriage; it was harnessed with a team of three good horses. Two strangers were clambering out of it; one was flaxen-fair, of tall stature; the other was somewhat shorter, of a dark complexion. The flaxen-fair fellow had on a dark-blue Hungarian jacket with frogs; the one with the dark complexion simply a short, striped Tatar kaftan, fastened with hooks. Another carriage, a most wretched and small affair, was dragging along at a distance, empty and drawn by some sort of shaggy team of four, their collars all rent and tattered and their harness of odds and ends of rope and haywire. The flaxen-fair man at once started up the steps, while the swarthy fellow stayed behind, groping for something in the carriage, talking with a servant near by and at the same time motioning with his hand to the carriage ambling behind them. His voice seemed somehow familiar to Chichikov. While Chichikov was looking the swarthy man over, the flaxen-fair fellow had already managed to find the door by groping and to open it. He was tall of stature and gaunt of face (or what they call shop-worn), with a small, reddish mustache. By his sunburned face one could conclude that he knew what smoke was —if not that of cannons, then that of tobacco-pipes, at least. He made a polite bow to Chichikov, to which the latter responded in kind. Within a few minutes they would have probably gotten into conversation and become well acquainted with each other, since a beginning had already been made and both, almost at one and the same time, had evinced satisfaction because the dust along the road had been completely beaten down by yesterday's rain and now it was both cool and pleasant to travel, when the flaxen-fair man's dark-complexioned friend entered, tossing the cap off his head onto the table and running his hand through his thick black hair, rumpling it up with a may-the-Devil-take-me gesture. He was a fine lad of medium height, very far from being badly made, with full rosy cheeks, teeth as white as snow, and side-whiskers as black as pitch. His was a strawberries-and-cream color; his face seemed simply to exude health.

"Ba, ba, ba!" he cried out suddenly, flinging his arms wide at the sight of Chichikov. "What fates bring you hither?"

Chichikov recognized Nozdrev, the same Nozdrev together with whom he had dined at the Public Prosecutor's and who, in the space of a few minutes, had got on such an intimate footing with Chichikov that he had begun calling our hero *thou*, even though the latter had given him no reason whatsoever to do so.

"Where have you been traveling to?" Nozdrev was saying, and, without having waited for an answer, went on: "As for me, brother, I'm coming from the fair. Congratulate me: I have lost my shirt at cards. Would you believe it, never in my life have I had such a losing streak. Why, I arrived here on something I had to hire from the natives hereabouts! There, just for the fun of it, take a look through the window!" Here he himself bent Chichikov's head down, so that the latter almost hit himself against the window-frame. "See what trash that is? They barely managed to drag me here, the damned crow-bait; then I shifted over to that fellow's carriage." Saying this, Nozdrev pointed a finger at his friend.

"Why, haven't you made each other's acquaintance yet? This is my brother-in-law, Mizhuev! We were talking about you all morning. 'You just watch and see,' I says to him, 'if we won't meet up with Chichikov.' Well, now, brother, if you but knew how I was cleaned out! Would you believe it, not only have I gotten rid of four trotters, but of everything. Why, not only have I no watch on me, but not even as much as a chain—"

Chichikov glanced at him and saw that the other certainly had no watch nor chain on. It appeared to him, even, that one of his side-whiskers was shorter and not so luxuriant as the other.

"And yet, if I had but twenty roubles in my pocket," Nozdrev went on, "just that, and no more, I would have won everything back—or rather, besides winning back all my losses, I would have —there, as I am an honest man!—I would have put thirty thousand in my wallet, on the spot."

"However, you said that even at the time," the flaxen-fair fellow answered him, "but when I gave you fifty roubles you sent them after the rest, on the spot."

"Oh, I never would have! By God, I never would have! If I hadn't myself done a foolish thing, I'd never have done it, really! If I hadn't come a cropper by doubling my stake on that damned seven after the others had doubled theirs I would have broken the bank!"

"Just the same, you didn't break it," said the flaxen-fair man.

"I didn't break it because I didn't bet double on that seven at the right time. And do you think that major of yours is such a good player?"

"Whether he's a good player or no, he trimmed you just the same."

"He isn't so great!" said Nozdrev. "If I were to pull some of his stunts, I could trim him too. Oh, no; just let him try to double, then I'll see—I'll see then what sort of a gambler he is! But then, brother Chichikov, what a high time we had during the first few days! The fair was certainly a most excellent one. The merchants themselves say that never before had so many people come together. Everything I had brought from the village was sold at a most advantageous price. Eh, dear brother, did we have ourselves a good time! Even now, when one thinks of it . . . the Devil take it! I mean, what a pity it is you weren't there! Just imagine, there was a regiment of dragoons stationed a couple of miles from town. Well, would you believe it, all the officers—and there must have been at least forty of them—were in town, to a man. . . . When we started in to drink, brother dear. . . . Second Captain of Cavalry Potseluev, what a glorious fellow he was! What a mustache, brother dear! He never called bordeaux anything but just slops. 'Brother,' he'd say to the waiter, 'bring us some slops, now!' Lieutenant Kuvshinikov . . . ah, brother o' mine, what an infinitely charming fellow! There, now, is what one would call a full-blown profligate! He and I went around together all the time. And what wines Ponomarev let us have! You must know he's a great swindler, and you can't get anything decent in his shop; he always mixes in all sorts of rubbish into his wines—sandalwood, burnt cork and, the scoundrel, he even rubs alderwood into it; but then, if he does at last drag some little bottle or other out of his furthest room, which is called the Special Room in his place, well, brother o' mine, then you simply float in the empyrean. The champagne we had was such that . . . well, what would the Governor's be beside it? Why, nothing but ordinary bread-cider! Just imagine, it wasn't Clicquot, but some sort of a Clicquot-Matradura; that means it's double Clicquot. And he also got out a bottle of French wine, by the name of Bon-Bon. Bouquet? A posy of roses and everything else you wish. Oh, we sure did have ourselves a good time! Some prince or other who arrived in town after we did sent to Ponomarev's shop for champagne—the officers had drunk it up, every last drop of it. Would you believe it, I alone drank up seventeen bottles of champagne at one dinner!"

"Well, now, you could never drink seventeen bottles," remarked the flaxen-fair man.

"As I'm an honest man, I'm telling you I did drink that many," answered Nozdrev.

"You can say whatever you like, but I'm telling you you won't drink even ten."

"Well, do you want to make a bet I will?"

"Why bet on a thing like that?"

"There, you stake the gun you bought in town."

"I don't want to."

"Well, just stake it—see what'll come of it!"

"I don't want even to try."

"Why, you'd be shy a gun just as sure as you're standing there. Eh, brother Chichikov, I can't tell how sorry I felt you weren't there. I know that you and Lieutenant Kuvshinikov would have become inseparable. How well we'd have gotten along together! This isn't the same thing as with the Public Prosecutor and all the provincial skin-flints in our town, who simply shiver in their boots over every copper. This fellow, brother o' mine, will go for faro or banker, and for anything and everything you like. Eh, Chichikov, how would it have put you out to come? Really, you're a swine not to have done it, you cattle-breeder, you! Kiss me, my soul, I'm no end fond of you! Look you, Mizhuev, fate itself has brought us together! There, now, what is he to me, or I to him? He has come God knows whence, and I happen to be just a fellow living hereabouts. . . . And how many carriages there were, brother, and all that *en gros*, on a grand scale. I had a whirl at the wheel of fortune, too, and won two jars of pomade, a porcelain cup, and a guitar; then had one more go and, deuce take it, lost everything and six silver cartwheels besides. And if you but knew what a man Kuvshinikov is for a petticoat! He and I were at almost all the balls. There was one fair creature at one of them dressed to kill, all frills and furbelows, and the Devil alone knows what else she didn't have on. . . . All I do is to think to myself: 'May the Devil take me!' But Kuvshinikov, now, what a scoundrel he is! He sits down near her and starts dishing out compliments to her in French, and what compliments! Would you believe it, he wouldn't let even common countrywives pass by him. 'Crawling after the strawberries,' he calls it. There were some wonderful fresh fish and salted sturgeon steaks brought to the fair. I managed to bring a dried and salted sturgeon with me —good thing I had brains enough to buy it while I was still in the money. Where are you bound to now?"

"Why, I just have to see a certain party," Chichikov told him.

"Oh, what does that certain party matter? Drop him! Let's go to my place!"

"Can't, can't; there's a certain business matter I must attend to."

"There, now it's business! Now you've even thought up a business matter! Oh, you Quacksalve Ivanovich!"

"Really, there is a business matter and an urgent one, at that."

"I'm laying odds you're lying! There, now, just tell me whom you're going to see!"

"Well, it's Sobakevich."

Here Nozdrev burst into that ringing laughter which only a vigorous healthy male peals forth who can show every tooth in his head, and each of those teeth as white as refined sugar, whose cheeks quiver and shake, while a fellow-lodger, behind two doors and in the third room from his, jumps up from his sleep, with his eyes starting out of his head, and says: "Something sure must have struck that fellow as funny!"

"Well, what's so amusing about that?" asked Chichikov, somewhat displeased by such laughter.

But Nozdrev went on with his full-throated laughter as he kept on saying: "Oh, have mercy! Honestly, I'll burst from laughing!"

"There's nothing amusing about it; I gave him my word."

"Why, you'll be sorry you were ever born when you come to his place—that fellow can simply milk a billy-goat into a sieve! Why, I know your nature, you'll come a bad cropper if you think you'll find a good game of banker there and a good bottle of Bon-Bon or something like that. Listen to me, brother o' mine, you just send that Sobakevich packing to the Devil, now! Let's you and me go to my place! What salted sturgeon steak I'll treat you to! How Ponomarev, the low-down beast, scraped and bowed as he told me: 'It's only to you I'd sell it; you could search the whole fair through,' he says, 'and never find the like of that sturgeon.' He's a terrible rogue, just the same. I told him as much to his face. 'You,' I told him, 'and our tax-farmer are first rate swindlers.' He laughs, the low-down beast, and just strokes his beard. Kuvshinikov and I breakfasted at his place every day. Ah, brother, here's what I forgot to tell you—I know you'll pester the life out of me after you see it, but I won't give it up to you, not for ten thousand I won't, I'm telling you that beforehand. Hey, there, Porphyry!" he began shouting, walking up to the window, calling his servant, who was holding a small knife in one hand and in the other a crust of bread with a piece of dried and salted sturgeon which he had had the luck to slice off as he had been taking something out of the carriage. "Hey, there, Porphyry!" Nozdrev shouted. "Fetch that pup, now! What a pup!" he went on, turning to Chichikov. "It's stolen; its owner would rather have given up his own life than give up that pup. I promised him the light-chestnut mare—you remember, the one I got in a swap from Khvostyrev—"

Chichikov, however, had in all his born days never laid eyes either on the mare or on Khvostyrev.

"Wouldn't you like to have a bite of something, sir?" said the old woman at this point, walking up to Nozdrev.

"No, I'm not having anything. Eh, brother, did we have ourselves a good time! On second thought, let me have a glass of vodka. What sort have you got?"

"Anise," answered the old woman.

"Very well, then, let's have the anise," said Nozdrev.

"Let me have a glass while you're at it," said the flaxen-fair man.

"There was an actress at the theater, the little rogue, who sang like any nightingale! Kuvshinikov, who was sitting next to me, says: 'There,' says he, 'brother, are some strawberries to crawl after!' There must have been half a hundred show-booths alone, I'm thinking. Fenardi somersaulted and whirled like a mill for four hours at a stretch." Here he took the glass from the hands of the old woman, who made him a low curtsy in return. "Ah, let's have him here!" he cried out, catching sight of Porphyry, who had entered with a puppy. Porphyry was dressed in the same style as his master, in some sort of short Tatar kaftan fastened with hooks and quilted with cotton but somewhat more soiled.

"Let's have him—put him down on the floor!"

Porphyry put the puppy down on the floor and, with all its four legs sprawled out, it fell to sniffing the ground.

"There's a pup for you!" said Nozdrev, picking him up with one hand by the loose skin on his back. The puppy let out a rather piteous whimper.

"However, you haven't done what I told you to do," remarked Nozdrev, turning to Porphyry and examining the puppy's belly painstakingly. "You didn't even think of combing him out?"

"No, I did comb him out."

"Why has he got fleas, then?"

"I wouldn't be knowing. Could be that they'd crawled onto him out of the carriage, maybe."

"You lie, you lie—you didn't as much as give a thought to combing him out; I'm thinking you've even let some of your own on him in addition, you fool. There, take a look now, Chichikov, what ears he has; there, run a hand over them."

"What for? I can see even so; he's of a good breed," Chichikov answered him.

"No, do take him—just you feel his ears."

Chichikov, just to please him, felt the pup's ears, saying: "Yes, he'll turn out a good hound."

"And the nose, now, do you feel how cold it is? There, just touch it."

Since he did not want to hurt the other's feelings, Chichikov felt the puppy's nose as well, saying: "He has a keen scent."

"A real pug," Nozdrev went on. "I must confess I've been hankering for a pug for a long time. There, Porphyry, take him away!"

Porphyry, picking up the puppy under its belly, bore it off to the carriage.

"Listen, Chichikov, you must come to my place right now, without fail; it's only three miles and a half or so to it. We'll make it in one spurt, and after that, if you like, you can even go on to Sobakevich."

"Well, and why not?" Chichikov reflected. "Guess I'll really drop in at Nozdrev's. In what way is he worse than the others? Just as human as they, and on top of that he's lost his shirt gambling. He's ready for anything and everything, apparently; therefore one may wheedle a thing or two out of him for a song."

"Let's go, then, if you like," said he. "But I warn you, don't detain me; time is precious to me."

"There, that's the way, my friend! That's good! Hold on, now, I'll kiss you for that!" Here Nozdrev and Chichikov kissed each other. "That's just glorious—the three of us will go tooling along together."

74 ·

"No, you'll really have to let me off, now, please," said the flaxen-fair man. "I have to be getting home."

"Nonsense, nonsense, brother; I shan't let you off."

"Really, my wife will be angry with me. Why, now you can simply shift to his carriage."

"Never, never, never! Don't even think of such a thing!"

The flaxen-fair fellow was one of those people in the makeup of which there is, at first glance, a certain streak of stubbornness. You hardly have time to open your mouth when they're already set to argue and, it seems, under no circumstances will they ever consent to that which is obviously contrary to their way of thinking, or consent to call that sensible which is stupid, and, in particular, never will they consent to dance to another's tune; and yet it will always wind up by a certain soft spot in their makeup coming to the fore, by their consenting to precisely that which they had been rejecting; that which is stupid they will call sensible, and will thereafter set off to dancing to another's tune in a way that could not be bettered—in short, they'll start off smoothly and end up uncouthly.

"Bosh!" said Nozdrev in answer to one of the objections of the flaxen-fair man, put the cap on his flaxen-fair head, and the flaxen-fair one trotted off at their heels.

"You haven't paid for the tots of vodka yet, sir," the old woman reminded Nozdrev.

"Ah, right you are, right you are, mother! I say, brother-in-law, dear, you pay for me, please! I haven't got a copper in my pocket!"

"How much is coming to you?" asked the brother-in-law, dear.

"Why, how much should it be, father o' mine? Twenty kopeks, all in all," said the old woman.

"You lie, you lie! Give her half of that, it'll be more than enough for her."

"Kind of little, sir," said the old woman; however, she accepted the silver coin with gratitude, and even made a headlong dash to hold the door open for them. She was not really out anything, inasmuch as she had asked four times as much as the drinks were worth.

The wayfarers seated themselves. Chichikov's carriage rode side by side with that of Nozdrev's brother-in-law, and therefore all three could freely converse among themselves during the whole way. Nozdrev's small, wretched calash, drawn by the hired skin-and-bones nags, trailed after them, continually falling behind. It was occupied by Porphyry and the puppy.

Inasmuch as the conversation which the travelers were carrying on among themselves is of no great interest to the reader, we will do better if we say something about Nozdrev himself whom, per-chance, it may befall to play by no means the least rôle in our epic.

Nozdrev's face is by now most probably familiar to the reader. There isn't a man but has had to encounter not a few individuals like him. They're called free-and-easy fellows, have the reputation, even during their childhood and schooldays, of being good friends, and yet, with all that, are quite painfully beaten up from time to time. Upon their faces is always to be perceived something frank, direct, audacious. They make your acquaintance quickly, and you hardly have time to turn around before they're already *thou*'ing you. When they form a friendship, you might think it is forever and a day, but almost always things so fall out that he who has become friends with one of these individuals will have a fight with him that same evening at a friendly drinking bout. They're always great chatterers, revelers, dashing horsemen—folk that strike your eye. Nozdrev, at thirty, was absolutely the same as he had been at twenty and at seventeen—a great hand for having a good time. His marriage had not changed him in the least, inasmuch as his wife had soon passed on into another world, leaving two urchins behind her, of which he had absolutely no need. However, there was a rather comely nurse to look after the children. He could not, somehow, stay at home for more than a day at a time. His keen scent could smell out even at a distance of a few score miles where a fair might be going on, with all sorts of assemblies and balls and, as fast as you could blink an eye, he'd be there, argufying and creating a rumpus at the green-baize tables, inasmuch as he had, like all his kind, a low-down passion for the Devil's prayer book. When it came to turning the leaves of this prayer book he was, as we have already seen from the first chapter, not altogether without sin, nor entirely fair and aboveboard, being wise in many and sundry sleights and other finesses, and for that reason the game would often wind up with another sort of game: either they drubbed him, kicking him with their boots, or else went in for doing sleight-of-hand tricks with his thick and very good-looking side-whiskers so that at times he would come home with only one and that one quite scanty. But his healthy and full cheeks were so well made and held such a power of growth that the side-whiskers would soon sprout anew, producing an even better crop than the preceding. And— which is the strangest of all, which can happen in Russia alone— after a lapse of some time he would again meet those friends who had given him a shellacking and, at that, meet them as though there had never been a thing between them; he paid no never mind to it, as the saying goes, and they paid it no never mind.

Nozdrev, in a certain respect, was a man of affairs: there was nary a gathering at which he was present where things got along without an affair. Some affair or other was inevitably bound to arise: either the gendarmes would lead him by the arm out of the hall, or none other than his own cronies would be compelled to heave him out. But if such an affair didn't befall, then nevertheless there would be some such thing as could never befall anybody else: either he would become so quiffy at the buffet that he would be able to do nothing but laugh, or else he would lie such a blue streak that he himself would become conscience-stricken. And he would tell a pack of lies utterly without any need therefor: he would suddenly relate that he had a horse with some kind of blue hide, or pink, and such-like poppycock, so that his auditors would, to a man, walk away from him at last, saying: "Well, brother, it seems you've started pulling the long bow!"

There are certain folk who have a low-down passion for playing some vile trick on their fellow-man, at times without any earthly reason for it. One, for instance, a man who has even attained to high rank, with a noble appearance, with a Star gracing his bosom, will be clasping your hand as he discusses with you profound subjects which call for meditative reflection; yet later on, right on the spot, you look and before your very eyes he will pull some vile stunt at your expense, and will pull it in such a way as a common Collegiate Registrar might, and not at all in the way a man with a Star gracing his bosom would who discusses subjects that call for serious reflection, so that you can but stand there and wonder, shrugging your shoulders, and there isn't a thing else on earth you can do. Just as strange a passion did Nozdrev have. The more intimate anybody became with him, the more willingly would Nozdrev put the skids under him, of all people; he would spread some wild tale, so silly that it would be difficult to think up a sillier to top it; he would break up a marriage or a business deal, yet would not at all consider himself your enemy; on the contrary, if chance ever led him to meet you again, he would treat you anew as a close friend and would even say: "Why, you're such a low-down fellow, you never drop in on me!"

Nozdrev, in many respects, was a many-sided man—that is, he was ready to try his hand at anything. In the same breath he would propose to go with you wherever you wished—to the end of the world, even—would propose entering with you on any enterprise you like, to swap everything in the world for anything you like. A gun, a dog, a horse, anything could form the basis for a swap, but not at all in order to gain something: the swap was undertaken only from some sort of turbulently indefatigable impetuosity and liveliness of character. If, at a fair, he had the good luck of coming upon a simpleton and trimming him, he would buy up a mountain of whatever things happened to meet his eye first in the shops: horse-collars, incense-pastilles, neckerchiefs for the nurse, a stallion, raisins, a silver wash-basin, Holland linen, farina, tobacco, pistols, herrings, pictures, a turning lathe, pots, boots, faience dishes—as long as his money lasted. However, it but rarely happened that these things reached home: almost the same day they would be lost to some other, luckier gamester, at times even his own pipe, with tobacco-pouch and an extra amber mouthpiece, would be thrown in and, on occasion, his whole team of four horses and everything that went with it—not only calash but the coachman as well—so that the master himself would have to set out in an abbreviated, wretched frock-coat, or a short Tatar kaftan, to seek out some friend of his, to get a lift home in his vehicle.

That's the sort of fellow Nozdrev was! Perhaps people will call him a hackneyed character, will start saying that there is no Nozdrev in existence nowadays. Alas, those who are going to say such things will be unjust. Nozdrev will not die off this earth for a long time yet. He is everywhere in our midst, merely walking about in a coat of a different cut, it may be; but men are frivolously unperceptive and a fellow in a coat of a different cut will look to them like an entirely different fellow.

In the meantime the three vehicles had already rolled up to the front steps of Nozdrev's house. There had been no preparation whatsoever for their reception within. In the middle of the dining room stood wooden trestles, and two muzhiks, standing thereon, were whitewashing the walls, chanting some endless song; the floor was all spattered with the whitewash. Nozdrev immediately ordered the muzhiks to clear out and take the trestles with them, and dashed off into another room to issue additional commands. His guests heard him giving orders for the dinner to the chef; Chichikov, who was beginning to feel his appetite somewhat, taking everything into consideration perceived that they would not sit down to table before five. Nozdrev, returning, led his guests off to inspect everything he had in his village and, in a little over two hours, showed them absolutely all, so that there was nothing more left to show! First of all they went to inspect the stable, where they beheld two mares, one a gray piebald, the other a light chestnut; then a bay stallion, not much to look at, but for whom Nozdrev swore he had paid ten thousand.

"You didn't give any ten thousand for him," remarked his brother-in-law. "He isn't worth even a thousand."

"By God, I did so give ten thousand," Nozdrev maintained.

"You can swear by God till you're blue in the face," his brother-in-law commented.

"There, now, would you like to lay a bet on it?" asked Nozdrev.

But his brother-in-law didn't want to lay a bet.

After that Nozdrev showed them empty stalls which had previously been occupied by other thoroughbred horses. In the same stable they beheld a goat, which, according to the ancient belief, it was necessary to keep with the horses, which goat, apparently, lived on good terms with them and strolled about under their bellies as if he were perfectly at home. After that Nozdrev led them off to have a look at a wolf whelp, who was kept on a tether.

"There's a wolf whelp for you!" he said. "I purposely feed him raw meat. I want him to be a perfect brute."

They went for a look at the pond, where, if Nozdrev's words were to be believed, fish were to be found so big that it was all two men could do to drag one of them out—which, however, was something that his relative did not fail to express his doubts about.

"Chichikov," said Nozdrev, "I'm going to show you a most excellent pair of dogs; the firmness of their black bodies will simply amaze you; they have hackles like needles!" And he led them to a very handsomely built little house, surrounded by a yard that was fenced in on all sides. When they entered the yard they saw all sorts of dogs there, shaggy as well as smooth-coated, of all possible colors and breeds: tan, black with markings of white, liver-colored-and-skewbald, tan-and-skewbald, red-and-skewbald, black-eared, gray-eared. . . . Here were all the nicknames, all the imperative tenses: Shoot, Scold, Flit, Scrape, Pester, Get Hot; Fire, Sloper, Northerner, Darling, Reward, Lady Guardian. Nozdrev in their midst was absolutely like a father in the midst of his family; all of them at once, turning up their tails—which dogkeepers call *rudders*—flew straight toward the guests and began to get acquainted. Half a score or so of them placed their forepaws on Nozdrev's shoulders. Scold evinced the same sort of friendship for Chichikov and, getting up on his hindlegs, licked him right on the lips with his tongue, so that Chichikov had to spit without much ceremony. They looked over the dogs, the firmness of whose black bodies would amaze you; and good dogs they were, too. Then they set out to look at a Crimean bitch, who was blind by now and, according to Nozdrev's words, due to peg out soon but, only two years back, she'd been a very fine bitch. So they looked this bitch over as well, and the bitch, sure enough, was blind. Then they set out to look over the water-mill, which lacked the part whereon the upper millstone rests as it quickly revolves on a shaft—the part called the *flutterer*, according to the wondrously apt expression of the Russian peasant.

"And now we're coming to the blacksmithy," said Nozdrev. And, believe it or not, after going on a little way, they did see a blacksmith's shop. They looked the blacksmith's shop over as well.

"On that field there," said Nozdrev, pointing his finger at a field, "there's such an awful lot of winter hares that you can't see the ground for them; I myself caught one by his hindlegs with my bare hands."

"Well, now, you'll never catch a winter hare with your bare hands," remarked his brother-in-law.

"But I tell you I caught one; I deliberately caught one!" Nozdrev answered him. "Now I'm going to take you"—he turned to Chichikov—"to see the boundary line where my land ends."

Nozdrev led his visitors through a field that, in many places, consisted of hummocks. They had to make their way between fallowlands and furrowed corn-fields. Chichikov was beginning to feel fatigue. In many places their feet made water spurt forth, so lowlying was this bog. At first they were cautious and set their feet down with care, but then, seeing that this was of no use, they sloshed right on, without choosing between the deeper or the shallower mud. Having gone a considerable distance they beheld, believe it or not, the boundary line, consisting of a stumpy, round wooden post as a marker and a narrow trench.

"There's the boundary!" said Nozdrev. "Everything that you see on this side is all of it mine, and even on the other side, that whole forest that shows so blue over there is mine, as well as everything beyond the forest—it's all mine too."

"But whenever did that forest become yours?" his brother-in-law questioned him. "Why, did you buy it recently? For it wasn't yours before."

"Yes, I bought it recently," answered Nozdrev.

"How did you ever contrive to buy it so quickly?"

"Oh, yes, I bought it three days ago and, the Devil take it, I gave a high price for it."

"But you were away at the fair at that time—"

"Oh, you yokel! For can't one be at a fair and yet buy land? Very well, so I was at the fair, but my steward up and bought it without my being present."

"Oh, well, the steward could have bought it," said his brother-in-law, but even then he had his doubts and shook his head.

The visitors returned by the same vile route to the house. Nozdrev led them off to his study, in which, however, there were not to be found any traces of that which is usual to studies—books and papers, that is; all they saw there in the way of adornment was two swords and two guns—one of the latter had cost three hundred rubles and the other eight hundred. Nozdrev's brother-in-law, having looked them over, merely shook his head. After that the host exhibited to them genuine Turkish daggers—one of which, however, through some error, was engraved with *Made by Savelii Sibiriakov*. Following this a hurdy-gurdy was exhibited to the guests. Nozdrev, right then and there, ground out a thing or two for them. The hurdy-gurdy played not unpleasingly but, apparently, something must have happened to its innards, inasmuch as a mazurka wound up with *Malbrouk to the Wars Has Gone*, while *Malbrouk to the Wars Has Gone* was unexpectedly terminated by some long-familiar waltz. Nozdrev had long since quit grinding, but the hurdy-gurdy had one particularly lively reed that would not quiet down, and for a while thereafter it kept on tootling of its own accord. Then came the exhibition of the pipes: of brier, of clay, of meerschaum, broken in and new, in chamois purses and without chamois purses, a chibouk with a mouthpiece of amber, recently won at play, a tobacco-pouch embroidered by a certain countess who, at some stage-post or other, had fallen head over heels in love with him and whose minim hands, according to his words, were the most subtle *superflues*—a word that, for him, probably signified the very acme of perfection.

Having had a snack of salted sturgeon, they sat down at the table about five. The dinner table, evidently, did not constitute for Nozdrev the main thing in life; the courses did not play a great rôle in the dinner; this dish and that had even become burnt; this dish and that had not even been thoroughly cooked. It was evident that the chef was guided for the most part by some weird inspiration and would pop into the pot the first thing that came to his hand: if the pepper-pot happened to be standing near by he would sprinkle in the pepper; if cabbage came handy, he would shove in the cabbage; he slopped in milk, ham, peas—in short, slap, dash, as long as it was hot, and as for the taste, well, some sort of taste would probably come out in the end. But to make up for all that Nozdrev leant heavily on wine: even before soup was served he had poured out for each guest a large glass of port, and another of Haut Sauterne, inasmuch as in provincial capitals and district towns there is no such thing to be found as ordinary sauterne. Next Nozdrev ordered a bottle of madeira to be brought, "and not even the field-marshal himself has ever drunk a better." The madeira, to be sure, actually burned one's mouth, inasmuch as the wine-merchants, knowing well by now the taste of the landed proprietors who were fond of good madeira, hocused it unmercifully with rum, and on occasion even poured therein vodka as well, the kind called Czar's vodka, the fieriest of all, trusting that Russian stomachs would bear up under anything and everything. Then Nozdrev also ordered a certain particular bottle to be fetched which, according to his own unorthodox terminology, was both a bourgognion and a champagnion rolled into one. He was most zealous in pouring the drink into the glasses to his right and left, both in Chichikov's and into his brother-in-law's; Chichikov happened to notice, however, that he did not add a great deal to his own glass. This compelled him to be cautious and, as soon as Nozdrev would happen to become absorbed in talk or would be filling up his brother-in-law's glass, Chichikov would on the instant tip his glass over into his plate. In a short while some sorb-apple cordial was brought in and placed on the table, which cordial, according to Nozdrev's words, tasted exactly like cream, but in which, amazingly enough, one could perceive moonshine in all its potency. Then they drank some balsam or other bearing a name that was hard to remember, and even the host himself gave it another name when he had occasion to mention it a second time.

The dinner had long since ended and all the wines had already been tasted, yet the guests still sat on at the table. Chichikov under no circumstances wished to broach his main object to Nozdrev in the presence of his brother-in-law; after all, his brother-in-law was an outsider, whereas the object demanded a private and friendly talk. However, Nozdrev's brother-in-law could hardly have been regarded as a person to feel apprehensive about, inasmuch as he had, apparently, taken on a sufficient load and, seated in his chair, kept going off to sleep every minute or so. Perceiving himself that he was in a rather precarious state he began, at last, begging to go home, but in such a drawling and listless voice as if, according to the Russian expression, he were putting a collar on a horse with a pair of pincers.

"Oh, never, never! I'm not going to let you go!" said Nozdrev.

"No, don't you be taking advantish of me, m'friend—really, I'm going," his brother-in-law was saying. "You mean to take a great advantish of me."

"Nonsense, nonsense! We're going to make up a game of banker right now!"

"No, brother, you go 'head and make it up by yourself, but I can't take a hand in it: my wife will be ver', ver' angry with me, really; I've got to tell her everything about the fair. I've got to, brother, really, I've got to give her that pleasure. No, don't you be keepin' me back."

"Eh, send your wife to. . . . Really, one could think you two were going to do something mighty important together!"

"No, don't say that, brother! She's such a good wife to me! That's a positive fact—she's an exemplary wife, so worthy of esteem and so true! She does such things for me . . . would you believe it, it makes tears come to my eyes. No; don't you be keeping me; I'm telling you, as an honest man, that I'm going. I assure you I am—cross my heart!"

"Let him go; what good is he?" Chichikov suggested to Nozdrev on the quiet.

"Why, that's true enough," said Nozdrev. "I have a mortal dislike of people who go all to pieces like that!" And he added, more loudly: "Well, the Devil with you; go and have a good time with your wife, you horse's tail, you!"

"No, brother, don't you go cursing me for a horse's tail," protested his brother-in-law. "I owe her my life. Really, now, she's such a kind soul, so darling; she's so loving to me . . . it moves me to tears. She'll ask me what I saw at the fair—I'll have to tell her everything. . . . Really, now, she's such a darling."

"Well, go on home, then; tell her a pack of lying nonsense! Here's your cap."

"No, brother, you oughtn't to be shaying things like that about her at all, at all; by doing that same you, one may shay, are doing a wrong to my own self, she's such a darling."

"Well, then, go to her—the sooner the better!"

"Yes, brother, I'll go; forgive me for not being able to stay. I'd be glad to, with all my soul, but I can't."

His brother-in-law for a long while kept on reiterating his excuses, without noticing that he himself had long been sitting in his carriage, had long since driven out of the gates, and that for a long while only the deserted fields were lying before him. It must be supposed that his wife did not hear many details about the fair from him that night.

"What trash!" Nozdrev was saying, standing before the window and watching the receding vehicle. "Look at him go! That little off-horse of his isn't bad; I've long since been wanting to get hold of it. But then there's no getting together on terms with him. A horse's tail, just a plain horse's tail!"

After that they came back into the dining room. Porphyry brought in candles and Chichikov noticed in the hands of his host a pack of cards that had bobbed up from no one knew where.

"Well, what do you say, brother?" Nozdrev was saying, squeezing the sides of the deck with his fingers and buckling it a little, so that the band about it burst and flew off. "I'm starting the bank at three hundred—oh, just to pass the time away!"

But Chichikov made believe he had not even heard what the host was talking about and said, as though he had just recalled it suddenly: "Ah! Before it slips my mind, I have a certain request to make of you."

"What is it?"

"Give me your word first that you'll grant it to me."

"But what is your request?"

"Well, you just give me your word!"

"If you like—"

"Your word of honor?"

"My word of honor!"

"Here's my request: you must have, I surmise, a large number of dead serfs who haven't yet been taken off the census in the Bureau of Audits?"

"Why, so I have. What of that?"

"Transfer them to me, let them stand in my name."

"And what would you be wanting with them?"

"Why, I happen to need them."

"But what in the world for?"

"Why, I just happen to need them . . . for reasons of my own; in short, I need them."

"Well, now, you must have cooked up something, for sure. Own up—what is it?"

"Why, what could I have cooked up? Out of a trifle like that one could hardly cook up anything."

"But what do you need them for?"

"Oh, what an inquisitive fellow! He'd like to lay his hands on every sort of trash—and stick his nose into it as well!"

"But how is it you don't want to say anything about it?"

"Yes, but how would it profit you to know? Well, I want them just so; I've gotten a sort of fancy into my head."

"Very well, then; until such time as you tell me I'm not going through with it."

"There, you see now; that's already actually dishonest on your part—you give your word, and then start backing out."

"Well, you may act as you wish; but I'm not doing anything until you tell me what you want them for."

"What could I possibly tell him?" Chichikov pondered, and, after a moment's reflection, declared that he needed the dead serf-souls to acquire a position in society; that he did not own any large estates, and so, until such time as he did, he ought at least to be able to lay claim to some wretched souls, of any sort.

"You lie, you lie!" said Nozdrev, without letting him finish. "You lie, brother!"

Even Chichikov himself perceived that his invention was none too adroit, and that his pretext was rather feeble.

"Very well, then, I'll be more straightforward with you," he said, having recovered himself, "only please don't let it out to anybody. I've gotten it into my head to marry; but you must know that my bride's father and mother are most ambitious folk. What a fix I'm in, to be sure! I'm sorry I ever became mixed up with them;

they want their daughter's bridegroom to have no less than three hundred serfs, without fail, and since I have practically all of a hundred and fifty peasants lacking—"

"There, you're lying, you're lying!" Nozdrev again began shouting.

"Well, now," said Chichikov, "this time I haven't lied even that much," and he marked off with his thumb the very least moiety from the tip of his little finger.

"I'll stake my head on it you're lying!"

"I say, though, this is insulting! What am I, after all? Really, why must I necessarily be lying?"

"Oh, come, after all, I know you; you're a great swindler, allow me to tell you that out of friendship! If I were your superior official I'd hang you on the first tree I came to."

Chichikov felt insulted by this remark. For he always found distasteful every expression that was to any extent coarse or derogatory to his dignity. He even did not like to tolerate familiar treatment of himself in any case whatsoever, unless, perhaps, if the person extending such treatment was of far too lofty a station. And for these reasons he now became thoroughly offended.

"By God, I'd hang you," Nozdrev reiterated. "I'm telling you this frankly, not so as to offend you, but simply as a friend."

"There are limits to everything," said Chichikov, with a feeling of dignity. "If you want to show off with speeches like that you'd better go to the barracks," and immediately added: "If you don't want to make me a present of them, then you might sell them to me."

"Sell them! Why, I know you—why, you're a scoundrel—why, would you give anything like a price for them?"

"Eh, but you're a fine fellow, too! Look here! What are your serf-souls like, made of diamonds, or what?"

"There, it's just as I thought. Why, I knew what you were like."

"Good heavens, brother, what a grasping disposition you have! What you ought to do is simply make me a present of them!"

"Well, look here, just to prove to you that I'm not some sort of a skinflint, I won't take anything for those souls. Buy the stallion off me, and I'll throw the souls in."

"Good heavens, what would I do with a stallion?" asked Chichikov, really astonished by such a proposal.

"What do you mean, what would you do with him? Why, I paid ten thousand for him, yet I'm letting you have him for four."

"Yes, but what would I be doing with a stallion? I'm not running a stud-farm."

"But look here, you don't understand; why, I'll take only a measly three thousand from you, and the other thousand you can pay me later."

"Yes, but I don't need a stallion, God be with him!"

"Well, then, buy the light-chestnut mare."

"I don't need a mare either."

"For the mare, and the gray horse that I showed you, I'll take only two thousand from you."

"Yes, but I don't need any horses."

"You'll sell 'em, they'll give you three times as much as you paid for them at the first fair."

"Then it would be better if you were to sell them yourself, since you're so sure you can make a triple profit on them."

"I know I could, but then I want you to get some good out of it too."

Chichikov thanked him for his good intentions and refused outright both the gray horse and the light-chestnut mare.

"Well, then, buy some of the dogs. I'll sell you such a pair as will make you tingle with delight; the bitch has whiskers, so help me; their coats bristle like a badger's; the way their ribs are rounded like a barrel is something beyond the mind to grasp; their paws are just like pads, they won't leave tracks on the ground!"

"But what would I be doing with dogs? I don't go in for hunting."

"Why, I'd like you to have dogs. Look here, now: if you don't want the dogs, then buy the hurdy-gurdy from me. A marvelous hurdy-gurdy! It cost me, as I am an honest man, a thousand and a half; I'll give it away to you for nine hundred."

"But what would I be doing with a hurdy-gurdy? For I'm no German, to be lugging it up and down all the roads, begging for coppers."

"But this isn't the sort of hurdy-gurdy the Germans carry around. It's an organ; take a special look at it, it's all made of mahogany. There, I'll show it to you once more!"

At this point Nozdrev, seizing Chichikov by the hand, began dragging him into the other room and, no matter how the latter held back, hand and foot, resisting and protesting that he already knew what the hurdy-gurdy was like, he nevertheless had to listen once more to just how Malbrouk to the wars had gone.

"If you don't want to lay out any money for it, then I'll tell you what I'll do, you just listen: I'll give you the hurdy-gurdy, *and* all the dead souls I own, as many as there are of them, and you give me your carriage and three hundred to boot."

"There, what else! And what am I going to travel about in?"

"I'll give you another carriage. There, let's go to the wagon-shed, I'll show it to you! All you'll have to do will be to give it a new coat of paint, and you'll have a marvelous carriage!"

"Eh, some fiend that won't be downed must have gotten into him!" Chichikov reflected, and decided, no matter what happened, to get out of acquiring any light carriages, hurdy-gurdys, and all dogs of any sort whatsoever, despite the barrel-like formation of their ribs, beyond the powers of the mind to grasp, and the pad-like nature of their paws.

"Why, you get the light carriage, the hurdy-gurdy, *and* the dead souls, all in one lot!"

"I don't want that!" Chichikov refused once more.

"But just why don't you want it?"

"Because I simply don't want it—and that's all there is to it."

"Really, now, what a man you are! I can see one can't deal with you the way one usually deals with good friends and comrades. . . . What a fellow, really! One can see at once that you're a two-faced fellow!"

"Well, what am I, really—a fool? You just judge for yourself: why should I acquire a thing I have absolutely no need of?"

"There, now, don't talk any more, if you please. I know you very well by now. What a rascally creature you are, to be sure. Well, look here: do you want to have a go at a game of banker? I'll stake all the dead serfs on one card, and the hurdy-gurdy, too."

"Well, to decide it by cards means to be subjected to the unknown," Chichikov said, and at the same time eyed askance the cards in his host's hands. Both of the shuffles which Nozdrev made looked very much like fake ones to Chichikov, while the very design on the back seemed quite suspicious.

"But why the unknown?" scoffed Nozdrev. "There's nothing of the unknown about it! If there be but any luck on your side, you can win a hell of a lot. There it is, what luck!" he was saying, beginning to throw out the cards, to arouse interest. "What luck! What luck! There, it just runs after you! There's that cursed nine on which I lost every stitch I had! I felt it would sell me out but, just the same, shutting my eyes, I thought to myself: 'May the Devil take you, go ahead and sell me out, and be damned to you!' "

While Nozdrev was speaking thus, Porphyry brought in another bottle. But Chichikov refused positively either to play or to drink.

"But why don't you want to play?" asked Nozdrev.

"Well, just because I don't feel so disposed. And besides, to tell you the truth, I'm not at all fond of playing."

"Buy why aren't you fond of it?"

Chichikov shrugged his shoulders and then added: "Because I'm not."

"What a rubbishy fellow you are!"

"Well, what can I do? That's the way God made me."

"You're just a horse's tail! I was thinking up to now that you're a decent fellow, at least to some extent, but you don't understand good treatment, nohow. There's no way of talking with you as one would with someone intimate, nohow. . . . There's no straightforwardness at all about you, no sincerity! You're a perfect Sobakevich, that's the sort of scoundrel you are!"

"But what are you cursing me for? Am I at fault because I don't play? Sell me the souls by themselves, if you're the sort of a man who shivers over such trash."

"You'll get fiddlesticks out of me! I wanted to give them to you for nothing, I did, but now you'll never get them! If you were to give me three kingdoms for them I wouldn't give them up to you. What a shark! You're as abominable as a chimneysweep. From now on I want to have nothing whatsoever to do with you. Por-

phyry, go and tell the stableman not to give any oats to his horses—
let them eat hay, that's good enough for them!"

This last decision was something utterly unexpected to Chichikov.

"It would be best if you'd simply never show me your face
again!" announced Nozdrev.

Despite such a falling-out, however, the host and his guest had
supper together, although this time there were no wines with fancy
labels whatsoever standing on the table. There was only one bottle
sticking up like a sore thumb, of some Cyprus wine, which was in
every way of the sort that is called red ink. After supper Nozdrev
told Chichikov, leading him off to a side-room where a bed had
been made for him: "There's your bed! I don't want to wish you a
good night, even."

Chichikov, after Nozdrev's departure, was left in a most unpleasant state of spirits. Inwardly he was vexed with himself, up-
braiding himself for having gone with Nozdrev and losing his time
for nothing; but still more did he upbraid himself for having
broached this business to him; he had acted incautiously, like a
child, like a fool, inasmuch as the business was not at all of such a
nature as a Nozdrev could be trusted to know. . . . Nozdrev, as
a man, was so much trash; Nozdrev was capable of telling a pack of
lies, of bruiting about the Devil alone knew what—likely as not,
there would be plenty of crazy rumors as a result. . . . It was
bad, bad! "I am simply a fool!" he kept saying to himself. He slept
very poorly that night. Some sort of tiny, exceedingly lively insects
were biting him, inflicting unbearable pain, so that he would scrape
the bitten place with his whole hand, adding: "Ah, may the Devil
take you, together with Nozdrev!" He awoke early in the morning.
The first thing he did, after putting on a dressing-gown and pulling on his boots, was to set out through the yard toward the stable,
to give Seliphan orders about harnessing the light carriage immediately. As he was returning through the yard he encountered Nozdrev, who was also in a dressing-gown, with a pipe clenched between his teeth.

Nozdrev greeted him friendlily and inquired how he had slept.

"So-so," Chichikov replied, quite dryly.

"As for me, brother," said Nozdrev, "I've had such vile things bothering me all night that it's a foul thing even to tell of them; and my mouth, after yesterday, feels as if a troop had bivouacked there. Just imagine, I dreamt that I was flogged—I swear it, I swear I dreamt that. And just imagine who it was that flogged me? There, you'll never guess it—it was Second Captain of Cavalry Potseluev, he and Kuvshinikov."

"Yes," Chichikov reflected, "it would be a good thing if you were really to be skinned alive."

"Yes, by God! And most painfully! I awoke and, the Devil take it, something was really making me scratch—probably those damned witch-fleas. Well, you go and dress now; I'll come to see you right away. All I've got to do is to bawl out my scoundrel of a steward."

Chichikov went off to his room to wash and dress. When, after doing so, he came out into the dining room the tea things and a bottle of rum were already standing on the table. There were traces of yesterday's dinner and supper in the room; the floor-brush, apparently, had not been applied at all. Bread crumbs were all over the floor, while tobacco ashes were to be seen even on the tablecloth. The host himself, who lost no time in entering, did not have a thing on under his dressing-gown, but his exposed chest sprouted a luxuriant something that looked like a beard. Holding his chibouk in his hand and sipping out of a tea cup, he would have made a very picturesque subject for a painter who had no overwhelming love for slicked-down and curlicued gentlemen, like to wigmaker's signs, or for those who are closely clipped.

"Well, what do you think?" asked Nozdrev, after a short silence. "Wouldn't you like to play for those souls?"

"I've already told you, brother, that I don't play; if you'd like me to buy them I'll do so, by all means."

"I don't want to sell them—that wouldn't be the friendly thing to do. What the Devil, I'm not going to start picking up coppers off a dung-hill with my teeth. A little game of banker, now, that's another matter. Let's have one little deal at least!"

"I've already told you, no."

"But would you want to swap?"

"No, I wouldn't."

"Well, look here, let's have a game of checkers: if you win, they're all yours. For I have a lot of souls that ought to be stricken from the census in the Bureau of Audits. Hey, there, Porphyry, bring the checkers and the checker-board here!"

"You're putting yourself out for nothing—I'm not going to play."

"Why, this isn't like banker; there can be no luck or trickery here—everything depends on skill. I'm even telling you beforehand that I can't play the game at all unless you give me a handicap."

"Suppose I do sit down," Chichikov mused, "and play him a game of checkers. I used to play checkers not so badly, and as for tricks, it would be hard for him to try any in this game."

"So be it, then, if you like; I'll play you a game of checkers."

"I'm staking the souls against a hundred roubles!"

"But why? It'll be enough if you staked them against fifty."

"No, what sort of stake is fifty roubles? Better make it a hundred, and I'll throw in a fair-to-middlin' puppy or a gold watch-seal."

"Very well, if you like!" said Chichikov.

"How many checkers do you give me as a handicap?" asked Nozdrev.

"Why should I? I'm not giving you any handicap, of course."

"Allow me two moves extra, at least."

"I don't want to; I play poorly myself."

"We know all about you fellows who claim to play poorly!" said Nozdrev, advancing one of his checkers.

"It's rather a long time since I've tried my hand at checkers!" said Chichikov, moving a checker.

"We know all about you fellows who claim to play poorly!" said Nozdrev, moving a checker but at the same time moving up another one as well with the cuff of his sleeve.

"It's rather a long time since I've tried my hand—hey, there! What's going on here, brother? You move that back from there!" said Chichikov.

"Move what back?"

"Why, that checker, now," said Chichikov, and at the same moment perceived, almost under his very nose, still another checker, which, so it seemed, was trying to sneak through into the king's row. Whence it had bobbed up, God alone could tell. "No," said Chichikov, getting up from the table, "it's absolutely impossible to play with you. People don't move like that, three checkers at one time!"

"But why three at a time? That was just an error. One must have been moved forward by accident; I'll move it back, if you like."

"And where did the other one bob up from?"

"What other one?"

"Why, this one, that's trying to sneak into the king's row?"

"There you go! As though you didn't remember!"

"No, brother, I kept track of all the moves, and remember everything; you put it there just now. There's the right square for it!"

"What do you mean? What square?" asked Nozdrev, turning red. "Why, brother, you're making things up, as I see it!"

"No, brother, it looks as if you were the one who's making things up—but not any too successfully."

"What do you take me for, then?" asked Nozdrev. "Why, am I the sort that goes in for cheating?"

"I don't think you're anything, only from now on I'm never going to play with you."

"No, you can't get out of it," said Nozdrev, getting steamed up, "the game has started."

"I have the right to get out of it, because you're not playing in a way that befits an honest man."

"No, you're lying, you can't say such things!"

"No, brother, you're lying yourself!"

"I wasn't cheating, and you can't back out of it; you must finish the game!"

"You'll never make me do that," said Chichikov coolly and, walking up to the board, mixed up the checkers.

Nozdrev flared up and walked up so close to Chichikov that the latter had to back away a couple of steps.

"I'll make you play. Your mixing up the checkers doesn't

matter! I remember all the moves. We'll place them back the way they were."

"No, brother; it's all over and done with; I'm not going to play with you."

"So you won't play?"

"You can see for yourself that it's impossible to play with you."

"No, you come right out with it: you don't want to play?" Nozdrev was saying, walking up closer.

"No, I don't want to," said Chichikov but, just the same, brought both his hands nearer his face, against any contingency, since things were really getting hot. This precaution was quite called for, inasmuch as Nozdrev swung his arm back . . . and there was a very great possibility that one of the full and prepossessing cheeks of our hero would have been covered with an ignominy that could never be washed out; but, having fortunately warded off the blow, he seized both of Nozdrev's eager hands and held them fast.

"Porphyry! Pavlushka!" Nozdrev kept yelling in fury, striving to free himself.

Hearing this, Chichikov released Nozdrev's hands so as not to allow the domestics to become witnesses to so temptingly demoralizing a scene, and feeling at the same time that it would have been useless to hold onto Nozdrev. At this very point Porphyry entered, and with him Pavlushka, a husky lout by the looks of him, with whom it would have been entirely disadvantageous to tangle.

"So you don't want to finish the game?" asked Nozdrev. "Come right out with it!"

"There's no possibility of finishing the game," said Chichikov, and glanced out of the window. He caught sight of his carriage, which was standing all ready, while Seliphan, it seemed, was merely waiting for a wave of the hand to roll up to the front entrance; but there was no earthly possibility of getting out of the room: there were two husky fools of serfs standing in the doorway.

"So you don't want to finish the game?" Nozdrev repeated, with a face that was as blazing as if it were actually on fire.

"If you had played like an honest man . . . but now I can't."

"Ah, so you don't want to, you scoundrel! When you saw that you weren't winning, why, you can't play? Beat him up!" he cried out frenziedly, turning to Porphyry and Pavlushka, while he himself clutched his chibouk, with its long cherrywood stem, as if it were a club. Chichikov turned as white as a linen sheet. He wanted to say something, but felt that his lips were merely moving without making a sound.

"Beat him up!" Nozdrev kept yelling, all ablaze and sweating, straining forward with his cherrywood chibouk, as though he were storming an impregnable fortress. "Beat him up!" He kept yelling in the same sort of voice that some desperate lieutenant, whose hare-brained bravery has already gained such a reputation that a specific order is issued to hold him back by his arms during the heat of battle, uses to yell "Forward, lads!" to his platoon during a great assault. But the lieutenant has already felt the martial fervor, everything has begun going 'round and 'round in his head: Suvorov, that great general, soars in a vision before him; the lieutenant strains forward to perform a great deed. "Forward, lads!" he yells, dashing ahead, without reflecting that he is jeopardizing the plan of attack already decided upon, that countless gun muzzles are thrust out of the embrasures of the fortress, the impregnable walls of which reach up beyond the clouds, that his impotent platoon will be blown up into the air like so much swan's-down, and that the bullet with his name on it is already whizzing through the air, just about to shut off his vociferous throat. But if Nozdrev was portraying in his person the lieutenant attacking the fortress, desperate and at a loss, the fortress he was storming did not in any way resemble an impregnable one. On the contrary, the fortress was experiencing such fright that its heart was in its very heels. Already the chair, with which he had conceived the notion of defending himself, was wrested out of his hands by the serfs; already, with his eyes shut tight, neither dead nor alive, he was preparing for a taste of his host's Circassian chibouk, and God knows what might have befallen him; it pleased the Fates, however, to save the sides, shoulders, and all the well-nurtured parts of our hero. In an unexpected fashion there suddenly came, as if from the clouds, the quivering sounds of jingle-bells; there came clearly the rattle of cart-wheels flying up to the front entrance, and the heavy snorting and labored breathing of the heated horses of a halted troika echoed even in the very room. All involuntarily looked out of the window; some mustachioed fellow in a semi-military frock-coat was clambering out of the cart. After inquiring in the entry, he entered at precisely the moment when Chichikov, not having yet had a chance to recover from his fright, was in just about the most piteous situation in which mortal man ever found himself.

"Permit me to ask, which one of you is Nozdrev?" said the stranger, after looking with a certain perplexity at Nozdrev, who was standing with the chibouk in his hand, and at Chichikov, who was barely beginning to get over his unenviable situation.

"Allow me first to ask whom I have the honor of talking to?" asked Nozdrev, coming nearer to him.

"I am Captain of the District Police."

"And what is it you wish?"

"I have come to inform you of the notice communicated to me, that you are subject to arrest until such time as a final decision is reached in your trial."

"What nonsense is this? What trial?"

"You were implicated in an affair involving a personal assault, with birch rods, upon one Maximov, a landowner, while you were in a state of intoxication."

"You're lying! I never even set eyes on any landowner by the name of Maximov!"

"My dear sir! Allow me to inform you that I am an officer. You can say such things to your servant, but not to me."

At this point Chichikov, without waiting for what answer Nozdrev would make to this, grabbed his cap as fast as ever he could and, shielding himself behind the Captain of the District Police, slipped out on the front steps, got into his light carriage, and ordered Seliphan to give his horses the whip and drive them for all they were worth.

CHAPTER FIVE

OUR hero, however, had had a considerable fright. Although his light carriage rushed along at a breakneck speed, and Nozdrev's village had long since vanished out of view, screened by fields, hillsides, and hillocks, he nevertheless kept on looking over his shoulder with fear, as though expecting that at any moment a pursuit would overtake him. He drew his breath with difficulty, and when he attempted to place his hand against his heart, he felt that it was fluttering like a caged quail. "Eh, what a fine kettle of fish he cooked up! Look you, what kind of a man he is!" At this point a great number of all sorts of hard and potent wishes were dispatched in Nozdrev's direction; one even came upon words that were not at all genteel. Well, what can one do about it? A Russian fellow, and heartily vexed, at that! In addition, this was not at all a jesting matter. "No matter what you say," said Chichikov to himself, "but if that Captain of the District Police hadn't hurried up in the very nick of time, perhaps I would never have had another chance to see God's daylight again! I would have disappeared like a bubble on the water, with nary a trace, leaving no descendants, and bequeathing neither property nor an honored name to my future children!" Our hero was very much concerned over his descendants.

"What a vile squire that was!" Seliphan was musing. "Never have I seen his like. I could spit at him for that, what I mean. You'd do better if you didn't give a man anything to eat, but as for a horse, you're bound to feed him, inasmuch as a horse loves his oats. Them's his vittles; what fine living, for instance, is to us, oats are to a horse—them's his vittles."

The horses, too, apparently entertained but a poor opinion of Nozdrev: not only were the sorrel and Assessor out of spirits, but so was the piebald himself. Even though the poorer sort of oats usually fell to his portion, and Seliphan never poured them into his manger without making the preliminary speech of: "Eh, you scoundrel!" yet, notwithstanding, they were oats after all, and not common hay; he champed them with pleasure, and frequently would thrust his long muzzle into the mangers of his mates, to taste what sort of victuals they had, especially when Seliphan was not around the stable; but this time all they'd gotten was hay—that wasn't so good! All of them were discontented.

But shortly all these discontented beings were interrupted, in the very midst of their effusions, in a sudden and altogether unexpected fashion. All, not excluding even the coachman himself, recovered themselves and came to their senses only when and as a barouche harnessed to a team of six ran full tilt on top of them, and, almost over their heads, there resounded the scream of the ladies seated in the barouche, and the curses and threats of the other coachman: "Ah, what a thimble-rigger! Why, I was yelling to you at the top of my voice: 'Turn to the right, you crow!' Are you drunk, or what?"

Seliphan felt that he had been negligent, but since no Russian likes to admit to another that he is ever to blame he consequently summoned all his dignity and had an immediate come-back: "And where do you think you're goin' at a clip like that? Have you left your eyes in pawn at a pot-house, or what?" Following which he began backing his carriage, in order thus to get free of the other's harness, but that was easier said than done—everything was in a tangle. The piebald sniffed inquisitively at the newly acquired friends he found on either side of him.

In the meantime the fair occupants of the barouche were looking on at all this with an expression of fright on their faces. One was an old woman; the other was a young thing of sixteen, with aureate hair quite deftly and endearingly smoothed back on her small head. The pretty little oval of her face was as rounded out as a small newly laid egg and, like an egg, exhibited a certain translucent whiteness, as when the fresh egg, just laid, is held up against the light in the swarthy hands of the housekeeper testing it, and allows the rays of the beaming sun to pass through it; her fragile little ears were also translucent, glowing rosily from the warm light penetrating them. With all this the fright on her open, motionless lips, the tears welling up in her eyes were, in her case, so endearing that our hero contemplated her for a few minutes without paying any attention whatsoever to the mix-up that had involved the coachmen and their horses.

"Back 'er up, why don't you, you Nizhegorod crow!" the other coachman was shouting. Seliphan drew his reins back, the other coachman did the same with his, the horses backed up a little, and then collided again, having stepped over their traces. At this conjunction of events the piebald found the newly formed acquaintance so much to his liking that he did not want, under any circumstances, to get out of the rut in which unforeseen circumstances had placed him and, having put his muzzle upon the shoulder of one of his new friends, seemed to be whispering something into his very ear, probably the most arrant nonsense, inasmuch as the newcomer kept twitching his ears incessantly.

The muzhiks from a village that was, fortunately, not far off had of course managed to gather at such a hullabaloo as this. Since such a spectacle is, to the muzhik, a veritable godsend, the very same thing that his newspapers and his club are to the German, there was consequently no end of them milling around in a short while, and only the old women and the veriest babes stayed behind in the village itself. The muzhiks unloosed the traces; a few taps on the muzzle of the piebald horse persuaded him to back away; in short, the horses were separated and parted. But whether it was due to the vexation which the newly-come horses felt over being torn away from their friends, or simply because of some foolish notion they'd gotten into their heads, the fact remained that no matter how much their coachman lashed them they would not stir and remained as if rooted to the spot. The concern of the muzhiks grew to an incredible pitch. Each one vied with the others in coming forth with his own advice.

"You go ahead, Andriushka, and lead off the off-horse that's on the right side, whilst Uncle Mityai mounts the shaft-horse! Git up there, Uncle Mityai!"

Uncle Mityai, spare and lanky, with a red beard on him, got up on the shaft-horse and, perched up there, could have doubled for a village belfry or, better still, for the long crane with which they get the buckets out of some wells. The coachman gave his horses the whip, but nothing came of it; Uncle Mityai was of no help at all, at all.

"Hold on, hold on!" shouted the muzhiks. "Let you, Uncle Mityai, git up on the off-horse, and as for the shaft-horse, let Uncle Minyai git up on him!"

Uncle Minyai, a broad-shouldered muzhik, with a beard as black as coal, and a belly that resembled the gargantuan samovar in which mulled mead is prepared for a whole shivering market-place, willingly mounted the shaft-horse, which caved in almost to the ground under him.

"Now we're gittin' somewheres!" shouted the muzhiks. "Make it hot for him! Make it hot for him! Give a taste of the whip to that feller there, that light bay. What's he buckin' for, like a *cora-mora?*" *

But, perceiving that they were not getting anywhere, and that no amount of putting on the heat had been of any avail, Uncle Mityai and Uncle Minyai both seated themselves on the shaft-horse, while on the back of the off-horse they seated Andriushka. At last the coachman, losing patience, chased away Uncle Mityai and Uncle Minyai both; and did right well, too, inasmuch as there was such steam rising from the horses as if they had covered the distance between two stage-posts without halting to breathe. He allowed them a minute or so for rest, after which they started off by themselves.

While all these horsy maneuvers were going on, Chichikov had been looking very attentively at the pretty little unknown. He made several attempts to start a conversation with her, but somehow it did not catch on. And in due course the ladies had driven off, the pretty little head with its very fine features, and the slender little waist, had disappeared from view, like something akin to a vision, and again there remained only the road, the light carriage,

---

* A *coramora* is a great, long, torpid mosquito; occasionally one may chance to fly into a room and stick somewhere on a wall all by himself. You can walk up to him calmly and seize him by one of his legs, to which his only reaction will be to arch himself, or to *buck,* as the common folk put it. *Author's note.*

A gallinipper. *Trans.*

the troika of horses familiar to the reader, Seliphan, Chichikov, and the smooth and empty expanse of the surrounding fields.

Everywhere in life, no matter where it may run its course, whether amid its harsh, raspingly poor, and squalidly mildewing lowly ranks, or amid its monotonously frigid and depressingly tidy upper classes—everywhere, if it be but once, man is fated to meet a phenomenon that is unlike all that which he may have chanced to meet hitherto; which, if but once, will awaken within him an emotion that is unlike all those which he is fated to experience all life long. Everywhere, running counter to all the sorrows of which our life is compact, a glittering joy will gaily flash by, as, at times, a glittering equipage with gold on its gear, with its picturesque horses, and sparkling because of its gleaming plate-glass, will suddenly, unexpectedly, speed by some backwoods poverty-stricken hamlet that had never beheld anything but a country cart, and for a long while will the muzhiks stand there, their mouths gaping and without putting on their doffed headgear again, even though the wondrous equipage has long since whirled away and vanished out of sight. And in much the same way has this blonde suddenly appeared in our narrative, in a perfectly unexpected manner, and has disappeared in the same way. Had there happened to be at the time, instead of Chichikov, some youth of twenty—whether he were a hussar, or simply one who has just begun the course of his life— and, Lord! what would not have awakened, what would not have stirred, what would not have found a voice within him! Long would he have stood on the same spot, bereft of all sensation, his eyes staring senselessly into the distance, grown oblivious both of the road and of all the reprimands and goings-over in store for him for having tarried, grown oblivious of self, and of his work, and of the world, and of all the things that there are in the world.

But our hero had already reached middle age and was of a circumspectly congealed character. He, too, was plunged into thought, and kept thinking on and on, but in a more sedate manner; his thoughts were not so irresponsible and, to some extent, were even most substantial. "A glorious little creature!" said he to himself, opening his snuff-box and putting a pinch up his nostrils. "But then what, chiefly, is so good about her? It is good that she has only just now, evidently, finished some boarding school or scholastic institute; that as yet there isn't anything womanish about her, as they say derogatively, i.e., precisely that which is most unpleasant about the dear creatures. She is now like a child; everything about her is simple—she will say whatever may come to her mind, will laugh outright wherever and whenever she may feel like laughing. One can fashion anything out of her; she can be a miracle, and she may turn out to be so much trash—and will! In one year they'll pump her so full of all sorts of womanishness that her own father won't recognize her. Whence will come both the stuffiness and the primness? She will take to being guided by precepts drilled into her, will take to racking her head and considering whom she may talk to, and how, and for how long she should talk, and how this one or that one should be regarded; at every moment she will be afraid of saying more than is necessary; she will become all mixed up herself, and it will all wind up by her lying all her life, and the upshot will be the Devil's own mess!"

Here he ceased his mental soliloquy for some time and then added: "But it would be curious to know, of what family is she? Well, what's her father like? A rich landed proprietor of well-esteemed character, or simply a prudent fellow whose capital was acquired in serving the state? For if, let us suppose, they were to give this girl a dowry of two hundred thousand or so, she might turn out to be a most dainty tid-bit. This might constitute, so to say, happiness for some decent fellow."

The two hundred thousand or so came to be delineated in his head so vividly that he began, inwardly, to be vexed with himself because during the to-do about the two vehicles he had not found out from the outrider or the coachman who and what the chance travelers were. In a short while, however, the appearance of Sobakevich's village distracted his thoughts and made them revert to their constant theme.

The village seemed to him quite large; two forests, one of birch, the other of pine, like two wings, the one lighter in hue, the other darker, were, respectively, on his right and left; between them one could see a wooden house with a mezzanine, red roof, and walls of dark (or, to put it better, a "wild," nondescript) gray—a house of the sort that we build for military settlements and German colonists. One could perceive that, during its erection, the builder had had to struggle incessantly with the taste of the owner. The builder was a pedant and had longed for symmetry; the owner had wanted convenience and evidently as a consequence of this had boarded up on one side all the windows corresponding to those on the other and, in place of them, had bored through a single, small one, which had probably been needed for some dark store-room. The frontal, too, had by no means come out in the center of the house, no matter how hard the architect had striven, inasmuch as the owner had ordered one of the side-columns to be chucked out, and for that reason only three columns had survived, and not four, as originally intended. The courtyard was surrounded by a fence of solid and inordinately thick wood. This landed proprietor, so it seemed, took great pains to attain solidity. Full-weighted and stout timbers, destined to endure through the ages, had gone for the construction of the stables, sheds, and kitchens. The rustic huts of the muzhiks had also been wondrously made of hewn logs; there were no planed walls, no fretwork designs, or the like doodads, but everything was driven home tight and right. Even the water-well was bound in such strong oakwood as is used only for mills and for ships. In a word, everything that our hero might look at was steadfast, without any sway or play, with some sort of staunch and unwieldy orderliness about it.

As Chichikov drove up to the front entrance he noticed two faces that had peered almost simultaneously through the window —one feminine in a house-cap, and elongated like a cucumber, and a masculine one, round, broad, like those Moldavian pumpkins called *gorliankas* or calabashes, out of which they make, in Russia, balalaikas, two-stringed light balalaikas, the pride and joy of some frolicsome, twenty-year-old country lad, a fellow who knows how to wink and is a dandy, and who not only winks at but whistles after the snowy-breasted and snowy-necked maidens who gather around to listen to his soft-stringed strumming. Having peered out, both faces hid at the same moment. A flunky in a gray jacket with a stiff blue collar came out on the steps and led Chichikov into the entry, where the host himself came out to him. Upon beholding his guest he said abruptly: "If you please!" and led him into the inner quarters.

This time, as Chichikov glanced at Sobakevich out of the corner of his eye, he looked to him like a bear, just a middlin'-sized bear. To complete the resemblance, the frock-coat upon him was absolutely the color of a bear's pelt; the sleeves were long, the trousers were long, he set his feet down lumberingly, this way and that way, and was forever stepping upon the feet of others. His face was a red-hot, fiery color, the ruddy color you find on a five-kopeck copper. As everyone knows, there are many such faces in this world, over the finishing of which Nature did not spend much thought or ingenuity, on which she did not use any small, delicate tools such as fine files, fine gimlets, and so forth, but simply hacked away with a full swing of the arm: one swipe of the ax, and there's the nose for you; another swipe, and there are the lips; with a great auger she gouged out the eyes and, without wasting any time on trimming and finishing, she let her handiwork out into the world, saying: "It lives!" Just such a sturdy and wondrously rough-hewn countenance did Sobakevich have; he kept it down for the most part, rather than looking up; he hardly turned his neck and, because of this unwieldiness, looked but rarely at whomever he was speaking to, but always either at an angle of the stove or at the door. Chichikov glanced at him once more out of the corner of his eye, as they were passing into the dining room: a bear! A perfect bear! And, as the last, inevitable, needed touch to round out so strange an affinity, his very name was actually Mikhail Semënovich.* Knowing his way of stepping on the feet of others, Chichikov placed his own very carefully and allowed him to go ahead. The host himself, apparently, felt conscious of this failing and immediately inquired: "I haven't inconvenienced you, have I?" But Chichikov thanked him, saying that no inconvenience had yet occurred.

When they entered the drawing room, Sobakevich indicated an easy chair, again saying: "If you please!" Seating himself, Chichi-

---

* The generic folk-name, combining both affection and respect, bestowed upon all bears in Russia. When the bear is trained or a pet the name is contracted to Misha. *Trans.*

kov cast a glance over the walls and the pictures hanging thereon. They were all of fine, daring fellows, those pictures; Greek military leaders, almost all of them, engraved at full length: Maurocordato, in red pantaloons and uniform coat, with spectacles on his nose; Miaoulis, Kanaris. All these heroes had such sturdy thighs and unheard-of mustachios that they made shivers run up and down your spine. In the midst of these stalwart Greeks—there was no telling how or why he'd gotten there—was the Russian Bagration, a gaunt little, thin little chap, with tiny banners and cannon below him and squeezed into the narrowest of frames. Then, next in turn, came the Greek heroine Bobolina, whose leg alone seemed bigger than the torso of any of those dandies who throng the drawing rooms nowadays. The host, who was himself a hale and stalwart fellow, wished, it seemed, to have his very room adorned with people who were likewise stalwart and hale. Near Bobolina, in the very window, hung a cage out of which peeked a blackbird, its dark plumes speckled with white, which bird likewise bore a very great resemblance to Sobakevich. The guest and host did not have to sit in silence for more than a couple of minutes when the drawing room door opened and the hostess entered, a very tall lady, wearing a house-cap adorned with ribbons that had been redyed at home, and with home-made dyes, at that. She entered staidly, holding her head as straight as a palm tree.

"This is my Theodulia Ivanovna," said Sobakevich.

Chichikov approached Theodulia Ivanovna to kiss her fair hand, which she all but shoved into his mouth, during which operation he had an opportunity to note that her hands had been washed in dill-pickle brine.

"Allow me to introduce you, my little pet," Sobakevich continued. "This is Pavel Ivanovich Chichikov! I had the honor of making his acquaintance at the Governor's and the Postmaster's."

Theodulia Ivanovna invited him to be seated, saying, just as her husband had done: "If you please!" and making a motion with her head like that of an actress portraying a queen. After which she seated herself on the divan, drew her merino shawl about her, and from then on did not so much as bat an eye or twitch an eyebrow.

Chichikov once more lifted up his eyes, and once more caught sight of Kanaris with his stout thighs and endless mustachios, of Bobolina, and of the blackbird in its cage.

For almost all of five minutes they all preserved silence, broken only by the pecking noise made by the blackbird's beak against the wood of its cage as it angled for grains of wheat at the bottom. Chichikov once more cast his glance over the room and all that was in it: everything was solid, unwieldy in the highest degree, and had some sort of strange resemblance to the master of the house himself. In a corner of the drawing room stood a pot-bellied walnut bureau on four utterly preposterous legs, a perfect bear of a bureau! The table, the armchairs, the chairs, all had a most ponderous and disquieting quality about them; in short, every object, every chair, seemed to be saying: "I, too, am Sobakevich!" or: "I, too, look very much like Sobakevich!"

"We were remembering you at a party given by Ivan Grigorye-vich, the Chairman of the Administrative Offices," said Chichikov at last, perceiving that neither one of the others felt inclined to start a conversation, "last Thursday, it was. We passed our time very pleasantly there."

"Yes, I wasn't at his place then," Sobakevich answered.

"And what a splendid man!"

"Whom do you mean?" asked Sobakevich, looking at an angle of the stove.

"The Chairman of the Administrative Offices."

"Well, perhaps he may have struck you that way; he may be a Mason, but just the same he's a fool whose like the world has never yet produced."

Chichikov was somewhat perplexed by this rather harsh charac-terization but then, recovering, went on: "Of course, every man has his weak points; but you take the Governor—what a superb fellow!"

"The Governor is a superb fellow?"

"Yes, isn't he?"

"A brigand—the biggest one on earth!"

"What—the Governor is a brigand?" said Chichikov, and abso-lutely could not grasp how the Governor could have joined the ranks of the brigands. "I must confess I would never think so," he went on. "But allow me to observe, however, that his actions do not at all indicate anything of the sort; on the contrary, there is rather a great deal of gentleness about him, actually." Here he adduced, in proof, the purses embroidered by the Governor's own hands, and commented, with praise, on the kindly expression on the Governor's face.

"And his face, too, is a brigand's!" said Sobakevich. "Do but put a knife in his hands and let him loose on the highway, and he'll slit your throat—he'll slit your throat for the smallest copper! He, and the Vice-Governor with him, Gog and Magog, that's what they are!"

"No, he must be on the outs with them," Chichikov reflected. "There, I'll try him out with the Chief of Police—he's a friend of his, I believe."—"However, as far as I am concerned," he said aloud, "I confess I find the Chief of Police to my liking most of all. What a straightforward, frank character he has; one can see something simple-hearted in his very face."

"A swindler!" said Sobakevich with the utmost sang-froid. "He'll sell you out and he'll take you in, and dine with you right after that. I know them all, they're all swindlers, every man-jack of them; the whole town is like that, one swindler mounted on a second and using a third one as a whip. Judases, all of them. There is but one—and only one—decent man; that's the Public Prosecutor, and even he, if the truth were to be told, is a swine."

After such eulogistic although somewhat brief biographies, Chichikov perceived that it wouldn't do to mention the other officials, and reminded himself that Sobakevich did not relish giving a good report of anybody.

"Well, now, pet, let's go in to dinner," said Sobakevich's spouse, turning to him.

"If you please!" said Sobakevich.

Following which, having approached a table on which were placed various cold delicacies, guest and host drank a pony of vodka each, as is the proper usage; they had a snack, as all spacious Russia does throughout all its towns and villages, of all sorts of salted delicacies, and other such appetite-arousing blessed dainties, and then floated along into the dining room, the hostess, like a stately goose, hastening ahead of them. The small table was set for four places. To take the fourth place there very soon appeared a—it is hard to say positively just who she was, a lady or a miss, a relative, a chatelaine, or simply some woman living in the house—something without a house-cap, about thirty, wearing a brightly colored and patterned shawl. There are faces which exist upon earth not as primary objects but as foreign specks or spots upon objects. They always occupy the same seat, they all hold their heads in the same way, you're almost ready to consider them as furniture, and you'd think that no cross word had ever, since birth, issued from such lips as those; but if you'd happen to hear her somewhere in the maids' room, or in a pantry, you would be simply amazed!

"The cabbage soup today, my pet, is very good," said Sobakevich, having sipped the soup and dumped into his plate an enormous helping of *nurse*, a well-known Russian variation of haggis, which is served with cabbage soup and consists of a ram's stomach, stuffed with buckwheat groats, brains, and trotters. "You won't get to eat a pudding like that in town," he turned to Chichikov. "They'll serve you the Devil knows what there!"

"However, the Governor doesn't keep such a bad table," remarked Chichikov.

"But do you know what all those courses are made of? You wouldn't eat them if you were to find out."

"I don't know how they're prepared, I'm not in a position to judge that; but the pork chops and stewed fish were excellent."

"It just struck you that way. For I know what they buy in the market. The buying will be done by that rascal of a chef, who learned his trade from a Frenchman; he'll skin a cat, and then serve it up to you at table for rabbit."

"Faugh, what a nasty thing to say!" said Sobakevich's spouse.

"Well, isn't it so, my little pet? That's how they do things; I'm not to blame, they do everything that way. Every sort of refuse, stuff that our wench Akulka throws into the cesspool, if you'll permit me to use the word, they pop into their soup. Into the soup with it! That's the place for it!"

"You'll always come out with something of that sort at table," Sobakevich's spouse again protested.

"Well, now, my pet," Sobakevich persisted, "if I did things like that myself it would be a different matter, but I'm telling you right to your face that I'm not going to eat any abominations. You can plaster frogs' legs even with sugar, as far as I'm concerned, and I won't take 'em into my mouth, nor will I take oysters, for the matter of that—an oyster's looks remind me too much of something else. Take some of the mutton," he went on, turning to Chichikov, "it's a whole side of mutton, with buckwheat groats. These aren't your fricassees, which are made in lordly kitchens out of mutton that's been knocking around on the market stalls for four days in a row. It's all a scheme thought up by the German and the French doctors; if I had my way, I'd string up all of 'em. They've thought up dieting, the hunger-cure! Since theirs is a chicken-boned German constitution, they imagine they'll make the thing work with the Russian stomach! No, it's all wrong, it's all pure invention, it's all—" at this point Sobakevich even shook his head angrily. "They're forever talking about enlightenment, enlightenment, but all this enlightenment is just so much . . . flapdoodle! I might even use another word, only it would be impolite at table. I don't do things that way. If it's pork I want, I order the whole swine to be served at table; if it's mutton, drag in the whole ram; if a goose, the whole goose! Better for me if I eat but two courses, but eat a goodly enough portion of each, as the soul craves." Sobakevich confirmed this by action: he overturned half the side of mutton onto his plate, and ate it all up, gnawing clean and sucking dry every last bit of a bone.

"Yes," reflected Chichikov, "this fellow is no fool when it comes to his belly."

"I don't run things," Sobakevich kept on talking, wiping his hands on his napkin, "I don't run things the way some Plushkin does; he owns eight hundred souls, yet he lives and dines worse than my shepherd does."

"Just who is this Plushkin?" Chichikov inquired.

"A swindler," Sobakevich answered. "Such a miser as it would be hard to imagine. The convicts in stocks at the prison live better than he does; he's starved all his people to death."

"Really?" Chichikov chimed in with concern. "And you say that his people are actually dying off from hunger in great numbers?"

"They're dying off like flies."

"Dying off like flies . . . can such things really be! But permit me to ask, how far away from your place does he live?"

"A little over three miles from here."

"A little over three miles from here?" Chichikov exclaimed, and even felt a slight heart tremor. "But, when one drives out of your gates, would his place be to the right or to the left?"

"I wouldn't advise you even to know the way to that dog!" said Sobakevich. "There's more excuse for going to some unseemly place than to his house."

"No, I didn't ask for any particular reasons . . . but only because I am interested in knowing all sorts of places," Chichikov said in answer to this.

The side of mutton was followed by round tarts, filled with curds, each one of which was considerably bigger than the dinner-plates, then a turkey as well-grown as a calf, stuffed with all sorts of good things: eggs, rice, livers, and goodness knows what else that is bound to lie like a stone on one's stomach. And with that the dinner was brought to an end; but, when they got up from the table, Chichikov felt all of five and thirty pounds heavier.

They went off to the drawing room, where a saucer of preserves had already appeared on the table—not of pears, however, or of plums, or any known berry; however, neither the guest nor the host touched it. The hostess went out for some additional saucers. Taking advantage of her absence, Chichikov turned to Sobakevich who, lying back in an easy chair, could only grunt occasionally after such a filling dinner and emit some indistinct sounds from his mouth, making the sign of the cross and putting his hand over it every minute or so.

"There's a certain little matter I'd like to talk over with you," Chichikov said, turning to him.

"Here are some more preserves," said the hostess, coming back with another saucerful. "Radish, cooked in honey!"

"Well, we'll tackle it later!" said Sobakevich. "You go to your room now; Pavel Ivanovich and I will shuck our coats and rest a bit."

The hostess was not slow in evincing a readiness to send for down-beds and pillows, but the host said: "Never mind, we'll take a rest in the easy chairs," and the hostess went off.

Sobakevich cocked his head slightly, getting ready to listen to just what the little matter consisted of.

Chichikov began in a sort of roundabout manner, touching, in a general way, upon the whole realm of Russia and commenting with great praise upon its vast extent; he said that even the ancient Roman Empire had not been so great, and that foreigners were justly astonished (Sobakevich merely kept on listening, with his head cocked to one side) . . . and also that, owing to the conditions existing in this realm, whose equal in glory was nowhere to be found, the serfs listed in the Bureau of Audits, even though they might have ended their earthly course, were nevertheless, until the submission of a new census to the Bureau of Audits, considered on the same basis as those alive, so as not to burden the Administrative Offices with a multitude of petty and useless inquiries and so as not to increase the complexity of the governmental mechanism, which, even without that, was quite complicated (Sobakevich kept on listening, with his head cocked to one side) . . . and also that, notwithstanding, with all the justice of this measure, it proved, on occasion, quite burdensome to many of the serf-owners, obligating them to keep on paying taxes as if these souls, not actually in existence, were still living chattels, and that he, Chichikov, out of a feeling of personal regard for him, Sobakevich, was even ready to assume, in part, this really onerous obligation. Concerning the main theme Chichikov expressed himself with the utmost caution: he by no means called the serf-souls dead, but merely not actually in existence.

Sobakevich kept on listening, just as before, with his head cocked to one side—and if but something, in the least resembling an expression, would appear on his face! It seemed as if there were no soul at all in this body or, if it were there, it was not at all in the place it should be but, as with Koshchei the Deathless in the fairy tale, somewhere beyond many hills and dales and sheathed in such a thick shell that everything which stirred at the bottom of his soul created absolutely no commotion on the surface.

"And so? . . ." asked Chichikov, awaiting, not without a certain agitation, the other's reaction.

"You need dead souls?" said Sobakevich, very simply, without the least surprise, as if it were grain they were talking about.

"Yes," said Chichikov, and again softened the expression by adding: "Those that are not actually in existence."

"They can be found; why not? . . ." said Sobakevich.

"And, should any be found, then, doubtless . . . you would be pleased to get them off your hands?"

"I'm ready to sell them, if you like," said Sobakevich, this time with his head somewhat raised, and surmising that the buyer must surely have some advantage in view here.

"The Devil take it!" reflected Chichikov. "This fellow is already selling them before I've let a peep out of me!" and said, aloud: "And what would the price be, for instance? Although, by the bye, this is such a thing . . . that it's even odd to talk of the price—"

"Well, not to be asking too high a price of you, a hundred rubles a head," Sobakevich told him.

"A hundred rubles a head!" Chichikov cried out, letting his jaw drop and, after looking right into the other's eyes, without knowing whether he had heard aright himself or whether Sobakevich's tongue, because of its heavy nature, had not worked right, blurting one word out instead of another.

"Why, now, is that dear for you?" uttered Sobakevich, and then added: "But, in that case, what is your price?"

"My price! We are making some mistake, probably, or we do not understand each other, having forgotten what the talk is really about. For my part, placing my hand on my heart, I propose paying eight ten-kopeck pieces for each soul—that's my top-notch price!"

"So that's what you're aiming at, eight ten-kopeck pieces per head!"

"Well, now, in my judgment, I think one can't give more than that."

"But it isn't bast sandals I'm selling."

"Just the same, you must agree yourself, these, too, aren't what you might call people."

"So you think you'll find a big enough fool to sell you for a couple of ten-kopeck pieces a soul listed with the Bureau of Audits?"

"But, if you please, why do you describe them that way? For the serf-souls themselves have long since died; all that is left of them is but an insubstantial sound. However, in order not to go into further talk on this matter, I'll give you a ruble and a half, if you like, but I can't give you any more than that."

"You ought to be ashamed to even mention such a sum. If you want to trade, talk a real price."

"I can't, Mikhail Semënovich; upon my conscience, believe me, that which is impossible to do, there's no possible way of doing," Chichikov maintained, but just the same tacked on another half-ruble.

"But what are you so tight about?" asked Sobakevich. "Really, the price isn't so high! Another swindler will take you in, will sell you trash and not souls; whereas mine are all as sound as a nut, all hand-picked—if it isn't some master craftsman, then it's some other husky muzhik. Just take a close look: here's Mikheiev, for example, a coachmaker! Why, he never turned out a vehicle but what it was on springs. And it wasn't the way they work in Moscow, to last you an hour or so; what solidity he put into his work . . . and he'd upholster it himself, and lacquer it as well!"

Chichikov opened his mouth to remark that, after all, this Mikheiev had long been not of this world; but Sobakevich had got into the vein, as they say. Whence came this gift of gab and the pace of his speech?

"And what of Stepan the Cork, the carpenter? I'll lay my head on the block if you'll find such another peasant anywhere! Why, what strength he had! If he had been serving in the guards, God knows what rank they would have given him—seven foot one and three-quarter inches in height, he was!"

Chichikov again wanted to remark that the Cork, too, was no longer of this world; but Sobakevich, evidently, had thoroughly warmed up to the subject; his speeches poured forth in such torrents that all one could do was listen.

"Milushkin, a bricklayer! He could build you a furnace or an oven fit for any house you like. Maxim Teliatnikov, a bootmaker: he'd just run his awl through a piece of leather, and there was a pair of boots for you, and not a pair but you'd want to thank him, and it wasn't as if he ever took a single drop of spirits in his mouth. And what about Eremei Sorokoplekhin? Why, that muzhik alone was worth all of the others put together; he used to trade in Moscow, bringing me in five hundred in quit-rent alone. There, that's the kind of people they are! Not the kind some Plushkin or other would sell you."

"But, if you please," Chichikov got out at last, amazed by such a copious inundation of speeches, to which, it seemed, there was never an end, "why do you enumerate all their good points? For there's no good in them now whatsoever—they're all dead folk. All a dead body is good for is to prop up a fence with, says the proverb."

"Why, of course they're dead," said Sobakevich, as though he had come to his senses and remembered that they were dead in reality, but then added: "However, it may also be said, what good are the people that are now numbered among the living? What sort of people are they? They're so many flies, and not people."

"Yet, just the same, they are in existence, whereas the others are but a dream."

"Well, no, they're no dream! Allow me to inform you that you'll never find such men as Mikheiev was; he was such a mountain of a man that he could never get into this room; no, he was no dream! And as for those hams of shoulders he had, there was such a store of strength in them as no horse has. I'd like to know what other place you'd find such a dream in!"

The last words he uttered with his face already turned to the portraits of Bagration and Kolokotronis, as usually happens during a conversation when one of the speakers will suddenly, for some unknown reason, turn not to the person to whom his words are directed, but to some third person who chances to come in, even a total stranger, from whom he knows he will receive neither an answer nor an opinion, nor any confirmation, but upon whom, nevertheless, he will fix his gaze as though he were calling him in as a mediator; and, somewhat confused during the first minute, the stranger does not know whether he should make any answer in a matter which he had heard nothing of, or simply to stand there a while, as an appropriate observance of the civilities, and only then take his leave.

"No," said Chichikov, "more than two rubles I cannot give you."

"If you like, in order that you may not hold anything against me, or claim that I am asking too much from you and am unwilling to oblige you in any way, if you like, I'll let you have them at seventy-five rubles a soul, but it must be in government notes—and really, I'm doing it only out of friendship!"

"Really, now, what is he up to?" thought Chichikov. "Is he taking me for a fool, or what?" and then added, out loud: "I find it strange, really; it seems as if we were going through some sort of a theatrical performance or a comedy; I can't explain it any other way. You are, it seems, a man who is quite intelligent, possessing knowledge and an education. Why, the matter under discussion has no more substance than a puff of air! What can such stuff be worth? Who needs it?"

"There, now, you're buying it, therefore there must be a need of it."

Whereupon Chichikov bit his lip and could not find any answer to make. He did begin talking about certain circumstances in his family and household, but Sobakevich's answer was a simple one: "There's no necessity of my knowing what your circumstances are; I don't mix into family affairs, that is your own business. You had need of souls, and so I am selling them to you, and you will regret not having bought them."

"Two round rubles apiece," said Chichikov.

"Say, really! *Teach a magpie to say Joe, and it will call all men so,* as the saying goes—you've gotten that tune of two rubles into your head and simply don't want to change it. You give me a real price!"

"Well, now, the Devil with him!" Chichikov reflected. "I'll give him a half-ruble more per soul, the dog, by way of a tip!"—"I'll add on half a ruble for each, if you like."

"Well, if you like, I, too, will give you my last word: fifty rubles a head. Really, I'm taking a loss; you can't get such good people cheaper anywhere!"

"What a tight-fisted fellow!" said Chichikov to himself, and then went on, aloud, with a certain vexation: "But what is all this, really? Just as if it were truly serious business! Why, I'll get them for nothing some other place. And everybody will hand them over to me right willingly, only to get rid of them as quickly as possible. Only a fool would want to hold on to them and pay taxes on them!"

"But do you know that purchases of that sort—I'm telling you this just among ourselves, out of friendship—aren't always permissible, and were I, or somebody else, to tell about it, the man that buys them would not have any standing as far as contracts are concerned, or if he wanted to enter into any advantageous transactions?"

"Just see what he's aiming at, the scoundrel!" thought Chichikov, and at once uttered, with an air of the utmost sang-froid: "Just as you wish; I am not buying them for any particular need, as you think, but just so . . . because my own ideas so incline me. If you don't want to take two and a half, I'll have to bid you good-by!"

"You can't make him yield his ground, he isn't the yielding kind!" Sobakevich reflected. "Well, God be with you, give me thirty rubles a head and take them as your own!"

"No, I can see you don't want to sell. Good-by!"

"Hold on, hold on!" said Sobakevich, without letting go of Chichikov's hand and stepping on his foot, since our hero had forgotten to be cautious and, as a punishment therefor, had to draw his breath in with a hiss and to hop around on one foot.

"I beg your pardon! I think I've inconvenienced you? Sit down here, if you'll be so kind! If you please!"

Here he plumped him into an easy chair, even with a certain dexterity, like one of those bears that have been through a trainer's hands and can both turn cart-wheels and go through sundry panto-mime routines in answer to such questions as "And now show us, Misha, how do womenfolk carry on in a steam-bath?"—"And how,

Misha, do little boys go about stealing peas in a truck-patch?"

"Really, I'm wasting my time here; I'm in a hurry."

"Sit here for just another minute; I'll tell you something that will please you right away." Here Sobakevich moved his seat nearer to Chichikov and said softly in his ear, as though it were a secret: "Do you want to clinch the bargain?"

"You mean at twenty-five rubles? Never, never, never! I wouldn't give in ever so little, I won't add on another kopeck."

Sobakevich fell silent. Chichikov, too, fell silent. Their silence lasted for two minutes or so. Bagration, he of the eagle nose, was looking down with exceeding attentiveness from his wall upon this trade.

"What, then, will be your last price?" asked Sobakevich.

"Two and a half."

"Really, you hold a human soul at the same value as a boiled turnip! Give me three rubles, at least."

"I can't."

"Well, there's nothing to be done with you, take them if you like. I'm taking a loss, but I guess that's just my dog-like nature,* I can't help making things pleasant for my fellow-man. And I guess we've got to put through a purchase-deed, so's everything will be in order?"

"That's understood."

"Well, there you are, then; we'll have to go into town."

Thus was the deal consummated. Both decided to be in town no later than tomorrow and attend to the purchase-deed. Chichikov asked for a list of the serfs. Sobakevich willingly agreed and, right then and there, having gone to the bureau, with his own hand began an abstract of all the dead souls involved, giving not only their names but even designating their good points.

As for Chichikov, he, for lack of anything to do, occupied himself with an inspection, since he was behind him, of Sobakevich's whole ample build. No sooner had he glanced at his back, as broad as that of the thick-set Percherons that are bred in the Viatskaya region, and at his legs, that were like those squat, thick cast-iron pillars which are placed along street curbs, then he could not help

---

* "Sobakevich" is derived from *sobaka*, a dog. *Trans.*

but exclaim inwardly: "God hath surely blessed you bounteously! There, it's just as they say: you're not well cut but stoutly stitched! Were you born the bear you are, or were you turned into a bear by your backwoods life, by the planting of grain and the pother with the muzhiks, and is it through these you have become what is called a kulak, a tight-fisted man? But no: I think you'd still be the same, even if you had had a fashionable education, if they had placed you amid the social whirl and you were to live in Peterburgh and not in the backwoods. The sole difference lies in that now you can put away half a side of mutton with buckwheat groats, chasing it down with a tart of curds as big as a plate, whereas in the capital you would dine on dainty cutlets of some sort with truffles. There, now you have muzhiks under your rule; you get along well with them and, of course, would take no advantage of them, inasmuch as you own them, and it would be so much worse for you if you did; but, were you living in the capital, you'd have a lot of petty clerks under you, whom you would ride hard, having figured out that, after all, they weren't your chattel slaves; or you'd be dipping your fingers in the public treasury! No, he who's tight-fisted is never fated to loosen up and become open-handed! But if you make a tight-fisted man unbend but a finger or two, it's so much the worse! If he skims but lightly over the surface of some science or learning he will later on, upon attaining a more prominent place, let all those who may have really mastered some science or learning feel his heavy hand! And, to boot, he's as likely as not to say then: "Let's show them who I am! And he'll cook up such a complicated decree that many a man will have the Devil's own time of it. . . . Eh, if only all these kulaks were to go to—"

"The list is ready," said Sobakevich, turning around.

"Ready? Let's have it, please!"

He ran his eyes over it and was struck by its accuracy and meticulousness: not only were the trade, position, years, and family status of each dead soul circumstantially written out, but there were even to be found, on the margins, special notations regarding that soul's conduct and sobriety—in a word, the list was a delight to behold.

"And now for a small deposit, if you please."

"But why do you need any deposit? You'll get all the money at once in town."

"Well, you know, it's the usual thing," Sobakevich retorted.

"I don't know how I can give it to you; I didn't bring any money with me. Well, yes, here are ten rubles."

"What do ten rubles mean? Let me have fifty rubles, say, at the least!"

Chichikov began making excuses that he did not have that much with him, but Sobakevich told him that he did have the money so affirmatively that Chichikov took out another note in no time at all as he said: "Here are fifteen more, if you like, a total of twenty-five. But please let me have a receipt."

"But what do you need a receipt for?"

"Well, you know, it's better to have a receipt. Who knows what any hour may bring? . . . Anything may happen."

"Very well, pass the money over."

"Why pass it over? I have it right here in my hand! You can take it the minute you've written out the receipt."

"But, if you please, how am I to write out a receipt otherwise? One must see the money first of all."

Chichikov's hands released the notes to Sobakevich who, drawing near to the table and covering them with the fingers of his left hand, wrote out with the other on a slip of paper that he had received, in full, five and twenty rubles in government notes as a deposit on certain serfs sold. Having written out this memorandum, he looked the bills over once more.

"This note is rather old," he pronounced, scrutinizing one of them against the light, "it's a bit torn; but among friends there's no use minding such a thing."

"Kulak, kulak!" Chichikov reflected. "And a low-down beast, to boot."

"And would you like to have any souls of the female sex?"

"No, thank you."

"Why, I wouldn't take much, actually. For friendship's sake, just a mere ruble a head."

"No, I don't need any females."

"Well, if you don't need any, then there's no use even talking about it. Every man to his taste; what's one man's meat is another man's poison, as the proverb says."

"There's one more thing I wanted to ask of you, and that is that this deal should remain in confidence between us," Chichikov said as he was taking his leave.

"Why, that goes without saying. There's no use mixing any third party into this; that which takes place among intimate friends in all sincerity must remain a part of their mutual friendship. Goodby! Thanks for paying me a visit; I ask you not to forget me in the future as well—if you ever have an hour or so to spare, drive up for dinner and to pass the time. Perhaps there may be another occasion when we can be of some service to each other."

"You've got another guess coming!" Chichikov was thinking as he took his seat in the carriage. "Not after skinning me two and a half rubles for each dead soul, you God-damned kulak!"

He was dissatisfied with the way Sobakevich had acted. After all, no matter what you say, he knew the man; they had met each other at the Governor's and at the house of the Chief of Police, and yet he had acted like an utter stranger, had taken money for actual trash! When the carriage had rolled out of the courtyard he looked back and saw that Sobakevich was still standing on the front steps and, it seemed, was keenly watching him, wishing to know which way his guest would head.

"The scoundrel! He's still standing there!" Chichikov got out through clenched teeth and ordered Seliphan, after turning toward the huts in the village, to drive off in such a way that the vehicle might not be seen from the direction of the proprietor's courtyard. He wanted to drop in on Plushkin, whose people, according to what Sobakevich said, were dying off like flies; but he did not want Sobakevich to know about this contemplated visit. When the carriage was already at the end of the village, he called over to him the first muzhik he saw, who, having picked up somewhere along the road an exceedingly thick log, was dragging it along on his shoulder to his hut, like some indefatigable ant.

"Hey, there, you with the beard! And how does one drive from here to Plushkin's place, but so's not to drive past the master's house?"

The muzhik, apparently, was in a quandary over this question.

"Well, don't you know?"

"No, master, I don't."

"Oh, you! And yet your hair is streaked with gray! Don't you know Plushkin the miser, the fellow who feeds his people so poorly?"

"Ah, the patched ———! The patched ———!" the muzhik cried out. There was also a substantive added to the word "patched," a very apt one, but not used in polite conversation, and for that reason we will let it pass. However, it may be surmised that the expression came very close to the mark, inasmuch as Chichikov, even though the muzhik had long since dropped out of view, was nevertheless still smiling as he sat in his carriage. The Russian people have a puissant way of expressing themselves! And if they bestow an apt word upon any man, it will follow him into his lineage and into his posterity; he will drag it along with him wherever he serves, and into his retirement, and to Peterburgh, and to the ends of the earth. And no matter how cunningly you contrive thereafter and glorify and ennoble your nickname, even though you set the scribbling small fry to derive it, for hire, from some ancient lordly line, nothing will avail you: the nickname will, of its own self, caw with all its corvine throat and will proclaim clearly what nest the bird has flown out of. That which is aptly uttered is tantamount to that which is written: there's no rooting it out, though you were to use an ax. And how very apt, of a certainty, is that which has come out of the very core of Russia, where there is no German, nor French, nor Finnish, nor any other sort of tribe, but the purest virgin gold, the living and lively Russian wit, that is never at a loss for a word, that doesn't brood over it, like a setting hen, but comes spang out with it, like a passport to be carried through all eternity, and there's no use your adding on later what sort of nose or lips you have: you are drawn, at a stroke, from head to foot!

Even as an incomputable host of churches, of monasteries, with cupolas, bulbous domes, and crosses, is scattered all over holy and devout Russia, so does an incomputable multitude of tribes, generations, peoples swarm, flaunt their motley, and scurry across the face of the earth. And every folk that bears within itself the pledge of mighty forces, that is endowed with the creative aptitudes of the soul, with a vivid individuality of its own and with other gifts of God, each such folk has become singularly distinguished by some word all its own, through which, expressing any subject whatsoever, it reflects in that expression a part of its own character. With a profound knowledge of the heart and a wise grasp of life will the word of the Briton echo; like an airy dandy will the impermanent word of the Frenchman flash and then burst into smithereens; finickily, intricately will the German contrive his intellectually gaunt word, which is not within the easy reach of everybody. But there is never a word which can be so sweeping, so boisterous, which would burst out so, from out the very heart, which would seethe so and quiver and flutter so much like a living thing, as an aptly uttered Russian word!

CHAPTER SIX

✶✶✶✶✶✶✶✶✶✶✶✶✶✶✶✶✶✶✶✶✶✶✶✶✶✶✶✶✶✶

In former days, long ago, during the years of my youth, during the years of my childhood, now as irretrievably fled as a gleam of light, it was a gladsome thing for me to be driving up for the first time to some unfamiliar place; it was all one whether it were some hamlet, some poor, wretched little town (yet the chief one of its district), or some settlement, or some borough—the curious eye of the child would discover a great deal that was curious about the place. Every structure, everything, as long as it bore upon it the impress of some noticeable peculiarity, everything would bring me to a stop and amaze me. Whether it were a stone government building of the familiar style of architecture, with half its windows false ones, sticking up all by its lonesome amid a cluster of the one-story little houses of hewed timber inhabited by the local burghers, or a well-rounded cupola, covered all over with white sheet-iron, rearing over a new church whitewashed so that it was as white as snow, or a market-place, or some dandy of the district whom one chanced upon in a town—nothing evaded the fresh, fine observation and, with nose thrust out of the traveling cart, I would stare at some frock-coat, of a cut hitherto never seen, and at wooden bins full of nails, full of sulphur that showed yellowly even from afar, full of raisins and soap, all these to be glimpsed through the doors of a greengrocer's, together with jars of stale candies brought all the way from Moscow. I stared, as well, at an infantry officer walking on one side of the street, blown thither by a chance wind from God knows what province, to endure the ennui of the district town, and at a merchant in a Siberian great-coat, who flashed by in a racing-sulky—and in my thoughts I would whirl off after these people, into their meager way of life. A petty clerk of the district administration might happen to pass by me, and I would already be in deep thought: whither was he bound, to an evening at the home of some brother quill-driver, or straight for home, in order, after having sat on his front porch for half an hour or so, before the dusk came down for good and all, to sit down to an early supper with his mother, his wife, his wife's sister, and his whole household; and what would the talk be about around the time when a serving wench with many beads about her neck, or a boy in a quilted short jacket, would bring in (this would be after the soup had been served) a tallow candle in an ancient candlestick that had seen endless service in the house.

As I drove up to the village of some landed proprietor or other, I would eye curiously the tall, narrow, wooden belfry, or the old, sprawling, weather-beaten, wooden church itself. In the distance I could catch enticing glimpses, through the leafage of the trees, of the red roof and white chimneys of the proprietor's house, and I waited impatiently until the gardens that screened it would part to either side and it would appear in all its entirety, with all its exterior, which at that time (alas!) did not appear at all vulgar, and by that exterior I tried to guess just who and what the landed proprietor himself was—was he stout, and did he have sons, or all of a half-dozen daughters, with sonorous maidenly laughter, forever playing games, and with the youngest little sister, as always, the greatest beauty of them all, and were their eyes dark, and whether the proprietor himself was a jolly fellow or as dour as September in its last days, forever consulting his calendar and discoursing on rye and wheat, which were such boresome topics for youthful people.

Now I drive up apathetically to every unfamiliar village and look apathetically at its vulgar appearance; to my time-chilled gaze things seem bleak, and I am not amused, and that which in former years would have aroused an animated expression, laughter, and unceasing speeches, glides past me now and an impassive silence do my expressionless lips preserve. Oh, my youth! Oh, my fresh vigor!

While Chichikov was mulling over and inwardly chuckling at the nickname which the muzhiks had bestowed upon Plushkin, he had not noticed how he had driven into the center of a far-spreading settlement, with a multitude of huts and lanes. In a short while, however, a most jarring jolt, brought about by a corduroy roadway, a roadway before which the cobbled one in town was a mere nothing, let him perceive where he was. The logs of this roadway now rose, now fell, like the keys of a pianoforte, and the incautious rider acquired either a lump on the back of his neck, or a livid bruise on his forehead, or might even chance to nip, most painfully, the tip of his tongue between his teeth. He noticed some sort of especial tumble-down air over all the structures in the village; the logs of the huts were darkened and old; many of the roofs had gaps through which one could see the sky as through a sieve; on some only the weather-vane, in the form of a little horse, remained up above—that, and the transverse poles which looked like ribs. Apparently the owners themselves had carried the shingles and deal off the roofs, reasoning, and quite justly at that, that the huts afforded no shelter from the rain, while in fine weather it's dry and there's no sense in coddling oneself indoors, when one can find room to spread out both at the pot-house and on the highroad—in short, wherever you list. The windows in the small huts were without panes; some were stuffed up with rags or a sheepskin jacket; the tiny railed balconies under the eaves which, for some unknown reason, are tacked onto some Russian huts, had become askew and weather-beaten, yet without acquiring any picturesqueness thereby. Behind the huts, in many places, were rows of enormous stacks of grain which had been stagnating there, as was very evident, for a long time; in hue they resembled old, badly baked brick; all sorts of weeds were growing on top of them, and here and there even a shrub would be clinging to one of the sides. The grain evidently belonged to the master. Out from behind the stacks of grain and the tumble-down roofs reared up and momentarily appeared and disappeared in the clear air, now on the right, now on the left, depending on the turns the carriage made, two village churches that were side by side; a deserted one of wood, and one of stone, with yellowish walls; it was all in stains and blotches and with cracks everywhere.

Parts of the proprietor's house began to emerge and, finally, it came into full view at the spot where the chain of huts ended and was succeeded by a truck-garden or cabbage-patch that had been allowed to become a wasteland, with a low picket fence, broken in some places, thrown about it. Like some decrepit invalid did this strange castle appear, long, inordinately long. In places it was of only one story, in others of two stories; on its darkened roof, which did not everywhere afford dependable protection to the house in its old age, two belvederes were sticking up, facing each other; both of them were rickety by now, devoid of the paint that had covered them at one time. The walls of the house showed cracks here and there that exposed the naked plastering and lath and, as one could see, had endured a great deal from inclement weather, rains, whirlwinds, and autumnal changes. Of the windows, only two were in use; the others were shuttered or simply boarded over. These two windows, for their part, were also purblind; on one of them, showing darkly, had been pasted a triangle of dark-blue paper, such as comes wrapped around sugar-loaves.

The old, vast garden, stretching away behind the house, extending beyond the settlement and then losing itself in an open field, a garden gone wild, overgrown and stifled with weeds, was the only thing that lent a fresh air to the widely scattered settlement and the only thing that was fully picturesque in its pictorial desolation.

The joined summits of trees that had attained their full growth in freedom lay in green clouds and irregular cupolas of trembling foliage against the skyline. The white, colossal trunk of a birch that had been deprived of its crest by some tempest or thunderstorm rose up out of this green, thick tangle and, high in the air, looked like a round, regular column of dazzling marble; the oblique, sharply pointed fracture in which it terminated in lieu of a capital showed darkly against its snowy whiteness, like a cap or some black-plumed bird. The hop-vines that stifled the elder, rowan, and hazel bushes below, and then ran all over the tops of the paling, at last darted half-way up the broken birch and entwined it. After reaching its middle, the vine hung down from there and was already beginning to catch at the tips of other trees, or else dangled in the air, its slender, clinging tendrils curled into rings and lightly swaying in the breeze. In places the green, sunlit thickets parted and revealed some depression in their midst, sunless and gaping like a dark maw; it would be all enveloped in shadow and one could barely, barely glimpse in its dark depths a white, narrow path running through it, fallen railings, a rickety arbor, the hollow, decayed trunk of a willow, a hoary Siberian pea tree that stuck out from behind the willow its thick, bristling tangle of twigs and leaves, dried and dead because of the fearful underwoods and, finally, a new maple branch, extending from one side its green paws of leaves. Getting under one of these leaves, God alone knows how, the sun would suddenly transform it into a thing of transparency and fire that shone wondrously amid this dense darkness. Off to one side, at the very edge of the garden, a few tall aspens, rising above their fellows, lifted high into the air the enormous raven nests upon their quivering summits. Some of these aspens had branches broken but not completely severed, which dangled, their leaves all withered. In short, everything was as beautiful as neither Nature alone nor art alone can conceive, but only as when they come together, when over the labor of man, often heaped up without any sense, Nature will run her conclusive burin, will lighten the heavy masses, will do away with the coarsely palpable regularity and the beggar's rents, through which the unconcealed, naked plan peers through, and bestow a wondrous warmth to everything that had been created amid the frigidity of a measured purity and tidiness.

After making a turn or two on the road, our hero found himself at last before the very house, which now seemed more woebegone than ever. Green mold had already covered the time-worn wood of the enclosure and the gates. A throng of buildings—quarters for the domestic serfs, granaries, store-houses, all almost visibly moldering away—filled the whole courtyard; near them, to right and left, one could see gates leading into other yards. Everything testified that once upon a time husbandry had been carried on on a large scale here; now everything here bore a dismal look. One could not notice anything that might animate the picture, neither a door opening, nor people coming out of anywhere, nor any of the living fuss and bustle which enliven a household. The main gate alone was open, and that one only because a muzhik had driven in with a laden, matting-covered cart, and seemed to have come on the scene for the sole purpose of animating this extinct place; another time this gate, too, would have been locked tight, inasmuch as it had a colossus of a padlock hanging on an iron staple. Near one of the structures Chichikov soon noticed some sort of figure that began bickering with the muzhik who had driven in the cart. For a long while Chichikov could not make out the sex of this figure, whether it were a peasant woman or a muzhik. The clothing upon it was utterly indeterminate, resembling very much a woman's gown; on its head was a night-cap, such as village serving women wear about the house; the voice alone sounded to Chichikov somewhat too hoarse for a woman's. "Oh, it's a peasant woman!" he thought, and added on the spot: "Oh, no! . . . Oh, of course it's a woman!" he decided at last, after a closer scrutiny. A visitor, it seemed, was a rara avis for her, inasmuch as she looked closely not only at him but at Seliphan as well, and the horses, too, beginning with their tails and ending with their very noses. By the keys that were dangling from her waist and from the fact that she was cursing out the muzhik in rather abusive terms, Chichikov concluded that this must surely be the housekeeper.

"I say, mother," he began, getting out of the carriage, "is your master—"

"Not to home," the housekeeper cut him short, without waiting for him to finish the question and then, after the lapse of a minute, added: "And what was it you wanted?"

"I have business with him."

"Go in the house!" said the housekeeper, turning around and showing him her back, soiled with flour and flaunting a great rent down below.

Chichikov stepped into a dark, wide entry, out of which cold blew upon him as from a cellar. From the entry he found his way into another room that was likewise dark, very, very meagerly lit by a light that came through a broad crack below a door. Opening this door he at last found himself in the light and was struck by the disorder that appeared before his eyes. It seemed as if a general house-cleaning were going on and all the furniture had been piled up here for the time being. There was even a broken chair standing on one of the tables and, side by side with it, a clock whose pendulum had stopped and to which a spider had already cunningly attached its web. Here, too, with one of its sides leaning against the wall, stood a dresser with antiquated silver, small carafes, and Chinese porcelain. Upon a bureau, with a marquetry of mother-of-pearl mosaic, which had already fallen out in places and left behind it only yellowish little grooves and depressions filled with crusted glue, was lying a great and bewildering omnium gatherum: a mound of scraps of paper, closely covered with writing, pressed down with a paper-weight of marble turned green and having an egg-shaped little knob; some sort of ancient tome in a leather binding and with red edges; a lemon, so dried up that it was no bigger than a walnut; a broken off chair-arm; a wine-glass with some kind of liquid and three dead flies, covered over with a letter; a bit of sealing wax; a bit of rag picked up somewhere; two quills, dirty with ink that had dried upon them consumptively; a quill toothpick, perfectly yellowed, which its owner had probably been picking his teeth with even before Moscow had been invaded by the French.

Hung about the walls, quite closely and without much discrimination, were several pictures. One was a long, yellowed engraving of some military engagement or other, with enormous drums, drowning steeds, and soldiers in cocked hats yelling fit to split their throats; it was unglazed, set in a frame of mahogany with very thin strips of bronze and with whorls, also of bronze, at the corners. Alongside of the other pictures hung an enormous, time-stained one that took up half a wall by itself, done in oils and depicting flowers, fruits, a cut watermelon, a boar's head, and a wild duck hung with its head down. From the middle of the ceiling was suspended a luster in a canvas bag, which because of its accumulated dust had taken on the appearance of a silk cocoon, with the silkworm still inside. In one corner of the room had been piled up a heap of those things which were of a coarser nature and unworthy of knocking about on the tables. Precisely what the heap consisted of it would have been difficult to determine, since the dust upon it was so copious that the hands of whosoever touched it took on a gloved appearance. More noticeable than the other things were two that stuck out of the pile: a piece broken off a wooden shovel and an old bootsole. One could by no means have told that a living creature inhabited this room had not an old, worn night-cap, lying on one of the tables, proclaimed the fact.

As Chichikov was examining the whole strange setting of the room, a side-door opened and the same housekeeper whom he had met out in the yard entered. But now he perceived that this was a chatelain rather than a chatelaine; a chatelaine, at least, has no beard to shave, whereas this fellow on the contrary had one and did shave it, although, it seemed, he did so rarely enough, since all his chin and his jowls resembled a wire-bristled curry-comb. Chichikov, assuming a questioning expression, waited impatiently for what this chatelain might want to tell him. The chatelain, for his part, waited for what Chichikov might want to tell him. Chichikov at last, astonished by such a strange misunderstanding, decided to ask: "Well, what about your master? Is he at home, or what?"

"The master is here," said the chatelain.

"But where?" Chichikov persisted.

"What's the matter with you, father, are you blind or what?" asked the chatelain. "Oh, you! Why, I am the master!"

At this point our hero involuntarily took a step backward and looked at the other intently. It had been his lot to see not a few of all kinds of people, even such folk as the reader and I may never have a chance to see; but such a specimen as this he had never yet beheld. His face did not present anything peculiar; it was almost the same as that of many gaunt old men, save that his chin alone jutted out far too much, so that he had to cover it with his handkerchief every time he spat, to avoid slavering it; the fire in his little eyes had not died out and they darted about under his high, bushy eyebrows very much as mice do when, thrusting out of their dark holes their sharp little snouts, their ears perked and their whiskers twitching, they are spying out whether the cat is lurking about in ambush somewhere or whether some mischievous boy is about, and sniff the very air with suspicion.

Far more remarkable was his attire. Through no means and efforts could one ferret out what his dressing-gown had been concocted from; the sleeves and upper portions had become greasy and shiny to such a degree that they resembled the sort of Russia leather which is used for boots; dangling in the back were four flaps instead of two, out of which the cotton-wool quilting was actually crawling in tufts! About his neck, too, he had tied a something that one could not make out; it might have been a stocking, or a bandage, or an abdominal supporter, but nothing that one could possibly consider a cravat. In a word, had Chichikov met him thus accoutered at a church door he would most probably have slipped him a small copper, inasmuch as it must be said to our hero's credit that his heart was a compassionate one and he could never hold himself back from giving a small copper to a poor man.

But this was no beggar standing before him; standing before him was a landed proprietor. This landed proprietor owned a thousand serf-souls and more, and there would be no use in trying to find another who had so much wheat, in grain, flour, or simply in stacks, or one whose store-rooms, warehouses, and drying sheds were cluttered with such a world of linens, cloths, sheepskins (both dressed and raw), dried fish of all sorts, and all kinds of vegetables and salted meat. Had anyone peeped into his work-yard, where there was a reserve laid by of every sort of wood and wooden utensils, never used, it would have seemed to him that he must somehow have strayed into the famous Chip Fair in Moscow, whither the wide-awake matriarchs resort daily, with their cooks behind them, to put in supplies for their households, and where every sort of wood rises in mountains of white: nailed, turned, joined, to say nothing of wickerwork; there are barrels here, and chopping bowls, and tubs, and water-casks, and noggins, with spouts and without, and dippers, and bast baskets, and slop-pails, wherein to keep mops and such-like, and hampers of thin, bent aspen wood, and cylindrical boxes of woven birch bark, and a great deal of all that goes to supply the needs of rich Russia and poor. What need, it seemed, had Plushkin of such a host of these wares? He would never have been able to use them up in his whole lifetime even if he owned two estates instead of only one, but even this accumulation seemed small to him. Not satisfied with this, he would also patrol the lanes and by-ways of his village every day, peering under small bridges, under planks, and in every nook and cranny, and everything that he came upon—an old sole, a woman's rag, an iron nail, a clay shard —everything would be dragged off to his place and piled on that heap which Chichikov had noticed in a corner of the room.

"There, the fisherman is setting out for his catch!" the muzhiks would say when they caught sight of him setting out to try his luck. And truly, there was no need of sweeping the street after he had passed by; if a cavalry officer riding by happened to lose a spur, that spur was on the instant on its way to the pile we know of; if a peasant woman, having grown absent-minded somehow at the water-well, would forget her bucket there, he would lug the bucket off, too. However, if some muzhik, having seen him, would catch him red-handed on the spot, he would not argue and gave up the purloined article; but if ever it landed on that pile, then it was all over and done with: he called God to witness that he had bought the article at such-and-such a time from so-and-so. Or it had come down to him from his grandfather. In his room he would pick up from the floor whatever met his eye—a bit of sealing wax, a scrap of paper, a feather—and all this he would lay on the table or on a windowsill.

And yet there had been a time when he had been but a thrifty householder! He had been married and had a family, and one or another of his neighbors would drop in on him for dinner, to listen to him and learn husbandry and a wise thriftiness. All things went briskly and were performed at a smooth, even pace: the mills, the fulleries turned; the cloth manufactories, the carpenters' benches, the looms were all busy; the keen eye of the master penetrated everywhere and into everything and, like the toil-loving spider, he ran bustingly yet smartly from one end of his husbandly web to the other. His features did not reflect any emotions that were too strong but one could see intelligence in his eyes; with experience and a knowledge of the world was his speech imbued, and it was a pleasure for his guest to listen to him; the affable and talkative mistress of the house was famed for her hospitality; two pretty daughters would come out to meet you, both with flaxen-fair curls and as fresh as roses; the son would come running out, a sprightly little urchin, and would kiss everyone, paying but little attention to whether the guest liked it or not. All the windows in the house were open; the attics had been taken for his own by the tutor, a Frenchman, who was exemplarily clean-shaven and a great hand with a hunting gun; he would always bring for dinner some black grouse or wild ducks, while at times there would be only sparrow eggs, which he would order to be made into an omelet, inasmuch as there was not another soul in the house that would eat them. There was also a fair compatriot of his living in the attics, a preceptress for the two girls. The master of the house himself would come to dinner in a frock-coat, somewhat worn, true, but neat, just the same—the elbows were in good order and there was never a patch showing anywhere.

But the good lady of the house died; some of the keys and, together with them, some of the petty cares, passed on to the master. Plushkin became more restless and, like all widowers, more suspicious and more miserly. He could not rely in everything upon Alexandra Stepanovna, his elder daughter, and he was right in this, inasmuch as Alexandra Stepanovna shortly ran off with a second captain of cavalry attached to God knows what regiment, and married him somewhere in a hurry, in some village church, knowing that her father had no great love for military officers, because of an odd prejudice that all military men, now, were inveterate gamblers and profligate scalawags. The father sent a curse after her by way of a godspeed, but did not bother with a pursuit. It became still emptier in the house. The miserliness of the master began to evince itself more markedly; the gray that gleamed in his coarse hair, a faithful mate of miserliness, helped it to develop still more. The French tutor was dismissed, inasmuch as the time had come for the son to enter the military service; Madame la gouvernante was sent packing, inasmuch as it had turned out that she had not been entirely blameless in the abduction of Alexandra Stepanovna. The son, having been sent to the capital city of the province in order to find some berth in the administration which in his father's opinion would benefit him, joined a regiment instead and informed his father only after doing so, when he wrote asking him for money to outfit himself; quite naturally he received in answer to this that which is called among the common folk a fig. Finally his last daughter, who had stayed on in the house with him, died, and the old man was left sole watchman, guardian, and possessor of his riches.

His lonely life afforded rich fare to his miserliness, which, as everybody knows, has a wolfish appetite and which, the more it devours, the more insatiable it becomes; the human emotions, which, even as it was, were none too deep within him, shoaled more with every minute, and every day this decrepit ruin would suffer some loss. And it so fell out, at such a moment, as though on purpose to confirm his opinion of military men, that his son lost heavily at cards; he sent him a father's heartfelt curse and thenceforth never evinced any interest to learn whether his son was still in this world or not. With every year more and more windows were boarded up in the house until at last but two remained unobstructed, of which one, as the reader has already seen, had been pasted over with paper. With every year the important aspects of his estate disappeared more and more from his view, while his petty outlook was turned upon scraps of paper and stray feathers, which he accumulated in his room. He grew more and more inaccessible to the commission merchants who came around to buy the produce of his estate—the commission men used to dicker and dicker with him, and finally gave him up for good, saying this was a fiend and not a man. His hay and wheat rotted; the grain-stacks and the hay-ricks turned into downright manure—you could just go ahead and grow cabbages on 'em; the flour in his cellars had turned into stone and you had to take an ax to it; it was a fearsome thing to touch his cloths, his linens, his homespuns—they turned to dust under your fingers. He was already beginning to forget how much he had of this or that, and remembered only in what spot the little carafe stood that held the heel-taps of some cordial, on which carafe he had put a secret mark, so that no one might thievishly swig a drink, and he likewise remembered where that old quill ought to be and where that stub of sealing wax was. And yet, in his domestic economy, the revenue and perquisites accumulated as hitherto: each muzhik was bound to bring in the same quit-rent, every peasant woman had to bring in the same allotment of nuts, each spinster had to work just as many linen looms. All these goods, wares, and produce were dumped into the store-rooms and all turned to rot and rents, and he himself had turned, at last, into a rent on the cloak of humanity.

Alexandra Stepanovna happened to visit him twice, somehow; the first time with her little son, trying to see if she mightn't get something out of him—evidently the nomadic life with her second captain of cavalry was not so enticing as it had seemed before marriage. Plushkin forgave her, it must be said, and even allowed his grandson to play a while with some button lying on one of the tables, but not a copper of money did he part with. The second time Alexandra Stepanovna arrived with two little ones and brought him an Easter cake for his tea and a new dressing-gown, inasmuch as father had a dressing-gown which it was not only a pity but an actual shame to look at. Plushkin petted both his grandchildren a little and, having seated one of them on his right knee and the other on his left, gave them an absolutely perfect hossy-ride; the Easter cake and the dressing-gown he accepted but gave his daughter absolutely nothing, and Alexandra Stepanovna went back even more empty-handed than she had come.

And so that's the kind of landed proprietor who was standing before Chichikov! It must be said that one encounters such a phenomenon but rarely in Russia, where all things love to open up rather than to shrivel into a ball like a hedgehog, and it is all the more striking when there turns up in the immediate vicinity of such a phenomenon some landowner roistering with all the expansiveness of Russian recklessness and seigniorage, burning his candle, as they say, at both ends. The unfamiliar wayfarer will stop in astonishment at the sight of his dwelling, wondering what prince of the blood had suddenly turned up amid the petty, drab landed proprietors; like palaces do his white, stone houses look with their innumerable multitude of chimneys, belvederes, weather-cocks, surrounded with a drove of built-on wings and all sorts of apartments for the accommodation of any and all guests who might come. What won't you find on his place? Theatricals; balls; all night will his garden glow ornamented with Chinese lanterns and lampions, and be pealing with the thunder of music. Half the province is attired in its best and gaily strolling under his trees, and no one will perceive anything wild or sinister amid this forced illumination when out of the woody thickness a branch, lit up by the artificial light yet devoid of its vivid greenery, leaps forth theatrically, while because of this light the night sky appears still darker, still more austere, and twenty times more terrible, and the trees, receding still further into the impenetrable darkness, their leaves quivering on high, make their austere summits protest indignantly at this tinselly brilliance below that lights up their roots.

Plushkin had been standing thus for several minutes by now, without uttering a word, while Chichikov still could not begin a conversation, being distracted both by the appearance of his host and by everything in his room. For a long time he could not hit upon the words in which to explain the reason for his coming. He was just about to express himself in some such high-flown vein as that, having heard such a great deal about his virtue and the rare qualities of his soul, he had deemed it his duty to pay him his due tribute of respect in person; but he brought himself up short and sensed that this was a bit too thick. Casting another look out of the corner of his eye at all the things in the room, he sensed that for such words as *virtue* and *rare qualities of the soul* one might well substitute the words *economy* and *orderliness,* and for that reason, having reworked his speech accordingly, he said that having heard of his economy and his rare skill in estate management, he had deemed it his duty to make his acquaintance and to pay him his respects in person. Of course, he might have given another and a better reason, but at the time nothing else popped into his head.

In answer to this, Plushkin mumbled something or other through his lips—inasmuch as he had no teeth; precisely what it was is not certain, but probably the sense was: "Eh, may the Devil take you, respects and all!" But since hospitality is so prevalent among us that even a miser may not transgress its laws, he at once added, somewhat more distinctly: "I beg of you to be seated!"

"It's rather a long while since I've seen any callers," he went on, "and, I admit, I see but little good in 'em. They've started a most indecent custom of gadding about from one to the other, and yet it means a detriment to your household . . . and besides, you've got to give their horses hay! I've long since had my dinner, besides my kitchen has such a low ceiling, as abominable a kitchen as you ever saw, and the chimney, now, has fallen all to pieces; if you light the stove you'll put the whole place on fire, like as not—"

"So that's the way he is!" Chichikov reflected. "It's a good thing, then, that I managed to stay my hunger with a tart of curds and a slice of the side of mutton at Sobakevich's."

"And what a vile come-uppance, there isn't as much as a wisp of hay on the whole place!" Plushkin continued. "And, really, how is one to store it up? There's so little land; the muzhik is lazy, not overfond of work; all he thinks of is how he might sneak off to the pot-house . . . like as not, one may have to go out into the world and beg in one's old age!"

"However, I've been told," Chichikov put in discreetly, "that you have over a thousand souls."

"And who was after telling you that? Why, father o' mine, you should have spit in the eye of whoever told it to you! He must have been a great wag; evidently he wanted to have a bit of fun at your expense. There, they're blabbing about a thousand souls, but you just go and count 'em, and you won't count up anything at all! The last three years the accursed fever has carried off no end of my muzhiks."

"You don't say! And has it actually carried off many?" Chichikov exclaimed with concern.

"Yes, a lot of them have been carried off."

"Yes, but permit me to ask, what was the exact number?"

"Eighty head."

"No!"

"I'm not going to lie about it, father o' mine."

"Allow me to ask you something else—you reckon these souls from the day when you submitted the last census to the Bureau of Audits?"

"I'd thank God if that were the case," said Plushkin, "but the trouble is that they would add up to a hundred and twenty since that time."

"Really? All of a hundred and twenty?" Chichikov exclaimed and even let his jaw drop a little from astonishment.

"I'm too old, father o' mine, to go in for lying now; I'm going on my seventh decade now!" said Plushkin. He had, apparently, taken umbrage at such an almost joyous exclamation. Chichikov perceived that such a lack of concern for another's woe was really unseemly, and for that reason immediately heaved a sigh and said that he commiserated with him.

"Yes, but commiseration isn't anything you can put in your pocket," Plushkin remarked. "There, now, there's a certain captain lives near me, the Devil knows where he had bobbed up from; he says he's a relative of mine. 'Dear uncle, dear uncle!'—and he kisses my hand. Well, when he starts in commiserating, he'll set up such a howl that you'd better watch out for your ears. His face is all ruddy—he must be clinging to strong brandy for dear life, I guess. Probably he squandered every copper he had at the time he was serving as an officer, or some play-acting jade wheedled everything out of him, so now he's taken to commiserating!"

Chichikov made an attempt to explain that his commiseration was not at all of the same sort as the captain's, and that he was ready to prove this not in empty words but in deeds and, without putting the matter off further, without any beating about the bush, announced right then and there his readiness to assume the obligation of paying taxes on all those serfs who had died through such unfortunate causes. This proposal, it seemed, utterly amazed Plushkin. For a long while he stared at his guest with his eyes starting out of his head and finally asked: "But I say, father o' mine, were you ever in the military service, by any chance?"

"No," Chichikov answered him, rather slyly, "I was in the Civil Service."

"Civil Service?" Plushkin repeated and fell to munching his lips, as though he were eating something. "But how can you do such a thing as that? Why, it would mean a loss to you, wouldn't it?"

"To afford you pleasure I am ready even to face a loss."

"Ah, father o' mine! Ah, my benefactor!" Plushkin cried out, not noticing in his joy that the snuff had slipped out of his nose quite unpicturesquely, looking like coffee-grounds, and that the skirts of his dressing-gown, opening, had revealed his underlinen, which was not a quite seemly object to contemplate. "There, how you have comforted an old man! Ah, my Lord! Ah, all ye saints!" After which Plushkin could not utter another word. But hardly a minute had passed when this joy, which had so momentarily appeared upon his wooden features, passed just as momentarily, just as if it had never been, and his face assumed anew an expression of care. He even mopped his face with his handkerchief and, having rolled it up into a wad, began passing it over his upper lip.

"But just how, if you will be kind enough to tell me, since I don't want to anger you—how are you undertaking to pay taxes on them? Will you pay them every year, and will you pay the money out to me or to the Treasury?"

"Why, here's how we'll work it: we'll put through a purchase-deed for them, just as though they were still living and as though you had sold them to me."

"Yes, a purchase-deed . . ." said Plushkin, falling into deep thought and beginning to chew his lips again, as if he were munching something. "That there purchase-deed, now, it all means expenses. The clerks are so conscienceless! In former days you could get away with giving them half a ruble in coppers, and a bag of flour, maybe, but nowadays you've got to send 'em a whole wagonload of all sorts of grits, and then add on a red ten-ruble note, that's how avaricious they are! I don't know why no one else ever gives a thought to this. There, if but someone would say a word or two to such a fellow that would be the salvation of his soul! Why, you can move anyone you like with a good word. No matter what anyone may say, there's no one can withstand a soul-saving word!"

"Well, you would withstand it, I think!" Chichikov commented to himself and at once declared that, out of personal regard for Plushkin, he was willing to take upon himself even the expenses connected with the purchase-deed.

On hearing that Chichikov was assuming even these expenses Plushkin concluded that his guest must be an utter simpleton and had merely pretended when he claimed having been in the Civil Service but, of a certainty, must have served as an officer and dangled after play-actresses. With all that, however, he could not conceal his joy and wished all sorts of pleasant things not only to Chichikov but even to his little ones, without having asked whether he had any or not. Walking up to the window, he rapped his fingers against the glass and called out: "Hey, Proshka!"

A minute later they heard someone come running hurriedly into the entry and fussing there a long while with much clatter of boots; at last the door opened and Proshka came in, a lad of thirteen, in such large boots that at every step he took he all but stepped out of them. The why of Proshka having such large boots can be learned without much delay: Plushkin had for all his domestics, no matter how many of them might be in the house, but the one pair of boots, which always had to be left standing in the entry. Everyone who was summoned to the master's chambers usually had to prance barefoot through the entire yard, but upon coming into the entry had to put on these boots and appear in the room only when thus shod. On coming out of the room he had to leave the boots in the entry again and set out anew on his own soles. Had anyone glanced out of the little window at the time of autumn, and especially when slight hoarfrosts set in of mornings, he would have seen all the domestics going through such leaps as even the sprightliest of male ballet dancers could hardly succeed in performing.

"There, have a look, father o' mine, what a phiz!" said Plushkin to Chichikov, pointing a finger at Proshka's face. "Why, he's as stupid as a block of wood, but you just try to leave anything lying around, he'll steal it in a moment! There, what did you come for, you fool? Tell me, what for?" Here he fell into silence for a short while, to which Proshka responded with a like silence. "Get a samovar going, do you hear? And here, take this key, give it to Mavra and let her go to the store-room; there, on a shelf, is a dried-up Easter cake that Alexandra Stepanovna brought me—let it be served with the tea! . . . Hold on, where are you off to? Eh, you, what a great fool you are! Has the fiend got you by the legs, or what, that you're itching to be off? You listen to all I've got to tell you first. The Easter cake must have gotten moldy on top, I guess, so let her scrape it off with a knife, but don't let her throw the crumbs away—let her bring them over to the hen-house for feed. And look you, now, don't you be going into the store-room, brother, or else I'll treat you to—you know what? A bundle of birch twigs, just to let you know what they taste like, now! There, you've got a glorious appetite as it is, but that'll whet it still more! There, you just try to set foot in the store-room, for I'll be watching you from the window all the time! . . . You can't trust them in a single thing," he resumed, turning to Chichikov after Proshka, boots and all, had cleared out of the room.

After that he began throwing suspicious glances at Chichikov as well. The various aspects of such an unusual magnanimity began to seem improbable to him, and he pondered: "Why, the Devil knows him, perhaps he's merely a common braggart, like all these profligate scalawags; he'll tell you a pack of lies, and then another, just for the sake of talking and getting his fill of tea, and then will be off in his fine carriage!" And therefore, out of precaution, and at the same time wishing to test him out to some extent, he said it might not be a bad idea to make out the purchase-deed as speedily as possible, since the life of man is so uncertain—today he lives, but as for the morrow, God alone knows.

Chichikov evinced a readiness to make out the purchase-deed that very instant; all he asked for was a list of the dead serfs.

This pacified Plushkin. One could see that now he was contemplating some action, and sure enough, taking his keys he walked up to the dresser and, having opened the door, rummaged for a long time among the tumblers and cups therein and at last declared: "There, I can't find it, and yet I had a fine cordial, if only it hasn't been drunk up, my people are such thieves! But wait, isn't this it?" Chichikov beheld a small carafe in his hands, which was all covered with dust, as if with a jersey. "Goes back to my late wife, she made it herself," Plushkin went on. "My scoundrelly housekeeper had thrown it aside altogether and didn't even cork it up, the creature! Little bugs and all sorts of trash managed to get in it, but I got all the rubbish out and now it's as clear as can be—let me pour a little glass out for you."

But Chichikov did his best to decline such a fine cordial, saying that he had already dined and wined.

"You have already dined and wined!" Plushkin exclaimed. "Why, of course, one can always tell a man who moves in good society no matter where he is—he doesn't eat, yet he's full; but when it's some petty thief or other, it doesn't make any difference how much you feed him. . . . That captain will come, for instance: 'Uncle dear,' says he, 'let me have something to eat!' And I'm as much of an uncle to him as he's a grandfather to me. Probably he must go without anything at all to eat at home, and so he's traipsing around! Oh, yes, you need a list of all those drones? By all means! I wrote all their names out on a separate piece of paper, to the best of my knowledge, so's to cross them out, first thing, when submitting a new census."

Plushkin put on spectacles and began rummaging among his papers. As he untied all sorts of packets he regaled his guest with such dust that the latter had to sneeze. At last the old man drew out a bit of paper, entirely criss-crossed with writing. The names of the peasants were as closely clustered on it as midges. There were all sorts of names on it: Paramons, and Pimens, and Panteleimons, and there even popped up a certain Grigoriy Doezhai-ne-doyedesh (Try-to-get-there-but-you-won't); there were actually more than a hundred and twenty of them. Chichikov smiled upon seeing such a host. Having put the list away in his pocket, he remarked to Plushkin that, to execute the purchase-deed, his host would have to go into town.

"Into town? But how can I? And how can I ever leave the house? For not a one of my people but is a thief or a swindler; they'll strip me so in one day that there won't be a nail left to hang my over-coat on."

"Haven't you some friend in town, then?"

"There, now, what friend? All my friends have died off, or have dropped their friendship. . . . Ah, father o' mine, how can a man not have some friend! Of course I have!" he cried out. "Why, I know none other than the Chairman of the Administrative Offices himself; in the old days he even used to come out to see me. How can I help but know him? We used to eat out of the same trough, we used to climb fences together! What else should we be but friends? And what a friend! . . . Should I write to him, then, per-haps?"

"Why, by all means write to him!"

"Surely, and what a friend, at that! We were schoolmates."

And suddenly some warm ray glided over those wooden features; there appeared an expression of—no, not of emotion, but of a re-flection of emotion: a phenomenon like that of the unexpected emergence upon the surface of the waters of a drowning man, which evokes a joyous shout from the crowd thronging the bank; but his brothers and sisters have rejoiced in vain, and in vain do they cast from the bank a rope and wait whether there will not ap-pear anew the drowning man's back, or his arms wearied with the struggle—he has come up for the last time. All is over, and yet more fearsome and desolate does the stilled surface of the irresponsi-ble element become thereafter. And so it was with Plushkin's face: immediately following the emotion that had glided over it, it be-came still more impassive and still more vulgar.

"I had a sheet of clean paper lying on the table," said he, "but I don't know where it has ever gone to; my people are all such a worthless lot!" Here he began looking for it on the table and under it; he groped all over and at last set up a shout: "Mavra! Hey, there, Mavra!" A woman appeared in answer to the call, carrying a plate on which lay the stale Easter cake, which the reader already knows about. Whereupon the following dialogue took place between them:

"Wherever did you hide that paper, you murderess?"

"Honest to God, master, I ain't laid eyes on any paper, save for a small scrap that you used to cover your wine-glass with."

"There, I can see by your eyes that you sneaked off with it."

"And what would I be sneaking off with it for? Why, I have no use for it at all: I don't know how to read or write."

"You lie; you carried it off to that young sacristan; he's forever scribbling away, and so you carried it off to him."

"Why, that sacristan, should he want it, can get his own paper. He never laid eyes on your scrap of paper."

"You just wait; on the dread Day of Judgment the devils will make it hot for you with their iron pitch-forks. You'll see how hot they'll make it for you!"

"But why should they be making it hot for me, when I never laid a finger on that paper? If it comes to some other womanish frailty, well and good, but thieving is something no one has ever yet reproached me with."

"Oh, but will the devils make it hot for you! 'There,' they'll be saying, 'take that, you conniver, for the way you fooled your master!' and they'll make it hot for you with their red-hot pitch-forks, that they will!"

"And I'll say: 'You got no call to do it! As God is my witness, you got no call to do it, I didn't take it. . . .' Why, it's lying right there on the table! You're always after reproaching a body, for nothing at all!"

And, true enough, Plushkin caught sight of the paper; pausing for a moment, he munched his lips and said: "There, why did you fly off the handle like that? What a touchy creature! You tell her but one word, and she'll come back at you with ten. Go on, now, bring me something so's I can seal a letter. Wait, hold on! You'll grab a tallow candle; tallow is too good, it will burn up and there's nothing left, just so much loss; guess you'd better bring me a rush-light!"

Mavra went off, while Plushkin, seating himself in an easy chair and picking up a quill, for a long while kept on turning the paper this way and that, figuring if there weren't some means or other of tearing even one-eighth off it, but finally became convinced that there was no possible way of accomplishing this, whereupon he

144 ·

thrust the quill into the ink-pot that held some sort of fluid with scum on top and a multitude of flies at the bottom, and fell to writing, forming letters that looked like musical notes, at every moment curbing the impetuosity of his hand to keep it from racing all over the paper and instead meanly adding crabbed line to crabbed line as he reflected, not without regret, that there would still be a great deal of white space left.

And is it to such insignificance, such pettiness, such vileness that a man could sink? Could a man change to such an extent? And does all this have any verisimilitude? All this has verisimilitude, all this can befall a man. The fiery youth of the present would recoil in horror were you to show him a portrait of himself in his old age. Take along with you, then, on setting out upon your way, as you emerge from the gentle years of youth into stern, coarsening manhood, take along with you all the humane impulses, abandon them not on the road; you will never retrieve them after! Sinister, fearsome is the old age that will come upon you farther along the way, and it never releases aught nor ever aught returns! The grave is more merciful than it; upon the grave will be inscribed: *Here Lies a Man*, but naught will you read upon the frigid, insensate features of inhuman old age.

"But do you know some friend of yours, perhaps," asked Plushkin, folding the letter, "who might have need of runaway souls?"

"Why, have you any runaways too?" Chichikov asked quickly, at once on the qui vive.

"That's just it, I do have. My son-in-law made inquiries; he says that apparently there's never a trace left of them by now; but then, he's a military man, the only thing he can do well is clink his spurs. Whereas if one were to try the courts—"

"And how many might you have of them?"

"Well, they may add up to as many as seventy."

"No?"

"Ah, it's so, by God! Why, not a year passes but what some of them run off from me. My people are no end gluttonous; out of sheer idleness they've gotten into the habit of stuffing their guts, whereas I haven't a thing to eat even myself. . . . Yes, and I'd take anything you'd give me for them. So you just advise that friend of yours, now; if he should recapture but half a score souls he would easily have a goodly sum. For, after all, a serf-soul registered with the Bureau of Audits is worth five hundred rubles."

"No, we won't let any friend have even a sniff of this," said Chichikov to himself, and then explained that one could never find such a friend as that, inasmuch as the mere outlay involved would cost more than any slave was worth, for once you got tangled with the law and lawyers you would have to cut off the skirts of your own coat to get out of their clutches as fast and as far as possible; but if he, Plushkin, was so hard pressed, then he, Chichikov, being motivated by sympathy, was ready to give him . . . but it was such a trifle that it was not worth while even talking about it.

"But how much would you give?" asked Plushkin, and became the utter miser; his hands began to quiver like quicksilver.

"I would give you five and twenty kopecks per soul!"

"And what would your terms be—spot cash?"

"Yes, you would get the money at once."

"Only, father o' mine, for the sake of my poverty, you ought to make it forty kopecks each, really."

"My most esteemed friend!" said Chichikov. "By right it should be not only forty kopecks a soul; I would, if I could, pay you five hundred rubles apiece! I'd pay that with pleasure, inasmuch as I behold before me a venerable, kindly old man who is enduring hardship because of his own kindheartedness—"

"Ah, by God, that's so! By God, that's the truth!" said Plushkin, hanging his head down and shaking it contritely. "It all comes of being so kindhearted."

"There, you see, it didn't take me long to grasp your character. And so, why shouldn't I give you five hundred rubles per soul? But . . . I haven't the wherewithal! I'm ready, if you like, to add on another five-kopeck piece, so that each runaway soul will stand me thirty kopecks."

"Well, father o' mine, it's all up to you, but you might tack on just two kopecks apiece to that."

"I will tack on just two kopecks apiece, if you like. How many of these runaways have you? You said seventy, I think?"

"No, they'll come to eight and seventy."

"Eight and seventy . . . eight and seventy, at two and thirty kopecks per soul, that'll come to—" Here our hero stopped to think, but only for a second, no more, and suddenly announced: "That'll come to twenty-four rubles and ninety-six kopecks!" He was strong in arithmetic. Right then and there he made Plushkin write out a receipt and handed the money over to him, which the latter took in both his hands and carried over to the bureau as though he were carrying some liquid, fearing at every moment to let it slop over. Having reached the bureau he examined the money once more and tucked it away, also with the utmost care, in one of the drawers, where in all probability it was destined to be buried until such time as Father Karp and Father Polikarp, the two priests of his village, would bury him himself, to the indescribable joy of his son-in-law and his daughter, and perhaps even that of the captain who had enrolled himself among Plushkin's kin. Having hidden the money, Plushkin sat down in an easy chair and apparently could find no other subject for conversation.

"Well, now, are you already preparing to leave?" he asked, noticing a slight movement on the part of Chichikov, who had only wanted to get a handkerchief out of his pocket. This question reminded our hero that there really was no use in tarrying any longer. "Yes, it's time for me to be going!" he announced, picking up his hat.

"And what about a cup of tea?"

"No, I'd better have a cup of tea with you some other time."

"But, I say! Why, I've ordered a samovar. I am no great lover of tea, I must tell you, it's a dear beverage, and besides that the price of sugar has gone up unmercifully. Proshka! We don't need the samovar! You bring that dried Easter cake back to Mavra, you hear? Let her put it back in the same place it was; or no, let's have it here, I'll carry it back myself. Good-by, father o' mine! And may God bless you! As for the letter, you hand it over to the Chairman of the Administrative Offices. Yes! Let him read it; he's an old friend of mine. Of course! We used to eat out of the same trough."

After which this strange phenomenon, this shriveled little dotard, escorted him out of the courtyard, ordering the gates to be locked immediately thereafter; then he made the rounds of his store-rooms, to make sure if all the watchmen were at their posts—they were stationed at every corner and had to pound small paddles against empty little casks that did duty for the traditional sheets of iron; then he looked in at the kitchen where, under pretext of seeing whether his people were getting good fare, he filled himself with plenty of cabbage soup and buckwheat groats and, having scolded every last one of his domestics for their thievish and loose ways, returned to his own room. Left to himself, he even thought of how he might show his gratitude to his recent caller for such a really unparalleled magnanimity. "I'll make him a present," he reflected, "of my pocket-watch; after all it's a good watch, of silver, and not just ordinary pinchbeck or bronze; it's a trifle out of order, true enough, but then he can get it fixed himself; he's still a young man, so he has to have a watch to make his fiancée like him. Or no," he added after some meditation, "I'd better leave it to him after my death, in my will, to remember me by."

But our hero, even without the watch, was in most cheerful spirits. Such an unexpected acquisition was a veritable gift. Really, no matter what you might say, there were not only the dead souls alone, but runaway souls as well, and two hundred-odd creatures in all! Of course, while he had still been driving up to Plushkin's village he had already had a premonition that he would gain something or other, but that it would be such a windfall he had never anticipated. All the way back he was unusually jolly; he whistled in a low key; he made music with his lips, putting a fist to his lips as if he were playing on a trumpet, and finally struck up some song or other, a thing so unusual that Seliphan himself listened, listened and then, with a slight shake of his head, said: "Just you listen how the master's singing!"

It was already dusk when they drove up to town. Light and shadow had become thoroughly intermingled and, it seemed, all objects had also become intermingled among themselves. The striped toll-gate had taken on some indeterminate hue; the mustachios of the soldier on sentry duty seemed to be up on his forehead and considerably above his eyes, and as for his nose, why, he seemed to have none at all. The thunderous rattling of the carriage and its bouncing made the occupant notice that it had reached a cobbled way. The street lamps had not been lit yet; only here and there were lights beginning to appear in the windows of the houses, while in the lanes and the blind alleys scenes and conversations were taking place inseparable from this time of day in all towns where there are many soldiers, cabbies, workmen, and beings of a peculiar species who look like ladies, wearing red shawls and shoes without stockings and who dart like bats over the street crossings at nightfall. Chichikov did not notice them, nor did he notice even the exceedingly slim petty officials with little canes who, probably after taking a stroll beyond the town, were now returning to their homes. At rare intervals there would come floating to Chichikov's ears such exclamations, apparently feminine, as "You lie, you drunk, I never let him take no such liberties as that with me!" or: "Don't you be fighting, you ignoramus, but come along to the station house and I'll show you what's what!" In brief, such words as will suddenly scald, like so much boiling water, some youth of twenty as, lost in reveries, he is on his way home from the theater, his head filled with visions of a Spanish street, night, a wondrous feminine image with a guitar and ringlets. What doesn't he have in that head of his and what dreams do not come to him? He is soaring in the clouds, and he may just have dropped in on Schiller for a chat, when suddenly, like thunder, the fatal words peal out over his head, and he perceives that he has come back to earth once more, and not only to earth, but actually to Hay Square, and right by a pothouse, at that; and once more life has begun strutting its stuff before him in its workaday fashion.

Finally the carriage, after a considerable bounce, plunged, as if it were sinking into a pit, into the gates of his inn, where Chichikov was met by his servant Petrushka, who held the skirts of his frockcoat with one hand (inasmuch as he did not like having them come apart) and with the other helped his master to climb out of the carriage. The tavern servant, too, came running out with a candle and the inevitable napkin over his shoulder. Whether Petrushka was gladdened by the arrival of his master, no one knows; but at any rate he exchanged winks with Seliphan, and his usual sullen air seemed on this occasion to clear up to some extent.

"You've been pleased to take a long holiday," said the inn waiter, lighting the stairs.

"Yes," said Chichikov, when he had ascended them. "Well, and what's new with you?"

"Everything's well, glory be to God," said the server, scraping. "Yesterday we had some lieutenant or other arrive; he's taken Room Sixteen."

"A lieutenant?"

"Don't know who he is; from Riazan; got bay horses."

"Fine, fine; keep on being a good lad," said Chichikov and entered his room. As he was passing through the entry he turned up his nose and said to Petrushka: "You might open the windows, at least!"

"Why, I did have them open," said Petrushka, but he was lying. However, his master himself knew that he was lying, but he no longer wanted to argue the matter any further. After the trip he had made he was feeling great fatigue. Having eaten the lightest of suppers, consisting only of a suckling pig, he immediately undressed and, climbing in under his blanket, fell into fast, sound slumber, fell into that marvelous slumber which is known only to those fortunate beings who are bothered neither by hemorrhoids, nor fleas, nor overdeveloped mental faculties.

CHAPTER SEVEN

Fortunate is the wayfarer who, after a long, tedious journey with its cold spells, slush, mire, stage-post superintendents grumbling from lack of sleep, the jingle-jangling of bells, carriage repairs, heated arguments, stage-coach drivers, blacksmiths, and all sorts of scoundrels whom one meets on the road, beholds at last a familiar roof and the little lights that seem rushing forward to meet him.

And he will anticipate in his mind's eyes the familiar rooms, the joyous shout of his people running out to meet him, the noise and running of children, and soothing, low-voiced converse, constantly interrupted by flaming kisses, which have the power of eradicating from memory all that had been disagreeable. Happy is the family man that hath such a retreat—but woe to the bachelor!

Happy is the writer who, after passing by characters that are tedious, repulsive, overwhelming in their sad actuality, is about to approach characters that manifest the high dignity of man; happy the writer who has picked out only the few exceptions from the great slough of everyday figures revolving about him; the writer who has not changed even once the lofty strain of his lyre, has never descended from his aerie to his poor, insignificant brethren, and who, without touching the common earth, has devoted himself wholly to his images and forms, far removed from that earth and magnified to heroic size. Doubly to be envied is his resplendent lot: he dwells amid these images and shapes as if in the midst of his own family; and, in the meantime, his fame is trumpeted far and wide —and loudly. He has beclouded men's eyes with incense that transports their senses; he has flattered them wondrously, concealing the seamy side of life and presenting to them Man, the Glory of Creation. All and sundry, with much clapping of hands, hasten after him and run headlong at the tail of his triumphal chariot. A great universal poet do they style him, soaring high above all the other geniuses of this world, even as an eagle soars above other high-flying birds. At the very mention of his name young ardent hearts will be overcome with awe and trembling; responsive tears will glisten in all eyes. . . . There is none that is his equal in power—he is God!

But not such is the lot and different is the fate of the writer who has dared to bring out all the things that are before man's eyes at every minute, yet which his unheeding eyes see not—all that fearsome, overwhelming slimy morass of minutiae that have bogged down our life, all that lurks deep within the cold, broken, workaday characters with which our earthly path, at times woeful and dreary, swarms. Different is the fate of the writer who has dared, as if with the puissance of an implacable burin, to bring out all these things in bold and vivid relief before the eyes of all men! It will not be given to him to reap the plaudits of the populace, not his will it be to behold responsive tears and the whole-hearted rapture of the souls he has stirred; not to him will come, fluttering as if on wings, the maid of sixteen with her head all in a whirl and moved by a hero-worshipping infatuation; not for him will it be to forget himself in the sweet fascination of the strains he himself has uttered; not for him, finally, is it to avoid the judgment of his times, which will style as insignificant and base the creations he has cherished; that judgment will consign him to an ignoble place in the ranks of those writers who have insulted humanity; it will ascribe to him the qualities of the heroes he himself has depicted; it will strip him of heart, and soul, and the divine flame of talent. For the judgment of the writer's own times does not recognize that equally marvelous are the lenses that are used for contemplating suns and those for revealing to us the motions of insects imperceptible to the naked eye; for the judgment of his times does not recognize that a great deal of spiritual depth is required to throw light upon a picture taken from a despised stratum of life, and to exalt it into a pearl of creative art; the judgment of his time does not recognize that lofty, rapturous laughter is worthy of taking its place side by side with a lofty, lyrical strain, and that there is a very abyss between that laughter and the tortured posturings of a show-booth scaramouch! The judgment of his times does not recognize him and will turn everything into a reproach and an obloquy for the unrecognized writer: without discrimination, without response, without concern, he will be left behind in the middle of the road, like some traveler without kith or kin. Austere is his course in life, and bitterly will he feel his loneliness.

But for a long while yet am I destined by some wondrous power to go hand in hand with my strange heroes, to contemplate life in its entirety, life rushing past in all its enormity, amid laughter perceptible to the world and through tears that are unperceived by and unknown to it! And still distant is that time when awesome inspiration will break forth like a storm and well up like a fountain in another head that is clothed in sacred horror and refulgence, and when men will sense, in abashed trepidation, the majestic thunder of other eloquent words. . . .

Let us be getting on—on! Away with the frown that has over-cast the brow and with the countenance of austere gloom! Let us plunge suddenly and head first into life, with all its inaudible blather and jingle-bells, and see what Chichikov is up to.

Chichikov awoke, stretched his arms and legs, and felt that he had had a good sleep. After lying for two minutes or so on his back, he snapped his fingers and recalled, while his face lighted up, that he now had just a little short of four hundred souls. Right then and there he leapt out of bed, without even first taking a look in the mirror at his face, which he was sincerely fond of and in which he found the chin, apparently, the most attractive of all, inasmuch as he used to boast about it quite often before one or another of his friends, especially if he happened to be shaving at the time of the call. "There, take a look," he'd usually say, rubbing his hand over it, "what a chin I have—it's perfectly round!" But this time he did not take a look either at his chin or at his face, but simply, just as he was, put on a pair of morocco boots with fancy appliqués of variegated colors (such boots as the town of Torzhok carries on a brisk trade in, owing to the easy-going ways and ease-loving incli-nations of the Russian's nature), and clad only in a nightshirt that reached no further down than a kilt and which made him look like a Scotchman, forgetting all about his dignity and his discreet middle age, he covered the room in two leaps, each time slapping his behind quite deftly with his heels. Then, on the instant, he got down to business; as he stood before his casket he rubbed his hands with the same pleasant anticipation as that with which an incor-ruptible judge of a rural police court, bound for some investigation, rubs his on approaching a table set with all sorts of cold delicacies; save for this, Chichikov did not lose any time in taking certain papers out of it. He wanted to conclude everything as speedily as possible, without letting any grass grow under his feet. He had decided to formulate the title-deeds himself, both original and duplicate, so as to avoid paying anything to the pettifogging quill-drivers. He knew the correct form perfectly; combining the work with his morning tea (with sweet pretzels and rich cream) which the tavern waiter brought in, placing it deftly, with much clatter-ing of the tea things, almost under his very nose, he speedily wrote out in majuscules: *IN THE YEAR ONE THOUSAND EIGHT HUNDRED AND*—; then, immediately following, in minuscules: *So-and-so, a Landed Proprietor,* and everything else that was required.

In two hours all was in readiness. When, having finished, he glanced at these papers, at these fantastic souls, at these muzhiks who, verily, had been muzhiks once upon a time, had worked, had plowed, liquored, driven horses, and fooled their masters or, it may be, had been simply good muzhiks, some strange feeling that he himself could not comprehend immediately took possession of him. Every one of these memoranda seemed to have some sort of character of its own, and because of this it seemed as if the muzhiks themselves took on their own characters. The muzhiks belonging to Korobochka had, almost to a man, supplemental qualifications and nicknames. Plushkin's memorandum was distinguished by its conciseness of phrase: frequently only the first syllables of his dead serfs' first names and patronymics would be written down, followed by two dots. Sobakevich's list struck one by its unusual fullness and particularization: not one of the muzhiks' qualifications had been passed over; of one it was said: *A good Joiner;* another had a notation opposite his name: *Knows his Work and doesn't touch Spirits.* Just as circumstantially had Sobakevich supplied not only the names of the dead soul's father and mother, but also stated what the behavior of both had been; only one, a certain Phedotov, had written opposite his name: *Father Unknown, but born of Capitolina, a House Wench; nevertheless is of Good Character and no Thief.*

All these details imparted a certain air of freshness: it seemed as if these muzhiks had been alive only yesterday. As he gazed long at the names, Chichikov's spirit was touched and, with a sigh, he uttered: "Good heavens, how many of you are crowded in here! What, my hearties, did you do in your time? How did you get along?"

And his eyes stopped involuntarily at one of the names. It was one already familiar to the reader, that of Peter Saveliev, or No-Respect-for-the-Pig-Trough, who had at one time belonged to Korobochka, the landed proprietress. Again Chichikov could not restrain himself from saying: "Eh, what a long fellow you are, you've spread over the whole line! Were you a master craftsman, or just a muzhik, and what sort of death were you carried off by? Was it in some pot-house, now, or were you run over by a lumbering cart as you lay sleeping off your drink in the middle of the road?

"Stepan the Cork—*Carpenter; of Exemplary Sobriety*. Ah, there he is, Stepan the Cork, there's the mighty giant who was fit to be in the guards! Guess he covered all the provinces on foot with his ax stuck in his belt and his boots slung over his shoulders; he'd eat a copper's worth of bread and two of dried fish, yet in his purse, like as not, he'd lug home a hundred solid silver rubles every time, and maybe even sew a government note in his linen breeches or put it in the toe of his boot. Where did death take you off? Did you, for the sake of bigger earnings, clamber up on a scaffold under the very cupola of a church, and maybe even pull yourself up on the cross itself and, slipping off the plank up there, smash against the ground, with only some Uncle Mikhei who happened to be standing near you to say, as he scratched the nape of his neck: 'Eh, Vanya, but you had to go and do it!' while he himself, with a rope tied around him, climbed up to take your place?

"Maxim Teliatnikov—*Shoemaker*. Ha, a shoemaker! *Drunk as a shoemaker*, says the proverb. I know you, I know you, dear man; if you like, I'll tell you your whole life's history. You learned your trade from a German, who fed all of you apprentices together, beat you over the back with a strap for slovenliness, and wouldn't let you out into the streets to skylark and carry on, and you turned out to be a miracle and not a mere shoemaker; and the German master could not sing your praises enough when he talked about you with his frau or a kamerad. And what happened after your apprenticeship was over? 'Why, now I'll start a little place of my own,' you said, 'but I won't do it the way a German does, who shivers over every copper; me, I'm goin' to get rich quick.' And so, having paid a considerable quit-rent to your master, you set up a little shop, after getting a heap of orders, and got down to work. You'd gotten yourself some rotten leather somewhere, at one-third the regular price, and, sure enough, you made yourself a double profit on every pair of boots you turned out; but within a fortnight the boots you'd made were all cracked and split, and you were cursed out in the vilest way. And so that little shop of yours became deserted, and you started in taking a drop now and then and traipsing around in the streets, saying all the time: 'No, but things are bad in this world! There's no such thing as making a living for a born Russian; them furriners won't never let you!'

"And what muzhik is this? Elizavet' the Sparrow! Hell and damnation and the bottomless pit—a wench! How did she ever get shuffled in here? That Sobakevich is a scoundrel; even in such a thing he had to take me in!"

Chichikov was right; this was a wench, sure enough. How she had ever got in there no one could tell; but so artfully had her name been written out that from a distance one might have taken her for a muzhik, and even her name had been spelled in such a way that, at a careless glance, it might pass for a masculine one. However, Chichikov did not take this into consideration and crossed her off his list right then and there.

"Grigoriy Try-to-get-there-but-you-won't! What sort of a man were you? Did you go in for hauling and, having gotten yourself a troika and cart covered with matting, renounced forever your home, your native haunts, and started transporting merchants to the fairs? Was it on the road that you surrendered your soul to God, or did your own friends do away with you over some stout and red-cheeked soldier's wife? Or did some vagabond lurking in a forest get a hankering for your strapped mittens and your troika of squat but sturdy ponies? Or did you yourself, perhaps, as you lay in your broad bunk near the ceiling, get to thinking, and thinking, and then, for no reason on earth, after first turning in at a pothouse, dive right into a hole in the ice and vanish out of sight and mind? Eh, what a folk the Russians be! It doesn't like dying a natural death.

"And what about you, my darlings?" he went on, shifting his eyes to the scrap of paper whereon the runaway souls of Plushkin were listed. "Even though you be among the living, yet of what good are you? You might just as well be dead, for all the use you are. And wherever are your spry legs carrying you now? Did you

156 ·

run off because you had a bad time of it at Plushkin's, or are you roaming the woods and robbing travelers simply of your own free will? Are you doing time in prisons, or have you attached yourselves to other masters and are again tilling the soil? Eremei Kariakin; Nikita Volokita (Ladies' Man), and his son, Anton Volokita. One can see by their very nicknames that these fellows knew how to get around.

"Popov, a domestic . . . probably had book-learning—he wouldn't take a knife to anybody, I guess, but became a thorough-going thief in some refined, genteel manner. But there, the Captain of the Rural Police must have nabbed you by now, and you with never a passport (though you call it *pash*port) on you. You stand there alertly enough during the confrontation. 'Whom do you belong to?' says the Captain of the Rural Police, putting in, on this most probable occasion, a pretty strong word or two for your benefit. 'I belong to such-and-such a landed proprietor,' you answer, right smart. 'What are you doing here, then?' says the Captain of the Rural Police. 'He's given me leave, so's I can earn my quit-rent,' you answer, with never a hitch. 'Where's your passport?'—'With the master that hired me, Pimenov, a burgher.' 'Call Pimenov! Are you Pimenov?'—'I am that.'—'Did he give you his passport?'— 'No, he didn't give me no passport at all, at all.'—'What are you lying for?' says the Captain of the Rural Police, with the addition of a pretty strong word or two. 'That's right,' you answer smartly. 'I didn't give it to him, 'cause I got into the house late, but instead I handed it over for safe-keeping to Antip Prokhorov, the bell-ringer.'—'Call the bell-ringer! Did he give you his passport?'—'No, I never got no passport off of him.'—'Well, what are you lying for again?' says the Captain of the Rural Police, driving the speech home with a rather strong word or two. 'Where's your passport, then?'—'I did have it,' says you, quick as a wink, 'but I must have dropped it on the road somehow, it looks like.'—'And what about that there soldier's overcoat?' says the Captain of the Rural Police, again nailing you with an additional strong word or two. 'What did you go and swipe that for? And also that box full of copper money from the priest?'—'By no manner of means, I didn't,' says you, without as much as shifting a foot. 'I've never yet been apprehended in a stealing matter.'—'But how come they found the soldier's overcoat in your possession?'—'I wouldn't be knowing—probably somebody else brought it in and put it down near me.'—'Ah, you low-down beast, you low-down beast, you!' says the Captain of the Rural Police, shaking his head and putting his arms akimbo. 'Why, clap him in leg-irons and take him to prison!'—'By all means! I'll go with pleasure,' you answer. And so, taking a snuff-box out of your pocket, you friendlily treat to a pinch each of the two invalided soldiers of some sort who are putting the leg-irons on you, and ask them whether they've been in retirement long and what war they'd been in. And now you're living your life in prison, whilst your trial is going on in court. And the court hands down its written decision: You're to be transferred from the prison at Czarevo-Kokshaisk to the prison at such-and-such a town; and the court there hands down another written decision: You're to be transferred to Vesiegonsk, or something like that; and so you travel from prison to prison, and you say, as you look your new dwelling place over: 'No; the prison at Vesiegonsk, now, is cleaner nor this; there you could even play at nine-pins, there's so much room there; and besides, it's more social there, like.'

"Habakkuk Phyrov! What are you up to, brother? Where are you, what regions are you knocking about in? Has fate carried you off to the Volga, and have you fallen in love with a free life, having joined the brotherhood of barge-haulers? . . ."

At this point Chichikov paused and fell into a slight daydream. What was it about? Was it about the fate of Habakkuk Phyrov, or had he gone into a daydream just so, as every Russian does, no matter what his years, rank, and estate, when he thinks of the riotousness of a free and reckless life? And truly, where was Phyrov now? . . . Why, he's having a noisy and merry good time on the grain-wharf, having come to terms with the grain-merchants. With flowers and ribbons on their hats the whole band of haulers is making merry, saying good-by to their mistresses and wives, tall, well-built, in necklaces and ribbons, they dance in a ring and sing songs; the whole square is seething, and in the meantime, amid shouts, curses, and urgings, the roustabouts hook on their backs loads of more than three hundred pounds, noisily pouring wheat and peas into the holds of the deep vessels and piling up bags of oats and groats, and farther on one can see all over the square heaps of bags, piled up into pyramids like cannon-shot, and enormous does all this arsenal of grain seem until it shall have been all repiled within the deep river barges, and the endless fleet will start down the river with the spring ice, in single file, like a flight of wild geese. That's when you'll have your fill of work, you barge-haulers! And all together, as before you had made merry and had played like so many friends, you will buckle down to toil and sweat, hauling the tow-rope to the strain of a song as endless as all Russia!

"Oho, ho! It's twelve o'clock!" said Chichikov at last, after glancing at his watch. "What have I been fussing around like that for? And it wouldn't be so bad if I'd been doing something useful, but this is just nothing at all; first of all I started talking bosh, and then I got to daydreaming. What a fool I am, really!"

Having said which, he shaved, changed his Scotch costume for a European one, pulling his plump belly in by another notch in his belt, sprayed himself with eau de Cologne, picked up his warm cap and put the papers under his arm, and was off to the Administrative Offices to execute the purchase-deeds. He was hurrying not because he was afraid of being late; he wasn't afraid of that, inasmuch as the Chairman was a friend of his and could prolong or abridge an interview at his desire, much like ancient Zeus who, in Homer, prolonged the days or sent quick-passing nights whenever the need arose either to bring to a close a martial contest between the heroes he favored, or to permit them to fight to a finish. Rather, Chichikov himself felt within him a desire to bring the matter to an end as soon as possible; until such time as it was ended, everything seemed to him to be in an uneasy and awkward state; despite everything the thought would occur to him that the souls were not quite the real thing and that in such cases it is always necessary and best to shed the onus from one's shoulders as quickly as possible.

He had hardly come out into the street, mulling over all this and at the same time feeling the weight of his coat of brown broadcloth, lined with selected bear pelts, which he was wearing thrown over his shoulders, not at all because it was cold but in order to inspire awe in pettifogging small fry, when at the very turn into a by-lane he ran into another gentleman, also wearing a coat of brown broadcloth, lined with selected bear pelts, and in a warm cap with ear-flaps; he had on fine kid gloves and there was a smile on his lips. The smile spread more and more; his face lighted up, and he called out: "Pavel Ivanovich!" It was Manilov. They immediately clasped each other in an embrace and for five minutes or so remained in that position right out in the street. The kisses each bestowed on the other were so hard that both of them felt their front teeth aching practically throughout the rest of that day. Only Manilov's nose and lips remained on his face for joy; his eyes had vanished altogether. For a quarter of an hour did he hang on with both his hands to Chichikov's hand and made it fearfully hot and uncomfortable. In most refined and pleasant terms he told how he had flown to town, as if on wings, to clasp Pavel Ivanovich to his bosom; his speech was concluded with such a compliment as might perhaps be appropriate only to some gentle maiden with whom one is about to waltz. Chichikov opened his mouth, not knowing yet himself how to thank the other, when Manilov suddenly took out from under his fur coat a paper rolled up into a tube and tied with a thin little pink ribbon.

"What's this?"

"The little muzhiks."

"Ah!" Chichikov unrolled it right then and there, ran his eyes over it, and wondered at the neatness and beauty of the handwriting. "That's splendidly written," said he; "it won't be necessary to rewrite it even. There's even a border around it! Whoever made that border so artfully?"

"Why, you mustn't even ask," Manilov told him.

"You?"

"My wife."

"Ah, my God! Really, I feel conscience-stricken over having caused you so much trouble."

"There's no such thing as trouble where Pavel Ivanovich is concerned."

Chichikov bowed in acknowledgment. Learning that he was going to the Administrative Offices to execute the title-deeds, Manilov expressed a willingness to accompany him thither. The friends linked arms and started off together. At every slight rise in the ground, or a hummock, or a step, Manilov would support Chichikov and almost give him a hand up, adding with a pleasant smile that under no circumstances would he permit Pavel Ivanovich to stub his small feet. Chichikov felt compunctions, not knowing how to thank him, inasmuch as he sensed that he was somewhat heavy on the hoof. Rendering each other such mutual services they managed, at last, to reach on foot the square where the Administrative Offices were located, a great, three-story building of stone, all as white as chalk, probably to convey an idea of the purity of soul of the functionaries who had their offices within. The other structures on the square were hardly in keeping with the grandeur of the stone building. These other structures were: a sentry box, near which a soldier with a gun was standing; two or three cab-stands, and, to conclude the list, long board fences with the familiar fenciana and wall art, sketchily executed in charcoal and chalk. There was nothing else to be found upon this barren (or, as it would be described by our writing brethren, beautiful) square. Several heads of the incorruptible priests of Themis popped out of the windows on the second and third stories and hid themselves the same minute: probably a superior was entering the room at that moment.

The friends did not walk up but rather dashed up the stairs, since Chichikov, trying to avoid being supported under the arm by Manilov, had quickened his step, whereupon Manilov, for his part, flew forward, striving not to allow Chichikov to become fatigued, and for that reason both were puffing quite hard as they stepped into the dark corridor. Neither in the corridors nor in the chambers were their eyes overwhelmed with cleanliness. At that time cleanliness was still not considered a matter to be greatly concerned about, and that which was dirty just remained dirty, without acquiring any attractiveness thereby. Themis in all her simplicity, just as she is, was receiving her guests in negligee and dressing-gown. The chancellery chambers through which our heroes passed really merit description, but the author cherishes a strong timidity insofar as all administrative places are concerned. Even when he has had occasion to traverse such of these chambers as had a resplendent and ennobled air about them, with waxed floors and highly polished tables, he has tried to dash through them as quickly as possible, with his eyes meekly lowered and fixed on the ground, and for that reason he is utterly ignorant of how well and flourishingly everything is going on there.

Our heroes saw a great deal of paper, both for rough drafts and of the finest white for final copies; they saw heads bent over their work, and broad napes of necks, and many frock-coats, and dress-coats of a provincial cut, or simply some sort of short jacket of light gray, which stood out quite sharply, which jacket, with its head twisted almost entirely to one side and all but resting on the very paper, was nimbly and with a full sweep writing out some protocol or other concerning a land-grab, or the inventory of an estate appropriated by some peaceful landed proprietor or other who was tranquilly finishing out his days while the suit was going on, and who had lived long enough to beget him not only children but grandchildren under the benign shelter of this suit. And one could hear, in snatches, brief remarks, uttered in a whisky tenor: "Lend me, Theodossei Theodossiev, the file on Number Three Hundred and Sixty Eight!"—"You're always dragging off the lid of the office ink-bottle somewhere!" At times a voice, more majestic and beyond a doubt belonging to one of the higher officials, would ring out imperiously: "There, transcribe that! And if you don't, I'll have them take the boots off you and keep you here for six days without food or drink." Great was the scratching of quills, and the sound thereof was as if several carts laden with brushwood were driving through a forest piled with dead leaves a yard deep.

Chichikov and Manilov approached the first desk, seated at which were two clerks who were still young in years, and inquired: "Where are the purchase-deeds attended to, please?"

"But just what is it you want?" both clerks asked, turning around.

"Why, I have to submit an application," said Chichikov.

"But just what was it you bought?"

"I would first like to know where the desk for making out purchase-deeds is; is this it, or is it elsewhere?"

"Yes, but tell us first what you bought and what you paid, and then we'll be able to tell you where to go; as it is, we don't know where to send you."

Chichikov perceived at once that these clerks were simply inquisitive, after the manner of all young clerks, and wanted to lend greater weight and importance to themselves and their duties.

"Look here, my dear sirs," said he, "I know very well that all matters relating to purchase-deeds, no matter what the amount involved is, are attended to in one place, and therefore I'm asking you to show me the desk; but if you don't happen to know what's going on around you, why, we'll ask some of the others."

To this the clerks made no answer, save that one of them merely jabbed his finger in the direction of a corner of the room, where an old codger was seated at a desk and shuffling some papers. Chichikov and Manilov made their way between the desks toward him. The codger was attending to his work very closely.

"May I ask," Chichikov began, with a bow, "whether this is the desk for purchase-deeds?"

The codger raised his eyes and said, articulating almost every syllable: "The purchase-deeds are not handled here."

"Where then?"

"You want the Division of Purchase-Deeds."

"And where is the Division of Purchase-Deeds?"

"That's under Ivan Antonovich."

"And where is Ivan Antonovich?"

The codger jabbed his finger in the direction of another corner of the room. Chichikov and Manilov marched off to see Ivan Antonovich. Ivan Antonovich had already sneaked a glance at them and looked them over out of the corner of one eye, but the same moment had plunged still more assiduously into his writing.

"May I ask," Chichikov said, with a bow, "is this the desk for Purchase-Deeds?"

Ivan Antonovich acted as if he hadn't even heard him and became utterly absorbed in his papers, without making any answer. One could see right off that here was a man who had already attained years of discretion, that this was no young chatterbox and flibbertigibbet. Ivan Antonovich, it seemed, had already put far more than forty years behind him; his hair was black, thick; the

· 163

whole middle of his face jutted forward and ran mostly to nose; in short, it was the sort of face that, in common usage, is called a mug.

"May I ask, is this the Division of Purchase-Deeds?" Chichikov asked again.

"It is," said Ivan Antonovich, turning his mug around and then again applying himself to his writing.

"Well, my business is this: I have bought up from various owners of this district serfs that I want to transport elsewhere. The purchase-deed is made out—all that remains is to execute it."

"And are the sellers present in person?"

"Some are here; from others I have letters of authorization."

"And have you brought the application with you?"

"I've brought that as well. I would like . . . I'm in a hurry . . . so could this matter be concluded today, let's suppose?"

"What! Today? . . . Today is out of the question," said Ivan Antonovich. "It's necessary to make further inquiries, whether there are any liens and the like."

"However, if it comes to that, in order to expedite matters, well, Ivan Grigoryevich, your Chairman, is a great friend of mine—"

"But then, Ivan Grigoryevich isn't the only one here, there are others, too," Ivan Antonovich remarked sternly.

Chichikov grasped the hint the other had thrown out and said: "The others won't suffer; I was in the service myself; I know what it's all about—"

"Go to Ivan Grigoryevich," said Ivan Antonovich in a somewhat kindlier tone. "Let him issue the order through the proper channels, and there won't be any hitch about the matter when our turn comes."

Chichikov, taking out a bank-note, laid it down in front of Ivan Antonovich, which the latter utterly failed to notice and instantly covered with a ledger. Chichikov was about to draw his attention to it, but Ivan Antonovich intimated with a motion of his head that there was no need of pointing it out.

"There, he'll bring you to the Chairman's office," said Ivan Antonovich with a nod of his head, and one of the ministrants near by, who had sacrificed at the altar Themis so arduously that both his sleeves had burst at the elbows and had long since been obtruding their lining, for which zeal he had even attained in his time to the first rung in the ladder of ranks, that of Collegiate Registrar, served our friends even as Virgil on a time had served Dante, and guided them to the Presence, in whose office there was but one capacious armchair wherein, behind a desk with two thick tomes and a trihedral column that was surmounted by the imperial coat-of-arms and a decree of Peter the First on each side, sat the Chairman himself, solitary as the sun. Before the portals of this place the new Virgil experienced such reverent awe that he by no means dared to set his foot over the threshold and turned about, showing a back that was as frayed as an old straw matting with here and there a bit of down sticking to it.

As they entered this official chamber they perceived that the Chairman was not alone; near him sat Sobakevich, who had been entirely screened by the trihedral symbol of authority. The arrival of the new-comers evoked an exclamation; the administration throne was shoved back noisily. Sobakevich also rose up from his chair and became visible on every side, long sleeves and all. The Chairman took Chichikov into his embraces and the chamber resounded with kisses; they inquired about each other's health, whereupon it turned out that each had a pain in the small of his back, which was at once explained by their sedentary mode of life. The Chairman, apparently, had already been informed by Sobakevich about Chichikov's purchase, inasmuch as he took to congratulating him, which at first embarrassed our hero somewhat, especially when he perceived that both Sobakevich and Manilov, the two sellers, with each of whom he had put the deal through privately, were now standing together and face to face. However, he thanked the Chairman and, immediately turning to Sobakevich, asked:

"And how is your health?"

"Thank God, I have nothing to complain of," said Sobakevich. And, true enough, there was nothing to complain of: iron was more apt to catch a cold and start coughing than was this wondrously fashioned landed proprietor.

"Why, you were always famed for your health," said the Chairman, "and your late father, too, was a strong man."

"Why, he used to go after bears single-handed."

"It seems to me, however," said the Chairman, "that you, too, could knock a bear over if you wanted to tackle one."

"No, I couldn't," said Sobakevich; "my late father was stronger than I." And, after heaving a sigh, he went on: "No, people aren't what they used to be; you take even my life, now, what sort of a life is it? Just puttering around—"

"Well, in just what way is your life so unattractive?" asked the Chairman.

"It isn't right, it isn't right!" said Sobakevich, with a shake of his head. "Just judge for yourself, Ivan Grigoryevich: here I'm going on my fifth decade and I haven't been sick even once— haven't had as much as a sore throat, never even as much as a boil or a carbuncle. . . . No, that doesn't bode any good! Some time or other I'll have to pay for it." And at this point Sobakevich was plunged into melancholy.

"Eh, what a man!" both Chichikov and the Chairman thought at the same time. "Just think what a thing he has picked to complain about!"

"I have a little note for you," said Chichikov, taking Plushkin's letter out of his pocket.

"From whom?" asked the Chairman and, after breaking the seal, exclaimed: "Ah, from Plushkin! So he's still vegetating in this world. . . . What a fate! Why, he was the most intelligent, the richest of men! But now—"

"A dog," said Sobakevich. "A swindler. He has starved all his people to death."

"By all means, by all means," said the Chairman to Chichikov, after reading the letter, "I am ready to act as his agent. When do you wish to execute the purchase-deed, now or later on?"

"Now," said Chichikov. "I'd even ask you, if it's at all possible, to put it through today, inasmuch as I'd like to leave town tomorrow. I've brought the purchase-deeds as well as the application."

"That's all very fine but, whether you like it or not, we shan't let you go so soon. The purchase-deeds will be ready today, but, just the same, you'll have to tarry with us for a while. There, I'm going to issue the instructions right now," said he and, opening a door that led into the general chancellery, all filled with clerks, who had made themselves like so many toil-loving bees clustering upon their honey-combs (if one can but compare chancellery papers to honey-combs). "Is Ivan Antonovich here?" he called out.

"He's here!" a voice answered from the room.

"Send him in to me!"

Ivan Antonovich, he of the mug, with whom the reader is already acquainted, appeared in the Chairman's office and made a respectful bow.

"Here, Ivan Antonovich, take all these purchase-deeds; they belong to this gentleman—"

"And don't forget, Ivan Grigoryevich," Sobakevich chimed in, "that you'll need witnesses, at least two for each party to the contract. Send to the Public Prosecutor's right now; he's a man of leisure and most probably is sitting home this very minute. Zolotukha, that shyster and the foremost bribe-taker in the world, does all his work for him. The Inspector of the Board of Health, now—he, too, is a man of leisure, and is most probably at home as well, if he hasn't traipsed off to play cards somewhere; and there are many others, besides, who are still nearer at hand: Trukhachevski, Begushkin—they're all useless and merely cumber the earth."

"Just so, just so!" said the Chairman, and immediately sent one of the chancellery clerks after all these gentlemen.

"I'd also ask you," said Chichikov, "to call in the agent of a certain landed proprietress with whom I have also made a deal. He's the son of Father Cyril, the Dean; this man is one of the clerks right here."

"Of course, we'll call him in too!" said the Chairman. "We'll attend to everything. And as for the clerks, don't give any of them anything; I beg of you, don't! Friends of mine must not pay." Having said this, he issued some order to Ivan Antonovich on the spot, which order evidently did not prove to his liking. The purchase-deeds had apparently produced a good effect on the Chairman, especially when he saw that the purchases amounted to almost a hundred thousand rubles in all. For several moments he gazed into Chichikov's eyes with an expression of great pleasure, and finally said: "So that's how things are! That's the way, Pavel Ivanovich! So you have made acquisitions!"

"I have," Chichikov answered him.

"A good thing! Really, a good thing!"

"Yes, I can see myself that I couldn't have done better. No matter how things are, man's goal is still indeterminate as long as he has not placed his foot firmly upon some solid foundation instead of some free-thinking chimera of youth." At this point, quite fittingly, he chided all young people for their liberalism, and justly so. Yet, remarkably enough, there was a certain lack of assurance in his words, as though he had at the same time said to himself: "Eh, brother, but you're lying, and mighty hard, at that!" He even avoided looking up at Sobakevich and Manilov, out of fear of detecting something on their faces. But his fears were groundless: Sobakevich's face did not so much as twitch, and as for Manilov, he, as though bewitched by an apt phrase, was so pleased that he merely kept tossing his head approvingly from time to time, having plunged into that state in which a lover of music finds himself when some cantatrice has outdone the violin itself and has squeaked out so fine and high a note as is beyond the power of even a bird's throat.

"Yes, but why don't you tell Ivan Grigoryevich," Sobakevich commented, "just what, precisely, you have acquired? And you, Ivan Grigoryevich, why don't you ask what an acquisition he has made? For what folk he has bought! Pure gold! Why, I sold him even Mikheiev, the coachmaker."

"No, not really, you sold him even Mikheiev?" the Chairman expressed his amazement. "I know this coachmaker Mikheiev, a splendid master craftsman; he rebuilt my droshky for me. But, if I may ask, how is it possible? Why, you told me at one time that he had died—"

"Who, Mikheiev dead?" Sobakevich said, not in the least at a loss. "It's his brother who died; but Mikheiev himself is as alive as can be and has become huskier than ever. Just a few days ago he constructed such a light carriage that a better couldn't be built even in Moscow. Really and truly, he ought to be turning out work only for the Emperor."

"Yes, Mikheiev is a splendid master craftsman," said the Chairman, "and I actually wonder how you were able to bear parting with him."

"As if it were a case of Mikheiev alone! But what about Stepan the Cork, my carpenter, and Milushkin, my brick-layer, and Teliatnikov, Maxim, my shoemaker? For they all went; I sold all of them!" And when the Chairman asked just why they had all been sold down the river, since they were people indispensable in a household and all masters of their crafts, Sobakevich made answer, with a hopeless wave of his hand: "Why, I simply must have had a fit of foolishness. 'Let's sell 'em,' I said, and sell 'em I did, foolish like!" After this he hung his head down, as though he himself repented this transaction, and added: "There, even though you see a gray-haired man before you, yet to this day he hasn't gotten any sense into his head."

"But allow me to ask, Pavel Ivanovich," said the Chairman, "how is it you're buying peasants without any land? Or are you buying them for resettlement?"

"Yes, for resettlement."

"Well, if it's for resettlement, that's another matter; and whereabouts will you resettle them?"

"Whereabouts? . . . In the province of Kherson."

"Oh, there are fine lands there," said the Chairman and commented most approvingly on the way things grew in that region.

"And have you sufficient land?"

"As much as will suffice for the peasants I've bought."

"Have you a river there, or a pond?"

"A river. However, there's a pond there as well." As he said this, Chichikov by mischance looked at Sobakevich, and although Sobakevich was as imperturbable as before, yet it seemed to Chichikov as if the landowner had written on his face: "Ouch, but you're lying! I doubt if there's any river and pond—or any land, for the matter of that!"

While these conversations were going on, the witnesses began to appear, little by little. The reader is acquainted with them: the blinking Public Prosecutor, the Inspector of the Board of Health, Truhachevski, Begushkin, and the others who, according to the words of Sobakevich, were all useless and merely cumbered the earth. Many of them were utter strangers to Chichikov; to make up the necessary number of witnesses, some of the clerks were recruited on the spot. They also brought not only the son of Father Cyril, the Dean, but even the Dean himself. Each one of the witnesses affixed his signature, with all his attributes and ranks, some in a backhanded scrawl, some in slanting pothooks, some almost upside down, putting down such characters as were never even seen in the Russian alphabet. Ivan Antonovich, whom we already know, had managed his end quite deftly and quickly; the purchase-deeds were recorded, marked, entered in the proper ledger and wherever else this was necessary, the tax of one-half of one per cent and the charge for the notices in the *Moscow News* had already been manipulated, and Chichikov somehow had to pay but a mere moiety. The Chairman even issued an order that only half the revenue tax be taken from him, while the other half, in some unknown manner, was transferred to the account of some other applicant.

"And so," said the Chairman, when everything had been concluded, "all that's left now is to wet the bargain."

"I'm ready," said Chichikov. "It all depends on you to name the time. It would be a sin on my part to refuse to open two or three bottles of the bubbly stuff for such a pleasant gathering."

"No, you haven't understood me aright; it's we ourselves who'll stand the bubbly stuff for you," said the Chairman. "That's our obligation, our duty. You're our guest; it's up to us to treat you. Do you know what, gentlemen? For the time being, here's what we'll do: let's all of us, just as we are, start out for the house of the Chief of Police; he is our miracle worker; he has but to wink as he passes by Fish Row or a wine-cellar, and then, don't you know, what a snack we'll have! And, to celebrate this occasion, we'll have a little game of whist as well."

No one could turn down a proposal like that. The witnesses, at the mere mention of Fish Row, felt their mouths watering; all immediately picked up their caps and hats and the session was over. As they were passing through the chancellery, Ivan Antonovich, he of the mug, said on the quiet to Chichikov, after making him a respectful bow: "You've bought up serfs for all of a hundred thousand, yet all you've given me for my work is a single white government note for twenty-five rubles."

"But then, what sort of serfs are they?" Chichikov answered him, also in a whisper. "The most worthless and insignificant sort, and not worth even half that." Ivan Antonovich perceived that this client was of a firm character and would not shell out any more.

"And why did you buy the souls from Plushkin?" Sobakevich whispered in Chichikov's other ear.

"And why did you tack the Sparrow onto the list?" Chichikov asked him in answer to this.

"What Sparrow?" asked Sobakevich.

"Why, the countrywife, Elizaveta Sparrow, and you even wrote her name out with a masculine ending."

"No, I never tacked on any Sparrow," said Sobakevich, but walked away to join the others.

They all made their way in a friendly crowd to the house of the Chief of Police. The Chief of Police, sure enough, turned out to be a miracle worker. No sooner had he heard just what was up than he had summoned a roundsman, a spry lad in patent-leather top-boots and, apparently, he had whispered but a couple of words in his ear and merely added, aloud: "Do you get it?" and, lo and behold! in a room adjoining the one where the guests were ardently at whist there had already appeared a table and, on that table, salted sturgeon (the huge white variety), salted sturgeon (the ordinary variety), salmon (both smoked and salted), caviar (both pressed and freshly salted), herrings, still a third species of sturgeon (the stellated), cheeses, smoked tongue, and dried-and-salted sturgeon fillets—all this had come in tribute from Fish Row. Then there appeared additional contributions from the master himself, the products of his kitchen: a fish-head pie, into which had gone the cartilage and head-trimmings of a three-hundred-and-twenty-five-pound sturgeon; another pie with pepper-mushrooms; fritters; dumplings fried in butter and dumplings boiled.

The Chief was, in a sort of way, the father and benefactor of the town. He was in the midst of the citizens altogether as if in the bosom of his own family, and as for the shops and the market-place, he dropped in on them as if into his own pantry. In general, he had found his proper niche, as they say, and had mastered his job to perfection. It was even hard to decide whether he had been made for the job or the job for him. So cleverly did he handle it that he made twice as much of a good thing out of it as his predecessors had done, and yet at the same time he had earned the love of the whole town. The merchants, first of all, loved him very much precisely because there was nothing stuck up about him; he was on hail-fellow-well-met terms with them and although at times he did take a powerful chunk out of their hides, yet he did it somehow with exceeding adroitness. He'd even pat you on the back, and laugh right hearty and treat you to a cup of tea; why, he'd give you his promise to drop in for a game of checkers, and would ask you how everything was going with you, how business was, and this and that; if he learned that one of your little ones happened to be taken sick, he'd actually advise you as to the right medicine. In a word, he was one fine fellow! He might be driving along in his droshky, watching that order was being maintained, yet he'd find time to say a word to this one or that: "Well, what's what, Mikheich! I ought to finish that game with you sometime!"—"Yes, Alexei Ivanovich," the merchant would answer, doffing his hat, "you really ought to." —"Well, Iliya Paramonich, you drop in on me, brother, and take a look at my trotter; I'll race him against yours—you harness yours to a sulky, too, and we'll have a go at it." This merchant, who was hipped on the subject of his own trotting horse, would, as they say, smile right heartily in answer and say, stroking his beard: "Yes, we'll have a go at it, Alexei Ivanovich!"

Even all the shop-help, who usually at such a time doffed their headgear, would look at one another with pleasant expressions, as much as to say: "Fine man, this Alexei Ivanovich!" In short, he had contrived to acquire thorough popularity, and the general opinion of the merchants was that this Alexei Ivanovich, now, even though he'll take summat, will, on the other hand, never go back on you, nohow.

Perceiving that the snack was ready, the Chief of Police proposed that his guests suspend their whist for a bite, and they all trooped into the room the aromas from which had long since been pleasantly titillating the nostrils of the guests and into which Sobakevich had long been peeping, having marked from afar a sturgeon placed to one side, on a special platter. The guests, having each drained a glass of vodka of a dark, olivine hue—such a hue as is to be found only on certain transparent stones from Siberia, which in Russia are graven into seals—armed themselves with forks and attacked the table from all sides, each one, as they say, revealing his nature and his leanings, this one pressing hard on the caviar, that one assaulting the smoked salmon, still another tackling the cheese. Sobakevich, paying no attention to all these trifles, settled down to work on the sturgeon he had had his eye on and, while the others were drinking, chatting, and eating, he, in just a little more than a quarter of an hour, finished it all off, so that when the Chief of Police did recall it, saying: "And how will this work of nature strike you, gentlemen?" and had walked up to it with the others, fork in hand, he saw that there was but an inedible tail left of this work of nature. As for Sobakevich, he bristled up as if this hadn't been his work at all and, having withdrawn as far as possible from the others, was prodding his fork into a plate of some sort of small, dried fish. Having put away the exceptional sturgeon, Sobakevich settled down in an easy chair and no longer ate or drank another thing, but merely puckered and blinked his eyes.

The Chief of Police evidently didn't like sparing potables—there was no counting the toasts. The first toast was drunk, as our readers may even have surmised for themselves, to the health of the newly baked landowner of Kherson; then came one to the well-being of his serfs and their happy resettlement, then another to the health of his future wife (naturally a great beauty), which evoked a pleasant smile upon the lips of our hero. They surrounded him on all sides and began imploring him most convincingly to stay on in their town for at least two more weeks: "No, Pavel Ivanovich! Say whatever you like, but it's just as if you were merely chilling the house, stepping on the threshold and then backing out! No, you really must spend some time with us! There, we'll marry you off. Isn't that so, Ivan Grigoryevich—we'll marry him off?"

"We will, we will!" the Chairman chimed in. "You can resist

hand and foot, but it won't do you any good! We'll marry you off just the same. No, father o' mine, since you've fallen into our clutches, you mustn't complain! We don't like to fool around."

"Well, now, what's the use of resisting hand and foot?" said Chichikov. "After all, a marriage isn't just one of those things . . . as long as a bride can be found—"

"Oh, there'll be a bride, all right! How else? There will be everything, everything you wish! . . ."

"Well, in that case—"

"Bravo! He's staying on!" they all set up a shout. "Viva! Hurrah for Pavel Ivanovich, hurrah!" And they all approached him, glass in hand, to clink his. Chichikov dutifully clinked glasses with all of them. "No, no, let's clink glasses some more," said those who felt especially lively, and they clinked glasses with him anew, and for a third time as well did they all clink glasses. In a short while they all grew extraordinarily merry. The Chairman (you couldn't find a more charming man, once he became thoroughly merry) embraced Chichikov several times, uttering in heart-felt effusiveness: "My soul! My little darling, you!" and even, snapping his fingers, went into a dance around him, singing as he did so the well-known song: " 'Ah, you Kamarinski muzhik, you're this and you're that!' "

After the champagne they uncorked some Hungarian wine, which added still more spirit and gaiety to the gathering. They had forgotten all about whist; they disputed and shouted and spoke of everything on earth, of politics and even of military matters; they propounded free and daring ideas for which, at another time, they themselves would have given their children a sound whipping. Right then and there they resolved a multitude of the most difficult problems. Never had Chichikov felt himself in so merry a mood; by this time he imagined he really was a landowner of Kherson; he spoke of various improvements, of the scientific rotation of crops, of the happiness and bliss of twin souls, and began reciting to Sobakevich Werther's versified epistle to Charlotte, in answer to which Sobakevich only batted his eyes as he sat in his easy chair, inasmuch as after the sturgeon he felt a great tendency to sleep. Chichikov surmised even himself that he was becoming too expansive, asked for a carriage, and gladly availed himself of the Public Prosecutor's droshky. The Public Prosecutor's coachman, as it turned out on the way, was an experienced lad, inasmuch as he directed the reins with only one hand while with the other, placing it behind him, he kept the gentleman right end up. In such fashion did the Public Prosecutor's droshky get him at last to his inn, where for a long while yet all sorts of nonsense kept coming to the tip of his tongue: about a flaxen-fair bride with rosy-red cheeks and a little dimple on the right one; about villages in Kherson; about lots of capital. Seliphan was even given certain husbandly instructions about getting all the newly resettled serfs together, so's to call a muster of them. Seliphan listened in silence for a very long while and then went out of the room, after saying to Petrushka: "Go and undress the master!"

Petrushka began taking the boots off Chichikov and almost dragged his master to the floor together with them. But at last the boots were taken off, the master properly undressed and, after tossing a few times in bed, which creaked unmercifully, he fell asleep, to all intents and purposes an out-and-out landowner of Kherson. And Petrushka in the meantime took out into the corridor his master's trousers and the frock-coat of scintillating bilberry red, which, after spreading it on a hanger, he began cleaning with a beater and a brush, filling the whole corridor with dust.

As he was about to remove the garment, he happened to look down from the gallery and caught sight of Seliphan in the court-yard, returning from the stable. Their eyes met and intuitively they understood each other: the master is asleep!—they would be able to drop in at a place or two. Right away, having carried the frock and trousers into the room, Petrushka went down and the two walked off together, without saying a word to each other about their destination and chaffing each other on their way about some-thing utterly irrelevant. Their jaunt was not a protracted one—to be precise, they crossed over to the other side of the street, to a house that was opposite the inn, and entered a small low glass door, all covered with soot, which led into something that was practically a basement, where there was already a number of all sorts of folk seated at wooden tables: those who were clean-shaven and those who were bearded, those who wore unlined sheepskin jackets and those who wore little more than a shirt, while here and there was a fellow in a frieze overcoat. What Petrushka and Seliphan did there God alone knows; but they came out an hour later, arm in arm, preserving a perfect silence, paying a great deal of attention to each other and mutually watchful of running into any sharp corners. Arm in arm, without letting go of each other, they took all of a quarter of an hour to climb the staircase until finally they got the better of it and reached the top. Petrushka stopped for a minute before his low cot, considering how he might lie down most conveniently and wound up lying right across it, so that his feet were propped against the floor. Seliphan, too, lay down on the same cot, pillowing his head on Petrushka's belly and forgetting entirely that this was not at all the place where he was supposed to sleep, which was in the domestics' quarters, perhaps, if not in the stable, next to the horses. Both fell asleep the same minute, raising a snore of unheard-of intensity, to which their master in the other room responded with a high-pitched nasal whistle.

Soon after the arrival of the two everything quieted down, and the inn was enveloped in profound sleep, save that in a single little window there was still a light to be seen, where some lieutenant, the one who had come from Riazan, lived. Evidently he had a great weakness for boots, inasmuch as he had already bought himself four pair and was now incessantly trying on a fifth. Several times he approached the bed in order to throw them off and lie down, but somehow could not bring himself to do so; the boots really were well made, and for a long while yet did he keep on lifting now this foot and now the other and inspecting the deftly and wondrously turned heel of each boot.

CHAPTER EIGHT

CHICHIKOV'S purchases became the subject of much talk. Surmises, opinions, and discussions as to whether it was profitable to buy peasants for resettlement now absorbed the whole town. Many of the disputants evinced a thorough knowledge of the subject. "Of course," some maintained, "that's very true; there's no arguing against it—lands in the southern provinces are undeniably good and fertile; but how will things be for Chichikov's serfs without any water? There's no river there at all."—"The lack of water wouldn't matter; it wouldn't matter in the least, Stepan Dmitrievich, if it weren't that resettlement is an unreliable thing all around. Everybody knows what the muzhik is: he'll be on new land, and he'll have to work that land with nary a thing—he won't have a hut nor a yard. Well, he'll run off as sure as two times two, he'll make himself that scarce you'll find nor hide nor hair of him."—"No, hold on, hold on, Alexei Ivanovich, I don't agree with what you're saying, that Chichikov's muzhiks will run off. The Russian can adapt himself to everything and become used to every climate. You can send him even to Kamchatka—the only thing you'll have to supply him with will be mittens; then he'll slap his hands together, take an ax in them, and be off to chop down timber for a new hut." —"But, Ivan Grigoryevich, you've left out one important factor: you haven't yet asked what sort of muzhik Chichikov has. Have you forgotten that no landowner will sell a good serf? I'm ready to lay my head on the block if the kind of muzhik Chichikov has isn't a thief and the most abandoned of drunkards, an idle vagabond and of violent conduct."—"Just so, just so; I agree with that; it's true no one will sell good serfs, and that Chichikov's serfs are drunkards; but it must be taken into consideration that that's precisely what the moral consists of: they're good-for-nothings now but, having resettled in a new land, they may become excellent and

obedient people in no time at all. There have already been not a
few such examples, not only in daily life but throughout history as
well."—"Never, never!" maintained the overseer of the government factories. "Believe me, such a thing can never be, since Chichikov's peasants will have two powerful enemies to contend
against. Their first enemy is the proximity of the provinces in Little
Russia where, as you know, spirits are freely sold. I assure you that
within two weeks they'll drink themselves into the blind staggers.
The other enemy is none other than wanderlust, which will be
inevitably acquired by the peasants during the process of their resettlement. If these are to be guarded against it'll be necessary to
keep them perpetually under Chichikov's very eyes and he'll have to
treat them with an iron hand and bear down on them hard for every
offense, no matter how trifling, and he won't be able to rely upon
anybody else to do it for him, either, but, should the occasion call
for it, he must be able himself, with his own two fists, to ram the
muzhik's teeth down his throat or plant a good, solid clout on the
back of his neck, or both."—"But why should Chichikov be
bothered himself and have to clout the backs of their necks? He
can find an overseer, can't he?"—"Oh, yes, you'll find an overseer!
They're all cheating rogues!"—"They're cheating rogues because
the masters don't attend to their business!"—"That's the truth!"
many chimed in. "If the master himself knows anything at all
about what's what in running an estate, and if he's any kind of a
judge of character, he'll always have a good overseer."

But the factory manager said that you couldn't find a good
overseer for less than five thousand. The Chairman, however, said
that you could dig one up for even three thousand. Whereupon the
factory manager said: "Where will you dig him up, then? In your
nose, maybe?"—"No," said the Chairman, "not in my nose, but
in this very district—Petr Petrovich Samoilov, to be precise; there's
the overseer you need for Chichikov's muzhiks!"

Many felt strongly about Chichikov's situation, and the difficulty of resettling such an enormous number of peasants frightened
them exceedingly: they even began to be greatly apprehensive lest
an actual uprising occur among such unruly folk as Chichikov's
peasants. In answer to this the Chief of Police assured them that

there was no need to apprehend an uprising; that for the averting thereof there existed the power of the Captain of the Rural Police; that, if, instead of coming himself, the Captain of the Rural Police were to send merely the cap of his uniform, that cap alone would drive the peasants to the very place of their resettlement. Many offered their opinions on how to root out the spirit of revolt that had swept like a storm over these peasants of Chichikov's. These opinions were of every sort; there were such as reeked far too much of military harshness, and of a severity that was all but excessive; there were, however, such opinions as were inspired with gentleness. The Postmaster remarked that a sacred obligation lay ahead of Chichikov, that he could become a father, in a sort of way, to his peasants; as he expressed it, Chichikov might even bring about benevolent enlightenment and, in connection with this, he commented with praise on the Lancasterian method of mutual education.

In such a manner did the good people of the town dispute and talk, and many, moved by sympathy, imparted to Chichikov certain of these counsels personally, even proposing a convoy for the safe transportation of the peasants to their new locality. For these counsels Chichikov thanked them, saying that should the need arise he would not fail to avail himself of them; but as for the convoy, he turned it down in positive terms, saying that it was absolutely unnecessary, inasmuch as the peasants he had bought up were extraordinarily docile in character, since they themselves voluntarily favored the resettlement, and that an uprising among them was quite out of the question.

All this talk and discussion, however, brought about the most beneficent consequences, such as Chichikov could hardly have expected—to wit, rumors spread that he was no more and no less than a millionaire. The citizens of this town had, even without this, as we have already seen in the first chapter, come to love Chichikov with all their hearts, and now, after such rumors, they came to love him with their hearts and souls both. However, if the truth were to be told, they were all kind-hearted folk; they lived in concord among themselves, treating one another like perfect friends, and their conversations bore the impress of a certain peculiar simple-heartedness and intimacy: "My dear friend Iliya Iliich! . . ."; "I say, brother Antipator Zakharievich! . . ."; "You've gotten all tangled up in your lies, Ivan Grigoryevich, my little darling!" In the case of the Postmaster, whose name was Ivan Andreievich, they always tacked on the tag: "*Sprechen Sie Deutsch?*"—thus: "*Sprechen Sie Deutsch*, Ivan Andreich?" * In short, everything was on a very homey footing; and many of them were not without culture: the Chairman of the Administrative Offices knew the *Liudmilla* of Zhukovski by heart, which poem was at that time a novelty hot out of the oven, and recited many passages in a masterly fashion, especially: "Sleeps the pine-grove; the dale slumbers," and when he came to "Hush!" he would pronounce it in such a way that one really seemed to see the dale slumbering; for the sake of greater verisimilitude he would at this point even half-shut his eyes. The Postmaster went in more for philosophy and read quite diligently, even burning the midnight oil, such things as Young's *Night Thoughts* and Eckartshausen's *The Key to the Mysteries of Nature,* from both of which he copied quite lengthy excerpts, but of just what nature these excerpts were no one knew. However, he was a wit, colorful in his choice of words, and fond, as he himself put it, of "garnishing" his speech. And the way he garnished his speech was through a multiplicity of sundry tag-ends and oddments of phrases, such as "my dear sir; some sort of a fellow; you know; you understand; you can just imagine; relatively speaking, so to say; in a sort of a way," and other such verbal small change, which he poured out by the bagful; he also garnished his speech, quite successfully, by blinking one eye, or puckering it up, all of which added quite a caustic air to many of his satirical innuendoes. The others also were more or less enlightened folk; this one would read Karamzin, that one the *Moscow News,* while a third, perhaps, read nothing whatsoever. One might be what is called a *hangman's blindfold*—that is, a man who has to be kicked in the behind to arouse him to anything; another simply a solitary sluggard who, as they say, lies abed all his life long, whom it would be even no use to arouse, he'd simply roll over on the other side. All the men were

---

* A very innocuous bit of paronomasia or echolalia on *Deutsch* and the *ich* ending of the Postmaster's patronymic. *Trans.*

of the sort upon whom their wives, during the tender talks that take place in privacy, bestow pet names, such as Dumpling, Chubby, Tummy, Blackie, Kiki, Zuzu, and the like. But, in general, they were a kindly folk and full of hospitality, and a man who had partaken of their bread and salt or had sat through an evening of whist with them already became something near and dear to them; all the more so a Chichikov, with his enchanting qualities and ways, who really knew the great secret of making oneself liked. They fell in love with him to such an extent that he could not see any means of escaping from the town; he never heard anything but: "There, one short week more, stay with us for just one short week more, Pavel Ivanovich!" In short, they simply dandled him like a baby, to use the common expression. But incomparably more remarkable was the impression (truly a matter to marvel at!) which Chichikov made on the ladies. In order to explain this, to however slight an extent, it would be necessary to say a great deal about the ladies themselves, about their society, to describe in living pigments, as the phrase goes, their spiritual qualities; but all that is a very difficult thing for the author. On the one hand he is held back by his boundless respect for the helpmeets of the dignitaries, while on the other hand . . . on the other hand it's simply a difficult thing to do. The ladies in the town of N—— were . . . no, I simply can't do it, I really do feel a certain timidity. The most remarkable thing about the ladies of the town of N—— was. . . . Why, it's actually odd, the quill absolutely refuses to move, just as if it were loaded with lead or something. So be it, then: the description of their characters will evidently have to be left to him whose pigments are more vivid—and who has a greater variety of them on his palette; as for us, we'll simply have to say a word or two, perhaps, about their appearance, and about that which is rather superficial. The ladies of the town of N—— were what is called presentable, and in this respect they might be boldly held up as an example to all others. When it came to such things as deportment, keeping up the tone, observing etiquette, as well as a multitude of the most refined proprieties, and particularly following the mode down to its very least trifles—why, in such things they were 'way ahead of the ladies of even Peterburgh and Moscow. They dressed with great taste, and drove about town in their carriages, even as the latest fashion decreed, with a footman swaying behind, and the livery on him all gold galloons. The visiting card, even if one were forced to improvise one out of a deuce of clubs or an ace of diamonds, was nevertheless a very sacred thing. Because of just such a thing two of the ladies, not only great friends but actually relatives, broke off their friendship for good and all; to be precise, one of them had been negligent about returning a call. And no matter how hard their husbands and male kindred strove afterward to reconcile them, it was no go; it turned out that one can accomplish all things in this world, save one alone: the reconciliation of two ladies who have fallen out over a neglected return call. And so both ladies remained "mutually disinclined," to use an expression current in the *grand monde* of the town.

The matter of precedence at social functions also brought about a great many quite stirring scenes, which at times inspired the husbands with perfectly chivalric and magnanimous notions of knight-errantry. No duels, of course, took place among them, inasmuch as all of them were Civil Service officials, but to make up for that each would try to pull some dirty trick on the other wherever and whenever possible, which, as everybody knows, can on occasion inflict greater damage than any duel.

When it came to morals the ladies of the town of N—— were strict, filled with noble indignation against vice of any sort and temptations of every sort, punishing frailties without any mercy. But if what is known as *a thing or two* did occur among them it occurred in secret, so that there was no hint whatsoever given of what was going on; propriety was entirely preserved, and the husband himself had been so well trained that, even if he did happen to catch a glimpse of *this and that,* or heard about it, he would answer succinctly and sensibly with the proverb: *He that would live at Peace and Rest, Must hear and see and say the Best,* or *Evil to him who evil thinks.* It must also be said that the ladies of the town of N—— were distinguished, like many ladies in Peterburgh, by an unusual fastidiousness and decorum in their choice of words and expressions. Never did they say: "I blew my nose; I sweated; I spat;" instead they said: "I relieved my nose; I had to use my handkerchief." One could not, under any circumstances, say: "This glass (or this plate) stinks," and one could not even say anything that would give a hint of this, but instead of that they would say: "This glass is misbehaving," or something else of that sort. In order to ennoble the Russian language still more, almost half the words therein were utterly rejected in conversation, and for that reason they frequently had to resort to the French language; also, to make up for their nicety in Russian, things were altogether different when it came to French—words far coarser than any of the examples given above were perfectly *propre* therein. And there you have whatever can be said (speaking quite superficially, of course) about the ladies of the town of N——. But if one were to look below the surface then, naturally, many other things would be revealed; however, it's quite dangerous to look below the surface of feminine hearts. And so, limiting ourselves to superficiality in this case, let's be getting on.

Up to now all the ladies had somehow discussed Chichikov but little, giving him his full due, however, for having such agreeable social graces. But from the time that rumors began to spread about his millionairehood they began finding many other good points about him. However, the ladies were not at all avaricious schemers: the fault of the whole thing lay in the very word *millionaire*—not in the millionaire himself but precisely in the very word, inasmuch as the very sound of the word contains, outside of any vision of money-bags, a something that has an effect not only on men who are scoundrels but on men who are fine by nature, to say nothing of men who are neither one thing nor another; in a word, it had an effect on everybody. The millionaire has one great advantage, that he can witness meanness that is utterly disinterested, meanness pure and unadulterated, meanness not based upon any ulterior motives whatsoever: many know very well that they won't get a thing out of him and that they aren't entitled to anything, yet they'll never fail at least to catch his eye, or to laugh ingratiatingly, or to doff their hats, or to wangle an invitation to the dinner to which, as they have learned, the millionaire had been invited. It can't be said that this tender predisposition to meanness had been experienced by the ladies; however, in many of the drawing rooms they began saying that while Chichikov was not, of course, the handsomest of men, he was, just the same, all that a man should be, that were he but a little stouter or fuller it would be a pity. In connection with this something would be said, even quite offensively, somehow, concerning the man who was decidedly thin, that he was something in the nature of a toothpick rather than a man. Many and sundry additional touches appeared on the attire of the ladies. There was a great stir in Drapers' Row, almost a crush. There was something very like a parade of carriages, so many of them had gathered there. The merchants were amazed on seeing several bolts of goods they had brought home from the fair, and which had been left on their hands because the price had seemed high, now suddenly become all the go and all but snatched out of their hands. During mass one of the ladies was seen with such a rouleau or hoop at the bottom of her dress that made it spread out over half the church, so that the usher, who was near by, had to issue orders for the commoner folk to move back—nearer to the porch, that is—lest Her Highness' raiment be rumpled somehow.

And as for Chichikov himself, he could not but notice, if only in part, such unusual attentiveness. As everybody knows, a feminine opinion approving a man's looks will buck him up considerably. This induces such a radiant mood that he actually becomes an Adonis. In a certain species of wild duck, for instance, the drake's plumage will, at the mating season, blossom out in such vivid hues as it never had before. Chichikov's mien became even more agreeable than hitherto, his motions and gestures more unconstrained, and his very collars were snowier, somehow, and hugged his jowls more caressingly. He sported a new watch chain. He became alluring.

On one occasion when he came home he found a letter on his table. Whence it had come and who had brought it he could not find out; the tavern waiter remarked that someone had brought it but hadn't wanted to say whom it was from. The letter began in very positive terms, precisely as follows: "No, I really must write you!" After that it went on to say that there is such a thing as a secret affinity between souls; this verity was clinched with a number of full stops that took up almost half a line. Then followed a few thoughts, quite remarkable for their incontrovertibility, so that we deem it almost indispensable to make an abstract of them: "What is our life? A vale of sorrows. What is the world? An insensate human herd." Next the fair writer mentioned that she was bedewing with tears certain lines written by her angelic mother— five and twenty years had gone since she had passed from this world; she called on Chichikov to come out into the wilderness, to leave forever the city, where people in stifling enclosures cannot breathe the free air; the end of the letter even echoed downright despair and concluded with the following lines:

> Two turtle doves will show thee
> Where my cold corpse lies;
> Their lovelorn cooing tells thee:
> She died amid tears and sighs.

There wasn't much meter, especially in the last line; this, however, mattered but little—the letter was written in the spirit of that time. There was no signature of any sort, either: neither first name nor last; not even a date line. The postscript merely added that his own heart ought to surmise who had written these lines, and that at the Governor's ball, which was set for the morrow, the writer herself would be present.

This piqued his interest very much. There was so much about the anonymity of the letter which was enticing and excited the curiosity that he read it through a second time, and a third, and said, at last: "Well, now, it would be curious to know just who wrote that!" In brief, the matter evidently became serious, for he kept mulling over it for more than an hour. At last, throwing up his arms and cocking his head, he said: "The letter is surely written in a very, very flowery way!" After which, it need hardly be said, the letter was folded up and tucked away in the casket, next to some theatrical handbill or other and an engraved wedding invitation which had been preserved for seven years in the same position and the same spot.

A little later, sure enough, an invitation to the Governor's ball was brought to him, balls being quite the usual thing in provincial capitals; where the Governor is, there's bound to be a ball, otherwise the proper affection and respect on the part of the gentry would never be forthcoming.

Everything immaterial was dropped and put aside by Chichikov that very minute, and everything was directed toward preparations for the ball, inasmuch as there truly were many exciting and stirring reasons for attending it. But then, it is probable that so much masculine time and energy was never expended on dressing since the very creation of the world. A whole hour was consecrated to the mere contemplation of his face in the mirror. He tried to impart to it any number of varying expressions; now an important and a dignified one, now a deferential one, yet not devoid of a certain slight smile, then simply a deferential one, without the smile. Several bows were dealt out in front of the mirror, accompanied by indistinct sounds bearing some resemblance to French, although Chichikov was entirely ignorant of that language. He even surprised himself with a host of pleasant mannerisms: he twitched his eyebrow as if winking, and moved his lips, and did something or other even with his tongue; in a word, what doesn't one do when left all to oneself, assured that nobody is peeping at one through a crack in the door, and when one feels, on top of that, that one isn't at all hard to look at. Finally he chucked himself under the chin, ever so slightly, saying: "Eh, you little good-looker, you!" and began dressing. A most contented mood never deserted him all the time he was dressing; as he put on his suspenders or tied his cravat he scraped and bowed with an especial adroitness and, although he had never danced, he performed a caper. This caper had a slight and harmless sequel: the bureau shook and a clothes brush fell off the table.

"Say what you will, but balls are a fine thing!" Chichikov mused. "It may be freezing, and the crops may have been poor, or there may be something else for you to fret about, but when people come together they forget all their troubles. There's something to amuse everybody—dancing for the young people, cards for those who've reached years of discretion. One can look on while others dance, and have one's fill of whist; and just the society, the throng around you, means a great deal. All is gaiety, all is bright. And then there's the supper—the Governor's chef is famous. There'll be hazel-grouse with mayonnaise. Maybe, also, a cold fresh sturgeon or two, with truffles, capers, herbs, and so on; then we'll give the fish some chilled bubbly stuff to swim in! The Devil take it, what a lot of all sorts of things there is in this world! I love pleasant, harmless sociability! . . ."

His arrival at the ball created an extraordinary sensation. Everyone there, without an exception, turned to greet him, even if he were holding cards, or was at the most interesting point of the conversation, just after saying: ". . . while the lower district court maintains, in rejoinder to this . . ." But just what the lower district court maintained was at once brushed aside by the speaker as he hastened to greet our hero. "Pavel Ivanovich!"—"Ah, my God, it's Pavel Ivanovich!"—"Dear Pavel Ivanovich!"—"My most esteemed Pavel Ivanovich!"—"Pavel Ivanovich, my soul!"—"So here you are, Pavel Ivanovich!"—"Yes, here he is, our Pavel Ivanovich!"—"Let me clasp you to my bosom, Pavel Ivanovich!"— "Let's have him here; there, I'm going to give my Pavel Ivanovich a real hard kiss!"

Chichikov felt himself in several embraces at the same time. He hadn't succeeded in freeing himself entirely from the embraces of the Chairman of the Administrative Offices when he found himself in those of the Chief of Police; the Chief of Police passed him on to the Inspector of the Board of Health; the Inspector of the Board of Health to the tax-farmer; the tax-farmer to the Town Architect. . . . The Governor, who at the time of Chichikov's entrance had been standing near the ladies, holding a snap-dragon motto in one hand and a small, fluffy white lap-dog in the other, upon catching sight of Chichikov threw both the motto and the lap-dog to the floor, so that the poor creature whimpered. In a word, Chichikov spread extraordinary rejoicing and gaiety on all sides of him. There wasn't a face that did not express pleasure or, at least, a reflection of the general pleasure. Thus do the faces of all the bureaucrats light up when some high official arrives for an inspection of the departments entrusted to them, after their first fright has subsided and they perceive that not a few things are to the liking of the great man; he himself has at last condescended to jest a little—that is, to drop a few words with a pleasant smile—

whereupon those bureaucrats who are around him, and somewhat nearer him in rank, laugh in response to his sally twice as hard as need be; those who, truth to tell, had heard but poorly the words he has let drop, make up for that by laughing with all their heart; and, finally, some policeman or other, stationed far off near the door, at the very exit, who has never laughed in all his born days and who just before had shaken his fist at the people outside—why, even he, in accordance with the immutable laws of reflection, expresses on his face some sort of smile, although this smile resembles rather the grimace of someone getting set to sneeze after a pinch of rappee.

Our hero responded to all and sundry and felt somehow extraordinarily adroit: he bowed right and left, bending somewhat to one side, as was his wont, but perfectly at his ease, so that he bewitched everybody. The ladies encircled him on the spot, forming a glittering garland about him and wafting whole clouds of fragrant odors; one breathed of roses, another spread an aura of spring and violets, a third was permeated through and through with mignonette—Chichikov could but lift up his nose and breathe in the fragrances. There was no end of tastefulness about their attire: the muslins, satins, and tulles were of such fashionable pastel shades that one could not even give their names, to such a degree had the refinement of taste attained! Bows of ribbon and flower corsages fluttered here and there over their gowns, in a most picturesque disorder, although a clever head and clever hands must have expended considerable thought and toil upon that disorder. Or one would come upon a gossamer head-dress that perched only on the shell-pink ears and seemed to be saying: "Watch out—I'm going to fly away! The only pity is that I won't lift with me the beauty wearing me!" Their waists were tightly laced and their forms most sturdily shapely and pleasing to the eye (it must be noted that the ladies of the town of N—— ran, on the whole, to plumpness, but they laced themselves in so artfully and had such pleasant ways about them that the plumpness was not in any way noticeable). They had premeditated and foreseen everything with unusual thoroughness; the neck, the shoulders were exposed precisely as much as need be and by no means one jot further; each one had revealed her possessions only to that degree which her inner convictions made her feel would just about suffice to seal a man's doom, while the rest was tucked away with unusual taste: either there was some sort of ethereal neck-piece, of some material as insubstantial as cotton-candy; or else small, crenelated ramparts of the finest cambric, known under the name of *modesties*, emerged from the dress. These *modesties* concealed, fore and aft, that which no longer could seal a man's doom, and yet at the same time compelled him to suspect that this was precisely where the doom lurked.

Their long gloves were put on not all the way up but with malice prepense left exposed the seductive parts of their arms above the elbows; many of these arms were of an enviable plumpness; in some instances the kid gloves had actually burst from having been pulled up a little too far. In short, everything seemed to bear the inscription: "No, this is no province; this is a metropolis; this is Paris itself!" Only here and there some such mob-cap as the earth has never yet seen would suddenly emerge, or even some weird feather, almost a peacock's, running counter to all modes, in keeping with the wearer's own taste. However, such things are inevitable; such is the nature of a provincial capital: somewhere it's bound to show its true nature.

"However, which one of them wrote that letter?" Chichikov wondered as he stood before them, and had even craned forward for a better look when a whole procession of elbows, cuffs, sleeves, ends of ribbons, perfumed chemisettes, and dresses scraped his very nose. The gallopade was going full blast; the Postmaster's good lady, the Captain of the Rural Police, a lady with a blue feather, a lady with a white feather, a Georgian prince by the name of Chipkhaikhilidzev, a bureaucrat from Peterburgh, a bureaucrat from Moscow, a French gentleman called Coucou, Perkhunovski, Berebendovski—they were up and away, all swirling and whirling.

"There she goes! The province is off on the light fantastic!" Chichikov muttered, staggering back and, as soon as the ladies had found their seats, his eyes began their search anew, to see if by some expression of face or eyes he might not discern the fair creature who had composed the letter; but no such expression, either of face or of feature, availed, and he could not discern her. Yet one could note everywhere something that was just the least bit revealing, something so imperceptibly exquisite—ooh, how exquisite! . . . "No," said Chichikov to himself, "women are such a thing that"— at this point he actually had to make a hopeless gesture with his hand—"there's really no use even talking! There, you just go ahead and try to describe or convey all that flits over their faces, all those slight emanations, hints . . . why, you simply won't be able to convey a thing. Their eyes alone are such a realm that, once a man has ventured therein, that's the last you've seen of him! For you'll never drag him out of there, not with an iron hook or anything else. There, for instance, try to tell merely about the light in those eyes, melting, velvety, honeyed—God alone knows what other kind of light there may not be!—both harsh and soft, or even altogether languishing or, as some put it, full of voluptuousness; or without any voluptuousness, but still worse than if it were full thereof; that light will catch at your heart and, as if it were a violin bow, will start playing upon every fiber of your soul. No, one simply cannot find the right words to describe them—women are the fancy-goods half of humankind, and that's all there is to it!"

Sorry—my fault! It seems that a phrase overheard in the street has escaped the lips of my hero. What's one to do, then? Such is the situation of the writer in Russia! However, if a word off the street has crept into a book, it isn't the writer who's at fault but the readers; and, first and foremost, the readers of the higher social strata: they are in the van of those from whom one will not hear a single decent Russian word, but when it comes to words in French, German, and English they will, likely as not, dish them out to you in such quantity that you'll actually get fed up with them, and they'll dish them out without spilling a drop of all the possible pronunciations: French they'll snaffle through their noses and with a lisp; English they'll chirp as well as any bird could, even to the extent of making their physiognomies bird-like, and will even mock him who is unable to assume a bird-like physiognomy; while German they'll grunt as gruffily as any boar. And the only thing they won't dish out to you is any good, plain Russian thing—save that, out of patriotism, they may build a log-cabin in the Russian style for a summer house. That's the sort readers of the higher social strata are, while all the others who try to number themselves among them simply follow suit! And yet, at the same time, how very pernickety they are! They want, without fail, everything to be written in the most austere language, refined and genteel; in a word, they want the Russian language to descend, suddenly and of itself, out of the clouds, all properly finished off, and to have it perch right upon their tongues, with nothing more for them to do than merely to open their mouths wide and thrust their tongues out. Of course, the feminine half of humankind is whimsical; but it must be confessed that worthy readers can be still more whimsical on occasion.

As for Chichikov, he in the meantime was becoming utterly bewildered as to which of the ladies was the one who had composed the letter to him. When he tried to fix his gaze more intently on this one or that one, he perceived that the ladies, for their part, were also evincing something that inspired the soul of a poor mortal both with hope and sweet torments, so that at last he was forced to say: "No, there's no possible way of guessing who she is!"

This, however, did not in any way diminish the merry mood he was in. Unconstrainedly and adroitly he exchanged pleasantries with some of the ladies, approaching now one, now another with brisk, small steps or, as they say, he minced along, as little aged beaux do upon built-up heels (they call such old gallants little mouse-stallions), prancing around the ladies quite spryly. At every few steps, mincing along rather deftly and turning right and left, he would suddenly throw in a punctuating scrape of his small foot, by way of a curlicue, as it were, or something like a comma. The ladies were very much pleased with him and not only found a heap of amiable and pleasant things about him, but even began to discern a majestic expression on his face, something actually Mars-like and military, which, as everyone knows, the women find very pleasing. They were even beginning to squabble over him a little: having noticed that he usually took his stand near the door, some of the ladies vied with one another and hastened to take a seat as near as possible to it, and if one of them had the good fortune to get ahead of the others in this an unpleasant scene would almost take place, and to many of them who had wished to do the very same thing such brazenness appeared much too revolting, my dear.

Chichikov became so engrossed in conversations with the ladies or, to put it better, the ladies engrossed him so and put his head in such a whirl with their conversations, which they peppered with such a lot of the most intricate and refined allegories—all of which had to be resolved, the effort of which caused his forehead to become actually beaded with sweat—that he had forgotten to fulfill an obligation of good manners: that of approaching his hostess first of all. He recalled this remissness only when he heard the voice of the good lady herself, who had been standing before him for several minutes by now. The Governor's lady uttered in a somewhat kindly and arch voice, with an agreeable toss of her head: "Ah, Pavel Ivanovich, so that's how you are! . . ." I cannot convey the exact words of the Governor's lady, but something full of great amiability was said, in that spirit in which the ladies and gallants make themselves understood in the novels of our worldly writers (who are great hands at and fond of describing salons and of boasting a knowledge of the highest *ton*), in some such vein as: "Can it be possible that others have taken such possession of your heart that there is no longer any room therein—nay, not the tiniest nook!—for those whom you have so compassionlessly forgotten?" Our hero instantly turned to the Governor's lady and was all set to deliver his answer to her—an answer probably in no way inferior to those which are delivered in the fashionable novels by the Zvonskis, Linskis, Lidins, Gremins, and all sorts of adroit military men— when, chancing to raise his eyes, he was suddenly rooted to the spot as if thunderstruck.

It was not only the Governor's lady who was standing before him; she was holding by the hand a young girl of sixteen, a dewy-eyed blonde, with fine and regular features, with a sharp little chin, her whole face a bewitchingly rounded-out oval, such as an artist would have taken for his Madonna and which one but rarely comes upon in Russia, where all things like to evince themselves on a sweeping scale—all things, with never an exception: the mountains, and the forests, and the steppes, and faces, and lips, and feet. It was the very same blonde whom he had met on the road while traveling from Nozdrev's, when through the stupidity of the coachmen or the horses their vehicles had so oddly collided, their harness tangling together, and Uncle Mityai together with Uncle Minyai had undertaken the task of disentangling them. Chichikov became so confused that he was unable to bring out a single sensible word and mumbled the Devil knows what, but something which neither a Gremin nor a Zvonski nor a Lidin would ever have said under any circumstances.

"You haven't been introduced to my daughter yet, have you?" said the Governor's lady. "She's just out of boarding school."

He answered that he already had had the good fortune to encounter her by chance; he made an attempt to add something else, but that something else did not turn out well. The Governor's lady, after a few more words, at last went off with her daughter to another part of the room to the other guests, but Chichikov still did not stir from the spot, like a man who has gaily sallied out of doors for a stroll, his eyes disposed to take in all the sights, and then suddenly comes to a dead stop, remembering that he has forgotten something, and when that happens you won't find anything sillier than this individual: in an instant the carefree expression deserts his face; he strives to recall just what it is he has forgotten: was it a handkerchief, by any chance? But the handkerchief is right in his pocket. Is it money, perhaps? But the money, too, is right in his pocket; he has everything with him, and yet at the same time some unseen demon is whispering into his ears that he has forgotten *something*. And by this time he's staring absent-mindedly and in a muddled way at the throng moving past him, at the vehicles dashing by, at the shakos and guns of a regiment on the march, or even at some sign, yet without really seeing a thing. And so it was with Chichikov: he suddenly became aloof from everything that was going on about him. At this point a multitude of hints and questions permeated with finesse and politesse was directed at him from fragrant feminine lips: "Is it permitted for us poor dwellers upon this earth to make so bold as to inquire what the subject of your reveries is?"—"Where are located those happy regions where your thought is soaring?"—"May one know the name of her who has plunged you into this sweet vale of pensiveness?"

But his response to all this was utter inattentiveness and the pleasant phrases were entirely lost on him. He was actually uncivil to such an extent that in a short while he left them and went over to the other side of the room, wishing to spy out where the Governor's lady had gone with her daughter. But the ladies apparently did not feel like giving him up so quickly as all that: each one had inwardly resolved to resort to all those weapons so dangerous for our hearts and to utilize all that was best and most effective in her armory. It must be remarked that certain ladies—I am saying certain ladies, which is not the same as saying all ladies—have a little weakness: if they should happen to notice some especially fine point about themselves, be it the brow, or the mouth, or the hands, why, they already think that the best feature will be the first thing to strike the eyes of all beholders, and that all these beholders will instantly begin saying in the same voice: "Look, look what a splendidly beautiful Greek nose she has!" or: "What a regular, enchanting brow!" As for her who has fine shoulders, she feels certain beforehand that all the young men will go off into utter raptures, and will be incessantly repeating every time she passes by: "Ah, what marvelous shoulders that one has!"—feels certain that they won't so much as glance at her face, or hair, or nose, or forehead; but, should they happen to glance at them, they will be regarded as merely extraneous. That's the way certain ladies think. Each lady took an inner vow to be as enchanting as possible during the dances and to display in all its splendor the surpassing excellency of whatever was most surpassingly excellent about her. The Postmaster's good lady, while waltzing, let her head loll to one side in such a languishing manner that one really sensed something not of this mundane sphere about her. One very amiable lady, who had come here not at all for the dancing, because of a slight *incommodité*, as she put it, which had befallen her, in the form of a pea-shaped growth on her right foot, and who in consequence thereof had actually been forced to wear plush booties, why, even she had not been able to hold out, in spite of everything, and circled a few times in her plush booties, for the specific purpose of not letting the Postmaster's good lady really get too many high and mighty notions into her head.

But all these maneuvers failed utterly in making the intended impression on Chichikov. He didn't so much as look at the figures the ladies performed as they danced, but kept ceaselessly rising on tip-toes to see if he could find where the engrossing blonde had gone; he bent his knees a little, too, keeping a sharp lookout between the shoulders and backs of the dancers; finally his search was successful and he caught sight of her, sitting together with her mother, over whose head some sort of feathered oriental turban was majestically swaying. Apparently he wanted to take them by frontal assault. Whether it was the mood of spring that affected him, or whether something else was egging him on, the fact remains that he resolutely pressed forward, regardless of everything. The tax-farmer received such a shove from him that he staggered and barely managed to balance himself upright on one foot: if he hadn't succeeded in doing so, he would have toppled over a whole row of others after him. The Postmaster also had to step back and looked at Chichikov in amazement, not unmixed with rather fine irony, but Chichikov did not even glance at these officials: he had eyes only for the blonde in the distance, who was pulling on a long glove and, beyond a doubt, was all consumed with a desire to be off whirling over the parquet floor. For in the meantime there, over to one side, four couples were going through a mazurka; their heels were splintering the floor, while an army officer (a second captain, to be precise) putting into his work body as well as soul, arms as well as legs, was performing such steps as no one had ever chanced to perform even in a dream. Chichikov darted past the mazurka, almost at the very heels of the dancers, and made directly for the spot where the Governor's lady and her daughter were sitting. However, he approached them with the utmost timidity; he did not mince along nimbly and gallantly as before; he had become a little halting, even, and some sort of awkwardness evinced itself in all his movements.

One cannot say with certainty whether the emotion of love had really awakened in our hero; it is even to be doubted if gentlemen of this sort—that is to say, those who aren't what you might call stout, yet who at the same time aren't exactly thin, either—are capable of falling in love; but at the same time there was something so strange here, something of such a nature as even he could not explain to himself: it appeared to him, as he himself confessed subsequently, that the whole ball, with all its chatter and noise, had for a few minutes moved somewhere far off, as it were; the violins and horns were caterwauling somewhere far beyond hill and dale, and everything had become misted over with a haze that resembled a hastily daubed-over background on a painting. And out of this murky, roughly sketched-in background only the fine features of the seductive blonde emerged clearly and definitely: the rounded-out oval of her little face; her waist, even, ever so slender, such as the boarding-school miss has the first few months after graduation; her white, almost simple little dress, lightly and deftly and closely draping her youthful, graceful small limbs, defining their pure lines. She seemed to resemble some sort of toy finely and cleanly carved out of ivory; she alone emerged white, translucent, and radiant from out the turbid and opaque throng.

Evidently that is how things are in this world; evidently even the Chichikovs, for a few moments in their life, turn into poets—however, the word *poet* might be too much in this instance. At any rate, he felt himself something quite like a young man—just the least wee bit short of a hussar, in fact. Seeing a vacant seat near them he instantly availed himself of it. The conversation did not catch on at first, but later it went well; he even began to feel a bit cocky, but . . . at this point, to our greatest distress, it must be observed that men of dignity and occupying important posts are rather on the ponderous side when it comes to making conversation with ladies; it is Messieurs the lieutenants who are master hands at this sort of thing, but by no means anybody above the rank of captain. How they do it, God alone knows; it would seem that they aren't saying anything so very ingenious, and yet the young girl they're saying it to will simply rock in her seat from laughter; as for a State Councilor, he'll say God knows what: either he'll start a conversation about how vast a realm Russia is, or will turn a compliment which, even though it may have been conceived not without wit, will nevertheless reek horribly of printer's ink; on the other hand, if he should somehow happen to say something funny, he'll laugh at it himself immeasurably more than will the fair creature listening to him. We are making this observation here so that the readers may perceive why the blonde began to yawn while our hero was telling his stories. Our hero, however, didn't notice this at all, relating a multitude of pleasant things, which he already had had occasion to deliver on similar occasions in various places, to wit: in the province of Simbirsk, at the house of Sophron Ivanovich Bezpechnyi, there being present at the time his daughter Adelaida Sophronovna with three of her sisters-in-law, Maria Gavrilovna, Alexandra Gavrilovna, and Adelheida Gavrilovna; at the house of Fedor Fedorovich Perekroev, in the province of Riazan; at the house of Frol Vasilievich Pobedonosnov, in the province of Penza, and at the house of his brother Peter Vasilievich, there being present at the time his sister-in-law Katherina Mikhailovna and her second cousins Rosa Fedorovna and Emilia Fedorovna; in the province of Viatka, at the house of Peter Varsonophievich, there being present his daughter-in-law's sister Pelagea Igorovna with her niece Sophia Rostislavna and two cousins, Sophia Alexandrovna and Maclatura Alexandrovna.

All the ladies found such conduct on the part of Chichikov not at all to their liking. One of them purposely passed by him, in order to let him see this, and even brushed against the blonde rather carelessly with the rouleau of her dress, while she managed the scarf that was fluttering about her shoulders in such a way that its tip flipped into the girl's very face; at the same time a rather pointed and malicious remark issued, together with the fragrance of violets, from the lips of a lady behind him. Whether he really had not heard it, or merely made believe he had not heard it, doesn't matter; this failure to hear it was still a bad thing, inasmuch as one should value the opinion of ladies. He did repent this, but only later on, and consequently too late.

Indignation, in all respects justifiable, was evinced on many faces. No matter how great Chichikov's weight was in society, and even though he was a millionaire and there was an expression on his face not only of majesty but actually of something Mars-like and military, there are nevertheless things which the ladies won't forgive anybody, no matter who he may be, and in that case you can simply write him off as lost! There are occasions when a woman, no matter how weak and impotent in character she may be in comparison with a man, will yet suddenly become not only harder than any man, but even harder than anything and everything in the world. The neglect shown by Chichikov, though it was almost unintentional, actually brought about among the ladies that accord which had been on the verge of collapse at the time they had been vying for a seat nearest him. They discovered trenchant innuendoes in certain ordinary words he had dropped briefly and utterly at random. To round out the sum of his misfortunes, some one of the younger men had improvised on the spot certain satirical verses on the dancing elite, without which verses, as everybody knows, virtually no provincial dance would be complete. These verses were immediately ascribed to Chichikov. Indignation grew, and in different corners the ladies actually fell to discussing him in a most inauspicious manner; as for the poor boarding-school miss, she was utterly annihilated; her doom was signed and sealed.

And in the meantime an unpleasant surprise, as nasty as nasty could be, was preparing for our hero; at the very point when the little blonde was yawning, the while he was relating to her certain minor incidents which had befallen him at sundry times, and had even just touched upon the Greek philosopher Diogenes—at that very point, coming out of the farthest room, Nozdrev appeared. Whether he had torn himself away from the buffet, or whether he had emerged from the small green drawing room, where a more ardent game than whist was going on, and whether he had emerged of his own free will or had been bounced out, the fact remains that appear he did: jolly, jubilant, clutching the arm of the Public Prosecutor, whom he had probably been dragging along for some time by now, inasmuch as the poor Public Prosecutor was turning his bushy eyebrows every which way, as if he were cudgeling his brains for a way to get out of this personally conducted tour. And, really, it was unbearable. Nozdrev, having sipped courage from two cups of tea (not without rum, of course), was lying away unmercifully. Catching sight of him from afar, Chichikov decided to make an actual sacrifice—that is, to leave his enviable position and, insofar as it was possible, to beat a hasty retreat; this encounter boded him no good. But, as sheer hard luck would have it, the Governor bobbed up, manifesting extraordinary joy at having found Pavel Ivanovich; he detained him and begged him to act as judge in his dispute with two ladies as to whether the love of woman were a lasting thing or no. And meanwhile Nozdrev had caught sight of Chichikov and was heading straight toward him.

"Ah, the landowner of Kherson, the landowner of Kherson!" he kept shouting, walking up to him and emitting peal upon peal of laughter that made his cheeks, as fresh and dewy as a spring rose, quiver. "Well? Have you done a great deal of trading in dead souls? For you don't know, Your Excellency," he bawled right then and there, turning to the Governor, "that he trades in dead souls! By God, he does! I say, Chichikov! Why, what a man you are—I tell you this in friendship, for all of us here are your friends—there, His Excellency is here too—why, I'd string you up, I would, by God!"

Chichikov was utterly dazed.

"Would you believe it, Your Excellency," Nozdrev went on, "when he said to me: 'Sell me some dead souls,' I simply split my sides laughing. I come here, and they tell me that he has bought three millions' worth of serfs for resettlement. What serfs—what resettlement! Why, he was bargaining for dead souls with me! I say, Chichikov, why, you're a beast, by God, but you are! There, even His Excellency right here . . . or you, Prosecutor: isn't that the truth?"

But the Public Prosecutor, and Chichikov, and the Governor himself were thrown into such confusion that they could not think of any answer whatsoever; yet in the meantime Nozdrev, without paying the least heed to anything, was grinding out his half-inebriate, half-sober speech: "Why, you, brother, you . . . you . . . I won't go away from you until I learn why you were buying up dead souls. I say, Chichikov, why, you really ought to be ashamed; you haven't a better friend than I, you know that yourself. . . . There, even His Excellency right here . . . or you, Prosecutor: isn't that the truth? You'd hardly believe, Your Excellency, how attached we are to each other; that is, if you were simply to say—there, I'm standing right here, you know—and you were to say: 'Nozdrev, tell me, upon your conscience, whom do you hold dearer, your own father or Chichikov?'—I'd say: 'Chichikov!' By God, I would. . . . Here, my soul, let me plant a *baiser* on your cheek. Really, Your Excellency, you must permit me to give him a kiss. Yes, Chichikov, don't you be resisting now, let me plant one teeny-weeny *baiser* on your snow-white cheek!"

Nozdrev was pushed back so hard with his *baisers* that he was sent flying and all but fell to the floor. Everybody drew away from him and no one listened to him any more. But just the same what he had said about the buying up of dead souls had been uttered at the top of his voice and had been accompanied with such loud laughter that it had attracted the attention of even those who had been in the farthest corners of the room. This bit of news appeared so strange that all those present stopped still, with some wooden, foolishly questioning air. Chichikov noted that many of the ladies exchanged winks among themselves with malevolent, caustic smiles, and in the expression of certain faces there appeared a something so equivocal that it increased his confusion still more. That Nozdrev was an arrant liar everybody knew, and it wasn't at all a rare thing to hear him spout downright nonsense; but mortal man . . . really, it is hard to comprehend how mortal man is fashioned: no matter how a bit of news may start on its course, just as long as it be news he'll inevitably impart it to some other mortal man, even though it be for no other purpose than to say: "Just see what a lie they've spread around!" And the other mortal man will with pleasure incline his ear, although he'll say in his turn: "Yes, that's a downright vulgar lie, unworthy of any attention what-soever!" And, right after that he won't waste an instant setting out in search of a third mortal man, so that he may, after having retailed the story to him, exclaim in chorus with the latter in noble indignation: "What a vulgar lie!" And this story will inevitably make the rounds of the whole town, and all the mortal men, no matter how many of them there may be, will inevitably have their bellyful of talk, and then will admit that the matter doesn't de-serve any attention and isn't even worth talking about.

This incident, apparently so nonsensical, perceptibly upset our hero. No matter how foolish the words of the fool, yet at times they will suffice to throw a wise man into confusion. Chichikov began to feel ill at ease and out of sorts, every whit as if he had set a beautifully polished boot into a filthy, stinking puddle; in a word, things were bad, downright bad! He tried not to think of it; he tried to distract himself, to find some amusement, to sit down to whist, but everything went as badly as a crooked wheel: twice he played out of turn and, forgetting that it was not up to him to cover the third card, swung back his arm and idiotically covered his own card. The Chairman of the Administrative Offices could not, no matter how he tried, understand how Pavel Ivanovich, who had such a good—and, one might even say such a fine—grasp of the game could make mistakes like that, and even got the best of Pavel Ivanovich's king of spades, in which, according to the latter's own expression, he had placed his trust as in God. Of course the Postmaster and the Chairman of the Administrative Offices, and even the Chief of Police himself, kept twitting our hero in time-honored fashion: Was he in love, perhaps, and we know, now, that Pavel Ivanovich's little heart has been smitten; we know, as well, who loosed the arrow that wounded it. . . . But all this didn't console him in the least, no matter how hard he tried to smile and to return their banter.

At supper, too, he found it impossible to relax, despite the fact that the gathering at the table was a pleasant one and that Nozdrev had long since been led out, inasmuch as the ladies themselves had at last remarked that his conduct was becoming far too *scandaleuse*. At the very height of the cotillion he had plumped down on the floor and begun grabbing the dancers by their skirts and coat-flaps, which, to use an expression of the ladies, was already beyond anything, really. The supper was a very gay one; all the faces, glimpsed between triple candelabra, flowers, bottles, and bonbonnières, were glowing with the most unconstrained pleasure. Army officers, ladies, frock-coated gentlemen—all became amiable, even to the point of being cloying. The gentlemen leapt up from their seats and ran to relieve the waiters of their platters, so as to offer them, with extraordinary adroitness, to the ladies. One colonel offered a sauce-boat to a lady at the end of his unsheathed sword. Men who had attained the decorous age, among whom Chichikov was seated, were carrying on loud discussions, driving home the point of their weighty words with gobs of fish or veal, ruthlessly smothered in mustard, and their discussions dealt with the very subjects in which he always took part; but he looked like a man fatigued or broken up by a prolonged trip, who can't get a thing into his head and who finds it beyond his strength to grasp any matter. He didn't wait for the supper to be over, even, and went home incomparably earlier than he usually did.

There, in that small room which is so familiar to the reader, with the door to the adjoining room blocked off by a bureau, and with the cockroaches occasionally peeping out of their corners, the state of his thoughts and spirit was just as uneasy as that misnamed easy chair in which he was sitting. His heart was troubled, confused; some oppressive void persisted therein.

"May the Devil take all of you who invented these balls!" he soliloquized, heartily vexed. "There, what are they rejoicing over, like so many fools? There are poor crops throughout the province; prices are sky-high—and so they go in for balls! They'll get together for three hours, and there will be enough gossip for three years thereafter. . . . You might think man was an intelligent animal, yet look at how he spends his time! Dances! What a thing to astonish one with, dolling themselves up in womanish rags! What a rare sight, one of them swathing herself in a thousand rubles' worth of trumpery! And all this is at the expense of the serfs' quit-rents or, which is still worse, at the expense of our brother's conscience. For everyone knows why you take a bribe and perjure your soul, so's to get enough for your wife's fancy shawl or all sorts of crinolines, or whatever they call 'em, may they all fall into the bottomless pit! And what's it all about? So that some gossiping Sidorovna, who goes about in a quilted blouse, mightn't say that the Postmaster's wife had a better gown on her than your wife, and over that dressmaker's word bang! goes a thousand rubles. 'A ball! A ball! What fun!' they shout. A ball is just so much rubbishy foolishness. It isn't in the Russian spirit, nor after the Russian nature. The Devil alone knows what it is; a full-grown man, of mature age, will suddenly jump out in the middle of the floor, dressed all in black, all tweezered and slicked up, his clothes so tight-fitting on him that they make him look like an imp, and starts off mincing and prancing. One of these fellows, even while he's paired off for the dance, will be talking some important matter over with another man, yet at the same time his legs will be cutting capers like a young goat's, now to the right, now to the left . . . as if there were fleas biting him! All this out of aping, all this out of aping! Since the Frenchman at forty is as much of an infant as he was at fifteen, let's do the same thing too! No, really . . . after every ball one feels just as if one had committed some sin; one doesn't want even to remind oneself of it. There's simply nothing at all inside your head, as after a conversation with a man from high society: he'll give you a heap of talk about all sorts of things, he'll touch on all things lightly, he'll tell you everything he has gotten a smattering of out of books—motley, pretty talk—but you just go and try to carry anything of it away in your head and you'll see later on that a talk with even a common merchant, who knows nothing but his own business, yet knows it soundly and through experience, is better than all these tinkly baubles. There, what can you squeeze out of it, out of this ball? There, what if we were to suppose that some writer or other had gotten it into his head to describe all this scene, as is? Why, even there, even in a book, it would turn out just as senseless as it is in nature. What is that scene? Is it moral or immoral? Why, only the Devil knows just what it is! You spit in disgust and then slam the book shut."

Thus did Chichikov inveigh against balls in general; but apparently there was still another cause of indignation mixed in here. His chief vexation was not against the ball, but because he had chanced to come a cropper, because he had suddenly appeared before the eyes of all in God knows what guise, because he had played some sort of bizarre, equivocal rôle. Of course, after looking at it with the eye of a prudent, sensible man, he saw that all this was so much bosh, that a foolish word didn't mean a thing, especially now, when the main business had already been fully put through, all right and proper. But man is a strange creature: Chichikov was powerfully aggrieved by the attitude of dislike on the part of those very people for whom he had no respect and of whom he spoke so harshly, condemning their worldly vanity and their gay raiment. This matter was all the more vexatious to him because, having analyzed it clearly, he perceived that he himself had been in part the cause of it. He did not, however, get angry at himself and, of course, was right in this. We all of us have a slight weakness of sparing ourselves a little; we'd rather try to seek out some fellow-man on whom we may vent our chagrin—a servant, for instance, or some petty clerk, some underling of ours who turns up at the opportune moment, one's wife or, finally, a chair, which will be thrown the Devil knows how far, against the very door, so that its back and one of its arms will fly off—there, take that, and know what it means to arouse our wrath!

And so Chichikov, too, speedily found a fellow-man who had to shoulder all that chagrin could inspire our hero with. This fellow-man was none other than Nozdrev, and it need hardly be said that he was so well basted on all sides and quarters as only a knave of a village elder or a stage-coach driver is basted by some experienced army captain who has been around, or occasionally even by a general who, in addition to many expressions which have become classics, will add a great many as yet unknown, the invention of which appertains to him alone. Nozdrev's entire family tree was splintered into kindling, and many members of his family in the ascendant line had to suffer grievously.

But while Chichikov was sitting in his uneasy chair, troubled by his thoughts and sleeplessness, heartily reviling Nozdrev and all his kith and kin, and before him warmly glowed a tallow candle, the wick of which had long since become covered with candle snuff as if with a black cowl and was threatening to go out at any moment, and sightless, black night was peering in at the windows, just about to turn bluish because of the approaching dawn, and roosters, afar off, were exchanging their clarion calls, and throughout the town, all sunk in slumber, there may not have been a soul out on the streets save for some frieze overcoat tipsily weaving along somewhere, some poor wretch, his class and rank unknown, and himself knowing only (alas!) the path, all too deeply beaten and much trodden by the unruly, loose, hard-drinking Russian folk—at this time, in another quarter of the town, an event was taking place which was about to augment the unpleasantness of our hero's position. To be precise, through the remote streets and by-lanes of the town a quite odd vehicle, which made one wonder what name one could give it, was jarringly lumbering along. It resembled neither

2 tarantass, nor a calash, nor a light covered carriage, but rather a round-cheeked, bulging watermelon placed on wheels. The cheeks of this watermelon—i.e., its small doors—which still bore traces of yellow paint, closed but poorly, owing to the sad state of the handles and catches, which were haphazardly tied together with bits of rope. The watermelon was filled to bursting with calico pillows shaped like tobacco pouches, like bolsters, or simply like pillows; it was stuffed with bags of bread loaves (plain and braided), rusks, biscuits, and pretzels of biscuit dough. There was even a chicken pie, and another of salted beef, both peeping coyly out of one of the bags. The foot-board behind was occupied by a person of flunky extraction, in a short jacket of homespun striped ticking, his chin unshaven and his head slightly grizzled—a person usually described as a *lad*. The noise and whining from the iron clamps and rusty bolts awakened, at the other end of the town, a sentry in his box, who, picking up his halberd, set up a shout with all his might, though still half asleep: "Who goes there?" But, perceiving that no one was going there and that there was only a clatter of wheels in the distance, he contented himself with catching some beastie or other on his coat-collar and, walking up to a street lamp, executing it summarily on his thumb-nail, after which, putting his halberd away in a corner, he again fell asleep, according to all the canons of his order of knighthood.

The horses were forever stumbling to their foreknees, inasmuch as they were not shod and, in addition to that, had but little acquaintance with the restful paved road of the town. This antediluvian shandrydan, having made several turns from one street to another, finally turned into a dark by-lane near the small parish church of Nikola-Out-in-the-Sticks, and stopped before the house of the Dean's wife. A wench with a kerchief on her head and dressed in a warm, sleeveless jacket, crawled out of the vehicle and began pounding with her fists on the gate as hard as any man could have done (the lad in the short jacket of striped ticking was only later on dragged off his perch by his feet, inasmuch as he was sleeping the sleep of the dead). Dogs began barking, and the gates, gaping open at last, swallowed, though with difficulty, this cumbersome conveyance. It drove into a crowded yard, cluttered with firewood, hen-houses, and all sorts of flimsy coops and hutches; a gentlewoman crawled out of the vehicle, this gentlewoman being none other than Korobochka the landowner, relict of a Collegiate Secretary. Soon after our hero's departure the little crone had been overcome by such uneasiness about a possible raw deal on his part that, after losing sleep for three nights in a row, she had decided to go into town—despite the fact that her horses were not shod—and there learn for sure what dead souls were fetching and whether she hadn't—God forbid!—missed a trick in selling them for what may have been next to nothing. What effect this arrival brought about the reader may learn from a certain conversation which took place between two ladies. This conversation . . . but better let this conversation come in the next chapter.

CHAPTER NINE

IN the morning, even before the time which is in the town of N—— set aside for paying calls, out of the doors of a wooden house painted orange, with a mezzanine and blue pillars, fluttered a lady in an elegant checkered cloak, escorted by a footman in a great-coat with a cascade of collars and with a gold galloon on his round, sleek hat. The lady instantly, with inordinate haste, fluttered up the let-down steps into a barouche standing near the entrance. The footman at once slammed the carriage door shut after his mistress, folded up the steps and, grabbing hold of the straps behind the barouche, shouted to the coachman: "Let 'er go!" The lady was the bearer of a bit of news she had just heard and felt an insuperable urge to impart it to somebody as quickly as possible. She looked out of the carriage window every minute and saw, to her unutterable vexation, that half her journey lay still ahead of her. Each house front seemed to her wider than usual; the white, stone poor-house with its narrow small windows stretched out for an insufferably long time, so that she could not restrain herself from saying at last: "What a confounded building—there's never an end to it!" The coachman had already received his commands twice: "Faster, faster, Andriushka! You're driving unbearably slowly today!"

Finally the goal was reached. The barouche came to a stop before a house that was also of wood, one-storied, of a dark-gray hue, with small white bas-reliefs above the windows and a high wooden trellis right in front of them, and a cramped little garden in front, behind the pallisade of which the puny little trees had turned white from the town dust that never forsook them. Through the windows one could glimpse flower-pots, a parrot swaying in its cage, hanging onto a ring with its beak, and two lap-dogs snoozing in the sun. In this house lived the closest and truest feminine friend of the lady who had just arrived. The author is very hard put to it to name both ladies in such a way as not to make them angry at him, as they used to be angry in the old days. To give them fictitious names is fraught with danger. No matter what name you think up, there will inevitably be found in some corner or other of our realm, blessedly great though it be, someone who bears it, and who will inevitably become incensed not only to the extent of wishing to beat me within an inch of my life, but actually to death, who will begin saying that the author had purposely made a secret trip to the town to find out everything and will tell you just what sort of creature the author himself is, and what sort of wretched little sheepskin jacket he walks around in, and which Agraphena Ivanovna he calls on, and what dishes he's fond of. But if one were to mention ranks —God save us, that would be still more dangerous! Nowadays all our ranks and classes are in so touchy a mood that anything and everything which may be between the covers of a printed book already has the appearance of personalities for them—such, evidently, is the spirit in the air. It suffices merely to say that there's a stupid man in a certain town, and that's already a personal reflection: a gentleman of respectable appearance will suddenly pounce upon you and set up a shout: "Why, I, too, am a man; ergo, I, too, am stupid!"—in a word, he'll surmise in the wink of an eye just what you're up to.

And therefore, for the avoidance of all this, let's call the lady whom the guest had come to see what she was almost unanimously called in the town of N——: a lady agreeable in all respects. This appellation she had acquired quite legitimately, inasmuch as she truly enough hadn't spared any pains to make herself amiable to the utmost degree even though, of course, there could be glimpsed through her amiability an—ooh, ever so brisk!—liveliness of a feminine nature; and even though, on occasion, pins and needles —ooh, ever so piercing!—would be poking up through some pleasant word of hers. And may God avert that which seethed within her heart against her who had in some way and through some means wormed her way through into the front ranks. But all this was clothed in the most refined social grace, such as is to be found only in a provincial capital. She performed every move with taste, was even fond of verse, even knew how to keep her head in a dreamy pose at times, and everybody concurred that she was, really, a lady who was agreeable in all respects.

As for the other lady—that is, the one who has just arrived—her character did not have so many aspects, and for that reason we'll call her a lady who was simply agreeable.

The arrival of the guest had awakened the lap-dogs snoozing in the sun: the shaggy Adele, who was forever tangling up in her long wool, and the darling little hound Potpourri, who had such darling, slender little legs. Both the one and the other, barking, their tails curled into rings, dashed into the foyer, where the guest was divesting herself of her cloak, revealing at last a dress of modish color and design, with long streamers at the neck; jasmine was wafted all over the room. Barely had the lady who was agreeable in all respects learned of the arrival of the lady who was simply agreeable when she had already run out into the foyer. The ladies seized each other's hands, kissed, and screamed, as boarding-school misses scream at a reunion shortly after graduation, before their mammas have yet had a chance to explain to them that the father of one of them is poorer and of lower rank than the father of the other. The kiss was consummated sonorously, inasmuch as the lapdogs had begun barking anew, for which they were flicked with a handkerchief, and both ladies went into the drawing room—blue, naturally, with a divan, an oval table, and even small screens, with ivy twining over them; after them ran the shaggy Adele, growling, and tall Potpourri, on his darling, slender little legs.

"Here, here, in this little nook," the hostess was saying, seating her guest in a corner of the divan. "There, that's it! There, that's it! There's a cushion for you, too!" Having said which she thrust a cushion behind her guest's back, which cushion had a knight embroidered in wool upon it, in that invariable fashion in which all knights are embroidered on canvas: the nose had come out as a ladder and the lips as a quadrangle. "But how happy I am that it's you! . . . I hear somebody driving up, and I think to myself, who could it be, as early as this? Parasha says: 'It's the Vice-Governor's lady,' and I say: 'There, that fool has come to bore me again!' and was on the very verge of saying that I was not at home—"

The guest was just about to get down to business and impart her news, but an exclamation emitted at this point by the lady who was agreeable in all respects suddenly gave a different turn to the conversation.

"What a cheerful little print!" exclaimed the lady who was agreeable in all respects, gazing at the dress of the lady who was simply agreeable.

"Yes, it's very cheerful. Praskovia Fedorovna, however, thinks that it would be better if the checks were somewhat smaller, and if the polka dots weren't brown but blue. I sent some material to my sister—it's so bewitching that one simply can't express it in words. Just imagine: teeny-weeny stripes, so-o-o narrow, as narrow as human imagination can picture; the background is blue, and running across the stripe is a design of little eyes and tiny paws, little eyes and tiny paws, all over. . . . In a word, it's beyond all compare! One can say positively that there's never been anything like it in all the world!"

"My dear, but that's so loud!"

"Ah, no! It isn't loud at all!"

"Ah, but it is!"

It must be remarked that the lady who was agreeable in all respects was very much of a materialist, inclined to negation and skepticism, and that she rejected quite a few things in life.

At this point the lady who was simply agreeable explained that it was not at all loud, and then cried out: "Yes, allow me to congratulate you—flounces are no longer being worn."

"What—they aren't?"

"Little scallops will be worn instead."

"Ah, that isn't pretty! Little scallops, indeed!"

"Little scallops—little scallops are all the go; a pelerine all of little scallops; little scallops on the sleeves; epaulets of little scallops; little scallops below, little scallops everywhere!"

"It isn't pretty, Sophia Ivanovna, not if the whole thing is in little scallops."

"It's darling, Anna Grigoriyevna, you'd hardly believe how darling it is: you sew them in two ruchings, with wide armholes, and then, on top . . . But there, here's something that will simply amaze you; here's where you'll say that . . . there, you'll be amazed: just imagine, they've started making the bodices still longer, with a sort of little peak in front, and the front whalebone going entirely out of bounds; the skirt is gathered all around, the way they used to have their farthingales in the old days—they even pad the back a little with cotton-wool, actually, so as to make one a perfect *belle femme*."

"Well, now, this is really . . . I must confess!" said the lady who was agreeable in all respects, tossing her head with a feeling of dignity.

"Just so, it really is, I must confess too!" answered the lady who was simply agreeable.

"You may do whatever you wish, but I'm not going to ape that for anything."

"Nor I. . . . Really, when one imagines to what lengths fashion will go at times . . . it's beyond anything! I wheedled a pattern out of my sister, just for the fun of the thing; my Melania has started in sewing it."

"Why, have you really got a pattern?" cried out the lady who was agreeable in all respects, not without a perceptible flutter of her heart.

"But of course; my sister brought it with her."

"Let me have it, my soul, for the sake of all that's holy!"

"Ah, I've already given my word to Praskovia Fedorovna. After her, perhaps."

"But who's going to wear anything after Praskovia Fedorovna? It would be far too peculiar on your part if you were to give preference to strangers above your close friends."

"Yes, but she's also a grand-aunt of mine."

"God knows what sort of an aunt she is to you, on your husband's side. . . . No, Sophia Ivanovna, I won't even listen to anything; it looks as if you actually wanted to insult me. . . . Evidently you've already tired of me, evidently you want to break off your whole friendship with me."

Poor Sophia Ivanovna didn't know what to do. She herself felt in what a terrific cross-fire she had placed herself. There, she had to go and brag! She was ready to stick her silly tongue as full of pins as a pincushion for this.

"Well, and what about our seductive Adonis?" the lady who was agreeable in all respects was asking in the meantime.

"Ah, my God! Why am I sitting here like this? That's a fine thing! Why, Anna Grigoryevna, do you know the reason for my coming to you?" At this point the visitor's breath failed her; the words were ready to start flying like hawks out of her mouth, one after another, and one had to be inhuman to the same degree as her bosom friend to venture upon stopping her.

"No matter how you may sing his praises and exalt him," that friend was saying with animation, "I'll nevertheless tell you outright, and I'll even tell him so to his very face, that he's a worthless man—worthless, worthless, worthless!"

"Yes, but do listen to what I'm going to tell you—"

"They've spread it about that he's a fine man, but he isn't fine at all, he isn't, not at all; and his nose . . . is a most odious nose."

"But allow me, do but allow me to tell you . . . Anna Grigoryevna, my dearest darling, do allow me to tell you! Why, this is a whole story, do you understand? *Ce qu'on appelle histoire!* * the caller was saying, with an expression verging on despair and in an utterly imploring voice. It might not be amiss to remark that very many foreign words were interspersed in the speech of both ladies

---

* "It's a story that one can call a story!" *Trans.*

and at times there would be whole long phrases in French. But no matter how imbued with reverent awe the author is toward those great benefits which the French tongue confers upon Russia, no matter how imbued he is therewith for the praiseworthy custom of our higher society, which expresses itself in that language at all the hours of the day and night (of course out of a profound feeling of love for their native land), yet with all that he simply cannot bring himself to introduce a phrase from any alien tongue into this Russian epic of his. And so, let's go on without any foreign phrases.

"But what's the story?"

"Ah, Anna Grigoryevna, my life! If you could but fancy the situation in which I found myself! Just imagine: the Dean's wife comes to me—the Dean's wife, you know, the wife of Father Cyril —and what do you think? Our visitor, now, in whose mouth butter wouldn't melt, what sort of a fellow do you think he is, eh?"

"What, can it be possible that he's been dangling after the Dean's wife too?"

"Ah, Anna Grigoryevna, if it had been only a matter of dangling it would be nothing. Do but listen to what the Dean's wife told me. A certain landowner, she says, by the name of Korobochka, arrived at her house, frightened out of her wits and as pale as death, and she has a story to tell—and what a story! Do but listen, it's for all the world like a story book: suddenly, in the dead of night, a most dreadful knocking resounds at her gates, such knocking as you can't imagine, and followed by shouts: 'Open up, open up, or we'll break down the gates! . . .' How does that strike you? What sort of a seductive Adonis is he, after that?"

"But what about Korobochka? Why, is she young and good-looking?"

"Not in the least; she's an old woman."

"Ah, how charming! So he's going after an old woman now? Well, after this, the taste of our ladies must be a fine one; they surely have found somebody worth falling in love with!"

"But it isn't that, Anna Grigoryevna, it isn't at all the way you suppose. Just imagine this to yourself: a man armed from head to foot appears on the scene, on the style of that great brigand Rinaldo

Rinaldini, and demands: 'Sell me,' he says, 'all the souls who have died!' Korobochka answers him, reasonably enough, telling him: 'I can't sell them to you, because they're dead.'—'No,' says he, 'they're not dead. It's up to me to decide,' he says, 'if they're dead or not; they are not dead, they aren't!' he yells. 'They aren't!' In a word, he created a terribly *scandaleuse* commotion: the whole village came on the run, children bawling, everybody shouting, nobody can understand anybody else—well, it was simply *horreur, horreur, horreur!* . . . But you can't even imagine, Anna Grigoryevna, how upset I got when I heard all this. 'My mistress, darling,' Mashka says to me, 'do take a look in the mirror, you're all pale!'— 'I've no time for mirrors now,' I tell her, 'I must dash over to Anna Grigoryevna and tell her everything!' That same moment I give orders to have the barouche harnessed; Andriushka, my coachman, asks me where he's to drive to, but I can't utter even a word; I stare him right in the eyes, like a fool. I think he must have thought me mad. Ah, Anna Grigoryevna, if you could but picture to yourself how upset I became over all this!"

"This is quite bizarre, though," said the lady who was agreeable in all respects. "What in the world could these dead souls signify? I understand precisely nothing of all this, I must confess. There, it's the second time that I'm hearing about these same dead souls, and on top of that my husband tells me that Nozdrev is lying: surely, then, there's bound to be something in it, after all."

"But do picture to yourself, Anna Grigoryevna, the situation I was in when I heard that. 'And now,' says Korobochka, 'I don't know,' she says, 'what I am to do. He forced me,' says she, 'to sign a forged paper of some sort and threw down fifteen roubles in government notes. I,' she says, 'am an inexperienced, helpless widow woman, I don't know a thing. . . .' So that's the kind of things that go on around us! But if you could only picture to yourself, if even just a little, how thoroughly upset I was!"

"Well, just as you will, but this isn't at all a matter of dead souls; there's something else going on, hiding behind all this."

"I, too, have been thinking the same thing, I must confess," said the lady who was simply agreeable, not without surprise, and instantly felt a strong urge to learn just what that something hiding behind all this might be. She even said, slowly: "And what do you suppose is going on?"

"Well, what do you think?"

"What do I think? . . . I am, I confess, totally at a loss."

"Well, just the same, I'd like to know what your ideas are about this?"

But the lady who was simply agreeable couldn't find anything to say at this point. All she knew was how to get upset, but the ability of forming some sagacious supposition was utterly lacking in her, and hence, more so than any other woman, she had need of tender friendship and of counsel.

"Very well, then, listen to what sort of thing these dead souls are," said the lady who was agreeable in all respects, and her visitor, at these words, became all attention: her little ears perked up of themselves, she sat up very straight, so precariously perched on the divan that one wondered how she retained her seat and, despite the fact that she ran somewhat to embonpoint, suddenly grew slimmer, and as light as a swan's down, apt to go sailing through the air at the least puff.

Thus a Russian squire, a great lover of dogs and a very Nimrod, on approaching a forest out of which a hare tracked down by beaters is about to emerge, becomes all transformed, with his mount and long whip, within one congealed moment, into gunpowder ready to be touched off at any instant. He is all eyes, piercing the murky air, and will infallibly overtake the beast, will infallibly finish it off, being irresistible, no matter how the whole snowy steppe may rise up and storm against him, hurling silvery star-shaped snowflakes against his lips, his mustache, his eyes, his eyebrows, and his beaver cap.

"The dead souls are—" began the lady who was agreeable in all respects.

"What are they, what are they?" her guest caught her up, all aquiver.

"—dead souls! . . ."

"Ah, do tell me, for God's sake!"

"All this is simply an invention that serves as a blind; but the real thing is this: he wants to carry off the Governor's daughter."

This conclusion was truly unexpected and an unusual one in every way. The lady who was simply agreeable, upon hearing this, just turned to stone where she sat; she grew paler and paler, as pale as death, and this time became upset in earnest.

"Ah, my God!" she cried out, wringing her hands. "Well, that's something I could never have supposed!"

"But I, I confess, as soon as you opened your mouth, had already surmised what was what," answered the lady who was agreeable in all respects.

"But, after this, Anna Grigoryevna, what do they teach these hussies in boarding schools! There's innocence for you!"

"What innocence! I heard her saying such things as, I must confess, I'd never have the courage to repeat."

"Why, do you know, Anna Grigoryevna, it simply rends one's heart when one sees what limits immorality has reached at last!"

"And yet the men lose their heads over her. But if you were to ask me, I must confess I can't see a thing in her. . . . She's unbearably affected."

"Ah, Anna Grigoryevna, my soul! She's a stone image—if only there were the least expression in her face."

"Oh, and *how* affected! Oh, how affected! God, how affected! Who taught her all that I don't know, I'm sure, but never yet have I seen a creature with so much namby-pambiness about her."

"Why, dearest darling! She's a stone image, and as pale as death."

"Ah, don't say that, Sophia Ivanovna: she rouges unmercifully."

"Ah, what are you saying, Anna Grigoryevna. She is chalk, chalk, simply chalk!"

"Darling, I was sitting right next to her, I ought to know: she had rouge on her a finger thick and peeling off in chunks, like plaster. Her mother taught her; she's a coquette herself, and the daughter will yet surpass her dear mother."

"Oh, no, if you please, oh, no; you can ask me to take any oath you like on it; I'm ready, right here and now, to lose my children, my husband, all our estate, if she has even one tiny drop, even one little particle, even a shadow of red in her cheeks!"

"Ah, what are you saying, Sophia Ivanovna!" said the lady who was agreeable in all respects, and wrung her hands.

"Ah, really, Anna Grigoryevna, how can you be like that! I'm really amazed at you!" said the simply agreeable lady and wrung her hands in turn.

But let it not seem strange to the reader that both ladies could not come to an agreement as to what they had seen at almost one and the same time. There really are in this world many things which do have that very peculiarity: if one lady will take a look at them, they'll turn out to be perfectly white, whereas if another lady takes a look at them they'll turn out to be red, red as bilberries.

"Well, here's one more proof for you that she's pale," the lady who was simply agreeable went on. "I remember, as if it were right now, that I was sitting next to Manilov, and I said to him: 'Look, how pale she is!' Really, one must be as addle-pated as our men are to go into raptures over her. And as for our seductive Adonis . . . ah, how repulsive he seemed to me! You can't picture, Anna Grigoryevna, how very, very repulsive he seemed to me."

"And yet, just the same, there were certain ladies who were not at all indifferent toward him."

"I, Anna Grigoryevna? There, now, you can never say that, never, never!"

"Why, I'm not talking about you. As though there were nobody else in the world outside of yourself!"

"Never, never, Anna Grigoryevna! Permit me to tell you that I know myself very well; but as for certain other ladies, perhaps, who assume the rôle of being unattainable—"

"Really, you must excuse me, Sophia Ivanovna! You must really permit me to tell you that I've never yet indulged in such *scandaleuse* goings on. In the case of anybody else, perhaps, but never in mine—you must really allow me to point this out to you."

"But just why have you taken offense? For there were also other ladies present there who had been the first to grab that chair near the door so as to sit nearer to him."

Well, now, after such words as these, uttered by the lady who was simply agreeable, a storm was inevitably bound to break; but, most amazingly, both ladies suddenly quieted down, and nothing whatsoever ensued. The lady who was agreeable in all respects recalled that the pattern for the latest thing in dresses was still not in her hands, while the lady who was simply agreeable surmised that she had not yet contrived to extract any details as to the discovery made by her friend, and therefore peace followed very shortly. However, it could not be said of both these ladies that a necessity for saying mean things was a part of their natures, and in general there was nothing of the malicious about their characters; but, just so, without their sensing it, a slight desire to be catty to each other would be engendered of itself in their conversation; one of them, for the sake of a little gratification, would, when the occasion arose, slip in a lively word or so: "There, now, that for you! There, have a taste of that!" Of various kinds are the urgings of the heart in mankind—and womankind.

"However, there's one thing that I can't understand," said the lady who was simply agreeable. "How could Chichikov, being merely a visitor in town, ever find the hardihood for such an escapade? It's impossible that there should be no accomplices involved here."

"And do you think there aren't any?"

"And who do you suppose could be helping them?"

"Well, why not Nozdrev himself?"

"Can it possibly be Nozdrev?"

"Who else, then? Why, that would be his very dish. You know he wanted to sell his own father or, better still, to lose him at cards."

"Ah, my God, what interesting things I'm learning from you! I could never under any circumstances have supposed that Nozdrev, too, is mixed up in this affair!"

"Well, I always did suppose that."

"When one comes to think of it, really, what things don't go on in this world! There, now, could one have supposed, at the time when Chichikov—do you remember?—had just arrived in our town, that he would create such a strange stir in the world? Ah, Anna Grigoryevna, if you but knew how all upset I was! If it were not for your affability and friendship . . . There, really, I was already on the very verge of passing out. Where was I to go? My Mashka sees that I'm as pale as death. 'Mistress, dearest darling,' she says to me, 'you're as pale as death!'—'Mashka,' I tell her, 'I have no time for that now!' So that's how things are! And so Nozdrev is in this too! Well, I never!"

The lady who was simply agreeable wanted very much to worm out further details as to the elopement—that is, what night and hour it was set for, and so on; what she wanted, however, was far too much. The lady who was agreeable in all respects reacted firmly by claiming to know nothing. She did not know how to lie; to suppose something or other was another matter, but even that held good only in a case where the supposition was based upon an inner conviction. Once an inner conviction was felt, she could stand up for herself; and were some expert advocate, celebrated for his gift of overcoming the opinions of others, to attempt a contest in such a case, he would have perceived what an inner conviction meant.

There is nothing unusual about the fact that both ladies became at last utterly convinced of that which hitherto they had merely assumed and known to be a mere assumption. Our fraternity—we intelligent people, as we style ourselves—acts in almost the same way, and our learned ratiocinations serve as a proof of this. At first the savant, when it comes to such things, will steal up on them as a most arrant knave, cringing and wheedling: he'll start off timidly, moderately; he'll start off by posing a most modest query: Is this not derived from that? Is it not from this locality that such-and-such a country has received its name? Or: Does not this document appertain to another, later period? Or: Do we not have to understand, under the name of this nation, that other nation? Without losing any time, he will cite this ancient writer and that, and no sooner does he perceive some hint or other of what he's after, or simply what seems a hint to him, than he already puts on speed and takes heart, talks with the ancient writers without standing on ceremony, puts questions to them, and even answers for them himself, forgetting altogether that he had started off with a timid assumption. It seems to him by now that he perceives the point, that it is clearly evident, and his ratiocination concludes with the words: And it was thus that this event came about! It is such-and-such a nation that we must understand under the name of that other! And so it is from this point of view that we must regard the subject. Then he proclaims it for all the world to hear, ex cathedra, and the newly discovered truth is off on its jaunty travels through the world, gathering unto itself followers and devotees.

Just as both ladies had so successfully and wittily resolved such a tangled situation, the Public Prosecutor, with his perpetually frozen physiognomy, his bushy brows and winking eye, entered the drawing room. The ladies, breaking in on each other, began imparting all these events to him; they told him about the purchase of dead souls, about the contemplated carrying-off of the Governor's daughter, and got him to the point where he absolutely did not know what was what, so that, no matter how long he continued standing on the same spot, batting his left eye and flicking his beard with his handkerchief, whisking the snuff off it, he still could make neither head nor tail of anything. In the end both ladies left him standing there and each went her way to stir up the town.

This enterprise they contrived to carry out in just a trifle over half an hour. The town was positively stirred up; everything was in a ferment—and if there were but one body that could make out anything! The ladies were so successful in beclouding the eyes of everybody that all, and especially the officials and clerks, were left stunned for some time. During the first moment their state was like that of a schoolboy up whose nose, while he's asleep, his mates, who have risen before him, have thrust a *hussar,* a small twist of paper filled with snuff. Having in his half-sleep drawn in all that snuff with all the heartiness of a sleeper, he awakens, jumps up, stares about him like a fool, his eyes popping in all directions, and can't grasp where he is or what has happened to him, and only later does he make out the walls lit by the indirect rays of the rising sun, the laughter of his mates, who have hidden themselves in corners, and the arrival of morning as it peeps in through the window, to the accompaniment of the awakened forest, resounding with thousands of bird voices, and a glimpse of a shining river, disappearing here and there in glittering eddies between slender reeds and with clusters of naked urchins everywhere, egging on one another to dive in—and only after he has taken all this in does the victim become aware that there's a hussar stuck up his nose. This, to perfection, was the state during the first flush of the inhabitants and officials of the town. Each one would come to a dead stop, like a ram, with his eyes bulging. The dead souls, the Governor's daughter, and Chichikov became churned and confounded in their heads in an extraordinarily odd fashion; and only later on, after the first stupefaction, they began, but only apparently, to distinguish each factor and to separate it from the others, began to demand an explanation and to become angry on seeing that the matter would in no wise explain itself.

"After all, what sort of a parable is this, really? What sort of a parable are these dead souls? There's no logic to dead souls; how, then, can one buy up dead souls? Where would you ever dig up a fool big enough to buy them? And what sort of fairy-gold would he use to buy them? And to what end, for what business, could one utilize these dead souls? And how on earth has the Governor's daughter gotten mixed up in here? If he really did want to carry her off, then why did he have to buy up dead souls for that? And if he really wanted to buy up dead souls, then what for would he want to be carrying off the Governor's daughter? Was he after making her a present of these dead souls, or what? And really, when you came down to it, what sort of poppycock had they spread through the town? What in the world are things coming to when, before you can as much as turn around, they've already up and spread a story like that? And if only there were the least sense to it. . . . However, spread it they did, therefore there must have been *some* reason to it. . . . But what reason can there be to dead souls? Why, there just isn't any! All this is simply the Devil riding on a fiddlestick, so much moonshine, stuff and nonsense, pigeon milk and horse feathers! This is, simply—oh, may the Devil take it all! . . ."

In a word, rumors upon rumors flew on their merry way and the whole town began talking of dead souls and the Governor's daughter, of Chichikov and the dead souls, of the Governor's daughter and Chichikov, and the whole mess stirred and rose. The whole town, which up to now seemed to be dozing, swirled up like a whirlwind. All the lie-abeds and sit-by-the-fires who had been lolling and vegetating at home in their dressing-gowns for years, placing the blame for their indolence either upon the bungling bootmaker who had made their boots too tight, or on their worthless tailor, or on their drunkard of a coachman, now came crawling out of their holes; all those who had long since terminated all their friendships and who, as the expression goes, knew only those two worthy landowners, Zavalishin and Polezhaev (famous terms, these, derived from the infinitives *to hit the hay* and *to lie down for a forty-winks,* which have great currency among us in Russia, on an equal footing with the phrase "to drop in on Sopikov and Khrapovitski" [Wheezer and Snoreaway], designating any and every manner of sleeping like the dead, on one's side, flat on one's back, and in all other positions, to the accompaniment of window-shattering snores, nasal flute arias, and other such obbligatos) ; all those whom you could never entice out of their houses even with an invitation to partake of a fish chowder costing five hundred rubles, cooked with sturgeons five feet long and served with all sorts of pastries that would melt in your mouth—well, even all these came crawling out of their holes. In short, it turned out that the town was bustling enough and great enough and as well populated as need be.

Some Sysoi Paphnutievich or other and a certain Macdonald Karlovich, both of whom no one had even heard of before, bobbed up on the scene; some sort of individual, as lanky as lanky could be, one of whose hands had been shot through, of a stature so tall that its like had never been seen, became a fixture in the drawing rooms. The streets became thronged with ordinary covered droshkies, with unbelievable droshkies of another sort, wide and of infinite seating capacity, with arks that clattered along and arks whose wheels squealed and whined—and the fat was in the fire. Some other time and under different circumstances such rumors might have attracted no attention at all to themselves, but it was a long time that the town of N—— had been getting no news whatsoever. There had not been, for the space of three months, anything occurring, even anything of that which, in our capitals, is called *commérages,* or comethers, which, as everybody knows, are the same thing to a town as the timely arrival of a food-supply transport is to an army.

Amid all this town tittle-tattle there suddenly turned out to be two diametrically opposed schools of thought, and two diametrically opposed parties were suddenly formed: the masculine and the feminine. The masculine party, being the most addle-pated, turned its attention upon the dead souls. The feminine party busied itself exclusively with the carrying-off of the Governor's daughter. In this party, it must be remarked to the credit of the ladies, there was incomparably more orderliness and circumspection. Such evidently is their very function, to be good mistresses of households and good organizers. In a very short while everything with them took on an animated, definite air, assuming clear and self-evident forms; everything became explained, clarified; in short, the result was a finished little masterpiece. It turned out that Chichikov had already been in love for a long time, and the pair had been meeting each other in a garden by moonlight; that the Governor would long since have given him his daughter, since Chichikov was simply made of money, had it not been for Chichikov's wife, whom he had abandoned (whence they had learned that Chichikov was married, no one could tell), and that the wife, who was suffering because she was hopelessly in love with him, had written a most touching letter to the Governor, and that Chichikov, perceiving that the blonde's father and mother would never give their consent, had decided upon an abduction.

In other houses this story was told somewhat differently: that Chichikov didn't have any wife at all, at all, but that he, as a man of finesse and one who always preferred to play a sure thing, had, in order to get the daughter's hand, begun matters with the mother, and had a secret affair of the heart with her, and that later on he had made a declaration concerning the daughter's hand, but that the mother, having become frightened lest such a sacrilege take place, and her soul experiencing the pangs of conscience, had rejected him flatly—and that was why Chichikov had decided upon an abduction. To all this there were joined many explanations and emendations, in keeping with the pace at which the rumors finally penetrated into the most god-forsaken blind alleys. For in Russia the lower social strata are very fond of chewing over bits of gossip about the upper strata, and therefore they began talking about this affair even in those humble houses where the people had never even set their eyes on or heard tell of Chichikov, launching addenda and even greater elucidations in their turn.

The subject was becoming more entertaining with every minute; it took on with every day more definitive forms, and at last, just as it was, in all its definitiveness, was brought to the very ears of the Governor's lady herself. The Governor's lady, as the mother of a family, as the first lady in town, finally as a lady who had not suspected anything of the sort, was absolutely insulted by such stories and was thrown into indignation, a just one in all respects. The poor little blonde went through the most unpleasant tête-à-tête that had ever befallen a girl of sixteen. Whole torrents of interrogations, inquisitions, reprimands, threats, reproaches, and exhortations were loosed, so that the girl threw herself down in tears, sobbed, and could not understand a single word; the doorman was given the strictest orders not to admit Chichikov at any time or under any pretext.

Having accomplished their work as far as the Governor's lady was concerned, the ladies exerted themselves to press the masculine party hard, trying to incline the weaklings to their side and asserting that the dead souls were all a fiction and that that fiction had been used merely to divert all suspicion and the more successfully to carry out the abduction. Many of the men actually deserted and went over to the feminine party, despite the fact that they were subjected to powerful recriminations from their very fellows, who cursed them out as old women and weak sisters, names which are, as everyone knows, most derogatory to the masculine sex.

But, no matter how the men armed themselves and resisted, in their party there was no such discipline as in the feminine. Everything with them was somehow coarse, unfinished, clumsy, unfit, ill-made, no good at all; their heads were filled with commotion, hurly-burly, muddlement, slovenliness of thoughts—in a word, everything manifested the nature of the male, which is vacuous in all things, a nature that is coarse, ponderous, incapable either of running a household or of heart-felt convictions, of little faith, lazy, filled with incessant doubts and perpetual apprehension. The men maintained that all this was so much bosh, that such a business

· 223

as the abduction of a Governor's daughter was work cut out more for hussars than for civilians, that Chichikov wouldn't do a thing like that, that the women were lying, that a woman was like a sack —she'll take in anything, carry it along, and then pour it out of her mouth; that the main thing to pay attention to was the dead souls; however, the Devil alone knew what they signified, but just the same there was something quite nasty, quite bad about them. Why it seemed to the men that there was something nasty and bad about these souls we shall learn immediately. A new Governor-General had been appointed for the province, an event which, as everybody knows, puts officialdom in a state of alarm: there would be a succession of shake-ups, dressings-down, rakings over the coals, and all sorts of such-like fare with which a superior in Civil Service regales his subordinates. "Well, now," the officials pondered, "what if he were merely to find out that silly rumors like that were going round in this town? Why, for that one thing alone he's likely to blow up, and it won't be a matter of saving your skin then, but your very life!" The Inspector of the Board of Health suddenly paled, seeing in his imagination God knows what: whether by the phrase *dead souls* were not meant those patients who had died in considerable numbers in the infirmaries and similar institutions from an epidemic fever against which no adequate measures had been taken, and whether Chichikov were not an official sent from the chancellery of the Governor-General to conduct a secret investigation.

He imparted these notions to the Chairman of the Administrative Offices. The Chairman of the Administrative Offices pooh-poohed the idea, and then turned pale, putting to himself the question: But what if the souls bought up by Chichikov were really dead? And yet he had permitted purchase-deeds to be executed, and not only that but he himself had played the rôle of Plushkin's agent, and were this to reach the knowledge of the Governor-General, what would happen then?

He did nothing more about this, outside of mentioning it to this one and that one, and suddenly this one and that one turned pale: fear is more catching than the plague and is communicated in an instant. All suddenly sought out in themselves such sins as they hadn't even committed. The phrase *dead souls* had such an ominously ambiguous ring about it that people began suspecting whether there might not be lurking therein some hint as to certain bodies that had to be hurriedly buried in consequence of two events that had happened not so long before. The first event had to do with certain merchants of Solvychegodsk who had come to town to attend a fair and who, after their trading, had tendered a small spree to their friends, certain merchants of Ustsysolsk, a little spree with a Russian sweep, but with a few German trimmings: orgeats, punches, balsams, and the like. The little spree had ended, as is usually the way, with a free-for-all. The men of Solvychegodsk had done in those of Ustsysolsk, even though they had received plenty from them in the way of broken ribs, wallops in the giblets, and biffs on the button, testifying to the inordinate size of the fists the late lamented had been endowed with. One of the victors even had had his air-pump, to use an expression of the fighters, broken off— that is, his whole nose had been beaten to such a pulp that there wasn't even half a finger's length of it left on his face. The merchants pleaded guilty in the affair, giving as an explanation that they'd been having a little fun. There were rumors current that in pleading guilty each of the defendants had apparently put in four additional pleas, printed by the government at some expense; however, the matter is too obscure; from the interrogations and investigations undertaken it turned out that the Ustsysolsk lads had died of charcoal fumes engendered by a faulty heating system, and hence they were so buried, as victims of suffocation by carbonic gas.

The other occurrence, which had happened not so long ago, was as follows: the government serfs from the hamlet of Vshivaya Spess (Lousy-Pride), having joined forces with the same category of serfs from the hamlet of Borovka, named after a species of edible mushroom, and also called Zadirailovo (or Quarrelsome), had, it would seem, wiped the Rural Police off the face of the earth, in the person of its Assessor, some Drobyazhkin or other; apparently the Rural Police—that is, Drobyazhkin the Assessor—had got into the habit of coming to their village far too often (which, in certain cases, is as bad as any epidemic fever), the reason therefor being that the Rural Police, having a certain weakness in matters of the heart, had been eying the wives and wenches of the village. However, the facts are not known definitely, although in their testimony the peasants expressed themselves forthrightly that the Rural Police, now, was as lickerish as a tom-cat, and that they'd given him warning more nor once, and at one time had even driven him mother-naked out of one of the huts into which he'd made his way. Of course the Rural Police deserved punishment for his frailties of the heart, but at the same time the peasants of Lousy-Pride, as well as those of the hamlet of Quarrelsome, could not be acquitted, either, for having taken the law into their own hands, provided they had really taken an active part in the slaying. But the affair was an obscure one; the Rural Police had been found out on a highroad; the uniform or jacket on the Rural Police was worse than any rag and as for his physiognomy, why, you couldn't even make out it had ever been a face, let alone identify it. The trial dragged along from court to court and finally reached a superior one, where it was first deliberated in camera to the following effect: Whereas it was not known precisely which of the peasants had participated in the crime, and yet there had been a host of them; and whereas this Drobyazhkin, he was a dead duck, and therefore there would be but little good to him even if he were to win the trial, whereas the muzhiks were still alive and kicking, ergo, a decision in their favor was quite important to them; therefore, and pursuant thereto, the decision was as follows: That Assessor Drobyazhkin had himself been the cause of the ruckus, inflicting injustice and oppressions upon the peasants of Lousy-Pride as well as those of the hamlet of Quarrelsome; and insofar as his death was concerned, it had occurred from a stroke of apoplexy, while he was on his way home in a sleigh. The matter, it would seem, had been disposed of, neatly and sweetly; but the bureaucrats, for some unknown reason, began to think that probably it was these dead souls that the present fuss was all about.

And things so fell out that, as if on purpose, at a time when Messieurs the bureaucrats were in a difficult enough position without this, two documents reached the Governor simultaneously. The contents of one informed him that, according to data and information received, there was in their province an utterer of counterfeit government notes, concealing himself under various aliases, and that the strictest search for him was to be instituted at once. The contents of the other document consisted of a communication from the Governor of an adjacent province concerning a brigand who had fled from the long arm of the law, and that if there should prove to be in their province any suspicious person who had not presented any credentials or passports he should be immediately apprehended. These two documents simply stunned everybody. Previous conclusions and surmises were all knocked galley-west. Of course, one could not by any means suppose that this had anything to do with Chichikov; nevertheless, when each one had mulled the matter over for himself, when they recalled that they still did not know just who Chichikov really was, that he himself had given but a vague report as to his person (true enough, he had said that he had suffered for the truth during his service, but then all this was somehow vague); and when, recalling all this, they also recalled that he himself had spoken of apparently having a great number of enemies who had even made attempts on his life— when they had reasoned all this out and recalled everything, they pondered still more deeply: consequently, his life must be in danger; consequently, he was being pursued; consequently, he must have been up to something or other, after all. . . . But just who was he in reality?

Of course it was unthinkable that he was capable of uttering counterfeit notes, and all the more unthinkable that he could be a brigand—his very appearance inspired confidence and respect— but with all that, who could he really be after all? And so Messieurs the bureaucrats now put to themselves a question which they should have put in the very beginning, in the first chapter of our epic, that is.

They pondered and pondered and at last came to the decision to make thorough inquiries among those whom Chichikov had traded with and bought these enigmatic dead souls from, in order to learn, at least, what each transaction had consisted of, and what, precisely, was the meaning of these souls, and whether he had not explained to somebody, even though perhaps by mere chance, even though in some indirect, incidental way, his real intentions, and whether he had not told somebody just who he was in reality.

To the Public Prosecutor fell the lot of having a talk with Sobakevich, while the Chairman of the Administrative Offices volunteered to go to Korobochka. And so let us, too, set out after them, and learn just what it was they found out.

CHAPTER TEN

SOBAKEVICH and his lady had taken quarters in a house somewhat remote from the more bustling sections of the town. The house he had chosen was of exceedingly solid construction; the ceiling was not likely to cave in and one could live there in safety and security. Its owner, a merchant by the name of Kolotyrkin, was also a solid fellow. Only Sobakevich's spouse was with him, but not his children. He was already beginning to weary of the town and was by now thinking of leaving it, staying on only to collect the ground-rent for some land that three burghers in the town had leased for growing turnips, and the completion of some modish capote quilted with cotton-wool which his spouse had got it into her head to order from a tailor in town. As he sat in his easy chair he was about to launch into a diatribe against both the prevalent knavery and the whims of fashion, without looking at his wife, however, but at an angle of the stove. It was at this point that the Public Prosecutor entered. Sobakevich said: "Please be seated," and, after rising a little in his easy chair, sat down again.

The Public Prosecutor approached to kiss Theodulia Ivanovna's little hand and then also took a chair. Theodulia Ivanovna, after duly receiving the kiss upon her hand, took a chair in her turn. All three chairs were enameled with green paint and had little jugs painted at the corners.

"I have called to discuss a certain matter with you," said the Public Prosecutor.

"Go to your room, my pet! The dressmaker is probably waiting for you there."

Theodulia went to her room.

"Permit me to ask," the Public Prosecutor began, "just what kind of serfs did you sell to Pavel Ivanovich Chichikov?"

"What do you mean, what kind?" Sobakevich countered. "That's what the purchase-deed is for, it specifies what kind; the coachmaker alone was—"

"However, throughout the town," the Public Prosecutor put in, "throughout the town there are rumors afloat that—"

"There is an awful lot of fools in town, that's why there are rumors," Sobakevich told him imperturbably.

"However, Mikhail Semënych, the rumors are of such a nature that they make one's head go round and round: that the souls aren't souls; that they were bought not at all for the purpose of resettlement; and that Chichikov himself is a man of mystery. Such suspicions have turned up . . . such tittle-tattle has been spread through the town—"

"But let me ask you this: are you an old woman, or what?" asked Sobakevich.

This question abashed the Public Prosecutor. He had never yet happened to ask himself whether he was an old woman or whether he was something else.

"You really ought to be ashamed even to come to me with such inquiries as that," Sobakevich went on.

The Public Prosecutor began to excuse himself.

"You ought to go to some of those housewives who sit around evenings spinning and knitting and chinning about witches. If God hasn't given you horse-sense enough to start a conversation about something more intelligent than that, you might go and play at knuckle-bones with little brats. Really, now, why have you come to muddle an honest man? What do you think I am, a laughing-stock for you, or what? You don't attend to your work the way you ought, you don't exert yourself to serve your country and to benefit your fellow-men, unless they happen to be your fellowgrafters; you never think of such things but only of how you can isolate yourself from other people as much as possible. Whichever way the fools may prod you, that's the way you'll plod along. And so you will disappear, having lived entirely in vain, and there won't be a single good thing left to remember you by."

The Public Prosecutor was at an utter loss for an answer to such an unexpected admonitory lecture. Pulverized, annihilated, he got away from Sobakevich, while Sobakevich called after him: "Git going, you dog!"

"How is it the Prosecutor left you so soon?" asked Theodulia, entering at this point.

"He felt the pangs of his conscience, so he up and left," Sobakevich told her. "There, my pet, you have an example before your very eyes. What an elderly man, with his head already gray, and yet I know that he's dangling after other men's wives to this very day. That's a way they all have—they're all dogs. And as if it weren't enough that they cumber the earth in vain, they'll also do such things as the whole kit and caboodle of them ought to be put into one bag for and thrown into the river. The whole town is nothing but a robbers' den. There's no use in our staying on here any longer; let's go away!"

His spouse made an attempt to make him see that the capote wasn't ready yet, and that, for the holidays, she had to buy some ribbons or other for her caps, but Sobakevich told her: "All those things are just stylish notions, my pet; they won't bring you to any good."

He ordered everything to be prepared for the trip; he himself, accompanied by a patrolman, went to the three burghers and got out of them the ground-rent for the turnip-patch; then he dropped in at the dressmaker's and took the capote in its unfinished state, just as it was in work, with the needle and thread stuck in it, so that it might be finished in his village, and drove out of the town, constantly repeating that it was dangerous even to visit it, inasmuch as it consisted of nothing but one swindler on top of another and that one could easily, together with them, be swallowed up in all sorts of vices.

The Public Prosecutor, in the meantime, was so nonplussed by his reception at Sobakevich's hands that he was perplexed how he might even tell about it to the Chairman of the Administrative Offices.

However, the Chairman of the Administrative Offices had also accomplished but little in finding any explanations for the Chichikov enigma. To begin with, having set out in his droshky, he at last found himself in so narrow and bemired a by-lane that during his entire ride through it the right wheel was higher than the left or the left was higher than the right. Because of this jouncing he had hit himself quite hard with his cane, first on the chin, then on the nape of his neck . . . and, to finish everything off, had splattered himself all over with mud. He drove into the courtyard of the Dean's house amid the champing of horses, sounds of churning mud, and the grunting of swine. Leaving the droshky and picking his way through all sorts of hutches and coops, he reached the house and at last got into the entry. Here, first of all, he asked for a towel and wiped his face. Korobochka met him in much the same way she had met Chichikov, with the same melancholy air. She had some rag or other wound around her neck, something in the nature of flannel. There was an incomputable host of flies in the room, and some dish of something extremely repulsive prepared especially for their benefit, to which mess, however, they seemed utterly accustomed by now.

Korobochka asked him to be seated.

The Chairman began by saying that he had known her late husband once upon a time, then suddenly shifted the conversation by asking: "Tell me, please, isn't it true that a certain person arrived at your house late one night and threatened to kill you if you didn't give up certain souls to him? And couldn't you explain to us what his intention was in acquiring them?"

"Oh, can't I though! You just put yourself in my place—fifteen rubles he gave me, in paper money! For really, I don't know anything; I'm a widow woman, I'm an inexperienced person; it's no hard thing to take me in when it comes to business, in which, I must confess and tell you, father o' mine, I don't know a thing. When it comes to hemp, now, I know the prices; I also sold some lard on the third of—"

"But do tell me first, as circumstantially as you can, just what happened. Did he have any pistols with him?"

"No, father o' mine, when it comes to pistols, God save and preserve us, I didn't see any. But mine is a widow's lot, you can't expect me to know what dead souls are fetching right now. Don't you fail me, now, father o' mine; enlighten me, at least, so's I might know the real price."

"What price? What price are you talking about, mother? What price, now?"

"Why, what price does a dead soul fetch now?"

"Well, either she's a born fool or she's gone batty," the Chairman reflected, staring into her eyes.

"What's fifteen rubles? For I don't know: maybe they're worth fifty rubles or even more."

"Suppose you show me the bank-notes," said the Chairman, and looked at them against the light to see if they were counterfeit or not. But the notes were all that notes should be.

"Now do tell me how he happened to buy anything from you. Just what was it he bought? I can't get a thing into my head . . . can't grasp anything——"

"Yes, he bought from me," said Korobochka. "But I say, now, father o' mine, how is it you won't tell me how much a dead soul fetches, so's I might know the real price for dead souls?"

"But, good heavens, what are you saying? Who ever heard of dead souls being sold?"

"But how is it you won't tell me the price?"

"What price are you talking about? Did he threaten you in any way at the time—did he want to seduce you?"

"No, father o' mine; but really, now, you're so. . . . Now I can see that you, too, are a commission merchant." And she peered suspiciously into his eyes.

"But, mother, I'm the Chairman of the Administrative Offices here——"

"No, father o' mine, say what you like, but you're really, now . . . you're also after doing the same . . . you want to take me in yourself. But just what good will that do you? Why, it's so much worse for you. I'd have sold you feathers, too; I'll have feathers around Christmas——"

"I'm telling you, mother, that I'm the Chairman of the Administrative Offices. What do I need your feathers for? I don't buy up anything."

"Why, now, trading is an honest business," Korobochka kept right on. "Today I sell to you, tomorrow you sell to me. Well, now, if we'll start in taking each other in that way, where is there any justice on earth, in that case? Why, it's a sin before God."

"Mother, I'm not a commission merchant but a Chairman!"

"Well, God knows who you are. Maybe you even are a Chairman—after all, I don't know. How should I? I'm only a poor widow woman. But why are you questioning me like that? No, father o' mine, I see that you yourself . . . now . . . are after buying them!"

"Mother, I'd advise you to see about your health," said the Chairman, growing angry. "You've got something missing here," he said, tapping his finger on his forehead, and left Korobochka.

Korobochka remained steadfast in her opinion that he was a commission merchant, and merely wondered how mean folks had become in this world, and how hard things were for a poor widow woman.

The Chairman of the Administrative Offices broke a wheel of his droshky and was spattered from head to foot with stinking mud. That was all he had got out of his unsuccessful expedition, including, of course, the smashing blow on the chin from his cane. As he was driving up to his house he encountered the Public Prosecutor, who was also riding in a droshky, out of sorts and with his head cast down.

"Well, what did you find out from Sobakevich?"

The Public Prosecutor hung his head still lower. "Never in all my life," said he, "have I had such a raking over the coals."

"Why, what happened?"

"He spat all over me," said the Public Prosecutor with an aggrieved air.

"How was that?"

"It seems that I'm of no use in my work at all: I've never handed in a single adverse report on my co-workers. In other places not a week passes by but that the Public Prosecutor hands in an adverse report; I've always put 'Approved' on every service record; even at times when one should really have sent in an adverse report I didn't keep any paper back."

The Public Prosecutor was really crushed.

"But just what has he got to say about Chichikov?" the Chairman persisted.

"What has he got to say? He called all of us old women, cursed us all for a pack of fools."

The Chairman of the Administrative Offices became pensive. At this point a third droshky came driving along, with the Vice-Governor therein. "Gentlemen," he said, "I have to inform you that we must be on the look-out. They're saying that a Governor-General is really being appointed for our province."

Both the Chairman and the Public Prosecutor let their jaws drop.

"There, he'll come just in time for the feast! What a fine kettle of fish—the Devil alone can find the taste in it! He'll see what a confounded muddle the town is in!" the Chairman of the Administrative Offices pondered.

"One damned thing after another!" thought the aggrieved Public Prosecutor.

"Do you know anything about who's been appointed—what his temperament is like, what sort of a man he is?" asked the Chairman.

"No one knows anything yet," answered the Vice-Governor.

Just then the Postmaster drove up, also in a droshky. "Gentlemen, I can congratulate you on your Governor-General!"

"We've heard that already, but nothing is known for a fact yet."

"Why, it's even known who he is," said the Postmaster. "It's Count Odnozorovski-Chementinski."

"Well, what do they say about him?"

"The strictest of men, my dear sir," said the Postmaster. "Most far-sighted, and of the shortest temper. He was formerly in some sort of a, now, you understand, important branch of the government. They got into certain sinful ways there. He gave them all a good dressing-down; he pulverized 'em so fine, you understand, that there wasn't even enough left of 'em to sweep up."

"Why, there's no need at all of any strict measures in this town."

"He's a treasure-house of information, my dear sir; a man on a colossal scale, you understand?" the Postmaster went on. "There

234·

was one occasion when—however," he remarked, "we're talking out in the street, in front of our coachmen. Let's better get indoors."

They all realized where they were. For in the meantime spectators had gathered in the street, gawking with gaping mouths at the four men in four droshkies carrying on a conversation among themselves. The coachmen shouted at their horses and the four droshkies trailed along to the house of the Chairman of the Administrative Offices.

"The Devil sure has brought this Chichikov at the right time," thought the Chairman, taking off his mud-spattered fur-coat in the anteroom.

"My head is going round and round," said the Public Prosecutor, taking off his fur-coat.

"I still can't make this business out, for the life of me," said the Vice-Governor, slipping out of his fur-coat.

The Postmaster didn't say a word; he simply threw off his fur-coat.

They all entered a room wherein all sorts of cold snacks suddenly appeared. The provincial powers that be can't do without cold snacks, and if, in any province, two officials happen to get together, the third boon companion to appear (of itself) will be a table set with cold snacks.

The Chairman of the Administrative Offices walked up to the table and poured out some of the bitterest wormwood vodka for himself, as he said: "If you were to kill me, I don't know just who this fellow Chichikov is."

"And that goes for me too," said the Public Prosecutor, "only more so. Such a mixed-up affair I've never yet come across, even in official papers, and I haven't the heart to tackle it—"

"And yet, what worldly polish . . . the man has," said the Postmaster, concocting a mixture of different vodkas for himself, beginning with a dark one and finishing with a roseate. "He's evidently been to Paris. I think he must have had a diplomatic post, or practically that."

"Well, gentlemen!" said the Chief of Police, the well-known benefactor of the town, the favorite of the merchants, and a miracle worker when it came to giving a feast, as he entered at this point. "Gentlemen! I haven't been able to find out a thing about Chichikov. I didn't have a chance to rummage through his personal papers; he never leaves his room—he has come down with something. I pumped his people: Petrushka, his flunky, and Seliphan, his coachman. The first wasn't any too sober, but then he's always been that way." Here the Chief of Police walked up to the liquid refreshments and made himself a mixed drink of three different vodkas. "Petrushka says that his master is like any master; that Chichikov has associated with apparently the better sort of people, with Perekroev, for instance. . . . He mentioned a lot of landowners—Collegiate and State Councilors, all of them. 'Not at all a foolish man,' Seliphan the coachman says of him; Chichikov was respected by everybody because he'd done his duty well in the Civil Service. He has worked in the Customs, and was connected with certain construction works for the government, but just which ones Seliphan couldn't say. 'There's three horses; one was bought,' he says, 'three years back; the gray horse,' says he, 'was swapped for another gray; the third was bought. . . .' As for Chichikov himself, his name really is Pavel Ivanovich, and he actually is a Collegiate Councilor."

All the officials became thoughtful.

"A decent man, and a Collegiate Councilor," reflected the Public Prosecutor, "and yet he decides on such an affair as carrying off the Governor's daughter, and gets such mad notions into his head as buying up dead souls and frightening aged ladies late at night—which may be becoming to some junker in the hussars, but never to a Collegiate Councilor."

"If he be a Collegiate Councilor, how can he embark on such a criminal offense as counterfeiting government notes!" reflected the Vice-Governor, who was a Collegiate Councilor himself, loved to play the flute, and had a soul inclined to the fine arts rather than to crime.

"Like it or not, gentlemen, this business must be wound up, one way or another. The Governor-General will arrive and see that simply the Devil alone knows what is going on among us," said the Chief of Police.

"Well, what action are you thinking of taking?"

"I think one must act decisively," the Chief of Police answered.

"But decisively in just what way?"

"By detaining him as a suspicious person."

"And what if he detains *us* as suspicious persons?"

"How can that be?"

"Well, and what if he turns out to be an undercover man? Well, and what if he has secret instructions? Dead souls! Hmm! Buying them up, apparently, but supposing it's really an investigation of all those deaths certified under 'cause unknown'?"

These words plunged everybody into deep thought. But the Public Prosecutor was staggered by them. The Chairman too, after having uttered them, became thoughtful. Odd, that the arrivals of both Chichikov and the Governor-General should coincide thus. . . .

"Well, now, how are we to act, gentlemen?" asked the Chief of Police, the town's philanthropist and the merchants' benefactor, and, after mixing himself a drink of a sweet vodka and a bitter he tossed it off, chasing it down with a cold delicacy.

A waiter brought in a bottle of madeira and fresh glasses.

"Really, now, I don't know what action to take," said the Chairman of the Administrative Offices.

"Gentlemen," said the Postmaster, after draining a glass of madeira and shoving into his mouth some edam cheese together with dried sturgeon steak and butter, "I'm of the opinion that this matter must be rather thoroughly gone into, that it must be considered rather thoroughly, and considered in camera, by all of us together, together assembled, in common, the way they do things in the British Parliament, you understand, so that everything may be explored definitely, following every twist and turn, you understand."

"Well, why not? We'll assemble," said the Chief of Police.

"Yes," said the Chairman of the Administrative Offices, "let's assemble and decide in a body just what Chichikov is."

"That's the most sensible thing of all, to decide just what this Chichikov is."

Having said which, they felt a simultaneous urge to partake of champagne, and then went their various ways, satisfied that this proposed committee would arrive at an explanation of everything and would show, clearly and definitely, just what Chichikov was.

CHAPTER ELEVEN

Having gathered at the house of the Chief of Police, the father and benefactor of the town whom the reader is already acquainted with, the officials had an opportunity of remarking to one another that they had actually lost weight because of all these worries and alarums. And truly, the appointment of a new Governor-General, as well as the recent receipt of those documents the contents of which were of so serious a character, and all those rumors the nature of which God alone knew, had all left perceptible traces upon their countenances, while the frock-coats upon them had become perceptibly roomier. Everybody there showed signs of wear and tear. The Chairman of the Administrative Offices had lost weight, and the Public Prosecutor had lost weight, and the Inspector of the Board of Health had lost weight, and a certain Semën Ivanovich, who was never called by his last name and who wore upon his right index finger a ring which he always permitted the ladies to examine—well, even he had lost weight. Of course, as is generally the case, there were to be found some courageous souls who hadn't let their spirits sink, but they were far from many— as a matter of fact there was only one: the Postmaster. He alone didn't change; his character remained as imperturbable and tranquil as ever. Whenever such occasions as the present arose it was his wont to remark: "We know all about you Governors-General! There will be three or four of you replacing one another; but it's thirty years by now, my dear sir, that I'm doing business at the same old stand." To which the other officials would usually remark:

"It's all very well for you to talk, *Sprechen Sie Deutsch,* Ivan Andreich. Your work has to do with the mail, receiving it and dispatching it. All the monkey business you can do is to close the post-office an hour earlier, maybe, or accept a little something from a belated merchant for taking a letter outside of regular hours, or you may forward a parcel or two that shouldn't be forwarded. In a case like that, naturally, any man would be a saint. But suppose the Devil took to turning up at your elbow day after day, so that, even though you didn't want to take anything, he persists in thrusting temptation upon you. You, of course, haven't much to worry you, all you've got is one little boy; but in my case, brother, my Praskovia Fedorovna has been endowed by God with such a blessed fertility that not a year passes without her bringing forth either a Praskushka or a Petrushka. In a case like that, brother, you'd strike up a different tune."

Thus did the officials discourse; but whether it's really possible to withstand the Devil or not is not an author's business to judge. In the council now convened there was very noticeable an absence of that indispensable something which among the common folk is called horse-sense. In general we Russians haven't, somehow, been created for representative bodies. In all our assemblies, beginning with the village meeting of the peasants and going all the way up to all possible sorts of learned committees and the like, a most impressive confusion will prevail if they lack a single leader who directs everything. It's difficult to say why this is so; evidently it must be so because we're that sort of folk. Only those conferences succeed which are undertaken with the ultimate goal of having a good time or a banquet, such organizations as clubs and all kinds of vauxhall pleasure gardens, patterned after the German style. But as for willingness, it's on tap at a moment's notice and for any purpose you will. We will, at the drop of a hat and with all the consistency of a weather-vane, launch societies for philanthropic purposes, for the encouragement of this and that, and for Heaven alone knows what else. The purpose will, every time, be splendid and beautiful, but with all that nothing will come of it. Perhaps this is due to the fact that we become quickly satisfied at the very beginning, and consider that everything has already been accomplished. For instance, having got up some society for the benefit of the poor and duly contributed considerable sums, we will immediately, to mark the occasion of so praiseworthy a deed, launch a banquet for all the leading dignitaries of the town, which banquet, in the nature of things, will eat up half the sums received; with the remaining funds magnificent quarters will be promptly rented for the committee, complete with the latest heating arrangements and all sorts of attendants. And, in the upshot, there remains for the poor all of five rubles and a half, but even then the members of the committee aren't in full accord as to the disposition of this sum, and each one proposes as the recipient some worthy person who had been godmother to his child.

However, the conference now convened was of an entirely different kind—it had been called out of sheer necessity. It wasn't with any poor folk or outsiders that it had to deal; it had to deal with matters that affected each one of the officials personally. It had to deal with a peril that threatened all of them alike; therefore, willy-nilly, the conference had to attain as much unanimity and camaraderie as possible. But, for all that, the result was the dickens knows what. To say nothing of the differences of opinion natural to all councils, a hesitancy that was downright incomprehensible was revealed about the views of those gathered here. One would say that Chichikov was a counterfeiter and utterer of government notes, and then would himself add: "And maybe he isn't, at that." Another maintained that our hero was an official from the chancellery of the Governor-General, and then immediately tacked on: "And yet, the Devil knows what he is; you can't read anything on his forehead." Against the conjecture whether he mightn't be a brigand in disguise all rose up in arms; they found that, outside of his appearance, which attested to his good intentions per se, there was nothing in his conversation that in any way betokened a man of violent deeds.

Suddenly the Postmaster, who for several minutes had been in some sort of meditation, moved by some inspiration or by something else, cried out unexpectedly: "Do you know, gentlemen, who this Chichikov is?"

The voice in which he uttered this was imbued with something so staggering that it compelled all of them to cry out at the same time: "No, who is he?"

"This, gentlemen, and my dear sir, is none other than Captain Kopeikin!"

And when all of them asked, as if with one voice: "And just who might this Captain Kopeikin be?" the Postmaster said: "So you don't know who Captain Kopeikin is?"

They all answered that they didn't know in the least who Captain Kopeikin was.

"Captain Kopeikin," the Postmaster began, opening his snuff-box only half-way, out of apprehension that someone of those near him might dip his fingers therein, in the cleanliness of which fingers he had but little faith, and was even wont to add: "We know all about it, father o' mine; who knows where you've had your fingers, and yet snuff is a thing that calls for cleanliness"— "Captain Kopeikin . . ." he repeated, but only after he had taken a pinch up his nostrils, "but then, really, if one were to tell you his story, it would turn out to be a most entertaining thing, even for some writer or other—a whole epic, in a sort of a way."

All those present evinced a desire to learn this story or, as the Postmaster had put it, this "most entertaining thing, even for some writer or other—a whole epic, in a sort of a way," and he began:

The Tale of Captain Kopeikin

After the campaign of eighteen-twelve, my dear sir—(thus did the Postmaster begin, despite the fact that the room held not one sir but all of six sirs)—after the campaign of eighteen-twelve a certain Captain Kopeikin was sent back from the front together with other wounded men. Whether it was at Krasnoe or at Leipzig, the fact remains that he had, if you can fancy such a thing, an arm and a leg blown off. Well, at that time none of those special provisions concerning the wounded had been made yet, you know, none whatsoever; any sort of a fund for invalided soldiers, as you may imagine, was formed, in a sort of a way, only considerably later. Captain Kopeikin sees that he'll have to get some work, but the Devil of it is that the one arm he has left is, you understand, his left. He did pay a visit home, to see his father; well, his father tells him: "I haven't the means to feed you; I"—just imagine such a thing—"I can barely win bread for myself." And so my Captain Kopeikin decided to set out, my dear sir, to Peterburgh, to petition the Sovereign as to whether there might not be some monarchal dispensation for the relief of such cases as his: "This is the way of things, and this and that, and I have, in a manner of speaking, laid down my life, have shed my blood. . . ."

Well, whichever way he did it, don't you know, whether through hitching rides on supply carts or on government army transports, the fact remains, my dear sir, that in one way or another make his way to Peterburgh he did. Well, you can just picture the thing for yourself: a fellow like that, a Captain Kopeikin of some sort, now, and suddenly he finds himself plumped down in a capital the like of which, so to say, isn't to be found anywhere in the world! All of a sudden the world, relatively speaking, unrolls before him, a veritable arena of life, as it were, such a Sheherazade fairyland, you understand. All of a sudden something like Nevski Prospect spreads out before him, if you will picture it to yourself, or, you know, some Gorokhovaya Street, the Devil take it, or some Liteinaya. Over here some spire or other soars in the air; over there are bridges suspended in some sort of a devilish way, without any visible contact with the earth, as it were—in a word, my dear sir, the hanging gardens of Semiramis, and that's all there is to it!

He did make a brash attempt to find rooms for himself, only everything was so dear and imposing: window-curtains, and window-blinds, all such devilishly expensive stuff, you understand; the rugs, my dear sir, are Persia itself, sort of . . . in a word, relatively speaking, as it were, you trod untold wealth underfoot at every step you took. You just walk along the streets, surely a simple enough thing, now, and yet, you know, your nose can sniff thousands upon thousands in the very air; but at the same time my Captain Kopeikin's entire First National Bank, you understand, consists of some ten blue V's and a trifle in silver. Well, you can hardly buy a country seat with that, not really, you can't—that is to say, you *can* buy a country seat with it, provided you add forty thousand to it; but when it comes to a matter of forty thousand you have to float a loan with the King of France, naturally. Well.

somehow or other, he found a snug nook in a low tavern run by a Finn, for a ruble a day, the dinner consisting of cabbage soup and a bit of chopped beef. . . . So he sees that there's no manner of use in holing in for a long stay.

He asked this one and that where he was to go and whom he was to see. They told him that there was a sort of a high commission, a department of the government, kind of, set up for such cases as his, headed by So-and-so as General-in-Chief. As for the Emperor, you must know that at that time His Majesty wasn't in the capital, as you may well imagine—he hadn't come back from Paris yet; everybody who was anybody was still abroad.

And so my Kopeikin, getting up very early, scraped the stubble off his face with his left hand, somehow, for even paying a barber would have put a dent in his finances, in a way; he pulled on his wretched little uniform and stumped off on his peg-leg, if you can fancy such a thing, to see none other than the grandee who headed the commission. He asked people where the official lived. "There," they told him, pointing out a house on the Palace Quai. Just a wretched tumble-down shack, it was, you understand, with nothing but marble for the walls and mere parquetry for the floors, with plate-glass windows ten and a half foot high, so that, if you can picture such a thing to yourself, it seemed as if you could reach out with your hand from the sidewalk and touch the vases and things on the inside. The least little metal door-knob, you understand, was such a work of art that before you dared as much as lay your hand on it you'd have to dash over to some shop first for a copper's worth of soap and put in an hour or two, so to say, scrubbing your hands, and only after that possibly get up courage enough to desecrate that door-knob by grabbing hold of it. In short, everything was so highly waxed and polished that, in a way, it was enough to turn your head. Why, the mere doorman out on the front steps looked nothing short of a generalissimo, if you follow me, with his gilt mace and a physiognomy on him like a count's— like some sort of a well-fed, fat pug-dog, you know, cambric ruffs on him, and no end of swank. . . .

My Kopeikin managed to drag himself up the marble steps on his wooden peg-leg, as best he could, and got into the reception room, where he made himself as small as possible in a corner, so's not to jostle with his elbow something or other that, as you can well imagine, might be as priceless as an America or an India—some gilded, porcelain vase, or something like that, if you follow me. Well, it goes without saying that he had his fill of cooling his one heel standing there, inasmuch as he'd come at a time when the General had, in a way, hardly risen from his bed, and his valet was bringing him some sort of a silver basin for his sundry, you understand, ablutions. My Kopeikin hangs around for four hours until an adjutant or some other official comes out and announces: "The General," he says, "will be coming out here right away." Well, by now the people in the reception room are as thick as peas. And all the folks there aren't just such country bumpkins as we, officials of the fourth and fifth grades, but colonels at the least, mind you; the room is simply chock-full of all sorts of epaulets and shoulder-knots and gold braid and macaronic stuff—in a word, the cream of the cream. Suddenly a barely perceptible stir runs through the room, like some ethereal zephyr springing up, you understand; there's a bit of shushing here and there and at last the stillness becomes unbearable. The grandee enters . . . well, you can imagine what's what for yourself. A statesman, actually! About his face, his person, his bearing there was, so to say—well, now, a certain air in keeping with his lofty calling, you understand, and with his high rank, that's the kind of air he had, I mean. Every soul in the room drew itself up at attention, expectant, quivering, awaiting, you know, the decision of its fate.

This grandee, or Prime Minister, or whatever, walks up now to one, now to another: "What is the purpose of your call? And yours? What is it you wish? What is your business here?" At last, my dear sir, he comes up to Kopeikin. Kopeikin screws up his courage. "This is the way of things, Your Excellency," he says, "and this and that, and I've shed my blood; I have lost, in a sort of a way, an arm and a leg; I'm so incapacitated that I can't work; I make so bold as to ask if there mightn't be some monarchal dispensation, some assistance, certain arrangements, of one sort or another concerning, relatively speaking, as it were, some remuneration, or pension, or what have you, you understand."

The Prime Minister sees that the man standing before him has a wooden peg-leg, and that the right sleeve of his uniform is pinned onto his breast.

"Very well," says he, "see me about it in a few days."

My Kopeikin walks out of there almost in rapture because, for one thing, he had actually been deemed worthy of an audience, so to say, with a grandee of the very first rank and, for another, because now at last the matter of his pension would, as it were, be settled. In such high spirits as you can well imagine he hops along the sidewalk; drops in at the Palkinski tavern for a glass of vodka; has his dinner, my dear sir, at the London, ordering a chop with capers and a pullet with all sorts of fixin's, and calling for a bottle of wine; in the evening he takes in a show—in a word, you understand, he had a bit of a fling. As he hops along the sidewalk he sees some graceful Englishwoman passing by, like some sort of a swan —as you can picture it all for yourself. My Kopeikin—his blood, now, begins coursing faster through his veins, you know—at first started running after her on his wooden peg-leg, tap-tap, hot on her trail. "But no," he reflected, "let that sort of thing go for the time being! Later, perhaps, when I get my pension, but now I've spent too much, somehow."

Well, my dear sir, three or four days later he shows up again at the Prime Minister's and waits until he comes out. "I've come," he says, after due preliminaries, "to find out Your High Excellency's decision in my case, seeing as how, because of my ill-health and the wounds I have sustained—" and the like of that, you understand, all in the proper style.

The grandee—just imagine!—recognized him right off.

"Ah," he says, "very good! But at present I can't tell you anything more than that you will have to wait for the arrival of the Emperor, when, without a doubt, arrangements will be made concerning wounded veterans, but without the Monarch's will in the matter, so to say, there is nothing I can do." A bow, you understand, and good-by. Kopeikin, as you can imagine, walked out of there in a most unsettled state. Here he'd been already thinking that, no later than on the morrow, they'd hand the money over to him on a silver platter: "There, dearest fellow, go ahead, eat, drink and be merry," but instead of that he's ordered to wait, and yet there's no definite time set.

So he clumps down those stairs as sore as a boiled owl, or like a poodle over whom a cook has thrown a pail of water, with his tail between his legs and his ears drooping. "Oh, no!" he thinks to himself. "I'll go to him again, will explain to him that I'm down to my last crust: 'if you don't help me now, I'll have to die, in a sort of a way, from hunger.' "

In short, my dear sir, he goes to the Palace Quai. "You can't go in," they tell him, "the General isn't receiving today; come tomorrow." The next day the same thing happens—the doorman doesn't even want to look at him. And yet, at the same time, out of those blue V's of his he has but one left in his pocket. Before this he used to eat cabbage soup, at least, and a bit of beef, but now he'll drop in at a grocer's and get him something like a herring, or a dill pickle, and two coppers' worth of bread; in short, the poor fellow's starving, and yet at the same time he has an appetite that's simply like a wolf's. He'd be walking past some restaurant where the chef—just imagine!—is a foreigner, a Frenchman, you know, with a frank, open countenance, the linen on him of the finest holland stuff, and an apron the whitness of which equals, in a kind of a way, the whiteness of snowy expanses, and this chef is working away at an omelet with *fines herbes,* or cutlets with truffles —in a word, some super-super-delicacy or other of such a tantalizing nature that you'd start eating your own self out of sheer appetite. Or he might happen to be going past the shops on Miliutinskaya; there, peeping out of the windows, in a manner of speaking, he'd behold such stunning smoked salmon, and little cherries at five rubles each cherry, and a colossus of a watermelon as big as your stage-coach, leaning right out of the window, so to speak, on the look-out for a fool big enough to pay a hundred rubles for it. In short, there's temptation at every step, making his mouth water, relatively speaking, as it were, yet all he keeps on hearing is the eternal "Tomorrow!"

Picture to yourself, then, what his situation was: here, on one hand, so to say, are the smoked salmon and the gigantic watermelon, while on the other he is offered the unvarying bitter fare called *Tomorrow*. Finally the poor fellow lost, in a way, all patience; he decided, at any cost, to get through to the Prime Minister, to storm the fortress, if you follow me. He hung around the front entrance, on the chance of some other caller going in, and then, with some general or other, you understand, he slipped through into the reception room, wooden peg-leg and all. The grandee comes out, as usual: "What is the purpose of your call? What is the purpose of your call? Ah," says he, catching sight of Kopeikin, "I've already informed you that you must await a decision."—"For Heaven's sake, Your High Excellency, I haven't, so to say, a crust to eat—"—"Well, what's to be done? I can't do a thing for you; try to help yourself in the meantime; seek out your own means of subsistence."—"But, Your High Excellency, you can judge for yourself, in a sort of a way, what means of subsistence I can find when I lack an arm and a leg."—"But," the dignitary buts right back at him, "you must agree, in a sort of a way, that I cannot support you at my own expense; I have many wounded veterans, they all have the same rights. Gird yourself with patience. When the Sovereign arrives, I give you my word of honor that the imperial graciousness will not overlook you."—"But, Your High Excellency, I can't wait!" says Kopeikin, and says it, in a certain respect, rudely. The grandee, you understand, had become actually irked by this time. And really, now, here were generals on all sides of him, awaiting his decisions, his orders; the affairs are, so to say, important, having to do with the State, demanding the most urgent execution—the loss of a minute may be of importance—and here you have a devil at your elbow you can't shake off, pestering you. "Excuse me," says the grandee, "I have no time now—matters more important than yours are awaiting me," reminding him in a way that was delicate, kind of, that it was time for him to go at last. But my Kopeikin—hunger was spurring him on, you know— he says: "Do what you will, Your High Excellency, I am not stirring from the spot until you issue instructions as to my pension."

Well, now, you can just imagine: answering like that a grandee who has but to give the word and you go flying head over heels, so far that the Devil himself will never find you. . . . Right here among us, if some clerk just a grade below ours were to say something like that to one of us, why, it would be considered rudeness. But there, what a contrast, just think of the contrast: a General-in-Chief and some sort of a Captain Kopeikin! Ninety rubles and a zero! The General, you understand, didn't do a thing but just give him a look, no more, but his look was as good as a firearm: you had no heart left, for it went down into your boots. But my Kopeikin, if you can imagine such a thing, doesn't budge from the spot; he stands as if he were rooted there.

"Well, what are your intentions?" says the General, and then decides to let him have it good and hard, as they say. However, to tell the truth, he treated him rather mercifully; another might have scared Kopeikin so that everything would have spun upside down before his eyes for three days thereafter, but he merely said: "Very well; if you find the cost of living too high here, and can't bide quietly in the capital until such time as your future is decided upon, I shall send you out of here at the government's expense. Call the state courier here! Have this man sent back to his original place of residence under convoy!"

Well, the state courier was already standing there, you understand, such a mountain of a man, all of eight foot high, and a hand on him, you can just imagine, that had been fashioned by Nature itself to handle stage-coach drivers—in short, as husky as they come. . . . And so they dump Kopeikin, that poor servant of God, into a small cart, and the state courier is off with him. "Well," thinks Kopeikin, "at least I won't have to pay my traveling expenses; thanks for that, at least." He's riding along with the state courier, and as he rides along with him he discourses to himself, in a manner of speaking. "It's all very well," he says to himself, "for the grand man to be saying that I ought to find my own means of subsistence and that I ought to help myself. Very well, then," says he, "I," he says, "will find the means, all right!"

Well, now, as to how he was brought back, and what place he was brought back to, nothing is known about all that. And so, you understand, even all rumors about Captain Kopeikin were plunged into the river of oblivion, into some Lethe or other, as the poets call it. But if you'll permit me, gentlemen, that's precisely where the thread that knots the plot of this romantic story begins. And so, where Kopeikin went to is not known; but, just imagine, no more than two months had passed when there appeared in the forests of Riazan a band of brigands, and the chief of this band was, my dear sir, none other than our Captain Kopeikin.

He had collected, as it were, a whole mob from among all sorts of deserting soldiers. This took place, as you can well imagine, immediately after the war; everybody had gotten used to a loose way of living; a man's life wasn't held at much more than a copper; everything was in such a state of rack and ruin that even the grass refused to grow; in short, my dear sir, he had what simply amounted to an army. There was no passing through the highways because of him, and his attention, so to say, was directed upon government property. If it were just a traveler going about his own business, well, they'd just ask him what his business was and then let him go on his way. But, when it came to a government supply transport, either of provender or money—in a word, anything and everything that could be described as government property—there was no such thing as its getting past them.

Well, as you can imagine, the government's pocket, so to put it, was being depleted horribly. If Kopeikin happened to hear that some village was due to pay its taxes, he'd be right on the spot. He'd immediately demand that the village elder be brought before him. "Come on, brother, let's have all those imposts and taxes." Well, the old muzhik sees a devil like that before him, with only one leg, and the collar of his uniform of a cloth as red as the plumage of the fire-bird in the fairy tale; he scents, the Devil take it, that he'll get plenty if he refuses. "Here, father o' mine," he says, "take it all, only let me be." And to himself he thinks: "Must be some Captain of the Rural Police, for sure, or mebbe someone still worse." But the Captain, my dear sir, never took the money save in a proper manner, as it were; he'd write out a receipt for those peasants on the spot so as, in a sort of a way, to make things easy for them: that the money had been received, for a fact, and that the taxes were all paid in full, and that they had been collected by such-and-such a Captain Kopeikin; he'd even top the whole thing off by affixing his seal thereto.

In short, my dear sir, there he was, robbing away, and that's all there was to it. Several times troops were sent out to capture him,

· 249

but my Captain Kopeikin didn't give as much as a hoot for that. He had such a fine collection of cut-throats around him, you understand. But at last, maybe because he got scary, seeing that the mess he had started, so to say, was no longer a joking matter and that measures for his apprehension were becoming intensified with every minute, and seeing also that he'd gotten quite a bit of money together by now—well, my dear sir, he ups and makes his way out of Russia and, once out of Russia, my dear sir, he heads for the United States of America.

And from there, my dear sir, he writes a letter to the Sovereign, as eloquent a letter as you could possibly imagine. All those Platos and Demostheneses of antiquity, of one sort or another, they were all, one may say, so much trash, so many pettifoggers, if one compared their eloquence with that of Kopeikin's letter. "Don't you be thinking, my Sovereign," he wrote, "that I'm this way or that way. . . ." What a world of well-rounded periods he let loose! "Necessity," he says, "was the cause of my actions; I shed my blood; I did not, by any manner of means, spare my life; and I have not, so to say, a crust of bread to subsist on now. Do not punish," he says, "my fellows and comrades, because they are innocent, since they were drawn in, properly speaking, as it were, by me, but rather manifest your monarchal graciousness, so that in the future, should there be any wounded veterans, as it were, they may, for example, have some provision, of one sort or another, made for them, as you may imagine. . . ." In a word, it was extraordinarily eloquent, that letter.

Well, the sovereign was touched, you understand. Really, his monarchal heart was profoundly stirred; although this Kopeikin was, sure enough, a criminal and deserved, in a sort of a way, capital punishment, yet seeing that such an oversight as the neglect of the wounded could come about, so to say, in a perfectly unintentional manner—although, however, it was impossible at that troublous time to arrange everything right off, for God alone, one may say, is never remiss or in error—in short, my dear sir, the Sovereign was pleased in this instance to manifest an unexampled magnanimity: he ordered the prosecution of the captured bandits to be stopped and at the same time issued the strictest decree that a committee be formed for the sole purpose of attending to the improvement of the lot of those, who had been, as it were, wounded or disabled in war. And there, my dear sir, you have the reason, so to say, because of which a basis was laid for funds to take care of invalided soldiers, which funds, one may say, now provide perfectly for all wounded soldiers, to such an extent that, truly, no similar solicitude for their care can be found either in England or among any of the other enlightened nations.

"And that, my dear sir, is who this Captain Kopeikin was. Now my present supposition is this: he has, beyond a doubt, gone through all his money in the United States, and so he has come back to us, to try once more whether he can't, in a sort of a way, so to say, carry out a new scheme—"

"But hold on, Ivan Andreievich," said the Chief of Police, suddenly breaking in on the Postmaster's story, "why, you yourself said that Captain Kopeikin lacked an arm and a leg, whereas Chichikov—"

At this point the Postmaster cried out and slapped his forehead with all his might, calling himself publicly, before all of them, a calf's head. He couldn't understand how such a circumstance had not occurred to him at the very beginning of his story and confessed that the proverb about hindsight being the Russian's strong point was most just. However, only a minute later he was already trying to be foxy and to squirm out of the situation, saying that, after all, mechanical ingenuity had reached a very high point of perfection in England, that one could see by the papers where someone had invented wooden legs so ingeniously made that at the mere touch of an imperceptible spring they could carry a man off to God knows what regions, so that thereafter there was no such thing as finding him.

However, they all expressed extreme doubts as to whether Chichikov was Captain Kopeikin, and found that the Postmaster had strayed much too far afield. Still, when it came to their turn, they kept up their end and, prompted by the ingenious surmise of the Postmaster, wandered off almost as far if not further. Out of a great number of suppositions, shrewd in their own way, one in par-

· 251 ·

ticular emerged at last (one feels oddly even mentioning it): whether Chichikov were not Napoleon in disguise; the Britishers, now, had long been envious because, forsooth, Russia was so great and vast; why, on several occasions caricatures had been actually put out depicting Ivan Ivanovich Ivanov talking with John Bull; John Bull stands there with a dog held on a rope behind him, which dog was supposed to represent Napoleon. "Look here, now," says John Bull, "if anything doesn't go just right, I'll let the dog loose on you right off." And so now, maybe, they'd actually let Boney out from the isle of St. Helena, and so there he was now, sneaking into Russia rigged out as Chichikov, but, when you got right down to it, he wasn't Chichikov at all, at all.

Of course, when it came actually to believing this, the bureaucrats did not believe, yet just the same they fell into deep thought and, as each one scrutinized this business to himself, they found that Chichikov's face, were he to turn and stand sideways, did bear a most striking resemblance to a portrait of Napoleon. The Chief of Police, who had served in the campaign of 1812 and had seen Napoleon with his own eyes, also could not but own that the Little Corporal couldn't possibly be of a greater height than Chichikov, and that in bodily build also Napoleon wasn't what you would call any too stout, even though you couldn't say he was any too thin, either.

Perhaps there are some readers who will call all this improbable; the author, too, just for the sake of pleasing them, is ready to call all this improbable; but, as ill-luck would have it, everything took place precisely as it is told here and, what's still more amazing, this town wasn't in some backwoods but, on the contrary, not far from both our capitals. However, it must be remembered that all this took place only shortly after the glorious expulsion of the French. At that time all our landowners, officials, merchants, bartenders, and all our literate folk as well as the illiterate, had become—at least for all of eight years—inveterate politicians. The *Moscow News* and the *Son of the Fatherland* were read through implacably and reached the last reader in shreds and tatters that were of no use whatsoever for any practical purposes. Instead of such questions as "What price did you get for a measure of oats, father o'

mine?" or "Did you take advantage of the first snow we had yesterday?" people would ask: "And what do they say in the papers?" or
"Have they let Napoleon slip away from that island again, by any
chance?"

The merchants were very much afraid of this contingency, inasmuch as they had utter faith in the prediction of a certain prophet
who had been sitting in jail for three years by now. This prophet
had come no one knew whence, in bast sandals and an undressed
sheepskin that reeked to high heaven of spoilt fish, and had proclaimed that Napoleon was Antichrist and was being kept on a
chain of stone behind six walls and beyond seven seas, but that later
on he would rend his chain and gain possession of all the world.
The prophet, as a reward for his prediction, has landed in jail, which
was just as it should have been; nevertheless, he had done his work
and had thrown the merchants into utter confusion. For a long
while thereafter, even during their most profitable deals, the merchants, on setting out for the tavern to wet their bargains with
tea, would talk a bit about the Antichrist. Many of the officials,
and the gentry and nobility, also involuntarily thought of this from
time to time and, infected by the mysticism which, as everybody
knows, was all the go at the time, saw some sort of peculiar significance in every letter that went to form the name Napoleon; many
even discovered Apocalyptic numbers in the same.

And so there's nothing to wonder at if the bureaucrats involuntarily fell into deep thought at this point. In a short while, however, they came to, remarking that their imagination was far too
frisky this time and that all this wasn't the right thing. They pondered and they pondered, they deliberated and they deliberated, and
the upshot was that they decided that it mightn't be a bad idea to
question Nozdrev rather thoroughly again. Since he had been the
first to put out the story about the dead souls and was apparently
on very close terms with Chichikov, and was consequently bound
to know, beyond a doubt, a thing or two about the circumstances
of the latter's life, they ought to have another go at it and see what
Nozdrev had to say.

Strange people, these Messieurs the bureaucrats—and, with them,
all the other ranks as well. For they knew very well that Nozdrev

was a liar, that one couldn't believe him—not in a single word he uttered, not in the least trifle—and yet, just the same, they had recourse to him. There, go and cope with man! Man does not believe in God, but he does believe that if the bridge of his nose itches he is inevitably slated to die soon; he will pass over the creation of a poet, a creation as clear as the day, all permeated with the accord and lofty wisdom of simplicity, but will eagerly pounce upon a work wherein some successful charlatan talks a lot of rot, tells a pack of lies, distorts nature and turns it inside out, and this will prove to his liking, and he will set up a shout: "Here it is, here is a genuine knowledge of the secrets of the heart!" All his life he doesn't value doctors at more than a bent pin, but in the upshot turns to some old conjure-woman who heals through whispered spells and gobbets of spit, or better still, he will devise for himself some decoction or other out of who knows what rubbish which, God knows why, he will consider the sovereign cure for what ails him.

Of course one may partly excuse Messieurs the bureaucrats because of their actually embarrassing fix. The drowning man, so they say, will clutch at the least straw, for he hasn't sense enough at the moment to reflect that only a fly, perhaps, might be able to ride it out atop a straw, whereas he weighs somewhere around a hundred and fifty pounds, if not all of a hundred and eighty; but this consideration doesn't enter his head at the moment, and he clutches at the straw. And so did our gentlemen clutch, at last, even at a Nozdrev. The Chief of Police that very instant dashed off a brief note to him, inviting him for that evening, and a roundsman in top-boots, with an attractive glow on his cheeks, ran off with it immediately, holding onto his saber and going lickety-split to Nozdrev's lodgings.

Nozdrev was taken up with very important business. For four days by now he had not left his room, would not admit anyone, and received his meals through the transom; in fact, he had actually grown gaunt and his face had turned a greenish hue. The business demanded the utmost application: it consisted of matching, out of several gross of playing cards, a single deck, but that one was to have the most recognizable features, so that one might pin one's faith on it as on a most tried and true friend. There remained enough work for another fortnight at least. During all this time Porphyry had to scrub the mastiff pup's belly-button with a special brush and wash him with soap three times a day (it had turned out to be no pug-dog, after all). Nozdrev was very much angered because his seclusion had been broken in on. First of all he sent the roundsman to the Devil, but when he read in the note that there might be a chance of winnings, because they were expecting a certain novice to attend that evening, he softened at once, hastily turned the key in the lock of the room, dressed himself any old way, and was off to attend the evening.

The statements, attestations, and suppositions of Nozdrev offered such a sharp contrast to those of the bureaucratic gentlemen that even their latest surmises were knocked into a cocked hat. Nozdrev was positively a man for whom there were absolutely no such things as doubts, and one could note just as much positiveness and assurance about his suppositions as one could note of faltering and timidity about theirs. He answered all their points without as much as a stammer; he declared that Chichikov had bought up several thousands' worth of dead souls from him, and that for his part he'd sold those souls to him because he hadn't seen any reason for not doing so. To the double-barreled question: Was not Chichikov a spy, and was he not trying to unearth something?—Nozdrev answered: Yes, he was; that even at school, where Nozdrev had been in the same class with him, Chichikov had been called a stool-pigeon, and that because of this propensity his schoolmates, Nozdrev having been of the number, had mussed him up somewhat, so that afterward it had been necessary to apply no less than two hundred and forty leeches to his, Chichikov's, temples alone—that is, he, Nozdrev, had meant to say forty leeches; the two hundred had popped out somehow of itself. To the question: Was not Chichikov an utterer of counterfeit bank notes?—Nozdrev answered: Yes, Chichikov certainly was and, since the opportunity offered, told an incident illustrating his extraordinary ingenuity. The authorities having learned that there were counterfeit government notes amounting to two million rubles in the house of the aforesaid Chichikov, they had sealed every door and window in the place and had placed guards, two soldiers to every door, but the said Chichikov had exchanged all these notes in the space of a single night, so that the next day, when the seals were removed, the authorities perceived that all the notes were genuine.

To the question, also double-barreled: Was it not a fact that the said Chichikov had intended to carry off, or abduct, or elope with, the Governor's daughter, and was it not a fact that he, Nozdrev, had himself volunteered to help and participate in this affair?— Nozdrev answered: Yes, he did help, and that had it not been for him, Nozdrev, nothing at all would have happened. At this point he did bring himself up short, perceiving that he had lied absolutely without any need and might bring trouble down upon his own head, but by then it was utterly beyond his power to curb his tongue. However, it also would have been a difficult matter to do so because such very interesting particulars turned up all by themselves that there was no possible way of turning them down. He even gave the name of the village where the parish church was wherein the eloping couple proposed to get married, the village of Trukhmachevka, to be precise; the priest was Father Sidor; seventy-five rubles was to be his fee for performing the ceremony, and he would never have consented to perform it for even that if he, Nozdrev, had not threatened to lodge information against him for having married Mikhailo, a flour dealer, to a woman who had been godmother to the same child he had acted as godfather for; * Nozdrev had even given up his own barouche to Chichikov and his bride and had made arrangements to have relays of fresh horses ready for them at all the stage-coach posts. The details had reached such a stage that he was already beginning to reel off the first names of all the stage-coach drivers involved.

The officials tried him out, gingerly, about their Napoleonic theories, but immediately had cause to regret the attempt themselves, because Nozdrev without an instant's hesitation went off into such a blue streak of drivel that it bore no resemblance either to truth or to anything else on earth, so that the officials, after heaving a sigh, all walked away. The Chief of Police alone kept on listening to him for a long while yet, thinking that perhaps eventually there might at least be a crumb or two of sense, but finally

* Such marriages were forbidden by the Greek Orthodox Church. *Trans.*

he, too, made a hopeless gesture, saying: "The Devil alone knows what all this is!" And they all concurred that *no matter how hard you sweat and pull, you'll never get any milk out of a bull.* And so the officials were left in a worse fix than they had been in before, and the whole business wound up with the conclusion that there was no way of their learning just what Chichikov was. And therein was clearly evinced what kind of creature man is: he is wise, he is clever and sensible in all things that pertain to others but not to his own self. What circumspect, firm counsel he will supply you with on the difficult occasions of life! "What a wide-awake head he's got on his shoulders!" shouts the mob. "What a steadfast character!" But let some calamity come swooping down upon this wide-awake head, and should it befall him to be placed himself in the difficult occasions of life, why, where in the world has his character gone to? The steadfast man of action is totally at a loss and has turned out to be a pitiful little poltroon, an insignificant, weak babe, or simply, as a Nozdrev puts it, a horse's tail!

All these bits of talk, all these opinions and rumors had for some reason affected the Public Prosecutor most of all. They affected him to such an extent that, upon getting home, he took to brooding and brooding and suddenly, without rhyme or reason, he up and died. Whether it was a stroke of paralysis or something else that carried him off, the fact remains that, just as he was sitting there, he went bang! off his chair, flat on his back. Those around him cried out, as is usually the way, while they wrung their hands: "Ah, my God!" and sent for a doctor to let his blood, yet perceived that the Public Prosecutor was already but a body bereft of its soul. Only then did they find out, with regret, that the Public Prosecutor had had a soul, although out of modesty he had never flaunted it. And in the meantime the manifestation of death was just as awe-inspiring in the case of a little man as in that of a great one: he who but a little while ago had been walking about, had been in motion, had been playing whist, signing sundry papers, and who had been seen so often among the other officials with his bushy eyebrows and his left eye always winking, was now laid out on a table, that eye not winking at all now, yet with one of his eyebrows still elevated with a certain questioning air. What the late lamented was asking about, why he had died or why he had lived, that God alone knows.

"But come, now, all this is absurd! This is utterly preposterous! It's impossible that these officials should frighten themselves so, should create such a pother over a rigmarole like that, should go so far astray from the truth, when even the veriest babe can see what the whole business is about!" That's what many readers will say, and they'll accuse the author of writing absurdities, or will call the poor officials fools, inasmuch as man is open-handed with the word "fool" and is ready to deal it out twenty times a day to his fellow-man. It suffices to have but one foolish point in one's makeup to be recognized as a fool, despite the other nine good points. It's easy enough for the readers to sit in judgment within their tranquil and lofty retreats, whence they have the whole horizon unobscured before them and can see all that is going on there, below, where only the object that is near at hand is visible to man. Even in the universal chronicle of mankind there are many unbroken centuries which one would, it seems, like to delete and do away with as unnecessary. Many delusions have overtaken this world, which delusions even a child, apparently, would not be subject to now. What twisted, god-forsaken, narrow, impassable by-paths that have diverted it far from the goal has not mankind chosen in its strivings to attain the eternal truth, when spreading right before it was an open way, like to a path that leads to a great fane, meant for a king's mansions! Than all other ways is it broader and more splendid, lit up by the sun and illumined all night by lights, yet it is past it, in a profound darkness, that men have streamed. And how oft, already guided by reason that had come down from heaven, have they not contrived, even then, to backslide and to stray off, how oft have they not contrived, even in broad daylight, to come upon impassable wildernesses, how oft have they not contrived to becloud one another's eyes anew with impenetrable fog and, pursuing will-o'-the-wisps, have contrived in the very end to make their way to the very brink of an abyss, only to ask one another: Where is the way out? Where is the path? The present generation sees everything clearly now; it wonders at the delusions and laughs at the lack of comprehension in its ancestors, not perceiving that this chronicle is written over with heavenly fire, that every letter therein is calling out to it, that from every direction a piercing forefinger is pointed at it, at it and none other than it, the present generation. But the present generation laughs and, self-reliantly, proudly, launches a new succession of delusions, over which its descendants will laugh in their turn, even as the present generation is laughing now.

Chichikov was utterly unaware of what was going on. As ill-luck would have it, he had contracted a slight cold at this time, and had a gumboil and a slight inflammation of the throat, in the distribution of which favors the climate of many of our provincial capitals is exceedingly generous. Lest his life, God forbid, be cut short somehow without his leaving any posterity, he decided that he had better keep to his room for three days or so. During those days he ceaselessly gargled his throat with milk and figs, the latter of which he would eat, and bound a little pad filled with camomile and camphor to his cheek. Wishing to occupy his time somehow, he had made several new and detailed lists of all the serfs he had bought, had even read an odd volume of the *Duchesse de la Vallière,* which he had dug up in his small trunk, had looked through all the various objects and little notes contained in his traveling casket, reading this one and that over for a second time, and all this had become very much of a bore to him.

He absolutely couldn't understand what the meaning might be of the way he was being neglected; not a single one of the town's officials had come to see him even once to find out about the state of his health, whereas only recently droshkies were forever stopping before his inn, now the Postmaster's, now the Public Prosecutor's, now that of the Chairman of the Administrative Offices. He merely kept shrugging his shoulders as he paced the room. At last he felt better and rejoiced God knows how when he saw he'd have a chance to go out into the fresh air. Without putting things off, he immediately tackled dressing; pouring some hot water into a tumbler, he opened his casket, took out his shaving things, and proceeded to shave. And it was high time he did so, because, after running his hand over the stubble and glancing into the mirror, he himself had to admit: "Eh, what a forest you've grown!" And true enough, although it may not have been a forest exactly, a rather dark crop had sprouted all over his cheeks and chin.

Having shaved, he began dressing quickly and briskly, so that he almost bounded out of his trousers even as he was putting them on. Finally he was all dressed and, spraying himself with eau de cologne and muffling up as warmly as possible, went out into the street, with his cheek still tied up as a precaution. His exit, just like that of every man after recovery from illness, was almost festal. Everything he ran across had taken on a laughing air: the houses, the muzhiks passing by; however, some of the latter looked rather serious, and one or two had already managed to clout a brother muzhik on the ear.

Chichikov intended to call on the Governor first of all. On his way all sorts of ideas popped into his head; the little blonde was continually on his mind; his imagination had even grown somewhat prankish, and he had even begun to laugh and poke fun at himself. It was in such a mood that he found himself before the entrance to the Governor's house. He was just about to throw off his overcoat in the foyer when the doorman stunned him with the utterly unexpected words: "I've got orders not to admit you."

"What! What are you saying? Evidently you haven't recognized me. Take a good look at my face!" Chichikov told him.

"How could I fail to recognize you! Why, this isn't the first time I see you," said the doorman. "But it's just you alone that I have been told not to admit—all the others can be received."

"There's a surprise! But why? For what reason?"

"Them's the orders, so it seems that's the way things has to be," said the doorman and added the word "Yes," after which he took his stand before Chichikov in a free and easy manner, without bothering about that genial air with which formerly he'd hasten to help him off with his overcoat. He seemed to be thinking, as he eyed him: "Eh, now, since the masters are chasing you off their front steps you must be just nothing at all, just some sort of common trash, I guess!"

"Can't understand it!" said Chichikov to himself and at once set out for the house of the Chairman of the Administrative Offices. But the Chairman of the Administrative Offices was thrown into such confusion on seeing him that he could not say two words in a row that made any sense and talked such a heap of rubbish that actually both of them felt ashamed. On leaving him Chichikov simply couldn't make out a thing, no matter how hard he tried, as he walked along, to penetrate what the Chairman had said and what his words could possibly have referred to. Then he dropped in on the others: the Chief of Police, the Vice-Governor, the Postmaster; but either they did not receive him, or, if they did, it was in most peculiar fashion—their conversation was so constrained and incoherent, they were so utterly at a loss, and the upshot was such a preposterous muddle, that he entertained doubts as to their mental soundness. He tried to see some of the others to find out, at least, the cause of all this, and did not succeed in gaining as much as an inkling thereof.

As though he were half asleep he wandered aimlessly through the town, unable to decide whether he'd gone out of his mind, whether the officials had lost their heads, whether all this was going on in a nightmare, or whether a crazy mess that was worse than any nightmare was coming to a boil in reality. It was already late, almost at dusk, when he came back to the room from which he had set forth in such high spirits. Out of sheer boredom he ordered tea. In a thoughtful mood and in some irrational brooding on the strangeness of his position he was beginning to pour out the tea when the door opened and Nozdrev appeared in an utterly unexpected fashion.

"There, doesn't the proverb say *seven miles is not too much out of one's way to see a friend!*" said he taking off his cap. "I was passing by and I see a light in your window. 'I guess,' I says, 'I'll drop in on him! Probably he isn't sleeping yet.' Ah, you've got tea on the table, that's good; I'll drink a cup with pleasure—today, at dinner, I stuffed myself with all sorts of trash; I feel my stomach starting in to fuss. Tell your man to fill my pipe. Where's your own?"

"Why, I don't smoke a pipe," said Chichikov dryly.

"Bosh; as though I didn't know you were an inveterate smoker. Hey, there! What do you call your man? Hey, there, Vakhramei, listen!"

"Not Vakhramei but Petrushka."

"But how come? Why, you used to have a Vakhramei."

"I never had any Vakhramei."

"Yes, that's right; it's Derebin who owns a Vakhramei. Imagine what luck this Derebin has: his aunt has quarreled with her son because he married a serf, and now she has willed all her estate to Derebin. 'There,' I thinks to myself, 'if only one were to have an aunt like that for one's future needs!' But I say, brother, why have you withdrawn yourself like that from everybody, why don't you go anywhere? Of course I know that you're at times taken up with scientific studies, that you're fond of reading." (Just why Nozdrev had concluded that our hero was taken up with scientific matters and was fond of reading, we must confess we cannot tell, and Chichikov would be still less likely to.) "Ah, brother Chichikov! If you had but seen . . . there, now, really, you would have found food for your satirical mind!" (Just how Chichikov had come to have a satirical mind is likewise unknown.) "Just imagine, we were playing cards at the house of Likhachev the merchant, and what an amusing time we had! Perependev was with me. 'There,' he says, 'if only Chichikov were here, why, this would be just the thing for him!'" (And yet Chichikov had never in all his born days known any Perependev.) "But own up, now, brother—why, you acted most abominably toward me that time, you remember, when we were playing checkers! For I had won. Yes, brother, you simply diddled me that time. But then, may the Devil take me, I simply can't bear a grudge. Just the other day, at the house of the Chairman of the Administrative Offices . . . ah, yes! I must really tell you that the whole town has turned against you. They think that you're turning out counterfeit bank notes; they started pestering me, but I stood up for you as firm as a rock; I told 'em a great deal about you, that I'd gone to school with you and had known your father. Well, there's no use talking even, I spun them a fine yarn."

"Me turning out counterfeit notes?" Chichikov cried out, jumping up from his chair.

"But why, after all, did you throw such a scare into them?" Nozdrev went right on. "The Devil alone knows what they're up to; they're scared out of their wits; they've rigged you up as a brigand and as a secret agent. As for the Public Prosecutor, he cashed in out of fright—his funeral is tomorrow. Aren't you going to attend it? They're all afraid of the new Governor-General, to tell the truth, afraid that there might be some fuss on account of you. But my opinion of the Governor-General is that if he should start walking around with his nose stuck up in the air and take to acting big, he won't be able to do a single thing with the gentry. The gentry demand cordiality, isn't that so? Of course, one can bury oneself in one's study and never give a ball, but what will he accomplish by doing that? Why, you can't gain anything that way. But, just the same, Chichikov, that's a risky business you've embarked on—"

"What risky business?" Chichikov asked cagily.

"Why, that of carrying off the Governor's daughter. I expected that, I confess, by God, I did! Right off, the minute I saw the two of you together at the ball. 'Well, now,' I thinks to myself, 'Chichikov surely isn't just wasting his time. . . .' However, it's a pity you made such a choice; I can't discover anything so fine about her. But there is one woman, a relative of Bikussov's, his sister's daughter—well, there's a girl for you! The finest piece of goods!"

"Why, what are you saying? What are you raving about? What's all this about carrying off the Governor's daughter? What are you saying?" Chichikov was asking, his eyes starting out of his head.

"Come, that'll do, brother; what a secretive fellow! I came to you, I confess, for that very purpose. I'm ready to help you, if you like. So be it: I'll hold the crown over you at the ceremony; I'll supply the barouche and provide the relays of horses, with but one condition: you must let me have a loan of three thousand. I need them, brother, as if I had a knife at my throat!"

All the time that Nozdrev was chattering away Chichikov had kept rubbing his eyes, wishing to make sure whether he were hearing all this in a dream or in reality. Turning out counterfeit notes—abduction of the Governor's daughter—the death of the Public Prosecutor, of which he was apparently the cause—arrival of the Governor-General—all these statements had thrown him into a considerable fright. "Well, if things have come to such a pass," he thought, "then there's no use hanging around here; I'll have to make tracks out of here as fast as I can."

He tried to get rid of Nozdrev as quickly as possible, then immediately called Seliphan and ordered him to be ready at dawn, so that they might leave the town no later than six o'clock in the morning, without fail; he gave orders to have everything in the carriage looked over, to grease the wheels, and so on and so on. Seliphan said: "Right you are, Pavel Ivanovich," but nevertheless lingered in the doorway for some time, without stirring from the spot. The master also issued immediate orders to Petrushka to drag the small trunk out from under the bed (it had gathered quite a coat of dust by now) and, with his assistance, began packing away, without being too particular, socks, linen (putting the clean and the soiled together), boot-trees, a calendar. . . . All this was put away just as it came to hand: he wanted to have everything ready that evening without fail, so that there might not be any delay on the morrow.

Seliphan, after lingering in the doorway for a couple of minutes, finally walked very slowly out of the room. Slowly, as slowly as one can possibly imagine, did he go down the stairs, leaving the imprint of his wet boots on the worn steps, and for a long while did he keep scratching away at the nape of his neck. What did this scratching signify? And what is its general significance? Was it vexation that the meeting set for tomorrow with some brother muzhik, in an unprepossessing broad-belted sheepskin jacket, would not now come off in some pot-house licensed by the Czar? Or had he already started an affair in this new place with someone who had pierced him to the very heart, and now he would have to leave off standing of evenings near the gates, leave off a politic holding of white hands at that hour when, as soon as the town had pulled the cowl of dusk over it, some husky lad in a red blouse strums his balalaika before all the house help, and working folk of all callings chat quietly among themselves after the toil of the day? Or, simply, did it signify that it was a pity to leave a place that had already been warmed in the domestics' quarters, under a sheepskin, near the oven, and cabbage soup served with a soft, city-made meat pie, only to go off anew out in the rain and the mire and all sorts of inclement weather that overtakes one out on the road? God knows —one cannot guess with certainty. Many and sundry are the things signified when the Russian folk scratch the napes of their necks.

CHAPTER TWELVE

However, nothing came out the way Chichikov had intended. To begin with, he awoke considerably later than he had thought he would—that was the first mishap. Upon getting up he immediately sent Petrushka to find out if the carriage was harnessed and whether everything was in readiness, but the report came back that it wasn't harnessed yet and that nothing was in readiness—this was the second mishap. He became very angry and even got set to give something in the nature of a drubbing to our friend Seliphan and was merely waiting with impatience to hear what explanation the other would offer as an excuse. In a short while Seliphan appeared in the doorway and his master had the pleasure of hearing those very same speeches which one usually hears from a servant on the occasions when one must make haste in leaving.

"Yes, but, Pavel Ivanovich, the horses have to be shod."

"Oh, you swine! You blockhead! How is it you didn't say something about it before? Wasn't there time enough, perhaps?"

"Why, yes, there was time enough. . . . But then, there's that wheel too, Pavel Ivanovich; the iron rim will have to be changed entirely, seeing as how the road is now full of holes, there's been such hard rains all over. . . . Also, if you'll allow me to tell you, the front of the carriage has been jarred all loose, so that, like as not, it may not make two stages!"

"You scoundrel!" Chichikov cried out, wringing his hands, and walked up so close to him that Seliphan, out of fear of receiving a free gift from him, backed away and side-stepped. "Do you want to be the death of me, eh? Are you after slitting my throat? Have you set your mind on slitting my throat on the highway, you robber, you damned swine, you sea-monster, you! Eh? Eh? We've been stopping on this one spot for three weeks now, haven't we, eh? If you'd only given me an inkling, you shiftless lout—but no, now,

at the eleventh hour, you let me have it all at once! When everything is all set to get in the carriage and be off, eh? So that's the
very time you have to go and play me a dirty trick like that, eh?
Eh? for you knew all this before, didn't you? For you did know it,
eh? Eh? Answer me! You did know? Eh?"

"Yes, I did know," answered Seliphan, casting down his head.

"Well, why didn't you tell me, then, eh?"

To this query Seliphan made no answer but, with his head cast
down, seemed to be saying to himself: "Look you, how oddly things
have fallen out; for I did know, but didn't say anything!"

"And now get along with you; fetch blacksmiths, and have
everything done inside of two hours. Do you hear? In two hours,
without fail, but if it isn't ready then I'll . . . I'll . . . bend you
into a horseshoe and tie you into a knot!" Our hero was very, very
angry.

Seliphan was turning toward the door to go and carry out his
orders, but stopped and said: "And another thing, sir, the piebald
ought to be sold, really; he's—he's altogether a low-down creature,
Pavel Ivanovich; what a horse he is—may God save us from such
another; he's just a hindrance."

"That's right! There, I'll go a-running to the horse market this
very minute to sell him!"

"Honest to God, Pavel Ivanovich, it's only that he's good to look
at, but when you come right down to it he's the orneriest hoss
there is; you won't find a hoss like that nowheres—"

"You fool! When I want to sell him I'll sell him. You've got to
start lecturing on top of everything else! There, I'm going to see:
if you don't bring me the blacksmiths right away, and if everything
isn't in readiness inside of two hours, I'll give you such a drubbing
that . . . you won't be able to tell your own face in the mirror!
Git! Go on!"

Seliphan went out.

Chichikov became thoroughly upset and threw to the floor the
sword which accompanied him on all his travels, to inspire appropriate awe whenever necessary. For more than a quarter of an hour
did he fuss and bother with the blacksmiths until he came to terms
with them, inasmuch as the blacksmiths were, as usual, out-and-

out knaves and having surmised that the work was urgently needed had jacked up their price exactly sixfold. No matter how heated he became, calling them swindlers, robbers, highwaymen, even hinting at what would happen to them on dread Judgment Day, he didn't penetrate their hides at all; they ran utterly true to form: not only did they not abate their price, they even fussed around with their work not for two hours but for all of five and a half. During this time Chichikov had the pleasure of experiencing those delectable moments which every traveler is familiar with, when everything has been packed away in the trunk and there is nothing in the room except bits of string, scraps of paper, and all sorts of trash littering the floor; when a man belongs neither to the road nor to any settled place, as he watches through the window the passers-by shuffling along and discussing their picayune affairs, as they lift up their eyes with some sort of silly curiosity to look up at him, then go on their way again, which irritates still more the bad spirits of the traveler who isn't traveling. Everything around him, everything that meets his eye—the wretched little shop opposite his windows, and the head of an old woman who lives in the house across the way, as she walks up to her window with its short curtains—everything is repulsive to him, yet go away from the window he will not. He stands there, now oblivious, now turning anew a sort of dulled attentiveness upon everything before him, whether it is moving or not, and out of vexation he will crush some poor fly that persists in buzzing and beating against the windowpane even as he crushes it.

But there is an end to all things, and the longed-for moment arrived. Everything was in readiness; the front of the carriage had been properly repaired; a new iron rim had been adjusted around the wheel, the horses were brought from their watering, and the brigand blacksmiths went off, after having counted over their silver rubles and having wished Chichikov godspeed. Finally the carriage itself was harnessed, and two hot twisted loaves, just purchased, were placed therein, and Seliphan had already thrust a thing or two for himself in the boot under his seat, and, while the tavern server in his invariable jacket of linsey-woolsey stood by and waved his cap in farewell, and while sundry other flunkies and

coachmen, from the tavern as well as outsiders, gathered to gape
at someone else's master departing, and amid all the other circumstances usually attendant upon a departure, our hero at last seated
himself in the vehicle, and the light carriage, of the sort that
bachelors ride in, which had for so long been stalled in the town,
and which the reader may have become so fed up with by now,
at last rolled out of the gates of the inn.

"Glory be to God!" Chichikov reflected, and crossed himself.

Seliphan lashed out with his whip; Petrushka, who had been
hanging on a foot-rest for some time, got up on the seat beside him,
and our hero, seating himself more comfortably upon a small
Georgian rug, put a leather cushion back of him, incidentally
crushing the two hot loaves, and the vehicle was once more bouncing and swaying along, thanks to the pavement, which, as we know,
had a resilient force. With some sort of undefined emotion did he
look upon the houses, the walls, the fences, and the streets, all of
which also seemed to be bouncing and swaying as they slowly fell
behind, and God knows if he were ever fated to see all these things
again during his whole life.

At a turn into one of the streets the carriage had to stop, inasmuch as an endless funeral procession was passing down its whole
length. Chichikov, leaning out, bade Petrushka ask whose funeral
it was and learned it was the Public Prosecutor's. Filled with unpleasant sensations, he immediately hid himself in a corner, pulling
the leather apron over himself and drawing the curtains to. At
this point, while the vehicle was thus halted, Seliphan and Petrushka, with their hats piously doffed, were observing who was
present, how everything was going, who was riding and who was
driving, what they were riding or driving, reckoning up the number of all the folk there, both afoot and riding, while their master,
having enjoined them not to recognize and not to return the salutes
of any of their acquaintances among the coachmen and footmen,
also began diffidently observing things through the little glass panes
in the leather curtains. The coffin was followed by all the officials,
on foot and bareheaded. Chichikov became apprehensive lest they
recognize his carriage, but the officials had other things on their
minds. They had not even gone in for the varied workaday small

talk, such as those escorting a dead man usually carry on among themselves. All their thoughts at this juncture were concentrated on themselves: they were thinking of what the new Governor-General would be like now, how he would set about his work, and what reception they would get at his hands.

Behind the officials came the carriages, driven at a walk, out of which the ladies, in mourning caps, were peeping. By the movements of their lips and hands one could see that they were taken up with animated talk; it may even be that they, too, were talking about the coming of the new Governor-General, and speculating as to what balls he would give, and were taken up with their eternal little scallops and their darling appliqués. Finally, behind the carriages, followed several empty droshkies, stretched out in single file; at last there was nothing more, and our hero could drive on. Drawing back the leather curtains, he heaved a sigh and uttered: "There, the Public Prosecutor lived on and on, and then he up and died! And now they'll print in the papers that a respected citizen, a rare father, an exemplary spouse, has departed this life to the great sorrow of his subordinates and of all mankind, and what sort of stuff won't they write! They'll add, likely as not, that he was followed to his grave by the lamentations of widows and orphans, and yet, if one were to go into this matter rather thoroughly, why, on investigation it would turn out that all there really was to you was your bushy eyebrows." Here he ordered Seliphan to drive on faster and in the meantime reflected: "That's a good thing, though, meeting this funeral; they say meeting a dead man is an omen of good luck."

The light carriage had meanwhile turned into more deserted streets; soon there were only long wooden fences stretching along, heralding the end of the town. And now the cobbled roadway had come to an end, then the toll-gate was passed and the city was behind him, and then there was nothing more, and he was again on his travels. And again on both sides of the highway began a new succession of mile after mile, with post-station superintendents, and water-wells, and strings of wagons, and drab villages, with samovars, countrywives, and the spry, bearded innkeeper running out of his stable-yard with a measure of oats in his hands; a wayfarer

in bast sandals all worn through, plodding along to cover a distance
of more than five hundred miles; little wretched towns, jerry-built
with miserable little shops, flour barrels, bast sandals, twisted
loaves, and other such small wares; striped toll-gates; bridges under
repair, fields so vast that the eye could not encompass them on this
side of the road and the other, antediluvian traveling coaches of
the landed gentry, a soldier on horseback, carrying a green box
with leaden grapeshot and labeled *Such-and-such an Artillery
Battery*; strips of green, yellow, and freshly furrowed black, flashing by on the steppes; a plaintive, long-drawn-out song afar off;
crests of pines in the mist; the pealing of church-bells, becoming
lost in the distance; crows as thick as flies, and a horizon with never
an end to it. . . . Russia! Russia! I behold thee—from my alien,
beautiful, far-off place do I behold thee. Everything about thee is
poor, scattered, bleak; thou wilt not gladden, wilt not affright my
eyes with arrogant wonders of nature, crowned by arrogant wonders of art, cities with many-windowed, towering palaces that have
become parts of the crags they are perched on, picturesque trees
and ivies that have become part of the houses, situated amid the
roar and eternal spray of waterfalls; I will not have to crane my
head to gaze at rocky masses piled up, without end, on the height
above; there will be no flash of sunlight coming through dark
arches thrown up on one another, covered with grapevines, ivies,
and wild roses without number—there will be no flash through
them of the eternal lines of gleaming mountains in the distance,
soaring up into argent, radiant heavens. All is exposed, desolate,
and flat about thee; like specks, like dots are thy low-lying towns
scattered imperceptibly over thy plains; there is nothing to entice,
nothing to enchant the eye. But just what is the incomprehensible,
mysterious power that draws one to thee? Why does one hear, resounding incessantly in one's ears, thy plaintive song, floating over
all thy length and breadth, from sea to sea? What is there in it, in
this song of thine? What is it about that song which calls one, and
sobs, and clutches at one's very heart? What sounds are these that
poignantly caress my soul and strive to win their way within it,
and twine about my heart? Russia! What wouldst thou of me,
then? What incomprehensible bond is there between us? Wherefore

dost thou gaze at me thus, and wherefore has all that is in thee and of thee turned its eyes, filled with such expectancy, upon me? . . . Yet still, filled with perplexity, I continue standing motionlessly, though an ominous cloud, heavy with coming rains, has cast its shadow over my head, and thought has grown benumbed before thy vast expanse. What does that unencompassable expanse portend? Is it not here, within thee and of thee, that there is to be born a boundless idea, when thou thyself art without mete or end? Where else if not here is a titan to arise, when there is space for him to open as a flower opens, and to stretch his legs? And thy mighty expanse awesomely envelopes me, with fearful might finding reflection in my very heart of hearts; through thy preternatural sway have my eyes come to see the light. . . . Ah, what a refulgent, wondrous horizon that the world knows naught of! Russia! . . .

"Whoa, whoa, you fool!" Chichikov yelled at Seliphan.

"I'll give you a taste of my cutlass!" yelled a state courier with mustachios a yard long, swooping down on them at a gallop. "Can't you see—may the Foul One flay your soul—that this is an official vehicle?"

And, like an apparition, the troika vanished amid thunder and dust.

How much of the strange, and of the alluring, and of that which carries you away, and of the wonderful there is in the words "the road"! And how wondrous it is itself, this road! A radiant day, autumn leaves, chill air. . . . Muffle yourself closer in your traveling cloak, pull your cap down over your ears, and let us settle down more closely and snugly in the corner of the carriage! For the last time has a passing shiver run through all your limbs, and has already been replaced by a pleasant warmth. The horses race on and on. . . . How temptingly drowsiness steals up on you and your eyes close, and by now it is through your sleep that you hear *Not the White Snows* and the snorting of the horses, and the rumble of the wheels, and you're already snoring, wedging your neighbor into the very corner. You awake: five stages have already sped by and been left behind; the moon is out; you don't know what town it is— there are churches with ancient, wooden cupolas, and sharp-pointed spires dark against the sky; there are dark houses of timber and white ones of stone; the moonlight falls in patches on this spot and that, as though kerchiefs of white linen were spread over the walls, over the paved way, over the streets; shadows as black as charcoal cut across them at a slant; the wooden roofs, under the oblique light of the moon, gleam like flashing metal; and there's never a soul abroad anywhere: everything slumbers. Save that, all by its lone, a little light may be glimmering in some small window somewhere: is it some burgher of this town cobbling his pair of boots, some baker bustling about his run-down oven? How do they concern us? But the night! . . . Heavenly powers! What a night is being consummated up in the heavens' heights! And the air, and the sky, distant, lofty, so unencompassably, harmoniously, and radiantly spreading there, in its inaccessible profundity! . . . However, the cold breath of night is blowing freshly into your very eyes and lulling you to sleep, and you are already slumbering, and sink into forgetfulness, and snore away, while your poor neighbor, wedged into the corner, angrily turns over on his other side, feeling your weight upon him.

You awaken—and again fields and steppes are before you; nothing to be seen anywhere: wasteland everywhere, everything is out in the open. A milestone with a figure on it flies into sight; morning is beginning; there is a pale golden streak against the chill skyey rim, now turned white; fresher and sharper becomes the wind— muffle yourself closer in your warm traveling cloak! . . . What a glorious cold! What wonderful sleep, enveloping you anew! A jolt—and you're again awakened. The sun is high in the heavens.

"Easy, there, easy, now!" you hear a voice urging; the vehicle goes down a steep declivity; there's a broad dam below, and a broad, clear pond gleaming like the bottom of a copper vessel in the sun; there is a village, its huts scattered over the slope of a hill; the cross of the village church glitters like a star off to one side; the muzhiks are chattering, and a ravenous, clamoring hunger assails you. God! . . . How good thou art for one at times, thou long, long road! How oft, like one perishing and drowning, I have clutched at thee, and every time thou hast magnanimously delivered me and saved me! And how many wonderful projects, poetic reveries, hast thou brought forth, how many impressions have I not experienced on the road!

Why, even our friend Chichikov felt himself under the spell of reveries that were not altogether prosaic. Let us see, then, just what it was he felt. At first he had felt nothing and had merely kept looking over his shoulder from time to time, wishing to make sure that he had really left the town behind him; but when he perceived that the town had long since disappeared, that one could no longer see any blacksmith shops, or mills, or any of those things which are to be found on the outskirts of a town, and that even the white spires of its stone churches had long since sunk into the ground, he turned his full attention exclusively to the road, looking merely to his right and left, and it was as if the town of N—— had never existed in his memory, as though he had passed through it long ago, in his childhood. Finally the road as well ceased to entertain him; his eyes began to close a little and his head to incline toward the cushion. The author confesses that he is actually very glad of this, since it will afford him an opportunity of saying something about his hero, inasmuch as up to now, as the reader has seen, the author has been incessantly hindered now by Nozdrev, now by balls, then by ladies, then by the tittle-tattle of the town, then, finally, by thousands of those trifles which seem trifles only when they are put into a book but which, while they are in circulation in the world, are held to be quite important matters. But now let us put absolutely everything to one side and get right down to business.

It is very much to be doubted if the hero we have chosen has proven to the liking of the readers. He won't be to the liking of the ladies, that we can state positively, inasmuch as the ladies demand that the hero be utter perfection and if there be any spiritual or bodily blemish in him, no matter how slight, why, it's just too bad! No matter how deeply the author peer into his soul, though he reflect his image clearer than a mirror, they won't have him at any price. The very corpulence and middle age of Chichikov will be much to his detriment, for corpulence is under no circumstances forgivable in a hero, and quite a great number of ladies will turn away and say: "Faugh! What a repulsive fellow!" Alas! The author is fully aware of all this, yet for all that he can't take a virtuous man as a hero. But . . . it may befall that in this very narrative other chords, as yet unstruck, will be heard, that the incalculable riches of the Russian spirit will be set forth, that someone worthy to be called a man, endowed with divine attributes of valor and virtue, or a wonderful Russian maiden, such as is not to be found anywhere else in the world, with all the wondrous beauty of a woman's soul, all compact of magnanimous striving and self-denial, may yet pass through our pages. And lifeless will seem beside them all the virtuous people of other tribes, even as a book is lifeless before the living word! Russian emotions will spring into life . . . and the readers will perceive how deeply has been implanted in the Slavic nature that which has but skimmed the surface of the nature of other peoples. . . .

But why and wherefore speak of that which lies ahead? It is unseemly in the author, who has long since been a man, schooled by a rigorous inner life and the invigorating sobriety of solitude, to forget himself like a mere callow youth. There is a turn, and a place, and a time for everything! But, just the same, we have not taken a man of virtue for our hero, after all. And one may even explain why he hasn't been taken. Because it's high time to give a rest to the poor man of virtue; because the phrase "man of virtue" is formed all too glibly and idly by all lips; because the man of virtue has been turned into a hack and there isn't a writer who doesn't ride him hard, urging him on both with a whip and whatever else comes to his hand; because they have overworked the man of virtue to such an extent that now there isn't even a shadow of virtue about him, and there's nothing but skin and bones left of him instead of flesh and blood; because it's only through hypocrisy that they trot out the man of virtue; because the man of virtue isn't held in much respect. No, it's high time, at last, to put an actual scoundrel in harness! And so let us harness a scoundrel.

Obscure and humble is the origin of our hero. His parents were of the nobility, but whether hereditary or from a new-baked lot, God knows. He did not resemble them in face; at any rate, a female relative who was present at his birth, a short little, squat little bit of a woman, one of those who are usually called peewees, cried out, as she took the child in her arms: "He didn't come out at all the way I thought he would! He ought to have taken after his grandmother on his mother's side, which would of course have been best of all, but instead of that he was born simply to bear out the saying: *neither like his mother nor like his dad, but like some unknown, passing lad."* Life, in the beginning, looked at him somehow sourly and dourly, as if through some turbid little window drifted over with snow; not a friend did he have in his childhood, not a play-mate! A tiny chamber, with tiny windows that were never opened, winter or summer; his father an ailing man, in a long frock-coat lined with the skins of still-born lambs, and knitted scuffs on his bare feet, gasping incessantly as he wandered through the room and spitting into a sand-filled cuspidor that stood in a corner; Pavlusha everlastingly sitting on a bench with a quill in his hand, ink on his fingers and even on his lips, the everlasting copy-book maxims before his eyes: *Tell No Lies, Obey Your Elders,* and *Cherish Virtue within Your Heart;* the eternal scraping and flip-flapping of the scuffs through the room; the voice, familiar yet always stern: "Up to your foolish tricks again?" resounding at the moment when the child, bored with the monotonousness of his task, would add some curlicue or a little tail to a letter, and everlastingly the familiar, always unpleasant feeling when, immediately follow-ing these words, the tip of his ear would be most painfully tweaked by the nails of the long fingers reaching out from behind him: there you have the poverty-striken picture of his early childhood, of which he had barely retained a pallid memory.

But in life everything changes quickly and briskly and one day, with the first spring sun and the spring freshets, the father took his son in a miserable little cart, drawn by a little brown skewbald nag, the kind that is known among horse-traders as crow-bait; the coachman who drove it was a small hunchback, the progenitor of the only family of serfs owned by Chichikov's father and filling almost all the domestic posts in the household. With that crow-bait they plodded along for a day and a half and a bit more; on the road they stopped over for a night, made their way across a river, had snacks of cold meat pie and fried mutton, and only on the morning of the third day did they make their way into town. The town streets dazzled the boy's eyes with their unexpected splendor, making him gape in open-mouthed wonder for several minutes. Then the crow-bait and the cart went kerplunk into a loblolly forming the beginning of a narrow by-lane that ran downhill and was practically a pond of mud; for a long while did the poor beast toil with all its poor might, churning the mud with its legs and urged on by the hunchback and the master himself, and finally dragged them into a tiny courtyard, standing on the slope of a hill, with two apple trees in blossom before the little old house and a scrap of a garden behind it, a squat, tiny garden, consisting only of mountain ash and alder bushes and hiding in its depth a small wooden arbor, roofed with laths and with a narrow little window with an opalescent pane.

In this house lived a relative of theirs, a decrepit little crone, who still went every morning to market and afterward dried her stockings while sitting at a samovar. She patted the boy's cheek and admired his chubbiness. He was to stay with her and attend classes daily in the school in town. His father, after staying the night, rode away the very next day. At the parting no tears were shed by the paternal eyes; all he gave the boy was half a ruble in coppers, for pocket-money and dainties, and, what is far more important, sage admonishment: "Mind, now, Pavlusha; study, don't play the fool, and don't be a worthless scamp; above all, please your teachers and superiors. If you'll please your particular superior, then, even though you may not be so successful in learning, and God may have given you no talent, you'll nevertheless get along and come out ahead of all the others. Don't be too friendly with your schoolmates, you won't learn much good from them; but, if you must make friends, let it be with those who are better off than the rest, so that if the occasion arises they may be of use to you. Don't treat and pamper anybody, but rather manage things so that you'll be the one treated and, most of all, take care of each copper and save it: money is the most reliable thing in this world. Your comrade or your friend will fool you and, when it comes to trouble, will be the first to betray you, but the copper will never betray you, no matter what trouble you may get into. You can do everything and overcome everything in this world with a copper."

Having delivered himself of this admonition, the father parted with his son and once more plodded off for home on his crow-bait, and from then on Pavel never saw him again; his words and admonitions, however, took deep root in his soul.

Pavlusha began going to school the very next day. He did not evince any special aptitude for any particular branch of learning, and was distinguished only for diligence and neatness; but on the other hand he did evince great intelligence in another direction—the practical. He had suddenly surmised and grasped what was what, and managed things in his relations with his schoolmates in such a way that they treated him, whereas he not only never treated them but even at times, having hoarded what he had received, would subsequently sell it to the very ones who had treated him therewith. Even as a child he already knew how to deny himself in everything. Out of the half-ruble given him by his father he did not expend a kopeck; on the contrary, that same very year he made an increment thereto, demonstrating an almost extraordinary resourcefulness: he modeled a bullfinch out of wax, colored it, and sold it very profitably. Then, for a certain period, he embarked on other speculations. For instance, having bought food of one sort or another in the market, he would pick a seat during classes near those boys who were better off financially and, as soon as he noticed that one of his schoolmates was becoming queasy—a sure sign of approaching hunger—he would thrust out from under his bench, as though by chance, the end of a pasty or a roll and, having aroused the other's appetite, would demand sums commensurate therewith. He spent two months fussing unremittingly in his room over a mouse, which he had imprisoned in a small wooden cage and, at last, attained his end: the mouse would stand up on its hindlegs, or lie down and get up, at command; then he sold it, also very profitably. When he had accumulated coins amounting to five rubles, he sewed up the little bag and began saving coins in another one.

In his relations with the officials of the school he conducted himself even more cleverly. Nobody could keep his seat on the bench as meekly as he. It must be noted that his teacher was a great lover of quiet and good conduct and could not bear clever and sharp-witted boys: it seemed to him that they must infallibly be laughing at him. It was sufficient for such a lad merely to stir in his seat or somehow, by mischance, to twitch his eyebrow, to fall a victim to his wrath. He would persecute and punish such a boy implacably. "Brother, I'll drive the insolence and insubordination out of you!" he would say. "I know you through and through, better than you know yourself. There, you'll stand on your knees plenty for me! You'll go without plenty of lunches!" And the poor urchin, without himself knowing why, had to scrape his knees raw on the floor and had to go without lunch for days at a time. "Aptitudes and talents are all bosh," this teacher used to say. "All I look for is conduct. I'll give good marks in all subjects to the boy who doesn't know his *a* from a hole in the ground, as long as he conducts himself meritoriously; but as for the lad in whom I see an evil spirit, and a mocking air, I'll give him a zero, even though he could give pointers to Solon!" Thus spoke this teacher, who hated Krylov mortally because the fabulist had said: "For my part go ahead and sing, if to your work but skill you bring," and was forever telling, with an actual delight in his face and eyes, how in the school where he had previously taught everything was so quiet that one could hear a pin drop, how not a single one of the pupils there coughed or blew his nose in class even once all the year round, and how, until the final dismissal bell, one could not hear whether there was a living soul in the room.

Chichikov instantly perceived the spirit of this schoolmaster and what a pupil's conduct was expected to consist of. He did not bat an eye or twitch an eyebrow during the whole session, no matter how hard his schoolmates pinched him from behind; as soon as the bell sounded he would make a headlong dash and fetch the teacher's three-cornered cap (that's what this teacher actually wore, a three-cornered cap); having handed him the three-cornered cap, he would be the first to walk out of the class and would try to come within the teacher's ken at least three times as the latter walked along, incessantly taking his cap off to the schoolmaster. This strategy was crowned with utter success. During his entire stay in the school his standing was excellent and upon graduation he received a full certificate of merit in all subjects, a diploma, and a book with an inscription in gold: "For Exemplary Diligence and Excellency of Conduct."

By the time he left school he was already a youth of rather enticing appearance, with a chin that called for the razor. At this time his father died. Chichikov's inheritance turned out to consist of four irretrievably worn jerseys, two old frock-coats lined with skins of still-born lambs, and an insignificant sum of money. His father evidently had known only how to advise saving coppers but hadn't saved many of them himself. Chichikov immediately sold the run-down little homestead and its trifle of land for a thousand rubles, and as for his family of serfs, he moved them into town, proposing to settle there permanently and enter the Civil Service. It was around this time that the poor teacher who had been such a lover of meritorious conduct and quiet was dismissed, for stupidity or some other failing. Out of grief the teacher took to drink; finally he didn't have anything for drink, even; without a crust of bread and without help, he was perishing somewhere in town in an unheated, forgotten little hole in the wall. His former pupils, the clever and witty fellows, in whom he had been forever imagining disobedience and insolent behavior, upon learning of his pitiful plight immediately took up a collection for him, even selling many things they needed. Pavlusha Chichikov alone talked himself out of contributing by declaring he had nothing to give, and merely gave a five-kopeck coin or some other small silver, which his schoolmates threw right back at him, saying: "Oh, you tightwad!" The poor schoolmaster buried his face in his hands when he learned about this action on the part of his former pupils: tears, like those of a weak child, gushed from his expiring eyes. "On my death-bed hath the Lord caused me to weep," he uttered in a faint voice, and sighed heavily when he heard about Chichikov, adding thereafter: "Eh, Pavlusha! So that's how a man can change! Why, how well behaved he was! Nothing unruly about him, smooth as silk he was! He's taken me in, taken me in no end. . . ."

It cannot be said, however, that the nature of our hero was really so harsh and callous and that his feelings were so dulled that he knew neither pity nor compassion. He felt both the one and the other; he was even willing to help, but only if that help did not call for a great sum, only if it did not involve his having to touch that money which he had definitely proposed to leave untouched. In short, his father's admonition, "Take care of each copper and save it," had had its beneficial effect. But essentially he did not have any attachment for money *qua* money; meanness and miserliness had not taken possession of him. No, it was not these that motivated him; he envisaged ahead of him a life all of ease, with all manner of good things: carriages, an excellently built house, delectable dinners—these were the things that incessantly swarmed through his head. It was in order that he might ultimately and inevitably partake of all this later on, in due course of time, that every copper was saved, was stingily denied for the time being both to himself and to others. When some Croesus whirled past him in a light, handsome droshky, drawn by thoroughbreds in rich harness, he'd stop as if he were rooted to the spot and then, upon coming to as if after a long sleep, would say: "And yet that fellow was nothing but an office clerk, and used to get badger hair-cuts!" And everything that had an aura of riches and well-being made an impression upon him which he himself could not analyze.

Upon getting out of school he didn't want to take any time out, so strong was his desire to get down to business and to obtain a post as quickly as possible. However, despite the certificates cum laude he had received, it was only with great difficulty that he got into the Treasury Department—even in the tallest of the sticks one needs protection! The place that fell to his lot was an insignificant one, the salary some thirty or forty rubles a year. But he resolved to buckle down fervidly to his work, to conquer and overcome everything. And he most certainly evinced unheard-of self-sacrifice, patience, and self-denial in even necessities. From early morn till late at night, with neither his spiritual nor his bodily forces flagging, he wrote on and on, plunged up to his ears in the chancellery papers; he did not go home but slept in the chancellery chambers upon the desks, dining at times with the chancellery watchmen, yet with all that was able to preserve his neatness, to dress decently, to impart a pleasing expression to his face and even a something that was genteel to his every movement. It must be said that the clerks in the Treasury were especially distinguished for their unprepossessing and unsightly appearance. Some had faces for all the world like badly baked bread: one cheek would be all puffed out to one side, the chin slanting off to the other, the upper lip blown up into a big blister that, to top it all off, had burst; in short, it wasn't at all a pretty face to look at. They spoke, all of them, somehow dourly, in such a voice as if they were getting all set to slap somebody down; they offered frequent libations to

Bacchos, thus demonstrating that there were still many vestiges of paganism in the Slavic nature; on occasion they even came to the office full to the gills, as they say, because of which the office was not any too fine a place and the air was not at all aromatic. Among such clerks Chichikov could not but be noticed and marked out, offering as he did a perfect contrast not only by the prepossessing appearance of his face but, as well, by the cordiality in his voice and his total abstinence from the use of strong spirits.

Yet with all that his path was a hard and thorny one. It fell to his lot to have as his immediate superior a Registrar who had already grown old in the service, who was the personification of indescribably stony insensibility and imperturbability, everlastingly the same, unapproachable; a man who had never in his life shown a smile on his face, who had not even once greeted anybody with so much as an inquiry about his health. Nobody had ever seen him, even once, being anything else but what he always was—not even in the street, not even at home. If he had even once evinced any concern for anything, if he had even once got drunk and in his drunkenness broken into laughter, if he had even once given himself up to wild merrymaking, such as a brigand gives himself up to in a moment of drunkenness! But there was not as much as a shadow of anything even as human as that about him. There was just nothing at all in him, either of wickedness or of goodness, and there was a manifestation of something fearful in this absence of everything. His face, as hard as marble, without any sharp irregularity, did not hint at any resemblance to any other face; his features were in severe proportionality to one another. Only the numerous pock-marks and bumps thickly strewn over them made his face one of the number of those upon which, as the folk expression has it, the Devil comes of nights to thresh peas.

It looked as if it were beyond any human powers to get at this man and win his good graces, but Chichikov made the attempt. As a beginning he started catering to him in all sorts of imperceptible trifles: he examined closely the way he cut his quills and, having prepared several modeled after his, put them close to the Registrar's hand every time he needed a quill; he blew and brushed grains of blotting-sand and snuff off the Registrar's desk; he dug up a new rag to clean the Registrar's ink-pot with; he would find the Registrar's cap for him, wherever he may have put it (and a most abominable cap it was too—just about the most abominable the world had ever seen), and would always lay it near the Registrar just a minute before the office closed; he brushed off the Registrar's back if the latter happened to soil it with whitewash off the wall.

But all this remained absolutely without any notice, just as though nothing whatsoever had been done. Finally he got wind of the Registrar's family life: he learned that the Registrar had a mature daughter, with a face that also looked as if peas were threshed on it of nights. It occurred to him to attack the fortress from this side. He found out what church she attended of Sundays and each time took his stand across the aisle from her, neatly dressed, with his shirt-bosom stiffly starched. And the ruse met with success: the dour Registrar was swayed and invited him to tea! And before the clerks in the chancellery had a chance to look around, matters were so arranged that Chichikov moved into the Registrar's house, became a useful and indispensable person there, doing the buying of the flour and sugar for the household, treating the daughter as a fiancée, calling the Registrar his dear papa and kissing his hand. Everybody in the Treasury assumed that by the end of February, before Lent, the wedding would take place. The dour Registrar even began working on the higher-ups for a better place for Chichikov, and after a while Chichikov was himself filling a Registrar's post that had just become vacant. This, apparently, was precisely what the chief purpose of his ties with the old Registrar had been, because right then and there he secretly sent his trunk back home, and the next day found him in another lodging. He stopped calling the old Registrar dear papa and no longer kissed his hand; and as for the wedding, matters there somehow got lost in the shuffle, as though nothing at all had ever happened. Just the same, whenever he encountered the old Registrar, he would cordially shake his hand and invite him to tea, so that the old man, despite his eternal stoniness and hard indifference, would shake his head every time and mutter under his breath: "He took me in, he took me in, the limb of Satan that he is!"

This was the most difficult threshold he had to cross, and he had crossed it. From then on things went more smoothly and successfully. He became a man of mark. He turned out to be possessed of everything necessary to get on in this world: affability in social intercourse and actions, as well as shrewdness and energy in business matters. With these for equipment he got himself in a short while what is called a soft snap and worked it to excellent advantage. The reader must be informed that just about that time the severest persecutions were launched against bribery of any sort. Chichikov did not become at all scared of these persecutions but immediately turned them to his own benefit, thus demonstrating a downright Russian ingenuity which appears only during times of stress. Here is how matters were arranged: as soon as a client came and shoved his hand into his pocket to pull out therefrom the well-known letters of recommendation (as we in Russia put it), signed by none other than the Minister of Finance, "No, no!" Chichikov would say with a smile, restraining the client's hands. "Do you think I'd ever . . . no, no! This is our duty, our obligation; we're in duty bound to do this without any extra compensation whatever! As far as all this is concerned, you may rest assured: everything will be completed by tomorrow. Please let me know where you're staying; you don't even have to bother about this, everything will be delivered at your residence." The client, enchanted, goes home almost enraptured as he thinks: "There, at last, is a man—we ought to have more like him! He's simply a gem beyond all price!" But the client waits a day, then another; nobody brings any papers to his residence, and the same holds true of the third day. He hies him to the chancellery: the papers having to do with his business haven't even been touched, whereupon he turns to the gem beyond all price.

"Ah, you'll have to forgive us!" says Chichikov, with the utmost deference, clasping both of the client's hands. "We were simply swamped with work; but no later than tomorrow all your papers will be done—tomorrow, without fail! Really, I feel conscience-stricken!" And all this is accompanied by enchanting gestures: if at that moment the client's coat happened to fly open, Chichikov's hand would try to correct the matter and hold the coat in place for him. But neither on the morrow, nor on the day after, nor on the third day, do the papers show up at the client's residence. The client begins getting the idea. "Come, now, what's up?" he asks those in the know, and is told: "You'll have to give something to the clerks who write out the papers."—"Well, why not? I'm ready to hand out a quarter of a ruble or even a couple of them."—"Not a quarter of a ruble but twenty-five rubles to each one involved." —"Twenty-five rubles to each of those quill-drivers?" the client yelps. "But why do you get worked up like that?" he is told. "That's just how it will work out: all the quill-drivers will get will be a quarter of a ruble each, while the rest will go to the higher-ups." The slow-witted client claps himself on the forehead and curses, for all he's worth, the new order of things, the persecutions launched against bribe-taking, and the polite, refined ways of the officials. "Before one used to know, at least, what to do: you brought the director a ten-ruble note and the trick was done. But now you have to shell out a twenty-five ruble note to each one in-volved and on top of that have to waste a week fretting and bother-ing before you as much as guess what's what. . . . May the Devil take all disinterestedness and official gentility!" The client is, of course, right; but then there are no bribe-takers now; now all the directors are the most honest and noblest of men; it's only the secretaries and the quill-driving small fry who are cheating rogues.

In a short time a far wider field opened up before Chichikov: a commission was formed for the building of some government edi-fice, quite an important one. He, too, found a snug spot thereon and turned out to be one of its most active members. The Commis-sion got down to business without any delay. For six years did this Commission fuss about the building; but either the climate or something stood in the way, or there was some peculiarity in the very nature of the building materials, for the government structure simply couldn't rise above the foundations, somehow. And yet at the same time, on the outskirts of the town, each one of the mem-bers of this Commission turned out to have his own handsome house of metropolitan architecture; evidently the nature of the ground was somewhat better there. The members of the Commission were beginning to prosper and started rearing families. Only now and at this juncture did Chichikov begin little by little to extricate himself from the stringent, self-imposed laws of abstinence and from implacable self-denial. Only at this juncture was his protracted fast mitigated at last, and it turned out that he had always been not at all averse to sundry delights which he'd been able to abstain from in the years of ardent youth, when no man is perfect master of himself. Certain extravagances made their appearance: he got himself a rather good chef, acquired the habit of wearing shirts of the finest holland linen. By this time he was buying such cloth as nobody else in the whole province wore, and began to adhere, for the most part, to scintillating brown and reddish shades. He had already set up an excellent pair of horses and would himself take one of the reins, making the off-horse prance and caracole; by this time he had got into the way of rubbing himself down with a sponge soaked in water mixed with eau de Cologne; he was already buying a certain soap that was far from cheap, to impart a satiny smoothness to his skin; by this time. . . .

But suddenly, to replace the stuffed shirt hitherto in power, a new chief executive was sent on; a military man, stern, a foe to all bribe-takers and of all that is called wrong-doing. The very next day he threw a scare into every last one of those under him; he demanded accounts, perceived discrepancies therein, coming upon shortages at every step; it didn't take him more than a minute to notice the houses of handsome metropolitan architecture—and the shake-up was on. Officials were removed from their posts; the houses of metropolitan architecture went to the Treasury and were turned into various charitable institutions and schools for soldiers' sons (or reservists); the well-feathered nests were scattered to the four winds, and Chichikov's more so than any of the others. His face, despite its amiability, suddenly proved not to the liking of the chief—just why, God alone knows: at times there just aren't any reasons for such things—and he conceived a mortal hatred for Chichikov. And the implacable new chief was a mighty terror unto them all. But since he was, after all, a military man, and consequently not wise to all the refinements of civilian chicanery, it followed that after some time, thanks to their appearance of righteousness and their ability to simulate and assimilate, other officials wormed themselves into his good graces, and the general in a short while found himself in the hands of still bigger swindlers whom he did not at all consider to be such; he was actually satisfied because he had, at last, chosen the proper men and boasted in all seriousness of his exceptional ability to discern capable people. It didn't take at all long for the officials to catch on to his temperament and character. All who were under his supervision became, with never an exception, awesome persecutors of wrong-doing; everywhere, in all matters, did they pursue it, even as a fisherman with a harpoon pursues some fleshy white sturgeon, and pursued it with such success that in a short while each one of them turned out to have a nest egg of a few thousands.

It was at this time that many of the former officials turned to the path of righteousness and were taken back into the service. But Chichikov no longer could, in any way, worm his way in, no matter how the general's head secretary, who had attained utter mastery in leading the general by the nose, exerted himself and stood up for him, urged on by certain notes signed by none other than the Minister of Finance himself; in this matter he could accomplish absolutely nothing. The general, true enough, was the sort of man who could be led about by his nose (without his knowing he was thus led, however), but, to make up for that, once he got any idea into his head it was fixed there once and for all, like a nail driven home flush, and there was no such thing as prying it out.

All that the clever secretary was able to accomplish was to do away with the blot upon Chichikov's service record, and he could move his chief to agree to this in no other way than through appealing to his compassion, depicting for him in lively colors the touching plight of Chichikov's unhappy family, which, fortunately, Chichikov did not have.

"Oh, well!" said Chichikov. "I got a bite and started pulling in the line, but the fish got off the hook, and don't ask me how! No use crying over spilt milk; I'll have to buckle down to work." And so he resolved to begin his career anew; to gird himself anew with patience, to limit himself anew in all things, no matter how freely and luxuriantly he had let himself blossom out before. It was necessary to shift to another town, and there begin all over again making a name for himself. Somehow nothing would catch on. He had to change two or three posts in the very shortest space of time. These posts, in some way, were mean, degrading. The reader must be told that Chichikov was the most fastidious man that ever existed on this earth. Even though in the beginning he'd had to elbow his way through a mean social stratum, yet in his soul he had always clung to cleanliness, he liked chancelleries that had desks of lacquered wood and where everything was on a genteel footing. Never did he permit himself to utter an unseemly word and always took offense if in the words of others he felt an absence of proper respect for rank or calling. The reader, I think, will be pleased to learn that he changed his linen every two days; while in the summertime, when it was very hot, he'd even change it every day; any odor that was in the least unpleasant was actually offensive to him. That was why, every time Petrushka came to undress him and take off his boots, he would put a clove up his nose, and in many instances his nerves were as sensitive as a young girl's, and therefore it was a hard thing for him to find himself anew in those ranks where all reeked of rotgut and indecorum.

No matter how he called upon his spirits for fortitude, he nevertheless lost weight and his face actually took on a greenish hue during these tribulations. On more than one occasion hitherto he had begun to put on weight and to take on those rounded and decorous contours which the reader had seen when he first made his acquaintance, and, time and again, as he contemplated himself in the mirror, he would ponder on many pleasant things—a little woman, a nursery—and a smile would follow such thoughts; but now, whenever by some chance he caught a glimpse of himself in a mirror, he could not but cry out: "Most Holy Mother of God! Why, how repulsive I've become!" And after that for a long while he would avoid looking into any mirror.

But our hero endured everything, endured it with fortitude; patiently did he endure it, and, at last, changed over to a position in the Customs. It must be said that this branch of the Civil Service had long been the secret object of his designs. He had noticed what elegant little foreign thingumbobs the Customs clerks acquired, what porcelains and cambrics they sent on to their sisters and their cousins and their aunts. More than once had he said with a sigh: "There's what one ought to get into: not only is the frontier right near by but the people are enlightened as well, and what a supply of shirts of fine holland linen one could put by!" It must be added that, besides this, he was thinking of a particular kind of French soap which imparted an unusual whiteness to the skin and a freshness to the cheeks; God knows just what it was called, exactly, but, according to his suppositions, it would infallibly be found at the frontier. And so he had long been longing to get into the Customs, but had been held back by sundry current benefits accruing from the Building Commission, and he had reasoned, justly enough, that the Customs was, after all, no more than the proverbial two birds in the bush whereas the Building Commission was an actual bird in the hand. But now he decided, come what may, to gain his way into the Customs—and gain his way he did.

He tackled his work with unusual zeal. It seemed as if fate itself had cut him out for a Customs clerk. Such smartness, penetration, and perspicacity not only had never been seen but even never been heard of. Within three or four weeks he had acquired such a grasp of the work that he knew absolutely everything: he didn't even weigh or measure anything, but found out from the bill of lading how many yards of woolen or other cloth there were in each bolt; by merely hefting a parcel he could tell you how many pounds it weighed. And when it came to searches, there, as even his co-workers expressed it, his scent was simply as keen as a hound's: one could not but be amazed at seeing that he had patience enough to tap and finger every tiny button, yet all this was carried through with a lethal sang-froid that was incredibly polite. And while those who were submitting to the search were going mad, beside themselves from rage and feeling an evil impulse to slap him all over his pleasant countenance, he, without changing either his expression or his polite behavior, would merely add: "May I trouble you to stand up a little, if you'll be so kind?" or: "Won't you please step into the next room, madam? The wife of one of our clerks will interview you there," or: "Permit me, I'll have to make a small rip in the lining of your overcoat with my pen-knife." And, as he said this, he'd start pulling shawls and kerchiefs out of there as coolly as if he were pulling them out of his own trunk. The only explanation even his superiors could offer was that he was a fiend and not a human being: he searched out contraband in wheels, in shafts, in horses' ears, and in who knows what other places, where no author on earth would so much as think of venturing into, and where only Customs inspectors are allowed actually to venture, so that the poor traveler, after crossing the frontier, still couldn't come to for several minutes and, as he mopped the sweat that had broken out in beads all over him, could but keep on making the sign of the cross over himself and muttering: "Well, well!" The poor traveler was in quite the same fix as the schoolboy who runs out of the principal's private study, whither the principal had summoned him to admonish him a little, but instead of that had given him a totally unexpected birching.

In a short while he made life utterly miserable for all contrabandists. He was the terror and despair of all Polish smugglers. His honesty and incorruptibility were insuperable—almost unnatural. He even passed up the opportunity of accumulating a tidy sum from the various goods that were confiscated and the sundry trifling objects that were impounded but never turned over to the government, to avoid extra clerical work. Such zealously disinterested service could not but become the subject of general wonder and, at last, come to the notice of the higher-ups. He was promoted to a higher rank and given an increase in pay, following which he submitted a project for catching all the smugglers, asking only for means to carry out the project himself. He was immediately entrusted with a command of men and unlimited authority to conduct searches of any and every nature. And that was just about all he had been after.

About this time a powerful smuggling syndicate had been formed along well-planned, thoroughly organized lines; the audacious enterprise promised to yield millions in profits. He had long since had information concerning it and had even turned down the emissaries who had been sent to bribe him, saying dryly: "Not yet." But the moment he had everything placed at his disposal, he let the syndicate know, saying: "Now's the time."

His reckoning was all too correct. He could now receive in a single year that which he might not have won in twenty years of the most zealous service. Hitherto he had not wanted to enter into any relations with the smugglers, inasmuch as he had been no more than a common pawn, ergo, he would not have received much, but now . . . now it was another matter: he could put whatever terms he liked to them. So that the business might be carried on without the least hindrance he won over another official, a fellow-worker who was unable to withstand temptation despite the fact that his hair was already gray. The terms were agreed upon and the syndicate went to work. The work began brilliantly. The reader must have heard, beyond a doubt, the oft-repeated story about the ingenious journey performed by some Spanish rams which, after crossing the frontier in double coats of wool, had carried through thereunder a million's worth of Brabant lace. This incident took place precisely at the time when Chichikov was serving in the Customs. Had not he himself taken part in this enterprise no free traders in the world, no matter how ingenious, could have brought such a matter to a successful conclusion. After those rams had crossed the frontier three or four times the two officials found that each one had a capital of four hundred thousand rubles. Chichikov, they say, had actually amassed more than five hundred thousand, since he was smarter than the other. God knows to what an enormous figure the goodly sums would have grown, if it were not that some black cat ran across their path. The Devil made both officials lose their wits: to put it simply, they waxed too fat and kicked their heels, and had a falling out over nothing at all.

Somehow, during a heated conversation, and perhaps even in his cups, Chichikov called the other official a priest's son, while the other, who actually was a priest's son, became for some reason sorely offended and answered Chichikov right then and there, forcefully and with unusual sharpness, in precisely the following terms: "No, you lie—I'm a State Councilor, and no priest's son; but as for you, why *you* are a priest's son for sure!" And immediately thereafter he added, just to pique and vex the other more: "So there, that's just what you are, now!" Although he thus won a crushing, all-around victory, having turned upon him the very name Chichikov had bestowed upon him, and although the expression "So there, that's just what you are, now!" might have been considered a strong one, yet not content with this he also lodged secret information against him. However, they do say that even without this there had been a quarrel between them over some female, as fresh and firm as a juicy turnip, to use an expression of the clerks in the Customs; it was also said that certain bravoes had been hired to waylay our hero some eventide in a dark by-lane and beat the daylights out of him, but that both officials were made fools of and that the female gave herself to a certain second captain by the name of Shamsharev.

Just how it all really happened, God alone knows; it would be better for the reader, if he is willing enough, to make up the end of that story for himself. The main thing is that their connections with the smugglers, hitherto covert, now became overt. Even though the State Councilor was ruined himself, he had also cooked his co-worker's goose for him. Both officials were arrested, all their worldly goods were inventoried, impounded, and confiscated, and all this broke suddenly, like a thunderbolt, over their heads. They came to, as if out of a daze, and saw with horror what they had done. The State Councilor could not stand up against his fate and perished in some backwoods or other, but the Collegiate Councilor did stand up. He had been able to secrete a part of his funds, no matter how keen the scent of the higher-ups who had trooped together for the investigation; he brought into play all the fine dodges of a mind by now all too experienced and knowing people all too well: on one he'd work through the charm of his manners, on another through a touching speech, on a third through thurification with the insidious incense of flattery, which in any case could do no harm in the matter; on a fourth he'd use a little palm oil; in short, he worked the business all around in such a way that at last he was dismissed with less ignominy than his co-worker, and got away without having to go through a trial on a criminal charge. But he had neither any great capital remaining, nor any of the sundry little thingumbobs from abroad; nothing remained to him: other willing hands had been found to grab everything that had been his. All that he had retained was some ten measly thousand, squirreled away for a rainy day, and two dozen holland shirts, and a small light carriage, such as bachelors like to drive about in, and two serfs: Seliphan the coachman and Petrushka the flunky; and, also, the clerks in the Customs House, moved by the goodness of their hearts, had left him five or six cakes of the soap for preserving the freshness of his cheeks. And that was all.

And so, such was the situation in which our hero found himself anew! Such was the mountain of woes that avalanched upon his head! This was what he called suffering for the truth while serving his country. At this point it might be concluded that after such tempests, tribulations, after such slings and arrows of outrageous fortune and the grievousness of life, he would retire with his remaining measly ten thousand, which he'd won with his heart's blood, into the peaceful backwoods of some small district town and there vegetate forever in a chintz dressing-gown, by the window of a squat little house, settling, of Sundays, the fights that sprang up under his windows among the muzhiks or, for exercise and fresh air, taking a walk to his hen-house to feel with his own hands whether the hen intended for the soup was plump enough, and would thus pass his quiescent yet, after a fashion, not entirely useless old age.

But things didn't work out that way. One must render full justice to the insuperable strength of his character. After all that which would have sufficed if not to kill, then at least to chill and tame, any man forever, his incomprehensible passion hadn't become extinguished within him. He was filled with grief, with vexation, he murmured against the whole world, he was furious against the injustice of fate and indignant at the injustice of men, and yet, despite everything, couldn't abstain from making new attempts. In short, he evinced a patience before which the wooden patience of the German is as nothing, since in the case of the latter it's due to nothing but the slow, sluggish circulation of his Teutonic blood. Chichikov's blood, on the contrary, surged mightily, and there was needed a great deal of rationalizing will to hold in check all that was fain to leap forth and have a free fling. He reasoned, and in his reasoning one could perceive a certain aspect of justice: "But why should it be I? Why has calamity crashed down upon me? Who is the man, working for the government, who isn't wide awake to the main chance? They all stuff their little tin boxes. I've never brought misfortune upon anybody; I've never robbed the widow and the orphan, have never ruined any man and sent him out into the world to beg; I have merely helped myself from the surpluses, I took mine where anybody would have taken his; if I hadn't helped myself, others would have helped themselves. Why, then, should the others prosper and wax fat and why must I perish like a miserable crushed worm? And what am I now? What am I good for? With what eyes can I now look into the eyes of any respectable father of a family? How can I help but feel the pangs of conscience, knowing as I do that I'm cumbering the earth in vain? And what will my children say to me later on? 'There,' they'll say, 'our father was a low-down animal, he didn't leave us any estate whatsoever.' "

As we already know, Chichikov was mightily solicitous about his descendants. What a touching subject! Here and there, perchance, one could come upon a man who perhaps mightn't plunge his arm quite so far into the grab-bag were it not for the question which, no one knows why, bobs up of itself: "But what will my children say?" And so the future founder of a line, like a cautious tom-cat, looking out of the corner of only one of his eyes to see if the master isn't watching from somewhere, hastily grabs at anything that's nearest him, whether it happens to be a piece of soap, or tallow candles, or lard, or a canary—in a word, whatever he can put his paws on; he won't let anything get by him. Thus did our hero complain and weep, yet at the same time enterprise didn't die out in his head; everything there somehow longed constantly to be a-building and merely waited for a plan.

Anew he curled up into a ball, like a hedgehog; anew he undertook to lead a hard life; anew he limited himself in all things; anew, out of cleanliness and a decent position in society, he came down into muck and a lowly life. And, while waiting for something better to turn up, he was actually forced to follow the calling of a legal agent, a calling whose followers have not yet won a status among us, being jostled on all sides, poorly respected by petty clerical creatures and even by the principals themselves, condemned to crawling and cooling their heels in anterooms, to rudeness and the like; but necessity compelled him to venture on anything and everything. There was one commission that came his way, among others: to see about mortgaging several hundred serfs in the Tutelary Chamber. The estate was in the last stage of disorganization. It had been disorganized by a murrain among the cattle, by knavish stewards, poor crops, epidemics that had killed off the best workers and, finally, by the lack of common sense in the landowner himself, who had decorated a house for himself in Moscow in the latest style, and who for the sake of this decoration had drained the life out of his estate, squeezing out the last copper, so that by this time he actually had no money for food. For this very reason the necessity arose, at last, of mortgaging the last remaining property, the serfs. This form of mortgaging, conducted by the government, was at that time still a new business, and people resorted to it not without apprehension. Chichikov, in his rôle of agent, having first predisposed everybody (without this preliminary of predisposing people one can't, as everybody knows, make even a simple inquiry or verification—a bottle of madeira must, no matter how trifling the transaction, be poured down each throat concerned)—having predisposed the proper people, Chichikov explained, among other things, the following circumstance: half the serfs had died off, henceforth he hoped there would be no objections raised later on. . . .

"Yes, but they're listed in the census of the Bureau of Audits, are they not?" asked the secretary.

"They are so listed," Chichikov told him.

"Well, then, why be so apprehensive?" asked the secretary. "There's a death and there's a birth, and each one has a certain worth." The secretary, obviously, knew how to talk in rhyme as well as prose. And in the meantime the most inspired idea that ever entered human head descended upon our hero. "Eh, but I am Simple Simon, I am!" said he to himself. "I'm looking all over for mittens, and they're stuck right in my own belt! Why, were I to buy all these souls that have died, now, before the figures for a new census are submitted. . . . Suppose I were to acquire a thousand of them, and also, let's suppose, that the Tutelary Chambers were to give me two hundred rubles a soul on a mortgage, why, I'd have a capital of two hundred thousand right there! And, too, it's the most proper time now: there's been an epidemic recently; not a few common folk, glory be to God, have died off. The landowners have lost their shirts at cards, have been having their good times and playing ducks and drakes with their money, sure enough; all of them have crowded into Peterburgh to work for the government; their estates are neglected, run any old way; it's harder and harder with every year to pay the taxes, so each one of them will be only too glad to let me have those souls, if only not to pay the serf-tax on them; and there may even be cases where I may come across a fellow whom I can actually charge a pretty penny for doing him this favor. Of course it's hard, there's a lot of fuss and bother, and there's always the fear lest, somehow, one get into hot water and land in a scandal over all this. But then, man hasn't been given his mind for nothing, after all. Yet the best thing of all is that this matter will strike everybody as improbable; no one will believe in its reality. True enough, one can neither buy nor mortgage serfs unless one has land. But then I'll buy them for resettlement—for resettlement, that's it! Tracts of land are now being given away, free and for the asking, in the provinces of Tabriz and Kherson, just so you settle there. And that's precisely where I'll resettle all my dead souls! To the province of Kherson with 'em! Let 'em live there! And as for the resettlement, that can be put through in a legal way, all fitting and proper, through the courts. Should they want to verify those serfs, by all means, I'm not averse even to that. Why not? I'll submit an actual affidavit of verification signed by some Captain of the Rural Police in his own hand. The village might be called Chichikov Borough, or by my Christian name—hamlet of Pavlushkino."

And that is how this strange scheme was formed in the head of our hero, for which scheme I hardly know if the readers will be grateful to him; but as for how grateful the author is, that would be hard even to express, for no matter what one says, if this idea had not come into Chichikov's head, this epic would never have seen the light of day.

Having made the sign of the cross over himself, after the Russian wont, he set about carrying out the scheme. Under the subterfuge of choosing a place of residence and various other pretexts he made it his business to drop in on various nooks and crannies of our realm and, for preference, those that had suffered more than the others from calamities: poor crops, high mortalities, and the like; in a word, wherever he could buy most conveniently and as cheaply as possible the sort of serfs he needed. He did not tackle just any landowner at random, but picked and chose those who were more to his taste, or those with whom one could put through such deals with the least difficulty, trying first to form an acquaintanceship, to predispose them in his favor, so that, if possible, he might acquire the dead muzhiks through friendship rather than by purchase. And so the reader must not wax indignant at the author if the personae that have appeared up to now haven't proven to his, the reader's, taste: it's all Chichikov's fault; he is full master here, and wherever he may get a notion of going thither must we, too, drag ourselves. For our part, if we should really incur censure for the lack of color in, and the unprepossessing nature of, our personae and characters, we shall merely say that one can never see in the beginning all the wide current and scope of any matter. Entering any town, even though it be a capital, is always a bleak affair; at first everything is drab and monotonous: one comes upon sooty factories and workshops without number and endless fences stretching on and on, and only thereafter will one glimpse the angles of six-story houses, and shops, and signs, and streets with tremendous perspectives, consisting entirely of belfries, columns, statues, towers, with all of a city's glitter, din, and thunder, and everything that the hand and mind of man have brought forth for man to wonder at.

How the first acquisitions were consummated the reader has already seen; how the affair will go on in the future, what the fortunes and misfortunes of our hero will be, how he will have to resolve and overcome still greater obstacles in store for him, how colossal figures will appear, how the hidden springs of a far-flung narrative will move, while its horizon widens still further and it adopts a majestic lyrical flow—these things the reader will see later on. There is still a great distance lying ahead of this whole nomadic outfit, consisting of one gentleman of middle age, a light carriage of the sort that bachelors prefer to drive about in, Petrushka the flunky, Seliphan the coachman, and the trio of horses, which the reader is now thoroughly familiar with, from Assessor to that scoundrel of a piebald.

And so there's our hero, warts and all, just as he is! But perhaps the demand may be made to define him conclusively through a single trait: just what sort of man is he as far as moral qualities are concerned? That he is not a hero all compact of perfections and virtues is self-evident. What is he, then? He must be a scoundrel, in that case. But why a scoundrel? After all, why be so severe toward others? There are no scoundrels among us nowadays: there are only well-intentioned, pleasant people, while as for those who would risk general disgrace by doing something for which their physiognomies might be slapped in public, why, you find only some two or three such, and even they are talking about virtue nowadays. The most just thing of all would be to call him a *proprietor,* an *acquirer.* Acquisition is the root of all evil; because of it deals have been put through upon which the world has bestowed the description of being "none too clean." True, there is about such a character a something actually repellent, and the very same reader who on the road he pursues through life will be friendly with a man like that, will gladly have him as a frequent guest at his hospitable board and will spend the time pleasantly with him, will start eyeing him askance if the same fellow turns up as the hero of a drama or an epic. But wise is he who does not contemn any character but, fixing him with a searching gaze, investigates him down to his primary causes. Everything transforms itself quickly in man; before one has a chance to turn around there has already grown up within him a fearful canker-worm that has imperiously diverted all his life-sap to itself. And more than once, some passion—not merely some sweeping, grand longing, but a mean, sneaky yen for something insignificant—has developed in a man born for great deeds, making him forget great and sacred obligations and see something great and sacred in insignificant gewgaws. As countless as the sands of the sea are the passions of man, and no one of them resembles another, and all of them, the base and the splendidly beautiful, are in the beginning submissive to the will of man and only later on become fearful tyrants dominating him. Blessed is he that hath chosen for himself the most splendidly beautiful of all passions: his bliss grows and increases tenfold with every hour and every minute and he penetrates deeper and deeper into the infinite paradise of his soul. But there are passions the choice of which is not of man's volition. For they were already born with him at the moment of his being born into the world, and he has not been given the forces to decline them. They are guided by designs from above, these passions, and there is in them something eternally summoning, something that is not stilled all life long. A great earthly course are they fated to perform, it is all one whether in a somber guise or flashing by as a radiant phenomenon that makes the world rejoice—they are equally called forth for a good that man is ignorant of. And perhaps, in this very Chichikov, the passion that is drawing him on is not of his choosing, and in his chill existence is contained that which will cast man down into the dust and on his knees before the wisdom of the heavens. And it is still a mystery why this form has arisen in the epic now seeing the light of day.

But it is not the fact that my readers will be dissatisfied with my hero which is heavy to bear; what is so heavy to bear is that there dwells within my soul an irresistible conviction that the readers might have been satisfied with that self-same hero, with that self-same Chichikov. Had the author not peered quite so deeply into his soul, had he not stirred at the bottom thereof that which glides away and hides from the light, had he not revealed his most secret thoughts, such as no man will confide to another, but shown him as he appeared to the whole town, to Manilov and all other people, why, all my readers would have been downright pleased and would have accepted him as an interesting fellow. There was no need to make either his face or his whole image to spring up so life-like before the readers' eyes; had the author restrained himself the readers' souls would not be troubled by anything after reading the book through, and they would be able to turn anew to the card table, that solace of all Russia, in all equanimity. Yes, my good readers, you would rather not see mankind's poverty exposed. "Why all this?" you say. "What does it all lead to? For don't we ourselves know that there's a great deal of the contemptible and stupid in life? Even as it is, it often befalls us to see that which isn't at all comforting. It would be better, then, to represent for us that which is splendidly beautiful, enticing. Better let us forget ourselves for a while!"—"Brother," says the landowner to his steward, "why do you tell me that things are going abominably with my estate?

Brother, I know that without you; why, haven't you got anything else to talk about, now? You just give me a chance to forget all this, not to be aware of it, then I'll be happy." And so the money that might have mended matters to some extent goes for various means of inducing self-forgetfulness. The mind that perhaps might have struck a sudden well-spring of great resources slumbers, and there goes the estate bang! under the hammer, and the landowner is sent forth into the world as a beggar to seek forgetfulness, with a soul that, out of extreme need, is ready to commit base deeds at which he himself would have been horrified once upon a time.

The author will also incur censure on the part of the so-called patriots who take it easy in their snug nooks and busy themselves with utterly irrelevant matters, accumulating tidy little bankrolls and arranging their life at the expense of others; but, should anything at all happen which in their opinion is an insult to the fatherland, should some book or other appear in which some bitter truth occasionally emerges, they'll come running out of all their crannies, like spiders on seeing a fly become tangled in a web, and will suddenly raise their voices to shout: "But is it a good thing to bring this out into the light, to proclaim this aloud? Why, everything that's described herein—everything!—has to do with our own affairs! Is it right to wash our linen in public? And what will the people abroad say? Is it so jolly to hear a bad opinion of our own selves? Do these people think this isn't painful? Do they think we aren't patriots?"

To such sage observations, especially touching on the opinion of the people abroad, there is but little, I confess, to be scraped up by way of an answer. Except the following, perchance. Once upon a time there were two citizens living in a remote little nook of Russia. One was the father of a family, by the name of Kipha Mokiyevich, a man of a mild nature, who passed his life in an easy-going, dressing-gown-and-slippers sort of fashion. He didn't bother himself with his family much: his existence was directed rather toward intellectual speculativeness and was taken up with the following philosophical, as he called it, problem. "You take an animal, for instance," he'd say, pacing the room. "An animal is born stark naked. But why, precisely, stark naked? Why isn't it born the way a bird is, why isn't it hatched out of an egg? Really, now, when you consider it, there's absolutely no understanding nature, the deeper one goes into it!" Thus did the citizen Kipha Mokiyevich cogitate. But that's not the main point.

The other citizen was Mokiy Kiphovich, his own son. He was what is called in Russia a *bogatyr,* a man of might, and, at the same time that his father was preoccupied with how an animal is born, the son's broad-shouldered, twenty-year-old nature was simply straining to unfold. He didn't know how to handle anything lightly; always, if he clasped anyone's hand, it would start cracking, or he'd raise a bump on somebody's nose; in the house and in the neighborhood every living thing, from the house wench to the house dog, would run off yelping at the mere sight of him; he had even smashed the bed in his room all to pieces. Such was Mokiy Kiphovich; yet, taking him by and large, he was a good soul. But that's still not the main point.

The main point is this: "Have mercy, our father and our master, Kipha Mokiyevich," he was appealed to both by his own domestics and by those of others, "what sort of man is this Mokiy Kiphovich of yours? There's never any rest for a body because of him, he's such a confounded pest!"—"Yes, he's playful, he's playful," his father would usually say in answer to this, "but then, what's a body to do? It's kind of late to take the strap to him, and besides I would be the one to be accused of cruelty by everybody. And yet he's a sensitive sort of fellow: you upbraid him before two or three people and he'll quiet down; but then there's the notoriety, now, there's the trouble! The whole town will find out and call him a downright dog. Really, now, what do people think, that it doesn't pain me? Am I not a father? Just because I am taken up with philosophy, and once in a while have no time to bother with him, does that mean that I'm not a father? But, oh, no, never, I am a father! I am a father, the Devil take it, I *am* a father! I've got Mokiy Kiphovich enthroned right here, in my very heart!" At this point Kipha Mokiyevich would thump his fist on his chest quite hard and become downright aroused. "Well, if he's bound to remain a dog, then don't let people find it out from me, don't let me be the one to show him up!" And, having evinced such a fatherly feeling, he would let Mokiy Kiphovich keep right on with his mighty exploits, while he himself turned anew to his favorite subject, suddenly posing some such question to himself as: "Well, now, suppose an elephant were to be born in a shell? Why, I guess the egg-shell would be mighty thick, then; there would be no breaking it through even with a cannon; one would have to think up some new sort of ordnance."

Such was the mode of life in their peaceful nook of these two citizens of Russia who have so unexpectedly peeked, as if out of a small window, at the very end of our epic, who have peeked out in order to furnish a modest answer to censure on the part of certain ardent patriots, who up to now have been quietly busying themselves with some philosophy or with increments in the sums acquired at the expense of the fatherland they love so tenderly, who are not concerned about avoiding wrong-doing, but are only concerned lest people get to talking about their wrong-doing. But no, it is neither patriotism nor the desire to do no evil which is the true cause of their censures; there is something else lurking behind these apparent causes. Why hold one's speech back? Who, if not an author, is bound to tell the sacred truth? You fear a penetratingly fixed gaze, you yourselves dread to fix your gaze penetratingly upon anything; you like to glide over everything with heedless eyes. You will even laugh with all your soul at this Chichikov, you may, perhaps, even praise the author, saying: "However, he has observed a thing or two quite deftly! He must be a merry sort of fellow!" And after saying this you'll turn to yourselves with redoubled pride, a smug smile will appear upon your faces, and you'll add: "And yet one must agree, one does come across the queerest and most amusing people in certain provinces—and quite considerable scoundrels, to boot!"

Yet which one of you, filled with Christian humility, not aloud, but in silence, when you are all alone, during moments of solitary communion with your own self, will let sink deep into the inward recesses of your own soul this onerous question: "Come, now, isn't there a bit of Chichikov in me, too?" But there isn't much likelihood of such a thing ever happening! And yet, if at this point some one or other were to pass by you, even actually a friend of yours. a fellow whose rank is neither too high nor too low, you would that very moment nudge the arm of the man next to you and say, all but snorting from laughter: "Look, look, there's Chichikov, there goes Chichikov!" And then, like a child, having forgotten all the decorum befitting your calling and years, you'll start running after him, teasing and calling him behind his back: "Yah, yah, yah! Chichikov! Chichikov! Chichikov!"

But we've begun talking rather loudly, having forgotten that our hero, who had slept throughout the entire telling of his story, has awakened by now and may easily hear his name, so frequently repeated. For he's a fellow who takes offense easily and is displeased if he's spoken about disrespectfully. A fat lot does the reader care whether Chichikov gets angry at him or not; but as for the author, he must under no circumstances quarrel with his hero; he still has to travel quite a long road arm in arm with him; there are still two long parts ahead of us, which is no trifling matter.

"Eh-heh! What are you up to?" Chichikov asked Seliphan. "What are you—"

"What is it?" Seliphan asked, none too briskly.

"What do you mean—what? You goose, you! Is that any way to drive? Come, now, give the horses a touch of the whip!"

And really Seliphan had long been driving along with his eyes closed and half asleep, merely flipping the reins at rare intervals over the flanks of the horses, who were also dozing; as for Petrushka, his cap had long since flown off, no one could tell where, and he himself, having slumped back, had propped his head against Chichikov's knee, so that the latter had to give it a rap to make him sit up. Seliphan bucked up a little and, having clipped the back of the piebald several times, whereupon that horse set off at a dog-trot, and having flourished the whip over all of them, uttered in a high, sing-song voice: "Don't you be scairt!" The nags bestirred themselves and dashed along with the light little carriage as if it were so much swan's-down. Seliphan merely kept brandishing his whip and adding the shouted encouragement of "Eh! Eh! Eh!" as he

smoothly rose and fell on his box, depending on whether the troika
was flying up a hillock or dashing with all its might down a hillock,
with which hillocks the entire highroad was strewn, although it
stretched away downhill in a barely perceptible slope.

Chichikov merely kept smiling, jouncing a little on his leather
cushion, for he loved fast driving. And what Russian is there who
doesn't love fast driving? How should his soul, that yearns to go
off into a whirl, to go off on a fling, to say on occasion: "Devil take
it all!"—how should his soul fail to love it? Is it not a thing to be
loved, when one can sense in it something exaltedly wondrous?
Some unseen power, it seems, has caught you up on its wing, and
you're flying yourself, and all things else are flying: some merchants
are flying toward you, perched on the front seats of their covered
carts; the forest flies on both sides of the road with its dark rows
of firs and pines, echoing with the ring of axes and the cawing of
crows; the whole road is flying none knows whither into the disappearing distance; and there is something fearsome hidden in the
very flashing by of objects, so rapid that there's no time for each
one to become defined before it disappears; only the sky in the in-
finity above and the light clouds and the moon breaking through
these clouds seem motionless.

Eh, thou troika, thou that art a bird! Who conceived thee? Me-
thinks 'tis only among a spirited folk that thou couldst have come
into being, in that land that is not fond of doing things by halves,
but that has evenly, smoothly spread itself out over half the world;
therefore, try and count its milestones until they turn to spots
before the eyes! And far from cunningly contrived is the vehicle
the troika draws; held together with no screws of iron art thou,
but hastily, with a slam and a bang, wert thou put together and
fitted out by some handy muzhik of Yaroslav, with nothing but
an ax and a chisel. No fancy Hessian jack-boots does thy driver
wear, he sports a beard and great gauntlets, and sits on the Devil
knows what for a cushion, but let him rise in his seat, and swing his
whip back, and strike up a long-drawn song and his steeds are off
like a whirlwind, the spokes of each wheel have blended into one
unbroken disk; the road merely quivers, and a passer-by on foot,

stopping short, cries out in fright, and the troika is soaring, soaring away! . . . And now all one can see, already far in the distance, is something raising the dust and swirling through the air.

And art not thou, my Russia, soaring along even like a spirited, never-to-be-outdistanced troika? The road actually smokes under thee, the bridges thunder, everything falls back and is left behind thee! The witness of thy passing comes to a dead stop, dumfounded by this God's wonder! Is it not a streak of lightning cast down from heaven? What signifies this onrush that inspires terror? And what unknown power is contained in these steeds, whose like is not known in this world? Ah, these steeds, these steeds, what steeds they are! Are there whirlwinds perched upon your manes? Is there a sensitive ear, alert as a flame, in your every fiber? Ye have caught the familiar song coming down to you from above, and all as one, and all at the same instant, ye have strained your brazen chests and, well nigh without touching earth with your hoofs, ye have become all transformed into straight lines cleaving the air, and the troika tears along, all-inspired by God! . . . Whither art thou soaring away to, then, Russia? Give me thy answer! But Russia gives none. With a wondrous ring does the jingle-bell trill; the air, rent to shreds, thunders and turns to wind; all things on earth fly past and, eying it askance, all the other peoples and nations stand aside and give it the right of way.

Rinehart Editions